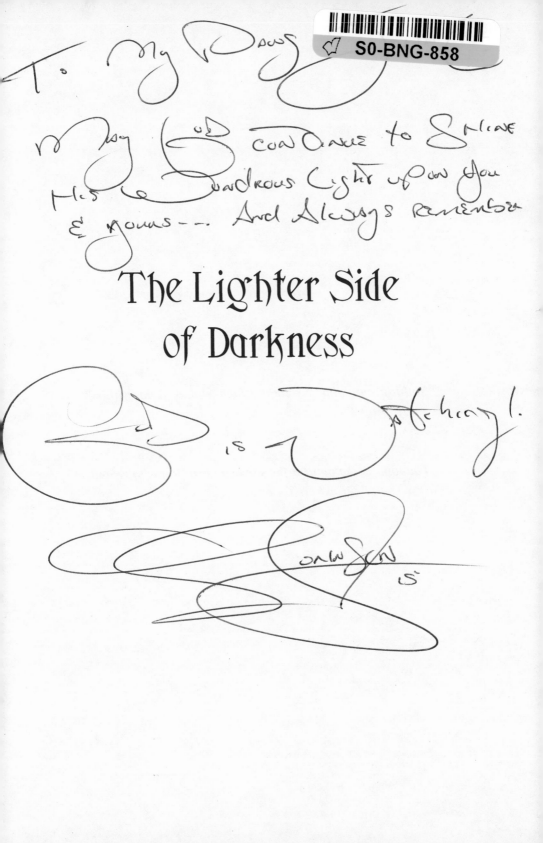

The Lighter Side
of Darkness

"Nothing can dim the light which shines from within." —*Maya Angelou*

"The light is too painful for someone who wants to remain in darkness."—*Eckhart Tolle*

The Lighter Side of Darkness

Troy Pappy Johnson

Library of Congress Control Number:		2014905793
ISBN:	Hardcover	978-1-4931-8913-7
	Softcover	978-1-4931-8915-1
	eBook	978-1-4931-8911-3

Rev. date: 10/16/2014

To order additional copies of this book, contact:
Xlibris
1-888-795-4274
www.Xlibris.com
Orders@Xlibris.com
536683

Contents

Artist Content

"I would like to dedicate this book to Jesus Christ, my Lord and Savior as well as my family for their inspiration and sacrifice; also to my friends for their support and encouragement."

As I walked through the magnificent doors of the church, there he was standing in the midst of everyone who was oblivious to his presence, the first face I saw was my old friend who is no longer here.

"**Hello** Forrest!" I said.

Forrest replied, "**Heaven High!**"

As I marveled at the wondrous site entered a luminous light that shone ever so bright, that exclusively shined upon him, which then consumed him. Called to a higher purpose, he ascended to the Kingdom of Heaven draped in his illustrious armor embellished with justice, and fortitude as all of God's soldiers would be when dress for battle . . . . A Guardian Angel he is; now forged to protect the Righteous as his new purpose in the Afterlife is clear.

He then said to me during his departure, "**Look Troy! God has made me an Angel yet not a fool**!" He then smiled due to his satisfaction; and then he was gone.

Overwhelmed with gladness as I watched in awe, a tear of Joy rolled down my face as I then walked into the sanctuary to give God the Glory, Honor and Praise in Jesus name . . . . While walking to my seat within the pews the congregation noticed my glee.

"**Hello** Brother Troy," said Chair Deacon Davenport as I sat down beside him.

With enthusiasm I responded, "**Heaven High!**" and then smiled.

(RIP) **Deacon, Forrest Lyman Elliott**
Until we meet again . . . .

Acknowledgements

While achieving this stupendous accolade of writing my book, first and foremost I'd like to thank *Jesus Christ: My Lord and Savior*, for giving me the wisdom and creativity to be able to bring this adventure to you. It is through His teachings; I was able to stay par the course by incorporating God's Word to support my thoughts and keep your interest. After reading this tale of enlightenment I pray that it reached the spirit that dwells deep inside of you in hopes that it activates the seed of Righteousness that's deeply embedded in your soul.

Secondly, a special thanks to *my wife Cynthia and my daughters: Dylan, Trystin and Madison)* who stood by my side, encouraging every thought, every word, sacrificing our quality time by allowing me my privacy to stay focused. It was due to their selflessness and love that I was able to stay committed to see this project to its end. *'I thank you my ladies for believing in me. I love you!'* Also, I would like to thank *my Church family* for keeping me grounded in the Word; while we worship and give honor and praise unto our Lord and Savior. It is due to their fellowship and unification that allows me to express myself willfully and openly with no hesitation to our God, as my relationship with Him continues to grow. It is with your support that I am inspired. *'Thank you Pastor for your stewardship as you preach to us in truth and love'*

A special shout out to *my Mom and Grandma* for those long conversations about life and holding me down emotionally keeping me in tuned to my tender side; which humbles me, and holds me accountable, may we continue these quality conversations as they are food for my soul . . . . Thanks to *my father* who've shown me strength as to which I've drawn my own and for always being there never leaving our side. To *my brothers* who share with me a common bond that can never be broken, may we strive to make our families proud by not wasting the talents that God has giving us; especially DJ who humbles you with his presence due to his autism. *'I love you all in more ways than you can imagine'*. **To *my brutha's*** from another mother, and the ***sistah's*** that holds us down; much gratitude for the camaraderie and solidarity of our kinship; as well as the Diaspora that bonds us spiritually. And a special thanks to ***Prof. William Neal McPheeters*** and the ***8 Artists*** that visually brought this tale to light . . . . Finally, I thank you for your support.

Prologue

Ladies and Gentlemen! Boys and Girls! With great pleasure, let me introduce to you; the Spiritual Warfare. It is a nonphysical phenomenon that is cloaked by adverse influences solely intended to seduce the secular realm of believers, and nonbelievers, in a higher power. Although it is unseen; it does exist. The fight for our very Souls' befalls daily in our lives. Yes, it's the ole Good vs. Evil theory. Is it real or unreal? Let your faith be your guide. As I see it, the supernatural war against mankind roars with a vengeance; undoubtedly causing unnecessary drama in our extraordinary lives. Although we are on the brink of damnation, have no fear. Forces of a pure nature have been established by God's Grace and Mercy to negate all dark efforts that rise against his children. Thus the Seraphim, aka Guardian Angels, were sworn to protect us all with the righteous swords of Divinity and Love. When I was a young Kat my Gran MaMa used to say, "Be nice! You never know when you'll run into an Angel." She was right but, as I became the well cultured dude that I am today (and if she were still alive) my reply to that would be, "Yeah Grammy, you're absolutely right but, demons were once angels who fell from God's Grace. So, you never know when you'll run into a demon perpetrating an angel." The Spiritual Warfare is real and true. To justify its existence, let us take glance at our daily lives.

Illegal drugs in the United States are brought in from overseas and neighboring countries via notorious Cartels and localized Drug Lords and found their way to our local ghettos, urban areas, and now suburbia. You may ask yourself; who has the finances and the muscle to pull off this elaborate scheme and get away with it with no questions asked? Surely, not the common street hustler trying to make a $1.00 out of $0.15 or the addicted benefactor cracked out of his mind. Times are hard. No wonder the old ski mask and glove way and selling drugs seem to be the popular route to gain a fast buck. The lack of financial prosperity dictates the method of madness. Unfortunately, crime does pay. Like vultures, big business has spread its wings into corruption, drugs and local governments. The rich get richer while the poor get poorer. Their profits weigh more than our lives. Then there are those who totally disregard life in general. The world is saturated with creeps who get their kicks from the suffering of others. Here's a short list of the demonically disturbed but amazingly successful: Adolph Hitler, Vlad the Impaler, Genghis Khan, Idi Amin Dada, Charles Manson, David Koresh, Jeffrey Dahmer and Saddam Hussein. Need I say more? Well, I will. Life's condition demands an extreme measure of survival. You do what you have to do in order to survive. Is life fair? You already know the answer to this commonly asked question. There has got to be a level of comfort, a level of complete-ness, a security blanket; if you will. Always striving to gain the advantage as; oppose to being at a disadvantage. Let us look to a higher power for answers and, together watch weight lifted.

As we journey through this tale keep in mind that although it is a fictitious tale graphed from a secular perspective, it is deeply rooted in Christian dogma. The story is not meant to add or take away from the true word of God, but it should be used to enlighten or plant the Seed of Righteousness. Let it be known that I am not an authority nor have obtained any religious ordinance that is sanctioned by man; to beguile those who teeter on the fence of righteousness. As a believer, it is a responsibility ordered by God to direct to all who seemingly are faithless and misguided. So, not to be a religious fanatic or tunnel vision-ed Christian, but yet striving to be a Disciple, it is my duty to minister the Gospel of Christ, which through this fictitious venue of adventure; I attend too. *(John 12:23) And I, if I be lifted up from the earth, will draw all men to me.*

My explanation and motivation to tell this kind of fairy-tale solely was discovered by reading scripture in the Bible. Particularly *(Psalms 16:10) for thou wilt not leave my soul in hell; neither wilt thou suffer thine Holy One to see corruption.* So, in contradiction to a contrite spirit and reaching out to those who refrain from establishing a relationship with God; I will not sugarcoat this venue I've chosen to aid in your salvation. The use of profanity, obscenities, sexual content and violence may offend some, but understand this: this is the world we've created. Let us not take a blind eye to what is present in our daily lives. In other words, let's keep it real. See if you can identify the realism by associating with each character and the complexities they face. Based on your findings, you may be able to manifest some of your own issues and solve them from a spiritual perspective. After all you have *'Free Will'* thanks be to God, the choice is yours.

I for one found my answer through the teachings of our Lord and Savior Jesus Christ. Hopefully, you will too. In *The Lighter Side of Darkness*, you will find that *all spiritual references are scripture based and found in the Word of God. (Please refer to the Holy Bible: King James Version or New International Version).* It is there that you will find God's word to be true; which will allow his spiritual Gift of Discernment **(Thessalonians 5:21-22)** to take hold and together let us no longer sit by and watch the evil that men do.

A typical day in these Modern times
Scenario #1

The heart of the city beats steady as the activity commences on the daily schedule of buses arriving and departing at Hustle and Bustle Bus Terminal. Patrons of this service are routinely slaved to this regimen. Unfortunately, this service is also utilized by wishful girls from small town USA who have dreams of becoming the next Fashion Super Model or Broadway Star. With this in mind, there is a bad element that realizes the need for a liaison to help this fantasy to become a reality. In most cases these innocent, eager and naïve damsels are mislead into a world of prostitution and, in a sense, modern day slavery. The Devil is always at work; weaving his web of deceit by causing Sin through the diligent efforts of his Demons, Minions and Agents of Chimera utilizing deception and persuasion, to primarily corrupt mankind.

Today, like any other day, two teenage Caucasian girls (friends), get off the bus from an impoverished mining town called Eunice, West Virginia. They are in search of high hopes and dreams. Due to the intense activity of the terminal, the girls are overwhelmed and confused, undoubtedly unaware that the eyes of a predator have spotted its prey. The girls seek direction from a helping hand and are confronted by the admiring eye. The predator engages its victims, imagine how reptiles slither along the grass as cute bunnies hop pass, monkeys and chicks trying to peep who has, it's a jungle in a city that ain't so pretty, so you better be in the comforts of your home when the sun goes down. While walking down the street watching people go by, a watching me-watching you—watching you—watching me paranoia takes a defensive stance, but in this city it's customary to take a blind eye toward the truth when, ignoring reality.

"Excuse me ladies, you look a little lost," said the Predator.

"Yeah, just a little. Hey mister, do you know how to get to Broadway? How about the Renaissance International Modeling Agency? You're looking at America's next Super Model and Broadway's next Superstar," boasts the silly girls.

"Well let me be the first to welcome you to the city that never sleeps; the place where dreams come true. How long do you plan to grace us with your presence?"

"What?" said one of the girls, not totally understanding the question?

"I think he said; how long are we going to be here?" whispered the other.

"Oh, however long it takes. I am not going back to Eunice. I'm going to be a star even if it kills me," she replied. "We're inspired. You don't understand, we've been dreaming about this our entire lives and now that we're here . . ."

"We'll do whatever it takes", her friend chimed in.

"Whatever huh, first of all, you should be careful. There's a lot of bad people here looking to take advantage of such fine, eager women such as yourselves. It just so happens, that today is your lucky day. Did I tell you I'm a talent agent?"

As he strategically plants the bait, the girls focus on what he has to say.

"I'm always looking for new talent. As a matter of fact, I'm waiting for one of my clients as we speak."

As he feeds the naïve girls a dream, he inconspicuously presses the button on his cell phone to give off a ringtone. He answers the phone as if someone called him.

"Hello. Hey baby, where are you?" He pauses as if he were in engaged in true conversation. "I'm here waiting for you . . . What! Are you okay? Don't worry about that, as long as you're alright. Yeah, yeah, I know. This puts me in a bind but, they'll have to understand. Look, I don't care how they feel! I told you before, my people come first. Don't worry, I'll find somebody to replace you. We'll be fine; Speedy recovery."

As he hangs up the phone, his demeanor changes; he appears to be desperate.

"Damn! My number one client broke her leg in a car accident on her way to the bus station."

The girls ask, "I guess she's not coming huh?"

He said, "Nah, now I need to find someone to replace her."

The gullible girls fall for his game. They look at each other as if a real opportunity has presented itself.

The girl says in unison, "Hey mister, look no further! You have all the talent you need right here."

Slowly, he raises his shades to reveal his eyes as he raises his eyebrow, "You know this just might work. Hey, I'm down to give this a shot!"

The dumb asses, oops! I meant damsels, hug each other.

"By the way what's your name?"

The grimaced look on his face turns into a huge smile and he replies, "Call me Silky, Baby."

The Clout of Grim strikes again! However, as soon as the girls' fate is sealed, two under cover cops close in on Silky.

"Hold it right there! You're under arrest for prostitution."

"What? This is crazy, you're making a mistake."

"You have the right to remain silent, anything you say can be held against you in a court of law."

"Wait a minute he's our agent," uttered the naive girls as the plain clothes men escort pimp daddy away. . . God is watching!

Scenario #2

Another travesty that comes to mind is the incarceration of minority men and women who fall victim to their own ignorance and a manipulative system that was created over 200 years ago by our so called forefathers; which is now utilized by big business for profit gain. That's right, I'm talking Wall Street, baby. Did you know that you can buy stock/shares for prisons on the Stock exchange? As long as the prison population remains full and occupancy steady, corporations steadily invest in its existence. Unfortunately, these penal habitats are heavily populated with confused individuals that deserve to be there or not, or, should be there on account that they got away with something that would've brought them there anyway. Fret not because things can change. On their own accord, they may seek rehabilitation or become what the system intended them to be: a repeat offender whose life condition has given him false hope and a bad attitude. This way of life has survival of the fittest, kill or be killed, get yours because I'm gonna get mine, or use what we got to get what we want attitudes that drive or motivate an aggressive consciousness. It's like 2nd nature that becomes an habitual way of living; especially for those who fall victim to financial depravity, hard times and crime. The way they see it: they didn't have a choice. In this story, 'The Clout of Grim' causes such drama, as instructed by Satan; to confuse and destroy mankind by stealing his will to live righteously. So, these temporary facilities and institutions are built to house penal residents whose low self esteem keeps them prisoners within their own minds and within the system. All the comforts of home are provided. Sometimes better than personal homes, if they had one to begin with, '3 Hots and a cot', prison walls, prison doors, prison guards, and prison rules. Am I forgetting something, oh yeah! Prison food. Damn! Lifestyles of the bitch that's blameless. Over 65% of prison occupants claim that they're innocent of the crime they've committed; although proven guilty without a reasonable doubt. Yet and still when allotted an opportunity to redeem themselves, 7 out 10 will fail. This is how the system was meant to be and how it shouldn't be: a revolving door of hopelessness and profit. Something is definitely wrong with this picture. God is watching!

Prelude

For thousands of years, Heaven has watched mankind corrupt itself with the aid of dark forces governed by Hell. Once again, man has lost his foolish way. The Angels in Heaven noticed that we are headed toward extinction which will flood Hell with the souls of the damned. They asked God to intervene, by giving us another chance.

"Lord Father God; do you not hear the cries from the eternal souls damned forever? Is there nothing you can do to save them?"

God replies, "If my children who are in Hell wish to be saved, all they would have to do is ask and I will save them, but they are disillusioned by Satan and not aware of this simple jest."

> **(2 Chronicles 7:14)** *If my people, which are called by my name, shall humble themselves, and pray, and seek my face, and turn from their wicked ways; then will I hear from heaven, and will forgive their sin, and will heal their land.*

The greatest gift God has given the world was Jesus Christ; his only begotten son. It was because of His love for us, Jesus was sacrificed so that we may enter His kingdom. The children of God took this gift for granted and became corrupt. As punishment is rendered, they now find themselves in the pits of Hell damned forever. Until now. When a man looks deep into his soul, he will find that he is not alone. The Lord promised the coming of a Redeemer who will bring the light into the darkness and the darkness into the light.

The Prophecy: As the Underworld is purged by the faith of the Redeemer, darkness will see the light, the four shall triumph and the Dark one will flee. Henceforth, Hell will be shackled and Heaven shall rein on earth forever.

Chapter One

(*The Awakening*)

In the Now: The Material world

Monastery of the Divine Saints in the Abruzzi Mountains, Italy

As the sun beams down on the so-called land of 'milk and honey' that is beautifully laden with flowers splattered with laboring bees, routinely harvesting nectar in an ivy courtyard of what is left of a mid 18th century monastery, refurbished by generations of committed men sworn to see its resurrection to completion. In its quad are two men bound by their wits pitted against each other in contest of cerebral dominance, faulted by strategy and costly mistakes. Father Gabriel and Chief Bishop Pietro Francis are engaged in a deep conversation over an intense game of chess. Due to the lack of concentration Gabriel's mind is elsewhere, thus he commits a blunder; putting his King into checkmate.

Bishop Francis says, "Today must be my lucky day, your mind seems to be elsewhere; what's the matter my son?"

Father Gabriel says, "Your Eminence, I've started having visions again but, this time they're different, they're more like premonitions. I feel that something is going to happen soon and, somehow I'm involved."

Gabriel by Todd T. Johnson aka Ness Tee

"What are these premonitions about?" Questioned the Bishop?

"Besides the usual Crucifixion dream, I think it has to do with the condition of the world. I sometimes wonder if God is looking at the destruction, the devastation, the all out war the Devil has raged against mankind. I see the souls of men crying out for help. Is there anything we can do to make the world a better place?" He pauses. "When is God going to do something?" Gabriel cries.

"All we can do is have faith and spread God's word throughout the land." the Bishop responded. "Our Mission is to help those who believe in God, understand God; it's not for us to question God's will." While standing up in a raged filled fervor, the Bishop slaps the chessboard knocking the pieces off the board sending them flying through the air. Sporadically they fall hitting the ground crashing like marbles during child's play. "Twenty Hail Mary's and twenty Our Fathers, read **2 Corinthians 5:7**; *for we walk by faith not by sight.*" Sternly grimaced, the Bishop walks away while continuously up holding his firm disposition of being the monarch of the holy establishment.

Speechless Father Gabriel sits baffled after the unexpected outburst. During his quandary suddenly, black clouds induce the sky with darkness; sprinkles begin to spill as a brazen crow intensely squawks signifying an omen.

Gabriel, a middle aged Italian man in his mid forties or so, obviously more concerned about the now than later, was raised by Gypsies of a traveling circus in Southern Europe. Due to his psychic parent's unexpected demise, he was befallen as a gifted orphan who inherited their clairvoyance. Conveniently placed in a profitable position, he was pimped for his ability of prediction. As no other opinion was available, he found his talents to be utilized for gain by those of crooked intentions. As a teen he was beset by the same dream that places him at the Crucifixion of Christ, allowing his curiosity to get the best of him; and needing to know the meaning of this dream, when the opportune moment arose, he then freed himself from his dark past by running away to the modified monastery for answers.

Rumble in the Jungle

While on a nighttime covert operation in a hostile jungle of South America, a merciless Reconnaissance Team "THE LUCKY 7" (Mercenaries) bound by honor yet unethical roughnecks all the same, led by MSgt. Dimitrius Steele encounter a testosterone free village inhabited by women and children. Due to the lack of men, the members of the team feel that this is a great opportunity to seize food, supplies and extra curricular activities. A horny need now motivates their intentions. Clandestinely, they enter the village via tactical maneuvers with precision. Quiet as a mouse they sleuth but, even a mouse on its quietest day can be caught by the slickest cat. Unexpectedly, they are noticed by a woman carrying a large basket of fish. The abrupt startle stuns her motion as she drops the basket. Paralyzed by her fear, she remained silent sweating profusely, trembling with merciful prayers muffled within. Cautiously, they aggressively approach her with weapons drawn with a new agenda. Witnessing her fear for some generated their salivary glands which made their mouths water.

"Donde estan los hombres?" (Where are the men), says Steele.

Nervously the woman replies, "Trabajando con Estaban Lopez y El Policia."

Sgt. Daxx surprisingly mutters, "Did she say what I think she said? They're working with the pigs and public enemy #1? Well damn, ain't that a bitch."

"Intel forgot to give us that info; how did we get picked for this duty?" Sgt. Sanchez stated.

"I'd rather be in Iraq where there's real action," proclaimed Sgt. Mayweather.

Sanchez says, "Then again, that was a waste of time and money. Not to mention lives . . ."

"I'm hip," chimed Sgt. Porter.

"Shut up punk," blurted Poole.

"This is all bullshit," Sgt. Massey includes.

"Yeah, fuck it! I say lets get some ass and get what we need. Then, get the fuck outta here," Sgt. Poole announces.

Daxx agrees as he spits his chew on a lizard that's perched on a branch, "Yeah I'm down wit that. Fuck it! I guess that means they're no rules to this engagement. Come here Baby!"

Sgt. Mayweather joins in the assault of the native woman by grabbing her left arm and pulling her close to him. The look on her face dictated that her end was near.

Simultaneously, Steele grabs her right arm and snatches her away from the eager, horny group of barbarians.

"Back Up! Forget it! We need food and supplies," barked Steele.

Porter says, "Come on guys. Let's stick to the mission."

"That's what I'm talking about, we're not here for that." chimed Sanchez.

Poole says, "Fuck it! I say we kill them all! It will send a message that we can get to them anytime we want."

"Hey why not, I say we do it," voiced Sgt. Massey.

"I said look for food and supplies," arrogantly spoken Steele announced, "Now that's an order! If you don't like it you'll have to go through me."

The defiant four glances at each other with a nonverbal agreement with raised eyebrows and gasp of breath. In unison, they decide to take MSgt. Steele up on his offer. Inconspicuously, they position themselves to have the advantage over their newly appointed opposition. When in sync they rush Steele, smacking him in the back of his head with the butt of an M16 A1 assault rifle.

"What the hell are you doing?" Sanchez rebelliously asked, at the same time, a shot is fired into his chest. His body falls lifelessly to the ground.

"No," Porter exploded "What are you doing? I'm not down with this."

"Shut up or you'll get the same, have it cho way," suggested Poole.

"Make your choice son we haven't got all day." Daxx demanded.

"Yeah hurry up bitch," chimed Mayweather.

"Alright, alright already, this is wrong, this is totally wrong." Porter proclaimed.

"Well okay then, that seals the deal, hurry up! You know what to do," commanded Daxx.

Lucky 7-1 by Christopher Romo

While the barbarians proceed to do what barbarians do best, rape and pillage, Daxx forces his way upon the lone woman. As the Master Sergeant awakens, he finds himself bound to a wooden post. Strangely enough he felt pinned down due to weight on his legs, and then he discovers it's a dead body. Quickly he jerks the body off his legs to find that it's Sanchez with a hole in his chest.

A demonic rage develops in his psyche as he observes the plunder. Chaotically, as the village burns and the cries of it inhabitants become helplessly louder, his compassion for the weak fuels his dark side and he begins his struggle to free himself from bondage. Porter nervously approaches him.

"Sarge, I had nothing to do with this, they've gone section 8, it's like they're possessed."

Steele replies, "They've been acting strange since Baghdad."

Oblivious to being in the enemies' line of sight, a shot is fired hitting Porter in the back of the head. His body plummets to the ground. Sprinkled with hot blood dripping down his face; now filled with adrenaline, Steele breaks free from his restraints. Resourceful, as he is trained to be, he confiscates Sanchez and Porter's weapons and scurries for cover. Quickly he assesses the situation which forces him to recall his superior tactical craft. Oddly as it may seem, he sits down on the ground placing his weapons before him, then assumes yoga like squatting position to marinate, Oops! I mean meditate on clearing his mind and focus on controlling his breathing. Step 1:.Control/ Rationalization. Step 2: Determine a method of execution—Ninja style. Step 3: Attitude adjustment-Kill or be killed. ATTACK!!!! And show no mercy. Revenge is a dish best served cold. An appetite for blood now motivated his mission. His plan is set and he is off and running. Like a hungry predator, Steele begins to stalk his prey until he has had his fill. Annihilate them 1 by 1 until they're all dead. A simple plan but effective all the same.

Due to a higher code of ethics and a strong practice of discipline, most high paid professionals and next level athletes are great at what they do because it's what the sport demands. Some excel to a higher plane, thus becoming the elite by reaching superstar status and masters of the game for example: Michael Jordan, Muhammad Ali or Kobe just to name a few. In Steele's case, considering killing as a sport, it became second nature. Now greatness he befalls. It is for this reason alone he was chosen to be the Alpha male of the group. Mastering the hunger game sport was his forte. Best of the best, if you will.

Unaware of the fury unleashed, the Conan's continue to ransack the feeble community. By utilizing a stealthy pursuit his approach surely would gain him the advantage; ninjas move independently in order to capitalize on the weak points of the opposition. A skill acquired from the hundreds of fallen victims that embellish his impressive resume. (Body count: 496)

Quietly but quickly, Steele approaches a shanty at the edge of the village by a slow flowing stream that runs behind all housing. The sound of clothes shredding and a woman grunting in pain captures his attention.

"No mas, ahhhhh!" excruciatingly the woman cries.

"Shut up bitch! You know you want it," barked Massey as he tries to hump his way into her ass. While fucking his mind into a sexual euphoria Massey is yoked from behind then gutted like a pig. The woman scurries into a corner and curls up with her eyes closed and head bowed on her knees. Steele secures her by humbly placing a blanket over her abraded body. She graciously accepts but can not express this to him because he is already gone . . . . 1 down 3 to go. (Body count: 497)

On a make-shift playground next to an oversized mound of hay, Sgt. Poole entertains himself by beating up 10 male juveniles who together try to stand up for their counterparts. All at once they rush him only to have their meager bodies tossed around like a Chef salad. Humorously amused by their feeble attempt to cause him pain, Poole overlooks one kid who manages to kick him in his jewels. *(Fellas, you know the pain I'm talking about; the kind that shoots up into your stomach, and breaks you down like a bitch, no matter how strong you may be).*

In a high pitched voice he says, "Oh shit! I'm gonna kill you, you lil son of a bitch!"

Fearful for his life, the boy runs and jumps into the mound of hay. Eagerly, yet stumbling, Poole approaches the mound with Machete drawn. He begins to hack away at the pile of dry shrubbery, swinging his blade back and forth to no avail. Meanwhile the frightened lads pummel him with sticks and stones, but they don't hurt him due to his leather tough skin.

Aggravated to say the least he proclaims, "Where are you? You piece of shit! Imma chop you're fucking . . ."

Before Poole can complete his sentence, the sound of a powerful wind whooshes by as his head slides off his shoulders which falls into a pool of blood gathering at his feet from his freshly drenched body. The kids are baffled because they never saw the assassin. Slowly the boy reveals himself and the cheers of joy shout aloud . . . . 2 down 2 to go. (Body count: 498)

Looking for a safe place to hide, desperate women with their babies try to escape the mayhem by crossing the stream. Unfortunately due to the ritually scheduled watering of the live stock, the task seemed impossible at this time, but worth the effort. They are hopelessly trapped, so they stay within the water hidden amongst the beef. Little did they know that a vulture already had them in its sights?

"Well, well, well where the hell ya'll think you're going? Target practice anyone," exclaims Sgt. Mayweather.

One by one, shots are fired missing on purpose to taunt the fearful. As they remain standing in the water, babies are crying while their mothers scream petitions for their lives. Due to the commotion the cattle become disturbed and restless.

"Looks like I'm about to start a stampede out this bitch and all of you cunts are going to be ran the fuck over. Ahhh! Haaaa! Yaaaw! Hoo!" Mayweather yodeled. Suddenly, Steele rises out of the water blasting away targeting Mayweather until he is shredded like Swiss cheese. Shocked yet relieved the helpless become hopeful once again . . . 3 down 1 to go. (Body count: 499)

In the center of the village lies an old dilapidated church with a garden filled court yard. Here, all of the villagers store their valuables for safe keeping; they're safe while on sacred ground. Consumed with greed, SSgt. Daxx tortures the lone woman to show him where the treasures may lie. He slaps her in the face then pushes her on a pew. He climbs on top of her and massages her lady lumps. Then he forced his hand under her skirt. His finger enters her womanhood as she gasps for air.

"Where is it? I'm not going to stop until you tell me. Look, I haven't got all night. Besides, they'll be here soon."

"Too late Daxx I'm already here." Steele shouts.

Daxx simultaneously removes himself off of the woman and riddles a barrage of bullets in the direction of where he thought Steele to be.

"What's the matter Daxx, you afraid all by your lonesome? That's right, I killed them all and you're next." proclaimed Steele.

Expeditiously Daxx vacates himself from the church and settles at the well in the court yard.

"Where are you? Come out you bastard, show your face so I can blow your fucking head off," raged Daxx as he looked side to side, right to left and front to back nervously unaware that behind him, his executioner lay hidden in the well below. He looks into the well only to see darkness due to the gloom of the night. He decides to climb into the well for cover. As he descends, Steele's voice saturates the well. Ignorant to the fact that the entrance of the well led to the basement of the church, and this is where the fortune laid dormant, Daxx goes insane trying to find out where the voice is coming from. So, he decides to ascend. When reaching the top he is met by Steele who snatches him by his collar and tosses him 10 feet into the air. His body hits the ground like a rotten bag of potatoes, po-ta-toes, whatever you decide. This causes him to separate from his guns.

"Come here punk, it's on now." Steele announced.

Forced into hand to hand combat, Daxx realizes he's at a disadvantage so he tries a final desperate attempt.

"Okay Steele, you got me. There's no need for us to end this way. The boys just wanted to have a little fun and things got out of hand," whimpered Daxx.

"Bullshit!" cursed Steele.

The beat down of Daxx's life continues for as long as 5 minutes until Steele decides to end it all by revealing Sanchez's bowie knife. Slowly he picks Daxx up by his collar with one hand and flips him around with his back against Steele's chest. Familiar with this position Daxx chirp one last statement: "I'll see you in hell."

Steele replies, "You can count on it."

Swiftly, the bowie knife glides across Daxx's neck ripping skin as it passes. As the life draws out of Daxx's body, Steele drops the fool at his feet. 4 down and 0 to go.

(Body count: 500) Pay back was truly a bitch.

Concurrently as Steele finishes his engagement, the rest of the platoon arrive to see him drenched in the blood of his team and Daxx's dead body at his feet with blood dripping from the bowie knife in his hand. Stunned by the gruesome sight his platoon stood baffled.

"Sgt. Ellis, Corporal Dobbs, arrest that man," ordered the next ranking soldier.

With no resistance Steele complies and willingly accept his fate, still in all satisfied all the same. He is arrested, court marshaled, tried and convicted for six counts of murder and treason. He is found guilty of these crimes which warrant him a death sentence. I'd say the "LUCKY 7" wasn't so lucky after all, which suggests that the devil is diligently doing his job; to kill, steal and destroy mankind. Ubiquitously watching what has unfolded, God witnesses the downfall of the avenging half breed who's base is black and whatever else you may decide. In His eyes he was a lost child now found.

(1 month later) Guantanamo Bay Detention Camp, Cuba: Death Row—Solitary Confinement

Dark and dreary is this dismal place where dusty walls confine men who are slaves to the sounds of grinding metal forged in to make-shift weapons of defense; while riotous gangs rule the tiers with an iron fist. The melody of men on men echo throughout the darkened hallways, while the stench of waste saturates the stifled air due to a busted HVAC system neglected. Crooked is this system as prison guards exploit opportunities to gain financial aid by smuggling narcotics in; not out. Most of its occupants believe it or not are comfortable to call this home due to the time already spent and, the time they have to look forward too. Slammed doors routinely bang shut signifying that it just accommodated welcome to someone new. As stated in Scenario #2, over 65% of prison occupants claim that they're innocent of the crime they've committed; although proven guilty without a reasonable doubt. In the case of ex-Marine MSgt. Dimitrius Steele, with no regrets he accepts full responsibility for his actions. Now residing in solitary confinement, a beautiful day in the neighborhood doesn't seem within reach. So to pass the time away by ignoring the mundane socialism that is exploited by cut-throats and thieves, Dimitrius does what every other jail bird does: sleep, workout, read the Bible or Quran or both depending on how much time he has and or, reminisce about how grand life use to be. Being an over achiever, he adds another activity to his list. In that familiar yoga-like squatting position, he mediates daily. While engaged in his reflection, an arrogant guard flings a letter through the cell bars hitting Dimitrius on the back of his head.

"You got mail punk. 3 days and counting until we take your dumb ass out," barked the guard.

Without flinching, Dimitrius ignores him and the letter at this time to finish his disciplined session of oneness. One hour passes, still he mediates. Two hours pass, his eyes open upon completion. Mysteriously, the television on the wall turns on by itself and the channel changes to **Breaking News: Hijacked Jet Liner crashes into UN during World Summit, killing US. President and General Assembly. World must chose new leaders. Local sleeper cell (Crimson Jihad) claim responsibility.**

"Damn! The world just got real ugly," said the condemned prisoner.

More concerned about how the TV turned on by itself rather than the news, slowly he gets up from the floor, then glances over at the letter and realizes that it's from his son; Donnie. Quickly he scurries over and picks it up, vigorously breaks the seal and begins to read. Donnie's voice filling his head:

To My Dearest Dead Beat Dad,

Living without you has caused me to screw up my life Mom says but, I am inclined to disagree with her. I want to thank you for the favor. Due to your neglect and unwillingness to step up to be a real man, I've found my true purpose in life. A calling of which to eradicate political governments that send idiots like you to do their dirty work. As they sit back stealing billions while the less fortunate scrounge to survive. It's time to give the people back the power. So, with that being said, I'm willing to sacrifice my life for the greater good and oh yeah, Mom's too.

Just think of it Dad. Your boy, immortalized as a martyr for a greater cause. And Mom? Oh well, Collateral damage. That's the least I can do for her, since she was weak and allowed you to get away with neglecting your responsibility. Hey! Since I haven't seen you much in this world, maybe I'll see you in Hell!

I humbly thank you once again for giving me life and for the airplane model you once gave me on my 10th birthday. Think of it as the gift that inspired me to fly the friendly sky.

Your not so-loving son,
Donnie the Destroyer, Crimson Jihad 4 life

After reading the letter, he balls it up and throws it across the cell. He then looks up to the ceiling in rage while falling to his knees with both arms rose and both fists clenched.

He yells at the top of his lungs, "AH, NO! WHY?"

He begin to ask God to spare their lives.

"Please God, don't let this happen! Take my life instead! What more do you want? If I have to go to hell to fight the devil himself to save them, so be it! Hurry up and kill me. I've got work to do." God is watching!

Dimitrius by Chris Brimacombe

Helplessly, he plunges his body flat to lie down. God heard his cry and decides to take him up on his offer. While on the floor mangled in the dirt, he curls up into fetal position as if he was in his mothers' womb. While engaged in the sad moment he views a white mouse entering his cell from the cell next door. In a delusional state of mind, Dimitrius notices a glow surrounding the rodent. The mouse stops running and stares at him and begins to speak to him telepathically. Totally bewildered, Dimitrius stares in awe. The mouse reveals his position of good intention.

"Go, Soldier of fortune. Go to Hell and save Gods' children."

The thought that he was going mad filled his head as he still answered the delusion.

"What is this some kind of trick? Who are you and what do you want from me," Dimitrius angrily replied.

"Would Satan send you to Hell to rescue souls, or deliver them as you have done? You will guide the Light into the darkness and Satan to the Lord our God."

Humbled by the angelic stab Dimitrius had questioned the rodent's authority but, soon realized that this was a divine intervention and that the mouse was dispatched from Heaven.

"Why me, who am I?" questioned Dimitrius.

"You are the liberator." muttered the mouse.

"What is it that you would have me do? How do I convince them to follow me? What do I say to them?" Dimitrius wondered.

"They will come to you like a moth to a flame. As you consult the Holy Spirit within you, for God is always with you, you'll know what to say when it is time to say it," answered the mouse.

Without hesitation and zeal willingly, Dimitrius accepts his duty and commits to his new found obligation.

"I am truly honored that I am chosen and knowing that He is with me in spirit, I accept this mission with no fear. When do we start?" inquired Dimitrius.

Applauded in the mind of the majestic, salvation is rendered accordingly.

"Do you accept Jesus Christ as your Lord and Savior and, believe that he died for your sins so that you may enter the Kingdom of Heaven?" asked the mouse.

"Yes, yes I believe in the Holy Trinity; thank you Lord!"

"You are now saved by Grace and bought with a price, you must die tomorrow to live another day. So for you, there is life after death." declared the mouse. As the mouse scurries away, so does the glow. Now content with his new responsibility, he begins to reassume the yoga position and continues to meditate but this time with a smile. You see, death is easier to accept when there is a purpose for dying but, in this case a purpose to be reborn.

Now that his new mission is set, he reflects on the life he once led. A vivid montage of 33 years flashes before him. Nurtured in a broken home and raised by a single black parent; a drunken abusive father frustrated for being alone due to his half-bred mother dying from cancer. Victimized by child abuse, led him to run away to escape the madness. Although alone, he was forced to fend for himself. Despite his commonly troubled condition, he still sort his education, played football and developed a work ethic that surpassed his peers; which by doing so gained him popularity and respect. As things became tough and his responsibilities warranted an illegal way to justify his needs; unfortunately, the 5 finger discount brought him the things he needed. When there were times he wanted more, selling product to turn a quick buck granted him 3 to 4 times the profit. Eventually, when you live by the sword, you die by the sword; which got him in trouble with the law. Knowing his story from whence he came, the town officials and local law enforcement gave him an out or face jail time. Thus, the Marines became his choice making him a career man, and the killing machine he is today. Despite his calamity; he was able to find love and father a child of his own. Understanding and respecting his profession his wife gave him his freedom to do his duty; although they were apart most of the time, left her to raise the child on her own. Like always this may prove to be a problem.

(Meanwhile) To Hell with the Prophecy: *Hell*

Deep down in the black hole of despair, smolders' fire and brimstone that grudgingly burn, perilous flames induces an inferno to rise due to active lava rocks bedding the ground. Crimson stains the blood as its color shadows the land, for in this world to live, is to let die, and you may live more than twice, therefore when caution speaks it better be heard, so that you may choose to die another day. Tormented, the tortured souls dwell; reliving their personal hell, as it replays over and over and over again. Melodious screams bellow out causing cringes deep down in their bones. Horrid is this home to many, a just punishment that is prized to all who led a toxic life when it meant something. Now without meaning or direction; you are lost, and may never be found. You may find your life to be a living Hell, because Hell is what you made it!

In the depths of the Dark Realm there are thousands of fields filled with lost souls waiting for their eternal retribution. The strayed souls', obliviously lurking, interest is redirected by two stars colliding in the sky. Fully unaware of the significance of this phenomenon, they wander about as though nothing ever happened. Having recollection of this fable unspoken, a small band of souls find hope.

Before you know it, the news spreads like wild fire until falling on an opportunist ear.

"I must inform Sire of the news, surely he'll be pleased that I brought him this pertinent information; hopefully, I'll gain position amongst the grand," he schemed. As he makes his way to the chamber where the evil one dwells, he is met by a servant with food and wine to serve.

Enoch asked, "Is that for the king?"

"Yes it is." answered the servant.

Nonchalantly a knife enters the servants' stomach killing him instantly. Hastily, Enoch disposes of the body by placing it behind some whopping drapes that cover an oversized window. As he confiscates the platter of food, the door opens slowly.

Hell by Hillary Wilson

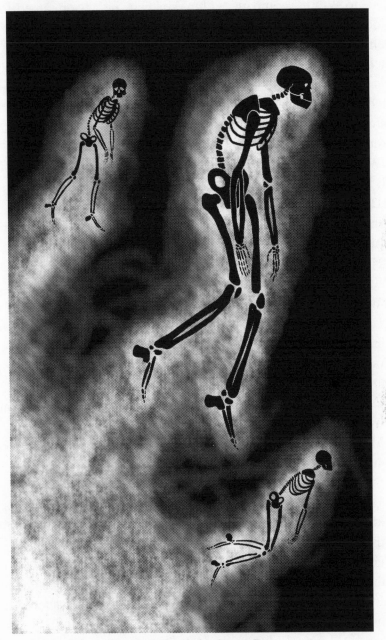

The Lost Souls by SpartaDog

"Hurry up slave!" demands Wrath the Henchman.

Due to Wraths' company within, he keeps his vision tamed for it is forbidden to gaze or speak unless you are told. In the suite we find the supreme ruler in lustful spirits. While engaged in an orgy, men on men, women on women, and the normal; Belial feels discomfort. Arrogantly he ceases his performance which concludes the session. He begins to scratch as though an itch has intensely aggravated his craw. Gifted with foresight, amongst many other things, he now knows of the plot that thickens as well as the new slave that has entered his chamber.

"Who is this slave? Where is the regular slave on duty? Answer me or I'll burn your ass like toast," demanded Belial.

"Do you want a lie or the truth?" questioned Enoch.

Angered but shocked Belial roars like a lion and answers Enoch with admiration.

"Hmmm that was ballsey of you. What is your name slave?"

"Sire, I am Enoch."

"Well, Enoch. What happened to my servant?" asked Belial.

"I killed him so that I could to talk to you, my Liege," blurted Enoch.

As the left eyebrow rises on Belial's face once again he is amazed at Enoch's response.

"I'm beginning to like this guy. So, what's so important that you had to kill your way in to talk to me?" Belial asked curiously.

"My Lord, there is talk amongst the damned that the Prophecy is soon at hand," replied Enoch.

"Silence!" commanded Belial.

Momentarily annoyed, once again he growls with the roar of a lion. Quickly Enoch takes a knee with his head bowed down trembling. Quietly the room stood still.

"Fool! Is there nothing that I don't already know? It appears that the Almighty wants me to once again become an angel in His kingdom. I wonder why the sudden change of heart. I should accept His invitation and, when I get there kill him. But, that will never work because He'll already know my intentions. Anyway, I'd rather rule in Hell than serve in Heaven. Let him send this Redeemer. I will unleash my army on the world and bring forth the Apocalypse. After all, which is more important? Ending my reign or saving his beloved children? Wrath! Unleash the beast and let us sit back and watch as it destroys his precious world," declared the Dark one.

"By your command," Wrath obediently replied.

With the swing of a huge club, Wrath bangs a massive gong on the far side of the chamber dispatching restless demons and more Clout of Grim.

"As for you Enoch, stick around, you're down with me now," suggested Belial.

As the weight is lifted, Enoch wipes his brow and exercises a sigh of relief. Timidly Enoch says, "Whew, anything you say Sire! Anything you say."

Suddenly the doors swing open, enters a beautiful half nude blonde woman built like an Amazon with a tan only a tanning bed could achieve. As pornographic thoughts fill his head, Enoch admires her as she struts across the room as she finally tosses herself on the royal bed.

"Ahh yes, Lilith! It's about time! I missed you baby. Come to daddy," boosted Belial.

Her movement dictates pure eroticism as she slowly gets up from the bed and sensually slides into Belials' arms. As they embrace, they kiss but while kissing Lilith stares at Enoch and Wrath to entice them with envy. Briefly caught up in his fantasy Enoch loses focus on his gain but, regains his senses as Wrath grips his shoulder due to sexual stimulation. Enoch shrugs Wraths' hand off.

"Sire, may I speak?" he asked.

Belial continued to get his cheap thrills by feeling Lilith up, all over her body.

"Speak and be quick about it," says Belial.

"It is my belief that the Redeemer will need help. A recruit if you will. I can be of use to you by being your eyes and ears," he proposed.

Sounding like music to his ears, Belial ceases his flesh grope.

"Hmmm, I could use a sneaky lizard to monitor my new found foe," engrossed Belial. "What do you gain by doing this?"

"But to serve you sire, in a place of nobility. If I have to be here why not be here as royalty," revealed Enoch.

"Ahh, I knew I liked this guy! That was a bold yet honorable request. So be it, when the time comes you will be my fly on the wall."

Satisfied with his new position Enoch turns to leave the Imperial chamber with a devilish grin.

Chapter Two

(Twice Chosen)

(In the Interim)

In the Material World: Late night at the Monastery, Italy

In the still of the night, silence consumes the hallways of this dwelling place. A place where disciplined men exercise celibacy in order to stay grounded. Is it just a shelter for monks and the religious recluse or, is it an escape? One can only lament the lifestyle chosen by these clients sworn to this mundane existence. Was life too stressful for these gents? Or maybe there comes a time in one's life when you must seek a higher calling?

While sleeping in his quarters, Father Gabriel becomes restless within his dream filled with slamming doors, screams of inflicted pain and blood splattered on a sign that says 'Gitmo.' Suddenly he wakes up in a cold sweat. As he regains consciousness, he gazes around the room until he notices the Crucifix on the wall hanging upside down. Simultaneously, the back of his neck and chest catch aflame; burning the Rosary beads and Cross into both. Concurrently, rope burns singe his wrists. Remarkably, he suffers no pain during this uncanny ordeal. Baffled and afraid, he rapidly gets up to look for Bishop Francis. At the end of the vestibule lies the master suite where the Bishop resides.

Gabriel briskly knocks on the door. No answer. He then darts to the sanctuary where the Bishop spends most of his time in prayer. Upon his arrival, he finds the Bishop accompanied by three Monks. With his hands clutched at his chest and a fistful of his garment, Gabriel approaches the group interrupting their prayer session.

"Your Grace! I need to show you something. May I have a word with you in private," humbly asked Gabriel.

"Gabriel, I'm warning you. I don't want to hear another blasphemous remark out of your mouth," barked the Bishop.

Gabriel replied, "I promise you, you won't."

As the Bishop stares at Gabriel, he notices the suspicious look on his face and how he is grasping his garment.

"Why are you clinching your chest like that? What are you hiding underneath your robe," questioned the Bishop.

"I told you something strange is about to happen and somehow I'm in the middle of it! Now, explain this," hollered Gabriel.

With no hesitation Gabriel removes his robe to reveal his markings. Instantly, every clergyman dropped to his knees with the exception of Gabriel.

"He bears the marks! It is time, let us pray." suggested the Monks.

One by one they bowed their heads and begin to pray.

Bishop Francis casually puts his hand on Gabriel's shoulder and says, "Come, let us have that private moment."

Together, the two men begin to walk toward the center of the sanctuary.

"The time has come? What are they talking about?" curiously asked Gabriel.

The Bishop replied, "God has chosen you to do his bidding."

"Do his bidding? What are you talking about? Bidding, what does that mean?" Gabriel puzzled.

"The time has come for you to fulfill the Prophecy. Mankind needs you to exercise your faith if it is to survive," preached the Bishop.

Baffled and confused Gabriel listens with an astute ear as Bishop Francis continued.

"This is a sure tale sign that the end of days is near. I will tell you what I've known about you from the first day you walked into the Monastery. For years my son, you've been having angelic visions of what your soul has experienced in the past. The reason you continuously have visions of the Crucifixion of Christ is because your soul witnessed the immortalizing event that took place on Calvary Hill. The premonitions you're having lately are the things to come thus, allowing your spirit to manifest whatever God has in store for you. This is why He has chosen you."

"Who am I to do Gods' bidding? I'm just a man who ran away from it all in search of answers to why I'm having these uncontrollable visions or dreams. Only to find out that I am the chosen one to take on some divine responsibility! Why me? What did I do to deserve this? I don't want it," protested Gabriel.

"Too late, the decision has been consecrated. Own it man. What an honor," admired Bishop Francis.

"Help me Lord." Gabriel cried out.

Suddenly, a white dove flies into the sanctuary with a soft yet settle glow surrounding its body. It lands on the Cross above the Pulpit. With all attention drawn to it; it begins to speak telepathically.

"Gabriel, fear not! For God knows your heart and, trust in your faith as did Job. Establish conviction in yourself and, believe in the spirit man within you. The mission before you is just and true."

As quickly as it entered, it exits.

"Oh my God, did you hear that?" asked Gabriel.

"No Gabriel we only saw the bird. We didn't hear anything," replied a Monk.

"You see? Even now God has dispatched an Angel exclusively for you," encouraged the Bishop. "Come let me show you something."

Together they walk to the Bishop's chamber. As they enter, the Bishop guides Gabriel to a large wooden table in the far corner of the room. On the table there are books, rolled paintings and scrolls collecting dust and mites. The Bishop ignites a lantern and diligently begins to rummage through the paintings until he finds what he is looking for.

"As you know I've been conducting research on the life of the Lamb. During his quest, our Lord allowed his followers to paint and record his wonders in order to tell his story to those who believed then and, for those who believe now. These paintings were banished and never to be revealed. What I have are copies. The originals are well hidden thanks to King Solomon and his Knights Templar. While viewing them I could not believe my eyes," the Bishop tells.

Gabriel inquires, "What did you see?"

Firmly Bishop Francis grabs Gabriel by both of his biceps, gets into his face and, looks into his eyes and says, "IT WAS YOU GABRIEL! Your face stood out as clear as day!" Gabriel continues to stand speechless as the Bishop schools him. "At first I thought I was seeing things, until now. This event has confirmed my suspicion. There were two thieves crucified along with our Savior, yes?"

"Yeah! What? You saw somebody who looked like me," questioned Gabriel.

"At first maybe but, your markings are in the exact placement of the thief who asked for forgiveness. While the other was burned on his forehead, he tried to persuade our Lord to save them with a miracle."

During the Bishop's explanation, sweat drips down Gabriel's forehead saturating his brow. Anxiety begins to build due to a piercing pain pounding in his head, he collapses to the floor as a flashback of two roman soldiers holding him down while a third soldier branded him with a smoldering necklace of metal beads attached to a cross signifying death by crucifixion. Immediately the Bishop grapples him to his feet.

Out loud the Bishop yelled, "Bring water, quickly!"

"What's the matter son, are you alright?" he nervously inquired.

Once Gabriel gathered his composure the Bishop continued his story.

"When the time came for you to die, you asked for forgiveness and this deed alone set the standard that God based his plan on by sacrificing his only begotten son. He knew our flesh was weak and that we were born and shaped in iniquity," explained the Bishop.

Hesitantly, Gabriel looks at the painting only to immediately and undoubtedly recognize himself. Astonished by the sight, he drops the painting like a hot potato.

"Time to fulfill your destiny," Bishop Francis announced.

"What destiny?" asked Gabriel?

"Are you familiar the Prophecy of the Apocalypse? It's the coming of Armageddon. Good vs. Evil. That's right the end of the world, as we know it. As the Underworld is purged by the faith of the Redeemer, darkness will see the light."

Before the Bishop could finish Gabriel chimes in, "the chosen will triumph and the Dark one will flee. Henceforth, Hell will be shackled and Heaven shall rein on earth forever."

"Ahh, so you do know of the Prophecy!"

"No, your Grace but, as you began to quote the verse . . . it came to me. What does the prophecy have to do with me? It says that Hell will be purged by the Redeemer. Does that suggest that I'm the Redeemer and that I must be dead if I'm to purge Hell?"

"No my Son; I believe your mission takes place here. As for your visions, what have they been showing you lately," quizzed the Bishop.

"My last dream had blood splattered on a sign that read: Gitmo."

"Ahh yes Guantanamo Bay: the military prison. I guess that's as good as any place to start. If I were you, I'd start my efforts there," suggested the Bishop.

"And do what? Give prisoners their last rites? It's a bit late to give confessions."

"Pray on it son. Pray on it. Now, get some rest. You should head out at sunrise."

"Something tells me, I probably won't get much sleep tonight," derived Gabriel.

As Gabriel leaves the Bishops' suite, the Bishop mumbled under his breath, "Peace be with you my Son."

Gabriel makes it to his room and crawls into his bed. Within five minutes, he is sound asleep. As the sunlight peeks through the clouds and birds begin to sing their songs, morning arrives; bringing purpose to a new day. KNOCK, KNOCK, KNOCK! on Gabriel's room door. It's the Bishop. There to encourage the Father on his new found mission but, to avail, no answer. Quietly, he opens up the door and finds the bed undisturbed. So, he does what he normally does every morning and makes his way to the sanctuary to pray. Upon his arrival, he finds Gabriel deep in prayer. Casually, the Bishop kneels down next to him and joins in. When completing their saintly conference, the

Bishop takes a moment to warn Gabriel of what to expect during his journey.

"Did you get any sleep?" asked the Bishop.

"Yeah I got a little. Guess I'm too pumped up. I still don't have a clue as to what I'm supposed to do," admitted Gabriel.

"That should be expected. You know more than you think. The answers will surface when you least expect them. Now, I must forewarn you of forces that are dedicated to negate your efforts. Surely Satan will dispatch demons to hinder your progress. They are called The Clout of Grim. These cloaked, menacing agents were once Angels who were in God's Grace until they found the women on earth sexually gratifying. Their lust inundated their souls, and the women became fruitful and multiplied. The offspring from this insolence warranted them to be banished from Heaven forever. From this act, they devoted their allegiance to the Dark one. Keep in mind that they're not the same Angels that were ousted with Lucifer by the Archangel Michael. They are a totally different breed of nuisance, but fear not! God has established his own beloved forces to compromise their efforts. These Guardian Angels are called the Seraphim. They will come to you in your time of need," warned the Bishop.

The two men casually walk toward the grand doors of the church.

"I will inform the Vatican of this pressing matter. I'm sure they will deem your mission to be the utmost of priorities. I'll ask for financial support. You will need the help of clergymen from various religious orders that stemmed from the 12 Tribes. Together you must be under one accord. I will text you a list of names that the Vatican will provide. They knew this day would come in our lifetime. Remember to maintain your faith and that you are protected by divinity. Peace be with you and glory be to God," advised the Bishop.

"I shall heed your advice and live by God's Word, **Isaiah 54:17 *No weapon formed against me shall prosper*,**" quoted Gabriel.

"Excellent, now go and allow the footsteps of the Lord to guide you. Recognize that there is power within His Word, and stay obedient; let your Faith strengthen you, as your life will depend on it."

The Clout of Grim by Peterson

49

Seraphim by SpartaDog

Exchanges of gratitude and appreciation are shared amongst them one last time. Hugs and kisses shared amongst them like we as blood related men do when they haven't seen each other for a long time. No shame in this game as it is purely fueled by genuine love.

Slowly the doors of the church open as the sun shine brightened the sky. Bishop Francis and the rest of the Monks watch Gabriel drive away in a taxi cab as he set forth on his wondrous journey.

Chapter Three

(A Good Day to Die)

Guantanamo Bay, Cuba (3 Days Later)

Built like an impenetrable fortress well guarded is this island getaway. Home to the diabolical and daunting dastardly doers. Today, just like any other day, inmates ritually commence with their duties. The activities scheduled have no bearings on their daily regimen, so life goes on without hesitation. Although for some, this day is a different day because it is a good day to die.

"Sgt. Wolf has the new Chaplain showed up yet?" inquired Warden Daniel T. Winfree.

"No sir," answered Sgt. Wolf.

"When he does, put him to work. We've got six executions scheduled today."

Just as soon as the inquiring mind wanted to know, a jeep pulled up to the front gate with a passenger.

"This is it Chappy," announces the driver.

Father Gabriel exits the cab dressed in the traditional priestly garb; black shirt, black pants, black shoes and let's not forget the contrasting white collar. Fully geared with christening oil and a Bible in hand, he struts to the gate and waits for his reception. In less than a minute he is greeted by Sgt. Wolf.

"Good morning, Chaplain! Welcome to Gitmo. We've got to hurry up and get you settled. Six prisoners are supposed to die today," boasted the Sgt.

"Ok skip the formalities, let's get straight to work, there are souls to be saved," requested Gabriel.

"Well I'll be damned. That's what I'm talking about a highly motivated Chappy. Next stop, Death Row," ranted the Sgt.

Immediately Gabriel begins to exercise his religious prowess on the condemned men until finally, he crosses Dimitrius' path. As he walks the tier where Dimitrius is housed a guard passes him with a grimacing look on his face. Suddenly, the lights begin to flash and the temperature becomes as hot as the Devils' breath. Upon his approach, Gabriel hears the sound of scripture resonating from a cell. It's Dimitrius reading the 23rd Psalm.

"If you continue to read without me, I may be out of a job," Gabriel gagged.

"Forgive me, Padre. I just like to stay ahead of the game," Dimitrius replied.

"Smart man, I see your heart is in the right place. That's good! Let us begin," encouraged Gabriel.

While administering and receiving the profound rites, simultaneously, the two men experience the same omen. Uncontrollably the lights begin to flicker as the guard begins to tremble. His eyes roll back into his head as slob drips from his mouth while his complexion turns gray. Disturbingly, the stench of a freshly made fart fills the air and finally, the wretched body falls to the floor. Blooming like a weed, Belial rears his wicked trunk.

"So, you are the Redeemer? The one who is suppose to deliver me to Heaven and end my reign in Hell? First of all, I don't think so. But, I would like to thank you for the souls you've sent to my realm. You are truly a monster! An all out killing machine! How many kills you have notched on the belt? Four, maybe five hundred or so . . . right? Eh, who's counting? You have earned your keep. Maybe, I'll hook you up with my boy Wrath. Together you guys would make a hell of a team. HAAAAAA! As for you Priest, I had you in pocket once before; until you flipped the script on me . . . That won't happen again. Twice you have been chosen to try my patience. This time, I can assure you, you won't make it. See you suckers on the dark side," Belial proclaimed as he withers away, while the guards' body slowly regains consciousness.

Totally oblivious to what just happened he asks, "What happened? Damn! It stinks in here. Smells like somebody busted their ass."

"Check your pants, son." Gabriel advised.

Embarrassed by the awkward position, the guard relieves himself, no pun intended, from the premises.

"Who the hell was that?" barked Dimitrius.

"I believe it was Satan himself. The battle has begun. Know that God is with you always. Have faith in Him and He will protect and guide you to victory. Listen to the Holy Spirit within you and not your heart. The heart can be fooled." Gabriel informed.

At the same time the Execution Team arrives outside of Dimitrius cell.

"Time's up Chappy," blurted a fresh Guard.

As they begin to restrain him, Gabriel exclaims, "While you're in Hell fighting the good fight, I will gather disciples and unite the 12 Tribes. Together, we can defeat Satan. Our faith must be strong. Do you believe?"

"Yeah no doubt," answered Dimitrius.

"Then know this to be true. WE ARE THE CHOSEN ONES," Gabriel proclaimed.

Chained by his wrist and ankles, slowly Dimitrius is escorted by four guards in a diamond formation to the Chamber of Death while Father Gabriel continues the ritual with prayer. Riotous clinging and clanging the cages are boasted as prisoners bang their cups on the steel bars that hold them at bay. On the way, Dimitrius reassures Gabriel.

"Hey Padre, I can assure you that after that ordeal, my faith in God has magnified."

"Excellent my son; you're going to need it to be."

"Okay you guys, hurry up! I've got things to do and people to see," Dimitrius demanded.

"Why are you so eager to go to Hell? You know that's where you're going," stated another Guard.

"Exactly, straight to Hell where all my friends are," reinforced Dimitrius.

"What, you think you're a tough guy?" asked a Guard.

Dimitrius replied, "Tougher than you, punk! Hey, do I have a choice? I am a soldier. I'd rather die by firing squad. That's right, guts & glory."

"Yeah, he's scared. That's why he's running his mouth," says another Guard.

"I would love to blow your fucking head off! Instead, we'll send you out like a bitch," states the other Guard.

Finally, they arrive at the chamber. When the door opens, the coldness of the room is overwhelming; it's the eerie presence of an electric chair and the demented souls who have falling victim to its vengeance.

Accompanying this gruesome piece of furniture is an equally daunting, massive, wooden table laced with leather straps and an EKG apparatus used to ensure death has taken its toll. Bypassing the chair, the guards push Dimitrius toward the table. They continue to taunt him during the process.

"Get on the table and lay down!" Ordered a guard.

As instructed Dimitrius accommodates their wish. While connecting the apparatus to his chest and strapping him down, their eyes flicker a flame.

"What was that?" he said. "You're freaking monsters."

Although Dimitrius notices, its too late. There is nothing he can do as an administrator injects him with a lethal dose of poison. Suddenly Dimitrius' body goes into convulsion and his heart beat slows down until finally stopped. The EKG sounds off; due to the flat line on its display. At last he is dead and, on his way. God is watching!

Recognizing his responsibility, Gabriel has undoubtedly found the answers he's been searching for. Unfortunately, so has The Clout of Grim. Upon exiting the penal complex, he is stopped at the gate.

"Come with us," the Guards demanded as their eyes flickered with flame.

Without resistance, Gabriel accommodates their command. Back into the main building they go. Where they'll stop? Only Satan knows.

He is taken to a section of the structure that is abandoned dusty and gloom, and tucked away like a secret with no chance of ever being discovered. To pass the time away, he sits on the dusty bed and begins to pray and then he falls asleep as if there were another choice.

It's midnight and all lights have been out since 10 pm. All are asleep with the exception of a few guards' playing cards in the command center and those who mischievously practice their sexual immoralities in seclusion. While lightly sleeping in his meager accommodations, Gabriel hears someone outside the door. Softly a key turns the tumblers and the door opens wide. It's the Warden.

"Come on man! We don't have too much time before they'll know that you're gone," whispered the Warden.

"Why are you doing this?" asked Gabriel.

With that being asked, the Warden enters the room and reveals his wings which suggests that he is a Seraphim.

"Thank you Lord," muttered Gabriel.

Together, thru back doors and hidden corridors the two men sneak their way out of the prison to rendezvous with a car for a ride to the airport, where a small plane awaits with plans to exit the country. Expeditiously they travel with mercy reaching their destination without resistance. As Gabriel gets on the plane, he realizes that there is only one seat available. He realizes that he'll be taking this trip alone.

"Come with me my friend," says Gabriel.

"Sorry my friend, this exit plan is meant for one. Go with God," spoke the Seraphim.

"Thank you!"

Forcefully, the door shuts and the plane jets down the runway ready for take off. Up, up and away! The plane is destined for the USA.

Now heading somewhere without a clue, Gabriel asks the pilot, "Where are we headed?"

"Miami. You've got another plane to catch that will take you to Los Angeles. We've got to get you as far away from here as possible. They'll be looking for you in Miami," explained the Pilot revealing his wings to comfort his passenger.

"Can I use your cell phone, please?" requested Gabriel.

The pilot reaches into his pants pocket and tosses Gabriel his phone.

"Thanks. This is going to be long distance," Gabriel warned.

"No problem! Knock yourself out. It's yours," allowed the Pilot.

Without a second to lose, Gabriel calls Bishop Francis. The phone rings twice then he answers.

"Hello, Bishop Francis speaking."

"Your Grace, you were right," shouted Gabriel.

"Gabriel is that you?"

"Yes it is me. You were right! There was a prisoner at the prison that I shared a vision with. Satan referred to him as the Redeemer."

"Thanks be to God! Then that means that you're on the right track.

"Thank you for your encouragement your Eminence. My mission is clear now. God willing, I will not fail. My faith is stronger than its ever been. I will contact you soon, God Bless."

"Like I told you, you know more than you think, you'll know what to do when the time is right. God's speed my son," ended the Bishop.

Simultaneously they hang up their phones. The Bishop then walks to his place of refuge and begins to pray with fervor. Gabriel on the other hand cops a snooze due to being exhausted and in safe keeping while in good hands.

Chapter Four

(Beginning of the End)

(Purgatory)

Now dead with someplace to go, Dimitrius body washes up on the shore of an exotic island beach with a beautiful edge line of a jungle and glamorous mountainous terrain. Taken back for a moment, he is dazed and confused as to his whereabouts. At first he thought he was back in South America; where his last encounter cost him his life. Instinctually his defense mechanism engages so he remains low, on his belly. While scoping out the scenery, he regains his senses and realizes that he is not alone. From a short distance of about 20 yards or so is a boy, of about 12 or so, perched on a wreckage of a canoe, carving a piece of wood. All clear in his mind, Dimitrius ascends from the sand dressed in pressed fatigues and jungle boots. He approaches the boy with a cocky attitude.

"Hey, hey boy, where am I?" barked Dimitrius.

The boy replied, "If I were to guess, I'd say you are where you suppose to be."

"Oh yeah, and where is that?"

"Wait a minute; I thought I was supposed to be going to Hell. This can't be Hell! This place is beautiful," wondered Dimitrius.

Purgatory by Hillary Wilson

"You're right. This isn't Hell. It's where souls wait for final judgment, and where you will find Mathyus," explained the boy.

"Purgatory are you serious? This place does exist," blurted Dimitrius.

"Serious as a heart attack Señor," said the boy.

"First of all, you act like you know me. Who are you and who is Mathyus?"

"I am Miguel. I was sent by Mathyus to greet you and bring you to him," explained Miguel.

"Well what's your story? What did you do to die so young? Dimitrius asked.

Miguel replied, "La historia de mi vida."

"I was born in the barrios of east L.A, the son of youthful parents who neglected me while deeply committed to a ruthless lifestyle as local gang members. Prior to their adopted life, my parents and I would spend a lot of time together. Frequently we would play hide & seek which was my favorite. Now-a-days with time hardly spent on La familia, anger and stress has filled the void. How does the saying goes, 'You should never bring your work home.' Someone forgot to tell my parents that as they would open our home to fellow members allowing them to call it their home too.

Not feeling the vibe I would find places to hide to keep out of harms way; until one day I decided to runaway to find a better life of my own. Wishful thinking on my part but, unfortunately I didn't go far due to my age, so I stayed in the neighborhood because it was what I knew. Now living off the streets for about six months but regularly attending school, my parents didn't mind just as long as I stayed in the neighborhood so that I could be monitored by their gang. I was allowed to become my own man as long as I stayed within their territory and away from gang life, I was on my own. Everyday my parents would leave a different opening to the house because they knew I would find it. Sometimes they would leave money and food on the kitchen table so that I would feel that this was my home and that it was open for me when ever I was ready to stay.

One day war was raged against a rival gang due to a tit-for-tat retaliation. Life in the barrio became plagued with drive by's and Molotov cocktails. Shots fired randomly killing the innocent as they got in the way. Being at the wrong place at the wrong time claimed many lives causing them to be collateral damage. Unfortunately, with that being said; which brings this close to home for me included unexpected victims who were killed; my parents were sprayed with armor piercing bullets intended for whoever was in the area,

Full of rage and driven by revenge, I decided to take matters into my own hands. This meant that I had to leave my territory. While spying on the gang who killed my family, I was able to find their headquarters which was well protected by steel doors and bars on the windows. Being the pro at finding a way in I was successful. Once in I found a lot of cardboard and newspaper, so I set it all on fire and chained the doors on the outside trapping all of them inside. As it burned I stood and watched them die, but one of them saw me out of the window with a box of matches in my hand, so he shot me in the chest. I died knowing that they died too. So that's how I got here."

"Well damn, I can relate, you and I have that in common; how old are you? Dimitrius asked.

"I'm old enough to be my own man," said Miguel.

"Speaking of that, what kind of man sends a boy to do a man's job? I don't like this guy already," declares Dimitrius.

"He is the Gate Keeper, and he is blind," Miguel enlightens.

"Oh, damn. Well then, the real question is: are you who you say you are? This could be one of Satan's tricks," inquired Dimitrius, intensely.

Out of nowhere, a pure white Cockatoo surrounded by that soft, yet subtle, glow lands on the opposite end of the wreckage.

"Fear not Dimitrius! I understand your distrust. For the evil one is tricky and, aware that you're coming. You are in an untouchable place where he can not consume you. The boy is not one you should fear! He is but, the eyes of the Gate Keeper. He will lead you to him, and there you will be taught the things you will need to do God's work. Remember, God is with you always! Have faith in him, and he will see you through this," telepathically clarified the bird.

Recognized and understood it to be an omen the bird takes flight.

Miguel says, "Are you okay? You act like you seen a ghost or something!"

"Yeah, something like that. Well then, lead the way my compadre," Dimitrius replied.

Miguel by Chris Brimacombe

Maintaining his composure, Dimitrius recognizes that the visit from the bird was exclusively for him. As they trek thru the jungle, Dimitrius experiences flashbacks of previous missions; not so proud of. After the five mile trek, they finally come to a clearing where a Fortress of Solitude lie with no gates; nor doors. It is an "all are welcome and trusted" type community. After all, you're waiting to be judged . . . Why 'F' it up by doing something stupid.

"We're here!" Blurted Miguel.

"Where are the doors, and where is the Gate?" Dimitrius inquired.

Miguel looks at Dimitrius with a smile. While walking thru the Fortress, Dimitrius realizes that Purgatory is a sabbatical of Peace and Tranquility. You know the kind of place I'm talking about. A sit back and have a brew while you wait retreat. Here's to good friends, tonight is something special, the beer we pour must be something more somehow, stay thirsty my friends type of place. Get it?! He is overcome by the serenity and splendor that relaxes you while in limbo but yet, he never lets his guard down.

"Surely, Heaven can't be too much better than this," Dimitrius admired.

"Oh but it is! Although I've never been there, but that will soon change, thanks to you," spoke an unseen woman as they walked past a hammock dangled between two palm trees.

As she raised her head, Dimitrius couldn't help but to notice her beauty.

Under his breathe he says, "Like I said, it can't be."

"I'm afraid you have me at a disadvantage. You are?" rapped Dimitrius.

Carefully yet sensually she climbed out of the hammock with an intricately embellished book tucked in a sling draped over her right shoulder, the woman replied, "Forgive my manners, I'm Sarah. The people around here call me the Librarian; aka, The Bookkeeper of Souls."

"The what?" questioned Dimitrius?

"I maintain the journals of all who enter Purgatory, and where they eventually end up," she explained.

"Well, I guess that explains the book you're carrying," says Dimitrius.

Always trying to stay ahead of the game, he uses this short encounter to gather some intel.

"So if I were to give you a name, you could tell me where that person is right now?"

"Yes I can. You see, in Heaven, all who are blessed to be there equally share God's grace. So, the blessed are all sent on the same plateau. With the exception of the higher plain; where God—the Father, the Son, and the Holy Spirit dwell. Hell on the other hand, has five plateaus. Each one is worse than the other. The deeper you go, the closer you are to the Devil. The closer you are to the Devil is based on the sin you committed," Sarah educates.

"So lets say, suicide. What plateau does that put you on?" Dimitrius inquires.

"I don't want to talk about that. Besides, what you really want to know is: where are your wife and son?"

Slapped in the face by her insight and truth, Dimitrius is embarrassed.

"I guess that was obvious huh?"

"Quite. I'm reluctant to answer that question but, I will. It just reminds me why I am here. The souls who have taken their own lives, fuel the fires that eternally burn in Hell. These souls are closest to Satan. It is by God's mercy, that I haven't shared their fate," Sarah explained.

"But for you I'll be more than happy to tell you my story."

"During the genocidal era of 1939-1945 when the Nazi Regime strong armed/ occupied Poland; I was a 25 year old Jewish woman growing up in Warsaw Poland, where I saw my entire community and family destroyed during the invasion. I vowed to do all that I could by assisting fellow Jews, who tried to flee from annihilation. For many years I worked as a Librarian in the centre of the city. The Library was centrally located there because underneath it laid a tunnel that led to the outskirts of the city.

Sarah by Chris Brimacombe

Everyday, I would save lives until one day I was captured and arrested by the Gestapo and penned for execution by incineration, for aiding and harboring fugitives and, simply for being a Jew. While imprisoned awaiting my impending doom, I decided to take my own life, committing suicide by hanging myself in the cell."

"I'm sorry. I didn't know," he apologized.

"Boy, you people have been through it, I too have a story to tell. Would you like to hear it?" he sympathized.

"No it doesn't matter, God sent you. I see you have a lot to learn. Come, let us find Mathyus! He'll whip you into shape in no time," assured Sarah.

Together, they walked to the last structure of the stronghold where Mathyus exercises true discipline as he attentively guards the Gate cloaked in black to ward off those with vile intentions. Upon entering the building, they're met by a magnificent dog whose purpose is to warn and protect its guardian from persistent Demons who constantly try to breach the gateway.

"Now that's a dog! Here boy, here boy! Yeah, that's a good dog. What did he do to get here," asked Dimitrius.

Instinctively, the dog approaches the stranger and begins to sniff his way into familiarity. Once the dog catches his scent, its tail begins to wag with zest. Dimitrius reciprocates by petting and rubbing him. The dog begins to get carried away; standing up on its hind legs and licking Dimitrius' face. Their bond has been established and etched in blood.

"SIT!"

A stern command is given. Combined with a snap from some fingers, immediately, the dog obeys. Mathyus enters into the foyer carrying an enormous key.

"His name is Thorn. He too, was not exempt. He was a search and rescue dog that saved the life of a child in a fire. Unfortunately, he inhaled too much smoke and died shortly after. He sacrificed himself to save the life of another. A noble deed and yes the ultimate sacrifice. Thus, forever he will remain in Purgatory assigned to be my companion. Along with Sarah and Miguel; they are my new family.

Enough about us! Welcome, Dimitrius! I am Mathyus. Glad you made it. Come, we've got a lot to discuss," he proposed.

"Thanks. You must be in pretty good shape carrying that key around," said Dimitrius.

"I don't carry it all the time. I've figured out a way to get multiple uses out of it," answers Mathyus.

At the same time he flips the key upright and uses it as a cane.

"See what I mean?"

"I gotcha."

"In the supernatural, it's mind over matter; one of the lessons I will teach you but first, we must train your inner man. I can see, you still have doubt in your heart. I can see thru you as clear as glass."

Dimitrius taps Sarah on her shoulder and under his breathe says, "He's blind, right?"

"Yeah I'm blind, and I have 20/20 hearing too! So whispering ain't gonna do you any good around here," warned Mathyus.

"I told you, you have a lot to learn," Sarah reminded Dimitrius.

Miguel starts giggling and takes off running around the room as Thorn chases him out the doorway.

"Come! We have a lot to discuss. I'd like to see where your head is at, and then I'll let you rest because at dawn, we begin," stated Mathyus.

As Sarah removes herself from the premises, a look of lust catches both of their eyes.

Together, the two men sit in front of the gate exchanging memories of good and bad until they become bonded in blood. Empathetic to each others tale, the term 'friendship' shines the possibilities of hope and trust. Mathyus ends the meeting of the minds with his story and something to think about.

"I was an Evangelist whose mission was to minister via revivals' to broken, troubled men and women up and down the renowned Bible belt. Reading scripture and sharing God's lessons through the teachings of Christ in areas most were afraid to go. On this day I was supposed to travel, but as plans do change, after service I decided to discontinue my trip, and go home early due to my wife who was ill earlier that morning. Usually I spend at least 7 hours every Sunday doing the Lord's work. Unexpectedly, unto her I came home only to find her in our bed with another man. In total rage I snapped. As a result of my madness I beat the man to death and strangled my wife. Afterwards I came to my senses, and realized what I had done. Ashamed of my sin; I self inflicted wounds to my eyes causing permanent blindness, so that I may never look upon the man that I'd become. Today as I sit here with you, I can assure you that God knows my heart and that temporary insanity drove me insane as Satan placed it in my mind. So the Lord Almighty accepted my sacrifice (Blindness) and sentenced me to Purgatory as the Gate Keeper along with Thorn by my side." Mathyus concluded . . . .

"Like I told Sarah, we all have had a rough way to go, this is why we must put a stop to this madness," declared Dimitrius.

"I am in total agreement with you. Get some sleep now my friend. Tomorrow starts the best days of our lives."

"I sure hope so," said Dimitrius.

"So tell me, how much do you know about our enemy; Satan that is?" Mathyus quizzed.

Dimitrius replied, "He's the ultimate bad ass that defied God, so Archangel Michael kicked him and his followers out. Now he's in Hell pissed off raring to destroy the planet, right?"

"Let me enlighten you about the Dark one. It is said that he was an angel, who was favored by God. While held high amongst all angels, Lucifer's vanity became his conceit. His yearn for power filled him with a rebellious fervor as his position became clear to him. His arrogance brought him strength and his disobedience soon became a threat to the enchanted. During his defiance 1/3 of the angels became bitter due to sanctions placed on them to cherish us as they did God Himself. Outraged by this command, Lucifer devised a Coup D' Etat to take over heaven; to reign supreme as King of Kings. God being ubiquitous in nature and all knowing saw this in Lucifer from the beginning, Thus the saying 'Keep my friends close, but keep my enemy closer.' Patiently He waited until Lucifer thought he had the advantage. Foolishly unaware that God was knowledgeable of his plot; Lucifer revealed his mutinous ploy. With a clap from God's hand, he was ousted from Heaven by the Archangel and casted in a place where darkness may never see the light. God had prepared Hell to enslave him but Lucifer, who now goes by many names waged a war on mankind, thus we are in conference now to end this war by any means necessary."

"Wow, thanks for the Intel. I knew it went something like that. Hey, time to hit the hay," said Dimitrius.

Mathyus replied, "Goodnight soldier."

As the two men parted Dimitrius said underneath his breathe, "What have I gotten myself into?"

Possessing 20/20 hearing Mathyus says, Stop worrying, you'll be fine."

Shocked Dimitrius crashes until the early morning dew.

Mathyus 'The Gate Keeper & Thorn by SpartaDog

Chapter Five

(*Iron Sharpens Iron*)

Purgatory

B eautifully the sun shines through the break of dawn as it peaks through the clouds, gleaming over the horizon. A Rooster crows twice; set as an alarm to start this glorious day. Today is an important day indeed; simply because on this day, actions for God are underway. Prior to Mathyus' plan to rudely awaken his protégé, the befriending of canine and man sets precedent. Awakened by the wet tongue of the brute, Dimitrius arise to eagerly assume the Yoga position. Upon Mathyus' arrival he surprisingly finds Dimitrius up and about. Without disturbing him, Mathyus leaves a lesson plan and a note; along with the Holy Bible, a concordance and a dictionary on the table. When completing his meditation he sees the items on the table and proceeds to inspect them. At first he notices the materials then the note, which says:

*In order to put on your Body Armor, we must fit you with your Battle Axe and Shield; so you must study to show thyself approved unto God. This quote is scripture, from **2 Timothy 2:15**. The best weapon I can give you is the Word of God. So, I've prepared a list for you to study and memorize. Remember, in the supernatural it's mind over matter. We will be on a ten hour schedule, eight hours of study and two hours of whatever physical regime you can come up with. God's speed.*

He opens the list and says, "You have got to be kidding."

Out of frustration he shakes his head back and forth and from side to side. The list reads as follows as Mathyus' voice fills his head:

*Due to your former occupation, you of all people should know this. Know your enemy before you engage him. Learn everything God has provided us through his never changing word. Read it, Study it, and know it until it becomes 2nd nature. Once you've mastered the Word then, and only then, will you will be ready for battle (**Ephesians 6:11-17**). But keep this little tidbit in mind, Satan is well versed and knows the Bible better than all of us. He goes by different names and yet, he is still the same. Hell is a place that God made; so for him there are no boundaries. He's with us, always.*

SATAN	**BELIAL**	**BAALZEBUB**
Genesis 3:1-7	*Deuteronomy 13:13*	*2 Kings 1:2-3*
Job 1:6-12, 2:1-7	*Judges 19:22*	*John 3:1-2*
Isaiah 14:12-15	*1 Samuel 1:15-16*	*Matthew 12:22-28*
John 8:44	*1 Samuel 2:12*	
2 Corinthians 4:4	*1 Samuel 25:17*	
2 Corinthians 11:3	*2 Samuel 20:1-2*	
Ephesians 6:11-18	*1 Kings 21:9-13*	
James 4:7	*2 Corinthians 6:14-15*	
1 Peter 5:8-9		
Revelation 12:9-10		
Revelation 20:10		

Read all of Psalms, Proverbs and The New Testament so that you can familiarize yourself with the teachings of Christ and the reason for his existence.

Time passes by in our era about 2 weeks or so; which in God's time may be equivalent to three milliseconds. During this time, Mathyus schools Dimitrius on what to expect while they're in Hell and diligently drills him on the lessons the scriptures implied. His workout, now maximized at full potential, rewards him with the resemblance of Hercules, Adonis, or an all out super hero if you will. He suspects that he has a new fan base as Sarah and Miguel admire his progress. While in training he finds that he has developed a sense of what compassion is all about. There is one particular individual he is drawn to more than others.

During his tenure flirtation manifest as giggles and smiles bring them to their fun days when things were at its best. Long walks and talks give insight to who they are while holding hands but not making plans. Flower picking and song singing brings them closer as they start to lose control. Noticing their puppy love is Mathyus, who takes a back seat for personal reasons of his own. Miguel too enjoyed the look of love; at last forgotten when the thoughts of his parents made him blue.

Is it because of the pure animalistic attraction between male and female, or is it temptation trying to sabotage the efforts before they start? But, what of his wife, you might ask? Confused and often confronted with this dilemma, Dimitrius learned from the training how to bring your burdens to Christ and leave them there. So he attempts to solve his problem with prayer.

"Father God, in the Blessed name of Jesus, I rebuke Satan and the lustful feelings he brings to my heart. Make me stronger, so that I may not offend you and I'll be careful to give you the honor, glory and praise in Jesus' name, Amen."

Listening to the prayer Dimitrius just petitioned Mathyus asks, "What's troubling you my friend?"

Dimitrius replied, "Whatever it was, I gave it to God. Let's get on with the show."

"Well, with that being said I would say that you are ready. At midnight, we'll go thru the gate. So prepare yourself and rest . . . We're gonna need it," suggested Mathyus.

"That's not a bad idea but, there is something I have to do. Where's Sarah?"

"She's on the balcony, looking at the stars," answered Miguel.

"What was the prayer about if you let your flesh dictate your actions," inquired Mathyus.

"Prayer changes things, I know. I'm trying my best," says Dimitrius as he leaves the room headed toward the balcony driven by lust and his craving flesh; although hypercritical at his best.

When he arrives, he can't help but to notice how delicious Sarah looks from behind. For a quick second he visualizes Jessica. As he regains his mind he continues to admire her tush. Again, lust has reared its ugly head.

"Beautiful."

"Yes they are," she agreed.

Casually he enters her personal space and puts his arms around her. Caught up in the sexual feeling, she welcomes his presence.

"This feels good," she says.

"Yeah it does."

Simultaneously he turns her around, looks into her eyes, and begins to passionately tongue her down until they've both had their fill.

"Wow! Why'd you do that?" she asked.

"The same reason you let me," he answered.

"Have you ever wanted something but, you know you couldn't have it?"

"My sentiments exactly. I've wanted you from the first time I saw you, but there's the issue with my wife so I kept my distance. The Spiritual Warfare is at battle all day, everyday. Even now it fights, and the only way I see us winning this war is if you come with us. I need the possibility of love in my life; even though we are not one. To have love present in a place where there is none, can only be a blessing," he pleads. "So will you come?"

"Yes! Yes, I'd thought you'd never ask," accepted Sarah.

Together they maintain their hold as they continue to watch the stars in awe until interrupted.

"Ahaarrrhhmm! Okay you two! Time to get some rest. Dimitrius, you come with me. Just like two teenagers; can't leave them alone for five minutes. Now get to bed before I sick Thorn on the both of you, and don't try to sneak! Thorn will be on guard. We'll be leaving in 7 hours," commanded Mathyus.

At the same time the 2 adults giggle as they separate with their eyes glued on each other like adolescents do when kissed for the first time.

Out of sight, out of mind. Or does separation weigh more than what people hope to bargain for? We struggle with our flesh daily because it is strong and relentless. Not to mention that we were born into iniquity. Prayer does change things but, don't stop praying if it doesn't happen right away. It may not happen when you want it but, the

God I serve is always on time. So don't be too hard on yourself. God foresaw that if depended on our own integrity, failure was inevitable. Hence the destruction of himself in human form. If we allow Jesus to bare our burdens and continue to give him praise, we grant him the right to stand as our advocate before God. Remember, Satan is always on the grind. So with that being said, in the case of Dimitrius and Sarah, is it love or is it lust?

(Infomercial #1)

The Lord directs our paths through the opening and closing of doors. When God closes one door, he opens another. If he didn't close the wrong door we would never find the right door. This constitutes that there is a wrong door and a right door. Choosing the right door and leaving the wrong door can be tricky. This concept may be hard to conceive. Don't give the Devil credit for what God has done for you. When things seem to go wrong, people have the tendency to give Satan power over them. *The devil is attacking me.* When in fact, it's God closing the wrong door for you. We must recognize when God is working his mojo. When a door closes, it forces you to change your course i.e. loss of employment or a toxic relationship. God will shut the door. Whether you choose to pursue another door is solely up to you. Your motivation should be that you have a choice. If you decide to be disenfranchised and content then you will procrastinate and may never receive your blessings but, if you are driven by the power that is within you—the power God has given you—you will realize that it is time to move and to open the right the door. So, I guess determining what is wrong or right depends on your faith. If you believe that our Lord and Savior Jesus Christ truly loves us and that he will never harm us as stated in **Jeremiah 29:11**, *For I know the plans I have for you, declares the LORD, plans to prosper you and not to harm you, plans to give you hope and a future.*

Believing in his Word of Truth will permit you to finally find the right door which allows you to walk into your blessing. So let us praise him for the closed doors that bring forth initiative, which pushes us forward, and keeps us out of harms way.

Chapter Six

(Open Sesame)

Purgatory

The best time to open the gate is at the twilight hour; Hell, meaning its residents are deep in slumber. Demons reprieve from a full day of torment exercised on condemned souls who are sentenced to torture and pain; not to include their incessant efforts to breach the doorway leading to limbo. As Dimitrius gathers his wits and weaponry, a beautiful white butterfly outlined with that familiar glow enters thru the window and lands on his shoulder. While perched, familiarity breeds content so with all due respect he ceases and listens to the heavenly creature.

"The time has come for you to fulfill your destiny. I anoint thee with divine power which will assist you in miraculous ways. This will be the last that I will come to you but, know that I am with you in spirit and in truth. Remember, your success is governed by your faith."

When completing the sentence it takes flight intensely swirling its way around the room causing a cold genuine draft. Graced like his predecessor Moses, he is armed with the power of God. Dimitrius makes his way to the foyer where the gate lies. Upon his arrival he realizes that he is the last; all accounted for. Reassured and raring to get the show on the road Dimitrius decides to start his leadership role with a motivational speech.

"We are about to embark on the greatest mission mankind has ever encountered. God has chosen us to save the souls of those who wish to leave Hell. It could be hundreds, or even thousands! Whatever it is, we'll be faced with challenges only God can withstand. Guess what people, God is on our side! So I say let the Devil come, because we are the DIVINE MILITIA! Mathyus, lead us into prayer."

"Let us hold hands, bow our heads, and close our eyes . . . Father God," begins Mathyus as Thorn starts to growl, interrupting the prayer. Suddenly the temperature drops to a frigid digit and the stench of death engulfs the air. All attention is drawn on the gate as they bare witness to an ominous dark shadow emerging from the doorway materializing into a shrouded humanoid carrying a scythe. Uncontrollably, Thorn goes into attack mode but is restrained by Dimitirus' grasp.

With an eerie voice the shadow utters, "Who amongst you claim to be the Redeemer?"

"Who wants to know?" Dimitrius asks.

"You are the one I seek. You are brave and strong; a wise choice indeed. Some call me the Harbinger of Death but, I am best known as the Grim Reaper. I come not to take your souls," claimed the mysterious one.

"Then why are you here? No one has died among us. What do you want?" inquired Mathyus.

Suddenly the cloak is removed and the creepy aura is interrupted, the stench of death is lifted. Dressed in a camel colored Safari outfit with a red ascot, cap and black riding boots is a flamboyant fella carrying a short whip, looking to negotiate terms?

"Look, rumor has it that the Redeemer is coming to put an end to this revolting place. I'm tired of this dreadful ass job! I'm stuck in this dismal gig for a hundred years, and then the next fool will take my place. Not to mention death, death, death! I am much bigger than that! I come to ask you, can I join the cause? The way I see it, this is my chance to get out of this dead end job; no pun intended. So, what do you say?" pleaded the Reaper.

The look on the Militias' faces appears to be that of flabbergast. Wise and blessed with hindsight Mathyus recognizes the gift.

"Give us a minute," requested Mathyus.

In the middle of the foyer the group huddles to consult.

"This is truly a blessing," implied Mathyus.

"Talk to me Mathyus," Dimitrius commands.

Sarah poses a question, "Can he be trusted?"

"He gives me the creeps," chimed Miguel.

Mathyus elaborates, "Let's take a look at what has presented itself. If we allow Death to join us, Hell would not be able to receive more souls. This will clearly be to our advantage. This must be a gift from God. He has allowed Death to cross the plains to be with us which means Death is not bound by eternal law; he can move about freely. This may be useful later on! Don't you get it? He was only doing a necessary job. Somebody had to do it. With Death on our side, we're in the winner's column."

As the consultation adjourns, Dimitrius warns the Reaper, "If you do this, surely there will be a price on your head," he says.

The Reaper responds, "The way I see it, I'm damned if I do and damned if I don't. Besides, you're down with God, right?"

Miguel replies, "No doubt. Are you?"

"Hell yeah! Oops! I mean yes, I believe in Christ Jesus," the Reaper admitted.

Now Sarah, being the Keeper of Souls, asks him, "what is your name?"

"Forgive my manners and allow me to introduce myself. Sebastian King, at your service," he eloquently states while taking a bow and tipping his skimmer.

Sarah sarcastically asks, "Ok well what's your story, everyone seems to have one."

"Well if you insist, I am a well cultured fellow a bit eccentric, flamboyant, witty and oh yeah, a cancer. I am proud to say that I am happy, carefree and I'm borderline gay; Why? Because I haven't crossed the line yet, but I'm very in tuned to my feminine side. I have a flare for the finer things in life that keeps me on edge; especially fashion as you can see. I was an aristocrat from the high society of

Sebastian the Grim Reaper by Christopher Romo

Paris, in a time when the magnificent city became the fashion cornerstone of the world. Traveling about Europe showboat style and setting a precedent for the whole world to see. In order to have freedom of travel thru the dimensions, I made a deal with the devil to do the mundane duties of retrieving souls and escorting them to Hell," he so colorfully explained.

Again the look on everyone's face left them flabbergasted to say the least.

"Well okay, back to business! Mathyus, how about that prayer? Assume the position everybody," demanded Dimitrius.

Graciously Mathyus says his prayer to completion. When finished, Dimitrius barks an order.

"Open the Gate!"

As the gate opens the stench of death resurfaces and the cries of tormented souls howl while the darkness overshadows the light. In unison, the Militia cautiously enters Hell. Suddenly the Gate slams shut behind them.

"Welcome to Hell. We've been expecting you," said an unknown spook that sat by the door accompanied by a hell hound drooling from its mouth.

Immediately Thorn pounces in its direction, daring it to reciprocate but, it doesn't. Growls and snarls percolate as their hairs rise to the occasion; establishing which of them are the Alpha male. Instead of confrontation, casually they circled about trying to sniff each other's butts. Once their scents were gathered, the Hell hound began to mark his territory; as any dog would.

"Who and what are you?" Dimitrius asked.

"He's my counterpart . . . I guess Satan isn't stupid after all," said Mathyus.

"I am Calixto, the Guardian. It is my duty to keep the malevolent from escaping Hell."

While explaining his position, he breaks the key off in the lock for precautionary measure.

Sebastian blurts out, "What are you doing?"

Miguel added, "We're trapped!"

"Right you are little one, and in case you were wondering, once you enter Hell, there is no turning back," cautioned Calixto.

Dimitrius boldly discontinued their conversation with this, "Doors are made to keep people in or out. We'll make one on the back end. Come on! Let's get this show on the road."

So they walked, as Calixto informed his master that company has arrived.

They're now in a place where there is no sense of time and space, only gloom and doom that marinates the spirit of all who dwell; like a shroud of eternal dismay.

"Oh my God what is that smell? Gross," exclaimed Sebastian.

Sarah snaps, "You've got to be kidding! Don't you recognize the scent of your own . . . ?"

Before she can finish her statement Sebastian defends himself.

"Oh, no she didn't! Excuse me miss thang, are you going to be a problem? Because if you are, let me read your little behind right now."

"Quiet! Satan is attacking us already; disruption amongst the troops. If we are going to be successful, we must respect and trust one another," barked Dimitrius.

"He's right. We must not allow Satan to disillusion us as he has done to the poor souls we come to rescue. Miguel, show us the way. Sebastian, study Proverbs and Ephesians. You're going to need them." Mathyus suggested.

"Wait a minute. If the kid has never been to Hell, how is he supposed to show us the way," asked Dimitrius.

Mathyus explains, "now Dimitrius, practice what you preach. Finding the way is his forte' and besides he has Thorn to assist him. Trust him. God does."

Humbled by the wise, Dimitrius looks at Miguel and nods his head in approval.

Calixto the Guardian by Peterson

(In the Interim) *Hell: The Devil's Lair*

While laid back trying to formulate a strategy, Belial has fallen victim to his own claim. He once declared that he will kill, steal, and destroy mankind by any means necessary. His number one method of destruction is to cause disruption by way of confusion. As part of his punishment, is he not exempt from the formidable things mere mortals are exposed to, or is confusion theoretically a universal concept that even monarchs may suffer?

"Ain't this a bitch? The Redeemer is about to begin his quest. Do you believe this shit? I'll be damned! Am I not the Lord of Darkness; the Incarnation of Evil? Don't I have dominion over men? How dare he attempt this feeble endeavor to end my rule?"

"Use the girl to distract him from his duty," Lilith suggests.

Belial admires, "that's a wicked idea! That's my girl, always on point. Enoch, bring me his wife! She will be my pawn to manipulate his mind; after all she's the reason he's here in the first place. So, let's give him what he came for. Then, his mission will be compromised. There will be no need for him to continue and then, business as usual."

At the door, Wrath stands guard and allows Enoch to enter with Jessica as ordered. Petrified of the unexpected, she remains silent. Belial and Lilith glace at each other with a sinister grin on their faces as if the outcome was inevitable.

"Come closer my dear," ordered Belial.

Jessica approaches with her head bowed.

"Damn! I can see what he saw in you; T&A for days! Where was I? Oh yeah, I have a task for you and if you value your husbands' life, you will do it with no questions asked," threatened Belial.

Amused by the situation, Wrath moves closer to get an earful.

Jessica timidly asks, "What is it that you would have me do, my Lord?"

Belial elaborates, "Your husband has entered my realm. I want you to tell him that there is no need to carry on his mission because I've released you."

In addition to her physical attributes, Dimitrius choose his wife because of her spunk, tenacity and her vivacious attitude.

Jessica boldly inquires, "Why are you doing this? Where's my son?"

"Silence bitch! You dare question me?"

Quickly Lilith rises from her sprawl and slaps the living shit out of Jessica's face causing her to fall on the floor.

"Wrath, have your way with her," barked Belial.

Wrath proceeds to snatch her up by her arm while grunting.

"No my Lord, please! Forgive me! I'll do it," apologized Jessica.

"Wrath Heel! Do that bullshit again, and I'll fry your ass like Popeye's. You get me?"

"Yes my Lord."

Wrath unleashes his grasp and pushes her to the door. As she scurried away Wrath begins to laugh. The kind of laugh that runs thru your body like finger nails screeching along a chalkboard.

"Well then go, Enoch you're up; go with her and handle your business." ordered Belial.

"By your command my Liege." obeyed Enoch.

"Wrath follow them but remain unseen, if she betrays me; kill her." instructed Belial.

Chapter Seven

(*City of Angels*)

(Meanwhile) *In the Now: Los Angeles*

T he transfer was completed with no resistance. Gabriel is safe and sound asleep on his way to the City of Angels via a commercial airline when a revelation enters his dream. It's him, kneeling in the rain at Calvary Hill in front of his cross overlooking the Valley of Death while reciting the 23rd Psalm. Suddenly he awakens due to plane turbulence. Immediately he grabs his Bible and reads to himself the referred Psalm. He commences reading and in a cross like pattern, covers his body. When finished he gazes at the text Bishop Francis provided by way of the Vatican. It is a list of names, locations, and instructions. Now he has all that is required to strategize a plan of action. Customarily, an announcement is made: *Ladies and Gentlemen this is your Captain speaking. Please return to your seats and fasten your seat belts. We're in the Los Angeles air space and will be landing shortly.* In compliance, Gabriel remains seated and indulges himself with prayer. Touchdown! It's a smooth landing. Welcome to Los Angeles, the City of Angels, home to the stars, the sexiest women, implants, bloods & Cripps and, according to Snoop, the best chronic (weed) money can buy.

First time at an International Airport, Gabriel is amazed at the variety of cultures stationed at LAX. He is approached by a Hare Krishna group. They offer him fruit, flowers and blessings of peace.

"Nourishment for the body strengthens the mind. You look like you could use something to eat. Can I offer you an orange?" offered the Guru.

He graciously declines, "No thank you but, that was kind of you. What religious order do you belong too? I'm not from this country. Please, excuse my ignorance."

The Guru responds, "Let me guess, Italian right? He who is ignorant is he who does not ask questions. We are Hare Krishna. We believe that in order to achieve peace it is thru one's original consciousness and goal of life, manifested from the pure love of God. Our mantra is of the purist intention."

"That's very interesting. A great God is he that he loves us all," Gabriel proclaimed.

"There're a lot of ignorant people here who do not appreciate their blessings and are willing to result to evil before good. Please watch your back."

"I will thanks. Peace be with you," granted Gabriel.

The two men shake hands as they part their separate ways. Finally, he finds his way to the taxi stand. He stands in line until it's his turn. The valet hales the next cab. Routinely, a cab pulls up and Gabriel gets in.

"Where to mister?"

Gabriel hands the driver the address on a piece of paper with a $100.00 bill.

"Are you familiar with this address? I need to get there as soon as possible."

The cabby replied, "For this kind of money I'll take you to Timbuktu!"

Swiftly the cab pulls away from the curb. During the ride Gabriel notices how the driver keeps looking at him through the rear view mirror but, he acts oblivious. The cabby delays on purpose and 45 minutes later, the cab pulls up to Mt. Zion Baptist Church in South Central.

"Okay mister this is it. Are you sure your at the right place? I mean people around here ain't too fond of white folk. You're gonna stand out like a faggot in prison," cautioned the Cabby.

Gabriel ignores him as he removes himself from the cab.

"Wait here. I may further need your services."

"As long as you're paying. As a matter of fact, I'll need an advance."

"Do I look stupid to you? I've already paid you more than enough. Don't try to hustle me my friend. You're better than that." Gabriel exclaimed.

"Alright, calm down slick. Just kidding. I'll stay right here," retracted the Cabby.

The door slams as Gabriel proceeds to the entrance of the church. While watching as his passenger walks away, his eyes flicker flame. Just like most churches the doors are always open for those in need of divine intervention. Fortunately, this church follows protocol so he enters. While crossing the threshold he hears a choir practicing which draws him into the sanctuary. As he enters, the choir ceases their song due to shock. Everyone stares at him as if he were Jesus himself. Approached by what appears to be an usher he is asked, "Can I help you sir?"

"Yes. Can you tell me where I might find Pastor James Grant?"

"Pastor isn't here today. Is there something I can help you with," asked the Usher.

"As a matter of fact, there is! It's of grave importance that he contact me as soon as possible, I'll give you my cell phone number. Please tell him that Father Gabriel from the Monastery of the Divine Saints from Italy wishes to meet with him about pressing matters," requested Gabriel.

Completely understanding what pressing matters the visitor is referring to, the charade is lifted by dialogue of a familiar dialect. The Usher begins to speak in Italian.

"We are the new Disciples that God trusts to unify his children."

Gabriel responds in his native tongue, "It is God's will that bless the chosen. Pastor Grant I presume."

"I apologize for the charade but, I had to be sure. The Vatican informed me that you were coming. Excuse me for a second. That will be all for today Deacon Elliot we'll pick up where we left off next week."

The two men proceed to the Pastor's office to get acquainted by discussing goals and objectives. Two hours pass before Gabriel realizes that he had a cab waiting.

They walk outside only to notice that the cab was no where insight.

"I guess he couldn't wait. Where do we go from here," Grant asked.

"Do you like Chinese food?"

"Who doesn't?"

"Good! Next stop, San Francisco. I was told of a chef there that specializes in Asian cuisine. Also, he's the man we seek."

"Well at least our bellies will be filled," jested Grant.

Gabriel welcomes humor in his stressful situation; which comes to be a temporary escape from his madness. He begins to laugh until he is tickled pink.

"It wasn't that funny, Gabriel. Come with me. I have something to show you."

The two men walk across the street to an old garage sitting unoccupied. Curious but silent, Gabriel is taken back when Grant presses a button on his key chain which opens the bay doors revealing a Winnebago.

"I don't think God would have a problem if we did this in comfort and style. Do you? Now, you can laugh," advised Grant.

Together, they laugh.

Chapter Eight

(Cry for Jesse)

Valley of Death

O nward now six miles within, they approach the world renowned Valley of Death; as if anybody's been there to talk about it. Although often mentioned and prayer ridden, this place does exist.

"I think this would be a fine time to recite the 23rd Psalm," suggested Mathyus.

"You took the words right out of my mouth," Sarah agreed.

In unison they begin the scripture. While reciting, Dimitrius notices with his keen sense of awareness two figures emerging from the ashes. Normally familiarity would breed content due to his tactical prowess, but there is something fishy about this situation as the figures become clearer upon their approach. The timing is off? It's too early, right? Why now? Questions one would ask if the trophy was given before the race began. Dimitrius recognizes Jessica immediately. Without hesitation, the has-been couple rushes into each others arms and kiss like never before. Caught up in the emotion Sarah's heart is briefly stunned but, her strength lies deep within her understanding; she remains calm.

"Jesse is it really you? Where's Donnie? This can't be happening," Dimitrius sobbed.

Valley of Death by Nolan Emme & Peterson

"Yes baby, it's me. I haven't got much time. I come to warn you, Belial knows you are here so he sent me to distract you. This is why I am here as soon as you entered. He's afraid of you. I now know my death was a part of God's plan. If you stop now then I would have died in vain," Jessica proclaimed.

"No! What have you done? You mustn't betray him," shouted Enoch. Due to the outburst all eyes draw to the stranger.

Miguel asks, "Who is he?"

"Good question," says Sebastian.

"I don't care! My life must have deemed some value, because God used me as bait to put an end to this forsaken place," declared Jessica.

Dimitrius stares at Enoch with a vengeance.

"Who is this guy, and why are you with her," he asked.

"He's the . . ."

Before Jessica could finish her sentence, Wrath, with superior accuracy, throws a flaming axe into her back which pierces her heart causing instant death.

"HaHaHaaaaha!!!" laughs Wrath as he runs away in the opposite direction.

Sarah screams while Dimitrius losses his cool.

Out of pure rage, he snatches the axe out of her back and lays her body down on the ground. Then, being the controlled person he is, he gives orders that stick to his cause.

"Sebastian grab him! Thorn, if he moves bite his freaking head off! Stay here. I'll be back."

Imagine a sprinter running as a shot is fired. That's how fast he takes off after Wrath with axe in hand as if it were a baton. As his momentum gains him closer to the assailant; he hurls the axe. Little does Wrath know, his nemesis is a skilled assassin, as well? Incredibly enough, he finds his own axe lodged in his back. Fortunately gifted with the strength of 100 men, he doesn't lose stride and successfully gets away. Realizing that continuing his pursuit would only gain him failure; Dimitrius decides to go back where he may find answers from the creep held under guard. In his head, thoughts of loosing her twice takes him to a place of retribution. Contradicting those thoughts are those of forgiveness. Still he struggles within. Angrily, he approaches

Enoch by Chris Brimacombe

the group; particularly the stranger. With one hand, he lifts the dude off his feet leaving them dangling in the air.

"Start talking punk! Who are you? The last thing she said, you were what? Fill in the blank. Now!!" Dimitrius demanded.

"I, I was the only friend she had in this place. I was the listening ear who allowed her to vent. She was fragile and I gave her support. I am Enoch. Please let me down."

Dimitrius drops him like a bag of dirty laundry. Drawn to her lifeless body he kneels and hugs her while grieving. As the revealed name is mentioned, Sarah tilts her head to the left and raises her eyebrow out of curiosity. "Enoch-Enoch" . . . repeats in her mind until she recalls his identity.

"There are two Enoch's that I know of: one who walked with God in Heaven, and one an accountant who stole money from the mob in 1940. Surely you are the lesser of the two."

"I'll beg your pardon, not one of my proud moments." He exclaimed

"Tell us something we don't already know; what's your story?" asked Mathyus.

Staring into space refrained from looking them in their eyes; he answers his interrogation.

"During the Great Depression I was an Accountant for the State and Local Government of Chicago, who moonlighted for the Mob. To their convenience I would adjust their books to accommodate their needs. Extortion was my business as we put the squeeze on local businesses and local officials. We had them all in pocket, from the Mayor to the Police Chief and everyone on down. It was a great time for business. Everyone had their hands in the pot. I too found opportunities to bank a buck, so I began to embezzle from them which led to my demise. When you make a deal with the Devil, you always get screwed."

"You got that right, working for him was a pain in the ass." Sebastian agreed.

"I'm afraid you have me at a disadvantage, and you are," asked Enoch.

"Never mind that! Who was that guy and why did he kill Jesse," Dimitrius inquired.

Enoch divulges, "His name is Wrath; the Devil's Henchman. Truly a wicked fella who enjoys torturing souls."

Wrath Smash by Chris Brimacombe

"I hit him square in his back with that axe! The force alone should've put him down, or at least slowed him down . . . it did nothing. As a matter of fact he became faster," astonished Dimitrius proclaimed.

Enoch continued to elaborate, "Because my friend, Satan has granted him the strength and agility of 100 men. He can never die. His tale is something out of the Dark Ages; gothic to say the least . . . .

In mid to late 16th century France, while serving under reign of King Louis XVI as an Executioner and Torturer; thousands of lives fell victim to the lustful swing of his axe. Inflicting pain brought him pleasure as did death; did the same. Putting fear in the hearts of men tickled his fancy until, the regions plagued with tyranny and strife united to revolt against their king; to halt his ruthless dread. Now force to fight for his life, Wrath showed no fear while killing 100 men; until fatigue set forth to start his demise. Wickedly filled with a vengeful spirit he came to a malice conclusion; that death was inevitable and, that hell was going to be his domain. In order to secure his place amongst the damned, with the aid of the guillotine he beheaded himself, welcoming death as did most deranged people do.

Admiring Wrath's character, Satan applauded the trifling act and honored him with the strength of every man he killed that day, thus making him the monster you met today. But it doesn't stop there; to include the authority to rule by his side as his henchman and torturer of souls. As you can see he is a nasty fellow; who can not die."

"I don't care how many lives he has. The next time I see him, his ass is mine," proclaimed Dimitrius while pissed off to the max."

Miguel asks, "Why did he kill her?"

"The reason the lady was assassinated was because she betrayed the Dark One." Enoch explained.

"She referred to him as Belial. Is that the name he goes by," questioned Mathyus.

"Why yes. Take your pick: Satan, Devil, Beelzebub, Nicodemus . . . you get the point. The Dark One has many names. This season, he's referred to as Belial."

"You seem to be well informed about the going-ons of this place. We can use his knowledge to gain the advantage! Will you fight for the cause," asked Mathyus.

Wrath by Chris Brimacombe

"The reason he is here is because he could not be trusted," blurted Sarah.

"The reasons why we are all here is because we did something displeasing against God's will. Who are we to judge? Our mission is to save everyone who wishes to leave; that includes the worst of the worst. It's not up to us to decide who comes and goes. Is that clear? All agreed, say I," mandated Mathyus.

One by one they responded, "I-I-I-I-I!"

Enoch realizes his window of opportunity, and exploits the offer.

"Okay, let me get this straight. Free my soul and end the Devil's reign? Sounds impossible. Unless, you are the Redeemer foretold by the prophecy. Are you him?"

"I don't believe in titles or labels my friend," Dimitrius informed.

"What difference does that make? Are you with or without us," bellowed Sebastian.

"Better yet, are you a believer in Christ," Sarah chimed.

"Yes, I believe in the lord," Enoch claimed.

(Notice the lower cased L, which signifies the Dark lord not Jesus.)

"Time will tell if our new recruit is true to our cause," wisely spoke Mathyus.

"We can't leave her here like this. She deserves a proper burial," suggested Dimitrius.

"If a soul dies in Hell, it becomes fuel for the eternal Lake of Fire. This is why it's always hot here. Death happens every day, all day," Mathyus educates.

"He's right. Their souls' burn forever," chimed Enoch.

"I don't care! I am not leaving her here to rot," Dimitrius roared.

Understanding his frustration, Miguel grabs Mathyus' staff and begins to shovel. Reluctantly Enoch joins in and as a team player; they begin to dig with what sturdy bones they could find. While they lay her to rest, he who mourns asks Mathyus for kind words.

Mathyus replies, "Of course, it would be my pleasure."

Simultaneously the group bowed their heads and held hands, to show their support. Sarah conveniently clutches Dimitrius' hand; he reciprocates with a firm but subtle grip. All are focused on the said prayer with the exception of Enoch who harbors his Judas mentality.

Chapter Nine

(Nothing but the Dog in Me)

The Devil's Lair

Caught up in lust mode, Belial wears a mink glove as he caresses Lilith's nude body.

"I must say, he knew what he was doing when he made the woman's body; perfection. Sheer perfection," admired Belial.

Abruptly Wrath enters the chamber with the axe still embedded deep in his back.

"Ahh Wrath, tell me the good news," requested Belial.

"She betrayed you."

"Really? I must be losing my Mojo or some shit. O well. Please tell me Enoch has joined the Band of Misfits."

"He seemed to be accepted," updated Wrath.

"What of our nemesis," inquired Lilith?

During the conversation, Belial notices how Wrath is hunched over and in pain.

"Wait just a minute, turnaround. Can somebody please tell me why is there a freaking axe in this mutha fucka's back," bellowed Belial.

"He was at least 50 yards away and was able to accurately gash me with my own weapon. He possesses the skills of a warrior and appeared to have the brawn only an average man would hope for; he is strong indeed. We must be careful with this one," reported Wrath.

Casually Belial walks behind Wrath and snatches the axe out of his back.

"Ahhhhhhh!"

Lilith is amused as Wrath suffers.

"Oh come now, take it like a man. You mean to tell me, he who tortures for a living can't take what he loves most; pure unadulterated pain? I find you to be pathetic," she said. Unenthusiastically, Wrath strolls away embarrassed.

"Okay, physically he is capable but, what of his will? Let's see where his strength truly lies. Who let the dogs out? Ruff, ruff-ruff-ruff! Wrath send them," commanded Belial.

"By your command, Sire."

As instructed Wrath reaches in his pocket and blows a high pitched whistle. Suddenly the sounds of howls, barks, and growls become prominent then, gradually fade away like a recording does at the end of its song.

(In the Interim) Valley of Death

Standing over Jessica's grave, the group decides to set up camp due to their emotions running high. While establishing their individual spaces the sound of howling catches their attention.

"Did you hear that?" Sarah asked.

Thorn snaps into a defensive stance and growls intensely.

"Heal boy! Heal! Miguel put his leash on! Now!" demanded Mathyus.

Quickly Miguel does what he's told.

"Oh damn, I hope that's not what I think it is," Sebastian cautioned.

"It is what you think it is, hell hounds," Enoch disclosed.

"Everybody listen to me, whatever you do, no sudden moves." Dimitrius advised.

Within the darkness the fearsome sound becomes closer as a horde of flaming red eyes surrounds them snarling, growling with tails wagging and mouths drooling.

Hellhounds by SpartaDog

"If you really are the Redeemer, then start redeeming damn it," shouted Sebastian.

"Quiet fool; we must be careful. If you are bitten by these hounds you become a Werewolf, they attack you to recruit you," counseled Enoch.

Realizing that they are in a no win situation, Dimitrius looks to a higher power and depends on his faith to see them through.

"Stand still and let me show you God's might so you will see and know that he is with us," announced Dimitrius.

As he moves forward he is confronted by the Alpha. Demonstrating that he is fearless, he slowly extends his left hand to establish trust. The Alpha sniffs his hand and welcomes his conviction. Unfortunately viewed from a distance, Wrath blows his whistle to disrupt their concentration. Suddenly the hound snaps as Dimitrius is bitten, causing the pack to move toward the group. One by one, the hounds leap forward only to meet a barrage of punches and kicks administered by the once bitten. Sensing the contamination of its victim, the canines stop their pursuit and flee; with the exception of the Alpha who sits awaiting validation. Now filled with adrenaline due to the excitement, the infection rapidly travels throughout Dimitrius' body causing him to collapse to the ground. Sarah runs toward him.

"Get away from him! He's infected," shouted Enoch.

"He's right, get back! In the name of Jesus, heal me Father," painfully cried Dimitrius.

As a matter of public opinion they automatically presume that he is doomed. The transformation initiates and hopelessly he is slaved to its alteration. The physical change brought out the worst in him, verifying that every dog will have his day. The whites of his eyes turn fiery red, while his hair began to spring as if he were a Chia Pet; his snout lengthens, as his teeth turn in to fangs. The gruesome transformation lasts for 7 long minutes then, suddenly as Dimitrius expected; the reverse process commenced on its own. Never under estimating the power of prayer, Dimitrius' faith brings him victory which guarantees that the Glory of God is reinforced for all attended; including Enoch who can't believe his own eyes. As Dimitrius rises from the ground, snarling due to his disposition, the Alpha approaches him to justify

Werewolf by Christopher Romo

their new found relationship. He licks the hand that was bitten and wags its tail in approval then runs off into the darkness howling to signal the others. Finally, Thorn calms down. In total amazement, the members of the Militia begin to give cheers and thanks to the Lord for their safety and disinfection of their fearless leader.

As he turned around toward his friends he says, "Now do you believe that He is with us?"

Joining Enoch's astonishment is Wrath; who once again must give a report of disappointing news.

"What the . . . ? This can't be so," Wrath sighed.

Quietly he mopes his way back to his master; like how a dog does when scolded with its tail tucked between his legs.

"How much further until we leave this valley," asked Dimitrius.

"Give or take ten, twelve miles," Sebastian answered.

"No, more like twenty," chimed Enoch.

"I hope our next encounter is less taxing than that last episode," Dimitrius anticipates.

"The City of the Dead waits," informed Enoch as he turns a stare at Miguel.

"La Ciudad de los Muertos," Miguel repeats in Spanish.

"Oh yeah. I hate that place. Nothing but pure d-trouble. There, you will find what the mean streets spit out: junkies, low-lifes, thieves, gangs, cut-throats, murders, rapists, stick-up kids, the mentally deranged, and cigarettes. I can go on for days. It's a hell hole within Hell," Sebastian informs.

"Well I'm sure you two will be comfortable. Isn't that your place of residence," Sarah sarcastically stabs her new found partners in crime.

Sebastian rolls his eyes at Sarah and says, "Keep it up . . . Heifer!"

While continuing their quest, they can't help but to notice the grimacing structures and objects that are oddly placed thru out the valley. Crosses mounted upside down laced with old flesh and torn clothes, pathways lined with broken bones and heads displayed as trophies. One would think that these monstrosities were warnings either to keep something in or keep something out. Vigorously they walk thirteen miles through Hell. The darkness turns into a fog and the stench of cigar and cigarette smoke fill their lungs.

City of the Dead by Dante Stuardi

They all fall victim to the smog and suffer an allergic reaction.

"Cough, cough, cough!"

"We must be close to the city. That's why it's so hazy. Everybody is enslaved to the nasty habit of smoking," explained Enoch.

Finally reaching the end of the valley, they come to a ridge overlooking a post apocalyptic city resembling NYC at its worst. Ladies and Gentlemen: lo and behold; La Ciudad de los Muertos. The City of the Dead," announced Enoch.

"There are a lot of bad people here. We must be careful," Sarah tells.

"Looks creepy. I try to bypass it as often as possible; due to the bad element and all," Sebastian includes.

"This looks like a good place to camp. There's cover and we're above the city, on higher ground. Tomorrow, we'll head into the city," Dimitrius advised.

Casually Sarah makes her way over to Dimitrius and says, "Come here. You, you scared me half to death! I thought we lost you. Let me give you a hug. You look like you could use one."

Dimitrius reciprocates by accommodating her request and comforts her with these words, "Lose me? Nah! We're just getting started. Besides I'm the star of this show, remember?"

Together they laugh.

"We should get some rest. I'll walk you to your bunk," Dimitrius says.

"After all that, you can help me move my bunk next to yours. The safest place too me, is being next to you," explained Sarah.

"Ok, I understand."

So together they move Sarah's stuff and set it up adjacent to Dimitrius' rest area.

"You people are foolish. You can't sleep in Hell! That's part of the irony. No one sleeps. The minute you close your eyes, a demon will try to take your soul. Because you are new to this place, you all smell like fresh meat . . . The creatures of the Netherworld will surely come to feast," warned Enoch.

"Good! Then we won't have to search for souls. They'll come to us," added Mathyus.

"Get some sleep, that's an order. Since you can't sleep Enoch, you and the dog have first watch," commanded the ex-MSgt. "Lights out."

"Good night, Miguel. Good night, Mathyus. Good night, Sebastian. Good night, Dimitrius. Good night, Sarah."

Deep into slumber they go while Enoch sneaks some winks whereas Thorn stands guard as the protector of his clan. He is well conditioned to do so from the many years of looking after his master while conducting his chores. Not intimidated by the sounds of ghostly screeches, tortured cries of pain, or the scent of burning flesh, the dog remains disciplined and focuses on his duty. Is he a Guard dog, a pet, or simply man's best friend? During the siesta, Enoch wakes to take advantage of this opportunity to converse with his boss. Trained to obey, he gives Thorn a command to stay while he walks into a nearby heavily brushed area. Enoch calls out to Belial.

"By your will Sire, come to me."

Responding to Enoch's call, Belial arrives as a black serpent with flaming red eyes. Flat on his belly, he slithers around the base of a decayed bush, hissing his way into discussion.

"Sssssssss! You have done well my ssservant. Your requesst ssshall be granted."

"As you wish my Liege," gratefully replied Enoch.

"Sssooooo, what have you learned," questioned Belial the snake.

"The Reaper has betrayed you," Enoch informed.

"Sssssssss! Betrayed me? Humm! I will deal with him later."

"As for the Redeemer, his faith is strong. With my own eyes I witnessed him bitten and as the transformation began, it reversed. It was as if Jehovah himself prevented it from happening," Enoch explained.

"Tell me sssomething I can ussse. I need weaknessssss."

"He looks to the Gate Keeper for guidance because he is wise and seems to have a great knowledge of the Underworld. There is a woman who recognized me from my fame and fortune; she is the Book Keeper. Together they're teamed with Death and as they move closer to you; their plan as I expected, is to recruit more."

"Ssssssss, good! Let them come! Thingsss are going according to plan with the exception of the Reaper. That comesss asss a sssurprissse indeed. Now, I musssst . . ."

Before the serpent could continue his sentence Thorn approaches growling.

"Grrrrrrrrrrrrrrrrrr!"

Being the coward that he is, Belial deems this an opportune time to vacate the premises. So immediately, in an 'S' like pattern, he slithers away at an incredible pace to avoid confrontation with the canine.

"Quiet, you'll wake everybody up," whispered Enoch.

Mathyus and Miguel approaches.

"He already has. His panting and pacing was enough to wake me up. I know my pooch. Something bothered him," Mathyus implied.

"We'll take over, can't sleep," Miguel offered.

With a disgusted look on his face, Enoch walks to his rest area.

"There's something about that guy I don't like," Miguel expresses.

Meanwhile as Dimitrius sleeps, the image of Jessica enters his dream. She encourages him to find comfort in Sarah.

"Love her as you loved me."

Suddenly he wakes up in a cold sweat. With the quickness, he gathers himself and makes his way to the guards on duty. Upon his arrival he noticed that his plan was altered.

"Where's Enoch? I thought he was on duty," Dimitrius asked.

"He was. We relieved him; couldn't sleep," stated Mathyus.

"I hear you but, I'll take over now. Thorn stay!"

"Okay, I'll try," Mathyus said.

Eager to go back to bed, he rushes to his make-shift bunk.

"Hey Papí, do you think there is someone who may wish to join us in the city?" questioned Miguel.

"Don't worry mi amigo. I'm sure if that's what God intended, it will happen," Dimitrius reassured.

"I guess you're right. God is with us. He proved that earlier . . . I thought you were a goner."

"Nah. I'm good. Get some rest."

"Yes sir, Sgt.! Hey! Mathyus! Wait up!"

Crouching down in that familiar yoga position Dimitrius focuses on his inner peace. Several hours pass by. Routinely programmed to wake up at the break of dawn, Dimitrius rises. One by one, he awakens his comrades and informs them to be ready to leave in a ½ an hour.

Impressed with Thorns' discipline, he solidifies their relationship with a warm greeting and praise.

"That's a good boy! Good job," he says while petting the dog and shuffling its ears.

Thorn counters with a hand lick. Maintaining his military protocol, Dimitrius decides to scout the outskirts of the city before leading his troops into an unknown situation.

"Wait here while I scout the border of Dead City, Dead Town, whatever it's called. Thorn, come," Dimitrius commanded.

"If you're not backing a 1/2 an hour, we're coming to look for you," affirmed Mathyus.

"I'm going to quote a famous poet; I'll be back," recited Dimitrius doing his Arnold Schwarzenegger, Terminator impression.

"That was so cliché, corny," Sebastian joked.

"When I get back, we're not stopping until we're out of the city," Dimitrius recommends.

Him and Sarah glance at each other and wink to show salutation.

(Meanwhile) In the Devil's Lair

Here we find Belial leaning back in his magnificent throne strategizing, overlooking the dark realm admiring the view; while vanity shares his company. Close by, Lilith is pampered by bisexual slaves. Abruptly, Wrath enters the chamber being the bearer of bad news.

Without turning around Belial asks, "So what's up?"

"The dogs failed."

Angered by the news, Belial stands up and grabs the nearest slave. He raises him up above his head and throws him thru the window, shattering it into a thousand pieces.

"Fool! I already know of this!"

Amused at his reaction, she chuckles. He looks at her, then Wrath.

"What are you laughing at?! Did any one else get bit," he asked.

"The Redeemer was the only one too suffered a bite but, the transformation reversed itself," explained Wrath.

"Obviously, there was a divine intervention," suggested Lilith.

"You think," yelled Belial.

"Gentlemen, what we need here is a woman's touch. Let me have at him. Surely a man who has lost love must need love. Especially from a beautiful woman who is in need of saving. When the time comes, it will be I who will slay the Redeemer," declared Lilith

"Come here you slut! So you plan to seduce him, and when he lets his guard down, you will kill him? Why you little trollop. I love it! When you kill him, bring me his head or Wrath will bring me yours. Come, I want to tap that ass before it becomes tainted," commanded Belial.

Together they stroll to the royal bed and have at each other like wild animals. In the meantime, Wrath claps his hands and a plethora of nude women tend to his needs; beginning with a bath, then a massage and finally, an orgy. During their session of extramural behavior, Belial has a revelation.

"While Lilith is seducing the fool, I must put a stop to the priest's activity. Wrath, I'm sending you to the material world to destroy the priest and all who may try to aid him. It is imperative that you eliminate them before they have a chance to unite. Then I want you to hunt him down and annihilate him like the dog he is. Kill him last, so that he can watch his friends die due to his failure. Oh, and one other thing, bring me the box and its treasures. If I possess the prize, I can rule the world. Then, there will truly be Hell on earth. The Monastery would be a great place to start. Kill two birds with one stone. Cut off his communication, and damage his heart. Be discrete. We don't want him to catch on until it's too late. Do you understand my reliable friend?"

"Yes Sire, with pleasure. Do I have to go now?"

"No, sit back, relax and enjoy yourself. Continue to have your way with these bitches and, let it be known that I was never a cock blocker . . . . Ha . . . . !"

Laughter fills the chamber as the sex fest resumes.

'As you can see, fornication is the favorite pastime sport in Satan's world. Then, there is pain and punishment. Practitioners of these extracurricular activities become Masters of Sin particularly lust;

which rules the flesh. Therefore as a consequence, we become weak for physical pleasure and our hearts desires.'

The story of Lilith

It is said that she was born in the time before Eve was created from Adam. In the very beginning when Satan fell to the Garden. She was forged to be his (Adam) wife but not his equal. Despite being crafted for love, her nature could not allow her to serve beneath him, so her deviance spawned a tiff against God's intention. Banishing herself from the Garden, she fled to serve another. One who did not place limitations, titles or judgment; one who gave her all that her heart desired, one who is called King amongst all that was ladled in black; for he is the Dark one; lord of the underground and, nemesis to all that is good? Accepting her deviance as a gift his admiration for her gained her respect and position over all.

Complacent with her status due to exile, her appreciation for her placement waged her to generously share her appetite for lust with all that wanted her. Thus the first whore was born. Sharing in her delights was Satan who found her to be his favorite. Allowing her to do his bidden by corrupting mankind with lust, greed and decadence. Her intentions are beguiling; and are boasted by flesh driven fools; who seek pleasure before and after business. Fruitfully she tamed their hearts as they continuously let themselves go.

She is the Mother of Evil and the Bride of Dread; scrupulous, conniving, carnivorous, lewd and lascivious. She is everything we have become and some . . . .

Lilith by Chris Brimacombe

Chapter Ten

(Deception)

In the Now: San Francisco

Vigilantly Gabriel ventures forth to recruit the Disciples as well as fight the ominous demons that plague us daily. The condition of the troubled world deteriorates day by day. Its mentality is selfish, carefree, and faithless. What were once concerns for the direction of the future is now based on present gain and prize possession. We are egotistical and our greed dictates our way of life. Our inhibitions are driven by our sins and iniquities which distracts us from the Glory of God. Society is in survival mode and religion is out the door. Attitude adjustments are occupations held by a hired hand. Total chaos renders havoc and bedlam. Anarchy rules the land. Kill or be killed is the motto to live by. The world is about to self destruct and only the strong will survive; the weak will be sacrificed. The Devil is winning, or is he? Let it be none that some positive propaganda have been posted, but no one is listening. God is watching!

Its midday hour and the traffic is as tight as dicks' hatband, a precautionary necessity for the promiscuous who exploit the city of open relations. The congestion is dense and the victims of the daily commute suffer accordingly; as expected. The pulse of the city is intense as everyday living constitutes the hustle. Although crowded, constant movement keeps the city alive, not to mention the Golden Gate Bridge as a backdrop. Signature trolley cars roll up and down Hill Street Blues and the infamous Chinatown where vacationers frequent due to its impeccable dining experience. Hungry and looking forward to capturing its glory is Pastor Grant. After overcoming battle traffic, he is ready to meet Master Peter Moon. The massive Winnebago pulls up to the shabbiest hole-in-a-wall take-out restaurant on the block. Looking around apprehensively, the Pastor hoped that this wasn't their destination.

"We're here! This is the place I was telling you about," Gabriel informed.

"You've got to be kidding. I thought you said that we were going to eat healthy. Look at this place! We're wasting our time," replied Grant.

Together they exit the rolling house and walk toward the entrance.

"Oh come now. Some of the best foods I've eaten came from less appealing places than this," boasted Gabriel.

"Well I haven't."

Upon their entry, behind the counter sat a middle aged Asian man cutting vegetables on a butcher block table along with a micro crew working uninterrupted. Sitting at a table closest to the kitchen is an older man eating a bowl of rice and fish with chop sticks; he ignores them.

"Hello!" bellowed Gabriel.

The host nods his head in acknowledgement.

"What's good on the menu," Grant asked.

This time the host stares at them without saying a word.

"I don't think he speaks English."

The host grins but still no reply.

"Do you understand what I am saying," asked Grant.

The host continues to chop-chop.

"I told you. We're wasting our time," said Grant as he impatiently walks out the door.

Finally igniting his conversation the host finally replies, "You shouldn't give up so easily."

Promptly Grant ends his departure and turns around.

"Ahh, he does speak!" to Grant surprise.

"Was the charade necessary my friend?" Gabriel inquired.

"It was to gauge your personalities. Now I have a question for you. How do you plan on saving the world, if you have no patience," questioned the host.

In unison Gabriel and Grant replied, "By the Will of God."

"Good answer, and now you shall have patience," claimed the host.

"Are you Master Peter Moon," Gabriel asked as the man put down his cutlery as he came from behind the counter.

"The world is hungry for vengeance but vengeance is mine; sayeth the Lord," Master Moon revealed.

"Great! Now that that's over, what do you have good to eat? I'm starving," says Grant.

"You should try my dumplings. They're to die for," bragged Moon.

"Thank you Jesus, Finally!"

As the gentlemen get acquainted, the rest of the restaurant crew, including the old man, leaves the premises.

"Where do we go from here?" inquired Moon.

"We'll head east hitting every major city until we end in New York," announced Gabriel.

Master Moon then locks the door, and flips the sign signifying that he is closed for business. Together the three men review strategy over fine dining prepared by Moon. They begin to contact the proposed Disciples in advance, to speed up the process, suggesting that they meet up in the Big Apple. God is watching!

(Meanwhile) At the Monastery, Italy

It's raining cats and dogs. While the thunder claps the sky, the lighting evokes fear as it searches for stable ground. Lurking within the raindrops is Wrath masquerading as a peasant. He approaches the front gate pleading for penance.

"Help me, please. I need to make this right. I know you can hear me. Please, let me in. I must make peace with him."

Selfless and warm hearted, a monk makes his way to the gate.

"Okay, okay, what's the matter son?" the Monk asked.

Still the gate remains locked. Wrath continues his farce.

"Father, I need confession. May I come in? I have sinned without remorse . . . . (Cough, cough) I am ill, and afraid that my illness will soon be my demise. Please summon the bishop. I need to make peace with the lord. Please! You must."

"Alright my son, come in. Our doors are open to all of God's children," the Monk proclaimed.

Finally, Wrath's ploy gains him access.

"Thank you. I am grateful," Wrath replied.

"Come let's go into the Sanctuary . . . Go into confession booth two. I'll find Bishop Francis and get some towels to dry off."

The Monk rushes off in search of the Bishop unaware that the man in need is a killer indeed. Once found, Bishop Francis necessitates the man's request.

He enters the opposite entrance of the booth and says, "Hello my son, God is merciful and just. It is wise that you make peace with him now."

"Spare me the God is good shit. Where is the priest called Gabriel?"

Now aware that the man on the other side of the booth is not who he appeared to be, Bishop Francis rebukes the Devil.

"In the mighty name of Jesus, I rebuke you Satan!"

"Sorry, wrong dude," Wrath revealed.

"I will see you in hell before I tell you anything," bellowed the Bishop.

"So be it."

Suddenly, without warning, he punches thru the wood with both hands in one swift motion snatching the Bishop thru. He breaks the Bishop's neck then rummages through his garments, finding the key to his office. Curious about the commotion the Monk, who had let him in, rushes to the scene, only to find the Bishops' dead body on the floor.

"What have you done?!"

"Come here," Wrath demanded.

The Monk tries to run in the opposite direction but, to no avail, Wrath is faster. He grabs the Monk by his hood and shows him the key, and then he forces him to take him to the Bishop's office. Once they arrive, Wrath breaks the clergyman's back and drops him to the floor. He enters the office and approaches the desk. He tries to open a locked drawer with the key but no luck. He decides to bash the desk up with his fists until he has full access to whatever is within. In the drawer, he finds the list of names and addresses that the Bishop texted Gabriel. Jackpot! He has found what he was in search of. Now, he begins to do what he does best; crush, kill, and destroy. After blocking all exits with pews from the sanctuary except for one, on which he stands, he sets the Monastery on fire. He stands at what is now the only exit so all who wishes to escape must come pass him. Facing death without recourse is their only means of salvation. One by one, they accept their fate and consequently die at the hand of their enemy. Humored by the heinous act, Wrath laughs with a demonic zeal.

"MuuuHaaaaaaHaaaaaaaaaaa!"

As the flames blaze out of control and the scent of burning flesh fills the air, Belial emerges from Hell's familiar surrounding.

"I thought I told you to be discreet! Anyway, what did you find," Belial asked.

"I found the list."

"Ahh, excellent! You know what to do. I dig what you've done here but, there's something missing. I know! Some flavor."

With a wave of his hand, the body of Bishop Francis is tossed onto the cross then, the cross is turned upside down signifying the worst is yet to come.

"Yeah, that's it."

Wrath continues to laugh, "MUHaaaaaaaaahhhhhaaaa! I like it Sire! I will use it as my signature, which will leave a trail, as if I were a serial killer."

"I'm afraid you're beyond that my friend."

Together they laugh as they both disappear into the burning flames by way of an ominous abyss. As the monastery burns to the ground with no witness to testify, the cross that mounts the Bishop remains untouched as if it were meant to be left as a warning.

Chapter Eleven

(The Good Samaritan)

(Meanwhile) City of the Dead

While confirming his plan with the faction, a loud cry of a woman in distress startles them.

"Yyyaaaaaaaa! No, No, Aaaaaaaaah!"

"What was that? Where's my knife? Don't let me have to cut someone out here," Sebastian declared.

Swiftly he whips out his over sized hack blade.

"Who was that, should be the question?" chimed Sarah.

"A woman's in trouble," Miguel implied.

"Help! Help! Somebody help me!"

The cries continue.

"There's always someone in trouble here," Enoch says.

"Stay here until I get back," demanded Dimitrius.

"Do you think it's wise to separate? This could be a trap," Mathyus cautioned. Dimitrius boldly replied, "That's a chance I'm willing to take."

"I'll go with you," volunteered Enoch. "I know these streets like the back of my hand."

As the cries for help continue, Dimitrius, Enoch, and Thorn quickly run to the boundary of city limits to find a woman surrounded by six men outside of a dilapidated Motorcycle bar. They torment the voluptuous woman by molesting her, the Goons continue as instructed, assaulting her by forcing her to the ground. During their race to rescue the helpless, Dimitrius picked up some rocks. Finally in range, he hurls one hitting a Goon in the back of his head.

"Get away from her! If you want to mess with someone, come get some of this," Dimitrius bellowed.

In the meantime, Enoch is startled at the identity of the distressed woman. It is the Devil's concubine: Lilith. She catches his eye and plays him off as though she ever knew him. The Tormentors proceed to surround the rescuers. Simultaneously, a voice comes from the inside of the bar.

"If you don't mind, I'll have some," said the voice unknown.

Exiting the bar is a tall, muscular, black man whose presence demands the utmost respect. Cool, calm and collected, he struts over to Lilith and helps her to her feet.

"Hey, baby. Are you alright?" asked the big black guy.

Amazed at his stature Lilith replied, "I'm okay, thank you. Who are you?"

The Black man answered in a 70s vernacular, "Not now baby, I'm about to get busy. I'll give you my 411 later; Ya dig! . . . . Now, as you were saying my brutha."

"I came to help the lady," Dimitrius clarifies. "Your goons need to learn some respect."

"They don't work for me."

Dimitrius and the unknown dude look into each others eyes. Instinctively, without a word being said, the two men become allies. To start their union, the black guy throws the first punch smashing a tormentor's face in. Dimitrius in turn picks up one and throws him back into the bar via window, breaking it. Thorn attacks one. The black guy puts another in a chokehold and puts him to sleep. Dimitrius double kicks one in the nuts. The remaining tormentor runs away like a coward. During the assault Enoch appeared to comfort the woman in need. Evaluating the situation, they are both impressed with the strength of the Redeemer and the brawn of the new guy yet, they continue the farce.

Now that the brawl is over and the rescue mission accomplished, the two men stand facing each other.

"Are you the one called the Redeemer?" the black man asked.

"Who wants to know? Friend, or Foe," inquired Dimitrius.

While shrugging his shoulders the big guy says, "If you are the Redeemer then I'm a friend. If not, well, I guess I'm just a Good Samaritan."

"I like to think that I'm your last chance to get out of here," Dimitrius informs.

"Cool! Xavier Dunn's the name. I'd been hoping you'd show up. The rumor is spreading like wild fire that you were coming; just didn't know when. Is there room for a brutha to join the bandwagon?"

"If you believe that Jesus Christ is your Lord and Savior," Dimitrius replied.

"To speak His name is grounds for death. The fact that you spoke it without fear, tells me that you are definitely the kat that I was waiting for, and to answer your question; yes, I am a believer."

"Good, we could use a bull like you to tame the opposition. Welcome to the struggle my brutha," Dimitrius greeted.

They shake hands to seal the deal.

"Cool! I'm outta here but before we get started, I believe in a fresh start, so I want to lay it all on the line, so that you know who and want you are dealing with as far as I'm concerned," Xavier behold.

"I was an underhanded New York City Detective whose ties ran deep in the bows of Organized Crime. You name it; I had my hands in it: Drugs, Prostitution, Gambling and Extortion just to name a few. I would frequently exploit the services of prostitutes on a routine bases as a part of a ritual; fulfilling my tenacious appetite for pure unadulterated sex. Keep in mind while doing all of this I still upheld the Law by serving justice. I'd extort sexual favors and commit bribery for money in lieu of jail time. Shaking hustlers down for their bread or face the system that'll keep them lost within. Yeah I was a crooked cop in a time when inhibitions' ran free, the British invasion faded while Motown made it, man took his first step on the moon and, Black Exploitation hit the movie scene. It was (1970). It was the best time of my life until The Player's Club decided to put an end to my game.

119

During a highly anticipated shakedown they set me up with 3 Hookers who possessed a hypodermic needle filled with a bad batch of dope. They knew I couldn't resist the threesome. I let my guard down which cause me my life, and my rep. The things I loved most were the things that took me out (Greed, Money and Sex). Now that you know my life story, am I still down?"

Thinking to himself, 'This guy is a piece of work' he let it go because he knows that it is not his position to judge.

So Dimitrius bragged but not boasted, "Actually I think I've got you beat; 500 bodies need I say more?"

Over hearing the tall tale of greed and lust Lilith found herself stimulated by its context and, then sought acceptance.

Finally the mysterious woman speaks to the two brutes, "Wait a minute! You are the one who is to free us from this place? Please, take me with you! I don't know how much more of this I can take!"

"It was your cries that brought me here. Of course you can come, provided you believe in Jesus Christ. What's your name?" Dimitrius asked.

"My name is Lilith and yes, I do believe," she said.

With no surprise, Enoch knew that she would lie like he did to conceal their secret. They are now connected like never before.

Dimitrius turns toward Enoch and asks him, "How long have we been gone?"

"Hmm, about 30 minutes or so."

"Well let's hurry back," Dimitrius replied.

He then looked toward Xavier who was staring at Lilith and vise-versa.

"If you have belongings you wish to bring, get them and meet us here in half an hour," he said.

In unison they replied, "Oh hell no! Let's get the heck out of here!"

Together they laugh as the group begins to walk back to the campsite.

During the trek back with his new editions, Xavier informs him of another who wishes to be saved.

"Yo man, I need to ask you a question."

"Go ahead, shoot," Dimitrius said.

Xavier by Chris Brimacombe

"Can anybody jump on this train or is it based on how deep the sin you've committed? The reason I ask is that's how it works around here."

"Nah man, God forgives all who wish to leave, despite the severity of their sins," Dimitrius enlightens.

"Because I know of a sistah who wants out but, she feels that she is where she should be due to the sins that brought her here," Xavier explained.

"Where is she? I want to meet her and let her know that God has sent me to bring her home. After we get the others, we'll look for her."

"Cool, I know where she chills."

"What's her name?"

"Rashida, Rashida Hollister. She a bad, fine ass chick," Xavier excitingly claimed.

"Ight! Calm down dude." Dimitrius playfully suggested.

"Oh excuse me, I forgot. My bad," Xavier apologized.

"No problem, Mon," Dimitrius spoke Jamaican style.

(Elsewhere) At the Devil's Lair

Sitting in a dark room brooding as he does, Belial becomes satisfied.

"Things are going according to plan. I now have two spies within the resistance and Wrath is in the Material World wreaking havoc. OH! What a beautiful day in the neighborhood!" Ecstatically he laughs.

"I need to pay them a visit to divert suspicion from my clandestine informants."

(Back to the Militia)

Patient but nervously waiting, the group is calmed as they view Dimitrius approaching from a distance accompanied by newfound others. Cheers of joy fill the air. As they get closer, Sebastian notices the blonde bombshell and the massive hulk.

Under his breath he says, "Get a load of Beauty & the Beast."

Now close enough and in the company of each other, a feeling of security calms their nerves.

"Glad you made it, and you're not alone! Who are your friends?" Mathyus inquired.

"Introduce yourselves," Dimitrius suggested.

At the same time Sarah runs and jumps into his arms. They share a brief kiss then he lets her down gently.

"Thank God! I was getting worried," she said.

While the acquaintances are met, Lilith focuses on the connection Dimitrius and Sarah share. Their hearts are filled with so much joy even a blind man could see. As jealousy rears it ugly head, Mathyus reflects on his past life and gets angry.

"It'll be a cold day in Hell before I see love again," he said to himself but loud enough for Dimitrius to hear.

"What was that Mathyus?" he asked.

"Oh nothing; I was just thinking out loud. Aaahh! Mathyus yells as he falls to his knees in pain covering his eyes, which triggers Thorn to bark ferociously. Sarah runs to his aid. Suddenly the sky fills with rain and the temperature increases. The raindrops are filled with boiling water. Saturating the ground making it suitable for a wicked weed to ascend; Belial in full bloom resembles an unwanted plant. The group takes cover as best they can without running away.

"The rain is burning me," Miguel cried.

"No shit Sherlock," Sebastian said.

Thorn jumps at Belial but is restrained due to his leash clenched in Dimitrius' hand. The burning rain tapers off into a lukewarm drizzle.

Belial speaks while blossoming, "Careful dog, your anger fortifies me like vitamins; kind of like a 'One-A-Day' Haaaaaa! Dimitrius, Dimitrius, or should I say Killer Man, I must tell you, you really have big balls coming here to destroy me. Do you truly think this is possible? He who calls himself 'I Am' has sent you to your doom. If you keep this up, surely you and your misfits will die."

They listen but ignore him; still focused on Mathyus who continues to suffer. Maintaining the spotlight Belial continues.

"Okay, let's make a deal. If you turn around now and stop this silly quest, I'll bring your wifey back and you all can leave together. No strings attached . . . Trust me."

"Oh hell no!" shouted Sebastian.

"Ahh Reaper, I'll deal with you later! You can believe that! That's a promise and a threat. No more souls entering Hell! Do you know what that means ass-wipe? The walking dead will roam and it will be Hell on earth. I'm okay with that, really, it's cool. Bet you didn't think of that thought, did you?" Belial taunted.

He then directs the conversation back to Dimitrius.

"So, Assassin's Creed, what's it gonna be? Door #1: Get your wife back and all of you can get the hell out of here or, Door #2: Death in the worst way you can imagine, then for kicks, I'll do it again, and again, and again . . . you get the picture."

Dimitrius replied, "Enoch, what was that you said earlier? When you make a deal with the Devil, you always get screwed? So, forget it Eddie Munster."

Laughter chuckled out loud.

"Oh snap! He called you Eddie Munster! Haaaa!" Xavier teased.

"Don't even try it, Magilla," Belial jested back.

"Don't listen to him he is a natural born liarrrrrraaaaahhh!" Mathyus said as he continued his agonizing pain.

"Release the old man! Spare him, I'm the one you want," Dimitrius requested.

"Whatever's happening to him is not my doing, although I do find pleasure within his pain. Look, I'll make this real simple for you. Do what I ask, or everyone you left behind in the material world will suffer. You know what I'm saying? That's right, everyone on your friends & family plan. I will unleash a plague so bad that it will make AIDS look like hay-fever . . . . Leave Now!"

"Dude, come on. If you were gonna do something like that, you would've already done it," Dimitrius boldly suggested. "Besides, you can't create! Your power is limited so, step off."

"You are mistaken my friend. This is Hell, boy. I run this shit. Why do you think he sent you? Because this is my house, he's not allowed . . . . I didn't make the rules so I can do whatever I want to, to you and your puny bastards," Belial enlightened.

"Whose he talking about, ain't nothing puny about me punk," Xavier said with a cocky attitude.

Suddenly Mathyus cries turns into laughter, "HaaaaaHaaaa, whew!"

"What in the world is he laughing at," Sebastian asked.

"Silence you fool! He stopped crying," Enoch barked.

Miguel asked Mathyus as he helps him to his feet, "Your eyes stop hurting, sí?"

Realizing that the fear that once filled their craw has now turned into courage, and the anxiety that held them down has graciously lifted. Sighs of relieve is shared by all who stood against the tumble weed.

Mathyus stands proud to emancipate his fear, "Sí mi amigo. You forgot one thing Satan, God is on our side and is with us even as we speak. Ask me how I know and I'll tell you so, I can see! That's right, I can see! Praise be to God!"

Taken by surprise his friends, including all that are evil, witness yet another miracle. Baffled by the event, Belial's eyes fill with dread and his face becomes astonished. Noticing his plight Lilith and Enoch spark a wonder. Nevertheless undetected, they look at each other in awe; simultaneously they both raise their eyebrows. Dimitrius uses this opportunity to their advantage.

"As you can see, we're not afraid of you! A word of advice, you should quit while you're ahead. As a matter of fact, let's change the subject . . . . Where's my son?"

Xavier chimes in, "Yeah! We rebuke you and your demons in the name of Jesus!"

Aggravated and disgusted, Belial loses his cool and begins to act like an ill-bred man who has run out of sarcasm. So he resorts to the ignorant way out by bellowing profanities more than usual.

"Bullshit! Fuck that! It'll be a cold day in Hell before I give this bitch up, and as for sonny boy . . . boy do I have plans for him."

As the nonsense spills from Belial's mouth, Dimitrius puts two and two together.

"That's it! That's what Mathyus said earlier! Miguel, give me his cane."

Quickly Miguel tosses the walking stick as instructed.

"Now stand back everyone and watch the power of God as Hell freezes over!" Dimitrius declared.

Now with all eyes focused on the task, Dimitrius raises the cane to the sky causing the lighting to strike; suddenly the rain intensifies causing a torrential down pour and hurricane flood like conditions. Vigorously he begins to swirl the cane around and around in a circular motion like Majorettes do when their doing their do, creating a whirlwind. As the twister gathers the wetness, it proceeds to travel throughout Hell dousing the everlasting flames; cooling things off to a tolerable temperature.

Upon completion, for all in Hell to see, a beautiful rainbow reveals itself signifying Gods' omnipresence. The expression of the damned as a whole is mystified by this sign and wonder.

Frustrated and confused Belial descends back from whence he came, vanishing into the ground. To show their appreciation they gather to praise God for what he has done. Including the newcomers who observed the Lord's Grace at its best.

"Hallelujah, Hallelujah, Hallelujah! Thank you Lord, in the blessed name of Jesus, thank you," they shouted.

Amazed at what has transpired Enoch begins to question his position. A righteous seed has been planted igniting the spiritual warfare that fights inside his mind. He begins to experience feelings that he has never felt before; the thoughts of repentance and forgiveness has sparked his heart which sets in motion a renewing of his mind. **(Romans 12:2)** Determined to forever enslave him to his sins, Hell itself refuses to allow him to change his disposition so confusion keeps him shackled down. Still he remains quiet as the battle within lay dormant, still he continued to maneuver as though nothing was wrong. After rejoicing, Mathyus greets everyone as if it were the first time.

"It is so good to finally see you all! I am truly blessed to have His mercy. I must say Dimitrius; you are a site for sore eyes. You're everything I'd imagined; you too Thorn! Come here boy!"

Thorn prances over to him vigorously waging his tail. Sarah hugs him expressing her love while Miguel smiles from ear to ear.

"My new family, just look at you, you're so beautiful."

Mathyus begins to shed tears of joy.

Dimitrius comforts him with words of encouragement, "Your faith has brought you your sight back. Enjoy the gift."

Mathyus replied, "A gift indeed. God is good."

Dimitrius customarily replies, "All the time."

Determined to stay on course, Dimitrius gets back to the business at hand.

"Guys and Gals gather around, shit oops! I mean; it's about to get real thick around here. We've only just begun and already we've been through a lot. Is there anyone who feels that they can't go on? If so, Sebastian can whisk you back to Purgatory where you can wait and be safe. By show of hands, who wishes to go back?"

Respectfully, no hands are shown as their decision is unanimous.

"If anytime during our escapade you decide you can't handle it, let me know," Dimitrius informed.

Once they gain their composure they begin to move forward into the city. As they walk in search of optimistic individuals, they can't help but notice the disregarding of their presence. It seems as if they were ghosts. Despite the fact that they stand out like minorities at a Ku Klux Klan meeting, they are avoided as if they had the plague. Yet and still they carry on their road march reluctantly witnessing sinful acts that warrant the city its name. Thievery, assault, rape and murder commonly abuse its existence as too much is happening at the same time.

"We couldn't save these people, evening if we wanted too. There is too much anarchy, no law and order; they're too caught up in the chaos." Sarah derived.

"This place is crazy! We need to hurry up and get out of here," Miguel advised.

"Something's not right. We're supposed to attract souls, not repel them," Dimitrius realized.

Xavier says, "The word is out my man, everyone knows you are here."

"There's a reason why they don't dare come to you," guessed Enoch.

Lilith adds, "He's right, the souls are afraid of you. Belial told us that the Prophecy was a ploy that was created by him to weed out the honest souls that infect Hell; their punishment is repeated torture by Wrath, his Henchman."

"Damn him!" Dimitrius shouts.

Mathyus includes, "I told you he was tricky. He's the master of deception. When it comes to scamming the people, he's the best. That's why there are an infinite number of souls condemned to this God forsaken place. He pulled the wool over their eyes without them even knowing it was there."

"Yeah, his greatest trick was convincing man that he never existed," Lilith injects.

Enoch bellowed, "Fools!"

"Uh, you are including yourself? I'm just saying," Sebastian verbally wondered.

Sarah humored by the conversation smiles at them but not with them. Her skepticism of their intentions is not genuine so she becomes a slave to another sin; the sin of judgment.

(Matthew 7:1-2) Recognizing her flaw, she begins to pray within and repents.

Repenting is essential when asking for forgiveness from one's sin **(Acts 2:38)**. Taken aback at the Redeemers' back up squad, Xavier musters up a question that's been bothering him since he first encountered the uncanny group of hero wannabes.

Boldly he asks Dimitrius, "Dude, let me ask you another question: Is this it? I mean an old blind man, a hottie, a boy and his dog, a James Cagney reject and this clown . . ."

Casually he points in the direction of Sebastian.

Offended by Xavier's statement Sebastian defends his honor.

"Yo King Kong, I ain't going to be taking too many more of your clowns."

Xavier apologizes and elaborates, "Sorry dude didn't mean to offend you. I just thought there would be more to this mod squad. If we're going to take on the Devil, we're going to need more troops and surely more fire power."

"The fact that we know God is with us is assurance enough. In the Bible, scripture tells the story of Gideon and the 300 men who fought against 32,000 soldiers **(Judges 7: 3-7).** God was with them which gained them victory and Israel," preached Mathyus.

"Right on, brotha. Thanks for the quick Bible study lesson. If God put this thang together, it's got to be funky," Xavier colorfully agreed.

Lustfully drawn to brutish men, and noticing his flavor Lilith begins to admire Xavier's style. Being accustomed to the pimp game, he hustled prostitutes back in the material world, gains him the advantage. He is already up on it so he chills until the time is right.

Baffled but determined to overcome this obstacle, they continue to walk. Together the group discusses the issue of how to convince souls to slight Belial's fib. Taking action, they devise a plan.

"Sebastian, can you still bounce around Hell at your convenience?"

A question raised by all.

"Of course I can. Why do you ask?"

"Good, then you can scout out the whereabouts of those who may be interested in leaving. This way, we'll be able to cover more ground. Mathyus was right; having you with us is an advantage and now is a good time to utilize our best asset," the group unanimously concluded.

"I'll be on a recon mission. Real tactical like, huh?" Sebastian asked.

"Keep your eyes and ears open for ambushes as well, and be careful. The Devil is pissed. If he wants you, this would be the best time to come after you. I suggest you jump sporadically; not creating a predictable pattern. Can you handle it," Dimitrius informed and inquired with a take charge attitude.

Sebastian yelled, "I'm your man Sergeant!"

Quick, fast, and in a hurry, he vanishes then pops back with a martini in his hand.

"What, back already? You couldn't have completed your mission that fast," Sarah implied.

"Of course not, I just wanted to get a drink before I embark on this James Bond, secret agent bullshiggity!"

"Is that a Martini?" Xavier asked.

"You damn skippy, and its shaken not stirred. Haaaaa!"

Sebastian jested as he vanished to begin his covert operation.

"Yo, that kat is crazy," proclaimed Xavier.

"Yeah, but crucial." Mathyus noted.

With so much going on and as tactical as the ex-Sgt may be, the thought of weaponry never crossed his mind until Xavier mentioned Rashida and her army. You see, even the best of the best sometimes isn't always the best.

He approaches the muscle man with curious intentions, "Okay Xavier, you were saying something about weapons."

"There's a group of militant kats who still believe in that: no justice, no peace revolutionary jazz. They're led by Rashida, and boy are they packing . . . If we get with them, we'll have our own army and a better chance to get this thang off. You know what I mean?" Xavier stated.

"I hear you but, what motivates them and why would they be a part of our movement?" Dimitrius asked.

"Because they're down with the cause! That's why I mentioned her in the first place. They've been preparing for the arrival of the Redeemer for a long time. They are your Crusaders, whose mission is to take Satan down; they believe in the Prophecy. The only thing though, the bullets don't kill you . . . . I mean you die but this is Hell, in a matter of minutes you come right back to live out your torment again; it's like a revolving door. The only way you die permanently is if the evil dude wants you too," explained Xavier.

"How is it that they're operating without being detected?" Dimitrius asked.

Mathyus implies, "Because God kept them hidden like a cancer that'll lay dormant until it's ready to fester."

Dimitrius says, "We need to find Rashida and her crew ASAP."

Over hearing the conversation Miguel makes a suggestion, "What if the bullets were blessed, you know like dipped in holy water."

At first, the comment seems to have gone over everyone's head, but as they continued to walk the thought peaks their curiosity.

"You know, the kid might be on to something," Mathyus says.

"You took the words right out of my mouth," said Xavier.

Enoch jumps at an opportunity to discourage.

"Let's not forget wooden stakes. Fools, this isn't television land! This is as real as real can get. That was a stupid idea."

"Well I beg to differ. Anything holy can be harnessed as a weapon," Lilith encouraged, beguiling and treacherous as she thinks ahead of the game.

If the blessed bullets work, she stands to inherit all of what Hell has to offer; then she'll rule as its queen.

Sarah adds her two cents, "All this talk about fire power you would think that we're preparing for war. Hasn't there been enough killing?"

"I believe our cause is of dire straits, not to justify the wars of today which are motivated by gain, ours is a different scenario, we fight for His Grace," stated Mathyus.

"He's right. You can't live your life complacent. Especially if you don't fight or stand on principles which may indicate that a conflict is needed to drive the will of the people, and to satisfy God; especially if we're shedding blood to defend his honor," Dimitrius supported.

Enlightened and humbled by the content of their conversation Sarah remembers that when you are around true disciples of God, the goodness of his word and the desire to learn his teachings become as exciting as a child on Christmas morning. You look forward to gaining understanding and know in your heart that God is in control.

So, she continues to ask questions as if she were a student during Sunday school. Mathyus entertains her by accommodating her need while they walk into the unknown.

As the journey continues, midway through Sebastian returns just like that . . . Puff!

"Hey there good people I'm back, sorry I took so long."

"Good to see you, mi amigo," stated Miguel.

"Yes it is," Sarah agreed.

"Why thank you. You guy's make me feel like family," says Sebastian sentimentally. Excited that the informant is back from completing espionage, Dimitrius drills him on the gathered Intel.

"Good job Sebastian, now talk to me," he demanded.

"Ok well the word is out baby, everyone knows you are here but, they're afraid of you like Goldie Locks said. Also, I did happen to see a well organized group just outside of the city at the baseball stadium, they looked like the Black Panther party but, that couldn't be because they were multi-cultural."

In unison Xavier and Dimitrius shout out, "RASHIDA!"

"Did they have a gold cross as their logo?" Xavier asked.

"Yep," confirmed Sebastian.

"That's them. They're not too far from here; actually give or take 30-40 blocks or so, heading east. If we put some pep in our step, we should make it in an hour," Xavier calculates.

"If they are as organized as I expect them to be, they probably won't accept strangers very well," Dimitrius implied.

Xavier responded, "Dude I'm not a stranger, Rashida and I use to bump uglies." Taken aback by Xavier's comment, Dimitrius begins to shake his head.

"That was a bit too much information. You could've kept that to yourself," tastefully suggested the hero man.

Their trek intensifies as they grow nearer to the revolutionary Madame of War.

(Infomercial #2)

Is it pride or is it determination that drives the will of a man to test unchartered waters, or venture forth in search of lands of new discovery? Is it stupidity, or could it be his faith that guides him? It is in his nature to question the unknown and to build upon what his mind can fathom. Since God has given him dominion over all animals **(Genesis 1:26)** it is his right and it is his duty to pursue happiness as long as it does not offend, hurt, or disrespect others. Thus he is faced with decisions that present choices; making a rational choice is the optimum goal, but making that choice may not be easier said than done. Once chosen, the outcome may have consequences and repercussions. Don't let the pressure from stress force you to make irrational decisions. The weight of one's choices may determine one's future so, chose wisely . . . your fate is counting on it.

(Infomercial #3)

In case you were wondering, Hell is what takes place in our present lives everyday. Your Hell maybe different than mine, therefore, some are in worse condition than others. In fact, Hell is unconditional. There are no special privileges or circumstances that will gain you favor. It is a pestilence that has infected all of mankind and I'm afraid that we all are bound by its ignorant rule. When trapped in a reprobated mind we fall victim to our own fears, and think that we can handle our own fate so we remain content and unenthused about pursuing a meaningful life because we believe God will forgive us no matter what we do. Unaware as to what truly has taken place is that God takes his hand off you and lets the devil have his way because, you chose to disobey the teachings of Christ. How does one break free from this stronghold? Seeking God places you in the right direction. Once you find Him, you can begin to build on your personal relationship with Him. Let the Holy spirit guide you through prayers, praise, and worship. Confess and repent your sins and most of all, believe in your heart that Jesus Christ is your Lord and Savior. Once this is done be mindful, because you made this choice Evil itself will try to tempt you from your positive quest. Actually, Satan will dispatch more demons to negate your progress by way of temptation. In order to maintain you must stand steadfast and be strong. Let God do his thing and when it is your turn, do it in love and in the name of Jesus and, you will be delivered. **(1 Corinthians 16:13-14).** So if the degree of which your problems are dire, know that it is not God because as mentioned in infomercial #1, God's word says that he will not harm you **(Jeremiah 29:11),** and to always know the enemy's intention; which is to kill, steal, and destroy you **(John 10:10).**

Chapter Twelve

(Prove Me Now)

City of the Dead

Have you ever wondered: did the bird pursue the bee originally for food? As a result, did the bee sting it? Did curiosity kill the cat? Or did the cat figure out how to capitalize on an opportunity as it presented itself. It's been a long time since she has been intrigued by anyone especially a man who has not pursued her with sexual intentions. Usually the male species can't resist her lady lumps or her sex appeal, so she flaunts about with a free-wheeling confidence unmatched by any woman. Tenacious, vivacious, and in full control she irresistibly seduces them without speaking a word but, something's wrong. The response she is accustomed to has eluded itself from these men of a different spirit. Itching to uncover what has tickled her fancy, she seeks knowledge from the only source that is familiar with the measures of a man from the female perspective. As she picks up her pace, Lilith utilizes this opportunity to get acquainted with Sarah.

"You sure are a lucky woman to have found such a man like Dimitrius."

Surprised at the subject matter of conversation in which Lilith approached her, Sarah informs her of God's Grace at work.

"I'm not lucky, I am blessed. God has selected me to be a part of something bigger than all of us. He has granted me another opportunity to redeem my soul unto him. So by loving Him, it's easy to find love. Dimitrius and I appreciate what God has done for us so in return, we openly share our compassion in the good Lord's name. Our affection is merely a symbol of his blessing."

After all that, Lilith wanted to shut her down by asking her about his wife but instead she remains tight lipped to keep up the masquerade.

"Wow! That was pretty deep. Do you think God will bless me the same way he has blessed you?" She asked.

"**(James 4:2)** says, *'yet ye have not because ye ask not'*. If love is what you want, speak it into your life and ask God **(Matthew 21:22)**. Pray on it, girl! Believe me, there's power in prayer," said Sarah.

"Thanks. I'll do just that. It has been a pleasure taking to you, we must do it again soon," Lilith says.

Sarah replied, "No problem, I'll look forward to it. I must admit it was nice talking to someone without testosterone."

Both ladies laughed suggesting that a bond has been established between them; after all it's a women thing. We as men wouldn't understand . . .

As Lilith ends her conversation with Sarah, she fell victim to confusion and begins to question her position. Whether or not she knows it, the Seed of Righteousness has been planted. Now an oblivious host, she too fights the spiritual battle within. Undoubtedly her evil is thick; the Holy Spirit will work on her patiently until it is time to manifest her destiny. So she carries on unaware of the wonder that's about to change her life forever.

Baffled and rarely unsure of herself she approaches Enoch with a whispering voice, "We need to talk . . . keep walking," she commanded.

Enoch customarily replied, "By your command mistress."

"We need to reconsider our plans. Suddenly I have a change of heart. Did you see the fear in Belial's eyes?! He was afraid to say the least. Evidently the Redeemer's God is more powerful," proclaimed Lilith.

"That's funny; I was thinking the same thing. Why should we serve a master who has fear of another God? I must say, I've only been with these people a short time and already I have seen enough. I'd rather be an Angel than continue to be a fool! Forgive me mistress, but I refuse to be under his rule any longer," declared Enoch.

While drawing the same conclusion as she treads lightly; Lilith warns him of his disobedience, "Be careful Enoch, you speak of treason."

"No I speak the truth," Enoch said under his breath.

Lilith cosigns his claim, "I must admit I like their spirit. They're alive and fearless. You can't help but to feel their joy; it's wonderful thus, I am confused."

Over hearing the last word of their conversation Xavier jumps in, "What are you confused about, baby? Is there something I can help you with?"

Finally the opportunity she's been waiting for so she replies with needful intention, "Why yes, there is something you can do for me."

"And what is that?" Xavier eagerly asked.

Guided by her lustful spirit and her craving for the flesh; she responds to him like an abandoned child seeking affection from anyone who will show him/her love.

"Hold me, hold me and tell me that everything is going to be alright."

"Ahh, come here Ms. Lady . . . what's got you frazzled?"

Being an opportunist, Xavier capitalizes on his window of opportunity.

"I got you, boo. Big daddy won't let anything harm you. Believe that! Now, talk to me."

Comfortable as well as intrigued by the colorful metaphors never spoken to her before, she willingly opens up to reveal her disposition.

"I'm just a little frightened that's all. The punishment for betraying Belial is enough to scare any man yet; you show no fear . . . Why is that?" Lilith questioned.

Xavier explains, "At one time or another I too was afraid. Then I heard about the Prophecy which gave me hope. While living in the world I did some bad things, and I promised myself that if I had a chance to make things right, I would. Besides, the true benefit is that I'm down with the Redeemer and he's down with the Big Man upstairs. It doesn't get any better than this. So, why fear the devil if I'm down with God?"

Without knowing what he has verbally done, Lilith receives confirmation. Now filled with a sense of safety and assurance, she shows her appreciation by attempting to kiss Xavier on his cheek. Smoothly, he turns his face just in time for her kiss to land on his lips. While engaged in this quick flash of sensual bliss, neither party refrains from its passion. Despite all eyes on them, the couple continuously welcomed the expression of love.

"Hmmmm! Check out Beauty and the Beast. There sure is a lot of love in Hell these days . . . Go figure," says Sebastian.

As the kiss ends, they stare into each others eyes and with a nonverbal agreement they accept compassion for each other. You see two can play that game, and both came out as winners. Together they walk holding hands while Sarah and Lilith smile at each other sharing that woman thing again. Sarah also filled with sentiment, catches up to Dimitrius and holds his hand as they continue. Due to the mere expression of love, Hell itself begins to lose its bravado. God is watching, and so is Satan!

(Meanwhile) In the Now: NYC

On an unusually brisk spring day in the infamous concrete jungle, demon spawn secretly infect the territory. It appears that Wrath is in New York City, actually, in the heart of Time Square. While walking down 8th Avenue, he admires the sights and sounds of street hustling at its best. Inconspicuously he blends in as winter gear is worn by all. Dressed in a thick, black cloak with his hood draped over his head, he casually approaches a group of listeners gathered around a small band of Black Israelites. He listens to the origins of descendants from the 12 tribes of Israel and the unjust system manifested by the white man's propaganda; which will lead to the destruction of mankind. Not to say the least he is amused by it all.

"Haaaaaaaa! Preach brother," barked Wrath whose voice dominates over the present speaker.

"Speaking of the devil . . . Yo my man, what's so funny?" asked the Israelite.

Wrath replied, "You speak the truth, the end is closer than you think."

"There, you see? Even the white man recognizes the truth," said the Israelite.

"Go ahead; continue your sermon of dismay. Haaaaa," said Wrath as he walks away laughing.

As he removes himself from the crowd an Israelite says to another, "That dude was creepy as hell."

In agreement, they both nod their heads. Continuing his sightseeing, Wrath is fascinated by the delight of which these modern times have to offer.

He says to himself, "Times have surely changed, and I like it."

As the day turns into night, Wrath has consumed his fill. The devil's business is still undone so he focuses on the task at hand.

Lurking within the darkness of the night, Wrath stands outside of a Roman Catholic Church; in his hand is the list of names and addresses confiscated from the monastery. He glances at it then, the street sign and the numbers on the building for verification. Once he confirms the target he grins; signifying assurance. Upon entering he gazes at the Priest and two Alter boys as well as the many holy statues which warrant him to become ill. He sits down in the last pew until the line for Communion dwindles down to six. As he gains his composure he stands at the end of the line until it's his turn. Patiently he waits with his head bowed and his hands clinched together; as if his nerves were getting the best of him. Finally he is where he is supposed to be.

"Are you ready to receive Communion, my son?" asked the Monsignor.

"By all means Father . . . . I was wondering, are you Monsignor Matthew Paul III?" Wrath inquired.

"Why yes I am," said the Monsignor.

Little did the Holy man know that his answer gave confirmation, sealing his fate? Wrath grins justifying his victim. As the Priest tries to give Wrath Communion, the chalice holding the wine that represents the Blood of Christ becomes hot. Simultaneously, he grabs the priest's hand and forcefully tightens his grip preventing him from dropping it.

"Aaaaah!" yelled the Priest as his hand begins to singe.

While initiating the torture, Wrath admires the ring on the finger of the condemned man.

"Hmmm! Nice ring," he said.

Realizing that pain is being afflicted on the Monsignor, the Altar boys try to pull Wrath's hand from the agonizing priest to no avail. Unfortunately, this merits their demise. With his free hand Wrath shatters the first Altar Boy's jaw with one blow. Then, he snatches up the second Alter Boy and tosses him into the pews as if he were skipping rocks on a pond. Amused by it all Wrath begins his sinister laugh.

Painfully the Monsignor cries out, "May God have mercy on your soul!"

Wrath replied, "I'm afraid it's too late for that."

With no remorse or mercy, Wrath carries out his orders in the cruelest way imagined. While doing so, a homeless man approaches the church but before he enters all he can hear is a combination of screams and laughter. Instantly, he changes his mind and goes about his business. Eager to begin his reign of terror, Wrath places the Monsignors' battered body on the cross in that Antichrist fashion with his ring finger severed. Satisfied with his signature piece he looks at the list for his next victim. Next stop, Brooklyn, Brooklyn for a date with a Rabbi and, then off to Atlantic City or bust.

(In the Interim) Father Gabriel in route across the USA

Exploiting their ability of rational thought, Gabriel and company decide to capitalize on time by parking the Winnebago when they arrive at the next destination. Moreover, due to the astronomical gas prices, the cost to push the oversized vehicle across country would financially break them. Utilizing the rail system would seem much more feasible. Taking advantage of a peaceful moment, Gabriel is sound asleep. Deep in his slumber, he has a dream of being pursued by an evil presence. In vivid color, Wrath's face shines through clear as crystal. Violently he wakes up in a cold sweat.

Noticing Gabriel's restless moment Master Moon asks him, "Are you alright?"

As he pours a glass of water, "Here drink this."

"We must hurry! Satan has deployed a demon to impede our assignment. How long do we have to get to Chicago?"

"Six, maybe seven hours," said Master Moon.

"Well then put your foot down my friend, time is of the essence," suggested Gabriel. Without hesitation Grant jumps into the fast lane and puts the pedal to the metal until he hits 85 on the speedometer.

"We're cooking with gas now," said Moon.

"That was a good idea to have the others meet us in New York. Undoubtedly, we will save a whole lot of time. Why are we going to Chicago?" Moon asked.

"Because there is a challenge that must be met head on," said Gabriel.

"What challenge?"

"The man we seek is of Islamic faith, so therefore he does not share our views. Persuading him to join our cause may prove to be difficult," Gabriel explained.

"His name is on your list, right?" Grant questioned.

"Yes, it is highlighted with a question mark beside it," Gabriel said.

"Being a man of God is why he was chosen like the rest of us," Grant concluded.

"What makes him so important compared to the others?" he asked.

"Nearly one-fourth of the world's population today is Muslim. Do you get the picture?" Gabriel said.

Based on that single fact, the two men understood and inquired no further. Next stop, Chicago. BAM! The left rear tire blows; a new problem.

(Meanwhile) at The Devil Lair

Stressed, troubled, and as tense as a defendant on a murder trail, Belial finds himself in an awkward position. He has fallen victim to his own persuasion. He see's a change in attitude in some and the buoyancy of his enemies. Something has to be done, this calls for an extreme measure. As cold and calculated he can be, instantaneously he devises a decadent plan of attack.

"This is some Bullshit! In order to defeat my enemy I must become my enemy. I know what I must do. I will infiltrate their so called *regime* by becoming a desperate soul who wants out. Better yet, I will possess the body of a coward, someone who's totally opposite of me in every way. But who? I really don't have time to conduct interviews. Ahh! I know, Enoch. Or maybe the Reaper! It doesn't matter. Neither of them would realize that I am within, and then I will play my role so well that no one will be able to tell the difference."

As he commemorates his demented scheme, he excitingly bursts into flames while vanishing into thin air. In the whole while, laughing his ass off.

(In the Interim) City of the Dead

Par for the course, all major cities of relevance feature a venue exclusively for sports and exhibitions. Rome had the Coliseum, London has Wimbledon, New York has Madison Square Garden and Hell has the Arena. Once alive and full of outlandish spectacle, this stage was set to entertain demons as they exercise their talents upon tortured souls. But that was then and this is now. Newly occupied by a militant regime waiting for the time to be right to fight for a dying cause, the stadium marinates until it is called to duty.

Quietly congregating two blocks away is Dimitrius and company, scoping out the situation before moving forward. While surveying, the ex-MSgt notices the hardware, the manpower as well as the location of posted guards and; Oh yeah! ATV's.

"Everybody keep quiet! Xavier this is major," said Dimitrius.

Gathered like mice before let in a maze, the group becomes anxious.

"Stay calm everybody, I'm sure we're being watched. Xavier you were right, this place is guarded like a fortress," he continued.

Xavier nods his head in agreement, "I told you these kats were serious. Dude, you and I will go in; the rest of you chill."

"No, we'll all go together," objected Dimitrius.

Xavier proposes, "Dude, I got this. Follow my lead, come on!"

As they take off, Dimitrius signals the rest of the group to remain silent until the coast is clear by putting his index finger in front of his mouth.

"Be careful baby," says Lilith.

Feeling her attention Xavier reciprocates by winking his left eye and flexing his pectoral muscles. Tickled by his gesture, she giggles. The others, on the other hand, remained obedient with the exception of Enoch. He's caught in a trance, and casually removes himself from their company, back tracking to an alley previously passed. Hearing voices in his head led him to the far-flung pathway; he then realizes that he's alone.

"What am I doing in this alley and where is everyone?"

Suddenly a gust of wind surges through the passage knocking him off his feet into a mound of rubble. Disgusted and now filthy, he gets up and brushes his clothes off. At the same time, Sebastian and Miguel enter the alleyway in search of their wandering friend.

"What are you doing, why did you wander off like that?" Sebastian asked.

Enoch replied, "I thought I heard someone, so I took a look."

Embarrassed and unsure of himself, he fabricates a lie to swaddle his pride.

At the far side of the alley rattling of trash cans and growls commence as a motley crew of flesh eating zombies amble their way toward the smell of fresh meat. Scared out of their wits, resembling a frightful scene from the television hit show of the mid 60's: The Munster's, quickly the three amigos haul ass. Like bats out of hell they run back to warn the others. As the feeble wait patiently for what drama Dimitrius and Xavier were about to unfold, out of the blue voices tremble as an alarm.

"Run! Run for your lives!"

Startled at the commotion they too flee toward the Arena. Due to Dimitrius' 20/20 hearing . . . lol, he too directs an earshot toward the hullabaloo.

"They're in trouble," he said.

"Dude, go check it out, I'll handle to guards . . . ight!" suggested Xavier.

In a dash before Xavier finished his sentence, Dimitrius jets to aid his comrades. As he arrives, the panicked group shoots past him as if they didn't see him.

"What the . . . ?"

He turns around to see them pass by and hears moans and groans coming from the opposite direction. Revealing themselves from around the corner, the zombies pick up his scent and begin to pick up their pace.

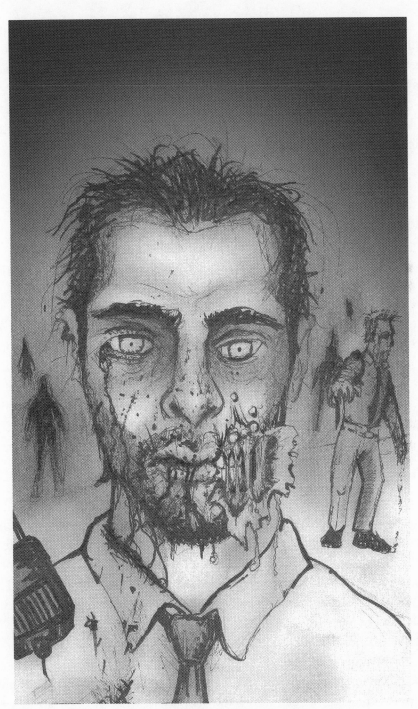

Zombies by Christopher Romo

Now having total understanding as to why the group shot past him, without hesitation, Dimitrius decides to join them. Quickly he runs back to the entrance of the Arena where the gang is gathered to await his rendezvous.

While approaching Scooby Doo and the Gang, Dimitrius says, "Okay, someone forgot to mention flesh eating zombies! That little tidbit of information could've cost us our lives."

Sarah moves closer to feel him as if he were her security blanket.

"Oh yeah, forgot about them," said Xavier.

"I apologize, I should've informed you of what to expect," said Enoch.

As he expresses his regret, Thorn growls and lunges at him as if he were the enemy. Thanks to his quick reflexes and Mathyus' firm grip of the leash, to no avail was the beast successful.

"Heal Boy!" bellowed Mathyus.

In the meantime, the zombies continue their pursuit. Cornered like a chicken by a fox, the group finds themselves in a vicarious situation.

"Uh Redeemer, you can start redeeming anytime now, really," Sebastian muttered.

During the episode, seemingly ignoring the state of affairs, the sentinels remain still as if they were Buckingham Palace Guards.

Xavier turns and says to the guards, "Hey, open up the gate! People are about to die here . . . Come on!"

Still they continued to pay no attention.

"What we need is a miracle," mumbled Sarah.

Instantaneously barrages of bullets are spewed, accurately piercing each zombie's head causing them to die instantly. (At least for a few hours) Automatically the gate opens slowly as the sentinels remained discipline to their sense of duty. Relieved nonetheless, but pissed off is Xavier who did not appreciate the cold shoulder. He steps to them with resentment.

"What the fuck was that?! Didn't you see what was happening?"

Approached and pressed within one of the sentinel's personal space, Xavier boldly bashes the guard in his face breaking the dudes jar in two places. In retaliation, the second sentinel swings but misses Xavier's head as he ducked the telegraphed swing. While crouched down in the ducking posture, Xavier tackles the kat like Terry Tate on that Office Linebacker Super bowl commercial for Reebok. After the beat down Xavier looks at Dimitrius and with no dispute they nod their heads in full agreement. KLAACK! KLAACK! KLAACK! Goes the sound of Sniper rifles locked and loaded on the defiant ones.

"Halt! Lower your weapons," barked the voice from an unknown woman.

All eyes shifted toward the figures entering the rotunda. It's Rashida in full militant garb resembling a member from the Black Panther Party being escorted by three men; one on each side holding automatic weapons and an Asian kat behind her playing with roped beads.

As she make her entrance Xavier says, "There she is; there's my girl."

As everyone heard, the look on Lilith's face suggests that she's not feeling their reunion.

Rashida approaches him and says, "Well-well-well look what the cat dragged in."

Entering in his space she wraps her arms around Xavier's neck as if she were going to hug and kiss him, comfortable with her approach he lets his guard down; unexpectedly she knees him in his family jewels. Helplessly, Xavier falls to the floor in pain. While the big man lie down curled up, Lilith steps to Rashida as if she were defending her man, but before she could say anything Rashida gives her the hand to halt any words spoken, then she pompously walks away to tend to her wounded men. Gradually Xavier stands up holding his nut sack.

"What was that for?" he asked sounding like a high pitched bitch.

"That was for leaving me for those two bimbos," Rashida replied.

"Damn Rashida, I was your lover not your man! I thought we were crystal on that," Xavier defended his misunderstood position.

"Yeah crystal, I bet you see clearly now asshole," she proclaimed . . . .

Rashida by Chris Brimacombe

Rashida (The Revolution will not be televised)

Rashida Hollister, a former black activist and member of the Black Panther party, in the late 60's and early 70's she taught African American studies at weekly meetings to those who were uneducated and out of touch with their Blackness due to impoverish conditions frequent in most ghetto communities.

During the civil rights movement on her way home, she was kidnapped by some good ole boys; that followed her with their van. She was assaulted, raped and left for dead by later claimed racist white southerners, the KKK. After recovery and set on revenge; while targeting the Bible belt, she began luring white men with her beauty and ethnicity to bed and then castrating them to avenge her rape. *'You see Massa could never turn down a nigger bed-warmer.'*

This sociopathic quandary continued for nearly 5 years before Rashida was caught by authorities. Militant to her core she chose to fight and was killed during a standoff with corrupt law enforcement. Her body was never found.

. . . . While observing the meager misfits Rashida asks, "Who are your friends?"

Somewhat amused at how Rashida got the best of his newly acquired cocky friend Dimitrius walks up to him and says, "Dude, you let a woman take you down." Then, he turns to answer her.

"I am Dimitrius and we are the Divine Militia. These are some of the souls who are going to help me put an end to the Devil's madness."

Amused at what was just said, Rashida looks at them and begins to laugh.

"Say what?! You're kidding right? This must be some kind of joke."

Rashida's men, the Crusaders, laugh as well.

Abruptly Xavier shouts out, "No, he's not kidding! It's him; he's the one you've been waiting for . . . the one the Prophecy spoke of."

Perplexed by the unexpected news Rashida digs for more information.

"Belial told everyone that he drummed up the prophecy to weed out all who wished to leave. So what you're telling me is that this dude is the truth? Ever since we got word of the prophecy we've banded together in hope that one day it would come true. Since then I've built an army. If you are the Redeemer, prove it. The Redeemer is supposed to have God's might . . . Do something that will convince me. If not, get the hell out of here."

"Look, I can assure you that God is on our side. We've come to ask you for help," Dimitrius said.

Irritated that her request gained no satisfaction, she decides to end the conversation.

"Alright that's it, just as I suspected . . . . Xavier, you and your friends need to get out of my face. I've had about enough of your bullshit."

Xavier desperately interjects, "Man, if you were going to cop a plea, now is a better time than any."

Dimitrius glances at Mathyus and Miguel then he turns toward Rashida.

Boldly he says, "Give me your weapon."

"Hell no!" bellowed Rashida.

"Give it to him, trust me," Xavier demandingly suggests.

Leery of what to expect, she tosses Dimitrius her M16 and the Crusaders point their hardware at his head, locked and loaded. Calmly, Dimitrius orchestrates a miracle right before they're eyes.

"Now the thing about these weapons is that they work, but they don't kill; until now. Mathyus do your thing."

"This is absurd! It was a theory created by a child that has not been tested, and what if you fail? Then the lady and her friends will send us back out there with those monsters," exclaimed Enoch.

Confidently Mathyus walks over to Dimitrius and places his hands on the weapon and begins his prayer.

"Pray with me everyone, for Jesus said, *'For where two or three are gathered together in my name, there am I in the midst of them.'* **(Matthew 18:20).** Now close your eyes and bow your heads. Dear Father God, bless this weapon with your might so that, a weapon used for destruction can be used as a tool to sanctify your glory. May the intentions behind the bullets bring you victory, oh Lord in a steadfast manner. Please allow these weapons to secure our path to triumph in Jesus most precious name I pray, Amen."

Unfortunately the look on Rashida's face dictates her disbelief as Dimitrius takes aim at a man brutally beating and attempting to rape a woman 300 yards away from the arena. Sadly but conveniently, there's always a heinous act or crime too be found in Hell.

"To prove a point I must sacrifice one to save millions, forgive me Father," said Dimitrius.

KA-CLAK! A single shot is fired, vigorously coasting to land center mass on its sacrificial casualty of purpose. While entering and exiting the casualty it begins to burn to a crisp.

Sarcastically Sebastian says, "Ain't no coming back from that."

The look on Rashida's face along with the rest of the attendance conveys admiration. The result of the lethal weapon is avant-garde to the existing eternal law in which Hell is governed. There's a new sheriff in town, let's see how the Devil likes that.

Entertained by their expressions Xavier boastfully blurts out, "There! Is that enough proof?"

Sarah yells, "Hallelujah!"

Mathyus adds praises as well, "Thank you Lord, thank you!"

Respectfully, Rashida adjusts her attitude by taking it down a notch or two, or maybe even three. Without hesitation she drops to one knee and humbly bows her head as if Dimitrius were a king.

"Forgive me, I needed to know. Then I guess the Prophecy is true. We've been waiting a long time for this day to come; which means our training and patients were not in vain . . . . So, when do we get out of here?"

Convinced that she's convinced immediately; Dimitrius get down to business.

"I'm glad you recognize the truth when you see it, but first things first; we need weapons and transportation."

Rashida looks at him with a serious look and says, "I'll give you more than that, I'll give you an army. Crusaders rise! The day we've been waiting for has finally arrived!

With the dawning of a new day comes a new era; we the Crusaders are now bonded by blood with the Divine Militia!"

Cheers permeate throughout the arena as their weapons are held high and gun claps applause the union.

Overwhelmed by the joyous occasion, Sebastian says, "Welcome to the party!" Unfortunately, Enoch is not enthused about what has taking place.

"This is going to slow us down. There are too many of us now, more people will surely die."

"Kill the negative vibes dawg, this is a good thing. Can't you dig it?" Xavier asks.

Lilith supports her new man by grasping and rubbing his left arm. Engulfed in the glory Dimitrius bows down and begins to pray as Mathyus and Sarah join him. Don't you just love it when a plan comes together? God is watching!

Inside the Devil's Head

"AAAAAAHHHH! This is some bullshit! Who are these people? How in the hell didn't I know about an army plotting against me in my own back yard?!! The only way this could've happened is if there were some intervention going on, and if so that means God has been here with me the whole time hiding and protecting them; only He can be everywhere due to his ***Omnipresence,* (Psalm 139: 7-12)** Ubiquitous indeed, well you want a war? You got it. Let me summon the Dogs of War . . . . Release the spawn and may His precious world crumble as I watch the hairless apes die."

Chapter Thirteen

(A Cold Cruel World)

City of the Dead: the Arena

Accepting their new position, Rashida and company gather around their new leader receiving instruction. While administering orders Dimitrius expresses his gratitude for their support by delivering a motivational speech.

"At first, when the Good Lord called on me to accept this mission, I had my doubts . . . I asked myself, would I be able to pull this off. I had very little faith or perhaps no faith at all, but as I stand here before you I must say, with His blessings and my new supporting cast there is nothing we can't accomplish. Look amongst yourselves . . . . God has had you in his plans from day one of what you thought were meaningless lives. They say the Lord works in mysterious ways; this is your chance to redeem your soul unto Him. We must complete our mission in order for the loved ones you've left behind to have a direct path to Jesus, no one gets to the Father unless they go to Christ (**John 14:6**). The world is depending on us and it doesn't have a clue that a spiritual war is being fought. Ladies and gentleman, we hold the future in our hands. Help me fight and I'll promise you victory! Together we will kick the Devil's ass and walk thru the Pearly Gates of Heaven as Reborn saints . . . . Are you with me?"

Celebrated cheers shout out flooding the hallways and stands. Concerned about another thought, Dimitrius turns to Mathyus and Sarah and says, "Things are moving little too fast. Keep an eye on our progress, it's about to get complicated . . . . We're about 20x the size we were when we started. In order to gain their respect I have to go strictly military so if I seem stern, it's nothing personal. Tell the others and make sure they understand. Okay?"

Sarah kisses him on his cheek then she sets off to inform the others.

"You do what you have too, we'll be alright. Focus on your responsibility, the rest of us will listen and obey. Don't worry, God knows what He's doing," said Mathyus.

Dimitrius replies, "I know God knows; I hope they do too. How they fight is from their heart, how deep is their faith is something else."

"This is true. I know your faith is where it needs to be," Mathyus believed.

"The troops are ready when you are," informs Rashida as the group disperses.

"Good," acknowledges Dimitrius. "First, I need you and your commanders to meet with me for a briefing in 30 minutes."

"My office is yours," She declares.

Looking around as if he lost something Dimitrius shouts out for Xavier.

"Xavier! Has anybody seen Xavier? Sebastian, Miguel, take Thorn. Find him for me and tell him that I need my enforcer."

Meanwhile, in an unoccupied room, Xavier and Lilith share an intimate moment that turns into an intense love session. For the first time ever, she is made to feel special due to his extraordinary technique in love making as opposed to the lustful sessions with Belial. She loves the way he handles her body as if he were playing an exotic instrument. He on the other hand has an appreciation for her beauty as well as her needy heart. In his mind the player is done playing, despite all the women he has conquered, finally love has come his way. Unexpectedly she captures his heart and gains his sentiment, she's got him now and never wants to let go. Jointly they reach their climax as they burst in unison. It was love at first sight that drove them mad. Never been loved or made love to in this manner she reveals to him her awkward position. Her secret is now his. Caught up on how good they were, his mind is clouded, so he does not care as long as they are one. Together they lie in each others arms and fall asleep. Twenty minutes go by as the search party stumbles into the room where the lovebirds are nude lying asleep in each others arms. Upon entering, Sebastian quickly covers Miguel's eyes. Quietly he wakes them up and informs Xavier as to what he was instructed to relay.

"Why did you cover my eyes?" Miguel asked.

Sebastian answered, "Some things are not for virgin eyes."

"I'm not a virgin, señor," retorted Miguel.

"Well, how old are you?" Sebastian asked.

Miguel boldly said, "I am thirteen, I'm almost a man."

"THIRTEEN, Damn! The kids of today are just too fast for their own britches," Sebastian barked.

In the middle of the playing field Dimitrius walks with Sarah.

"Before I meet with the commanders, I want to make sure you're alright. Is there anything you would like to talk about? Like, you and me for instance," Dimitrius pose.

Sarah responds, "What is there to talk about? I like you and you like me, what more can a girl ask for? Plus, you're taking us home. I don't want to distract or complicate things. You've got a lot on your plate."

"That's what I love about you, you are so selfless," he says.

Smack dab in the center of the field on the 50 yard line they passionately kiss as Xavier and Lilith walk up cheering and clapping.

"Well alright, look at the love birds. We ain't the only ones getting it in around here," boasted Xavier.

When finishing their lip-lock Dimitrius says, "Where have you been? I'm having a briefing with the commanders and I need you with me; let's go."

Together they trot off to the meeting leaving the women behind.

While walking, they share their love stories. Upon entry to the office they notice lustful eyes glued upon them from some of the soldiers. Suddenly Sarah picks up the pace to avoid further discomfort.

Lilith on the other hand, felt no discomfort but for a minute welcomed the scavengers as she was so accustomed. Then, the thought of Xavier smashing them gave her pleasure so she respected the big fella by trotting along Sarah's side to avoid the clash. At the same time Enoch suffers a crucial conflict within himself, his mind proceeds to play tricks on him as he continues to see Belial in his head.

Baffled about betrayal, and his new found faith in God, he runs and hides in a secluded area weeping.

"What is happening to me? I am losing control; confusion has taken hold of me," he says to himself out loud.

Suddenly excruciating pain pounds in his head as if he were suffering a migraine. Unexpectedly rising from an empty gun crate, Belial reveals himself.

"I guess it's true for what is said about an idle mind being the Devil's playground **(Philippians 4:8)**. Be my puppet."

Frightened out of his mind Enoch, like a chameleon, adjusts to the situation, "Let it be your will Sire, forgive me!"

Enoch whimpers with his head bowed.

"You thought my powers were weakened by your knight in shining armor feeble attempt to destroy me?! On the contrary! I have more than one trick up my sleeve. While consumed, your mind will be conscious but your soul will lay dormant. No one will suspect a thing thanks to your shitty attitude. Together, we will infiltrate their army and foil progress when best suits my need; now shut up and stay still."

Without a moment's notice Belial posses Enoch's body as it absorbs him like a sponge. Now fitted like a glove, Belial uncovers all of Enoch's thoughts.

"This maggot was about to betray me! I can use this to gain the Redeemer's trust," schemed Belial.

By unveiling his plot he hopes to gain the trust of his opposition. An uncanny plan but risky all the same, although the attempt is worth it, this would develop a comfort zone for his position; the concept of trust is a hard pill to swallow especially when you find it hard to trust yourself being the devil and all. Eager to set his plan in motion, Enoch/Belial moves forward toward sabotage. The first person he stumbles upon is Mathyus.

"Where is Dimitrius? It is imperative that I talk to him."

Noticing the sense of urgency, out of concern Mathyus asks, "Are you alright? Is there something that I can help you with? Cause, you seem very nervous. If you are heavy laden, and if you must know, he's in a meeting with the commanders."

The look on Enoch's face dictates that he is discussed and with a snippy remark he replies, "I'm fine, don't you worry your bald little head."

Marveled at his response, which was totally out of left field, left Mathyus curious, but as quick as from wherever Enoch's whimsical thought came; so went his curiosity.

Obliviously, he continues to walk away patting his head and says in a baffled but softly spoken tone, "I like my head like this."

Witnessing the meaningless exchange Sebastian puts Enoch in check, "Well excuse me Mr. Scrooge, what was that about? Disrespecting folk is totally uncalled for. Didn't your mother teach you to respect your elders?"

Entering the company at hand, Sarah and Lilith joined in the few.

"What's the matter?" Sarah asked.

"Nothing, mind your business." Enoch barked.

Lilith, who is used to giving orders and commands, says in a demanding voice, "Relax! You fool."

Boldly apprehensive to the instruction, thanks to his recently acquired personality harboring within, Belial Oops! Enoch obeys.

"We need to talk, now!" he says.

"Talk about what?" Xavier says upon entering the congregation. "What's with the attitude?"

"Good, your meeting is over. Where is Dimitrius?"

"I thought the lady asked you to relax," Xavier continues, "and I'll ask you again, what do you need to talk to her about?"

"That's none of your business," Enoch denies.

Modestly he stares at Lilith with the eyes of a child whose hand was caught in a cookie jar after he was told to stay out of it.

"I've decided to come clean . . . to tell the truth."

Simultaneously Dimitrius enters the area of discomfort.

"Tell the truth about what; Enoch?"

Secretly Enoch asked, "Can I have a word with you in private?"

Dimitrius replies, "Whatever you have to say, say it in front of everybody; there are no secrets here."

"Well, alright if you insist. Belial has planted a spy amongst you and I'm reluctant to say, it is I."

Immediately the group begins to heckle him for his dishonesty. Shocked at the unveiling, Lilith and Xavier remain silent; in fear of Enoch answering Xavier's pressing inquisition. Dimitrius stares at Enoch with a disappointed look on his face and shakes his head from side to side.

He then sighs and says, "Quiet everybody, please! Continue."

Now that Enoch has the floor he explains his position.

"Before I met you people my life was condemned to the evil that was the best Hell had to offer, I was a servant to the devil himself. In order to become a pillar in his melancholic community I volunteered my services. My task was to report your progress and weaknesses. I thought it would be better to be of nobility than a servant. Belial promised me royalty amongst the demons; I saw this to be an offer that I could not refuse, but as I got to know you all I realized that God will forgive me for my misguided ways and I too have a chance to redeem my soul unto him. So the real question is . . . Can you all forgive me?"

The hecklers continue but in a volume lesser, the common voiced Miguel expresses his disposition, "I knew there was something fishy about that guy."

Sebastian adds his two cents, "As the saying goes, "If it looks and smells like a duck, well then it must be a duck . . . . AFLACK!"

Sarah too voices her opinion, "I told you he couldn't be trusted."

Set out to cause mayhem, the Devil once again does his job. But as believers of Christ we know that **(Proverbs 19:21)** *many are the plans in a man's heart, but it is the Lord's purpose that prevails.*

Mathyus rears his rational head, "**John 8:7**, let he without sin cast the first stone. You people tend to forget that we're in Hell."

Piggy backing off of Mathyus' proclamation, Dimitrius supports his statement with his own.

"Mathyus is right! Who did you think was going to be here? Sinners, that's right. This isn't the world in which you all have grown accustomed too; this is the home of condemned souls who didn't get it right the first time. That's what this mission is about; to rescue those souls. It's not up to us to decide, if God can forgive them; than who are we to pass judgment? As disappointing as it may be God is at work here, because the truth has set this man free . . . As I look around at each and every one of you, I feel I could speak for us all and say that we forgive you."

Humbled by his acceptance, Enoch sheds a tear of joy while deep down in his craw Belial laughs because now he has gained their trust. Uncomfortably the small crowd remains silent and a bit displaced. Dimitrius, noticing the awkwardness, bellows a necessary question.

"Is there anyone else who wishes to give a testimony? Speak now or forever hold your peace."

Now that suspicion has grabbed a hold of the group they look at each other with different eyes. Enoch looks at Lilith hoping that she confesses her alliance to Satan. Lilith in turn looks at Xavier while holding his hand. Due to her new sense of joy and happiness, she wishes to confess her secret. As she attempts to moves forward, Xavier squeezes her hand to prevent her from saying anything. So she pauses following his lead but unfortunately curiosity already killed the cat. Sebastian scratches the surface by posing the unwanted question to Enoch.

"Why was it so imperative you talk to Goldie-Locks? Is she a spy too?"

Not realizing the weight the question carried, having to answer it places a stale taste in Lilith's mouth. As promised Xavier provides her protection.

"Dig; there is an old saying I think we should take heed too: 'A drop of water never thinks it's responsible for the flood.' Leave well enough alone fancy pants. Don't you see this little situation has messed up our groove?"

Sarah adds, "He's right. Now we have trust issues."

"No we don't because **Proverbs 3:5** says, '*Trust in the LORD with all thy heart; and lean not to your own understanding.*' Do you all know what this means? We have been born in sin and shaped in iniquity **(2 Timothy 1:10)**, don't ever put your faith in Man, he'll let you down 80% of the time. To add to this, don't think you can handle your situations all by your lonesome; trust in the Lord by bringing your burdens to him and allow him to handle it. Stand firm on this belief and reap the blessings in stored. Know this my friends, the only perfect man who walked the earth was Jesus Christ; need I say more?" Mathyus passionately preached.

With that tidbit of information the room became silent as everyone looked within themselves and found forgiveness in their hearts. Once again the Master Sergeant takes charge.

"Okay, let's focus on the mission. Rashida, gather the troops. We'll deploy in 15 minutes."

As the room disburses, Xavier consoles Lilith, "Are you alright; baby?"

"Why did you stop me?"

". . . Because you didn't need the spotlight. Don't worry, I'll tell Dimitrius about your status. Like I told you . . . I got your back. Does Enoch know?"

"Yes," she said.

Upon his departure Enoch is prevented from leaving the area by Xavier.

Xavier suggests, "Dude, we need to talk. First of all, I wanted to let you know, it took big balls to do want you did. Take it from me; honesty is the best policy, which brings me to my point. Lilith told me about her situation. So I need for you to cut her some slack, you dig? Don't worry, I'll tell Dimitrius."

Boldly Enoch replies, "You better because if you don't, I will."

Offended by Enoch's response Xavier becomes defensive, "Are you threatening me little man?"

"By all means no, I just think she should come clean. It feels good to have lifted that burden," Enoch explained while deep down, Belial is immensely amused.

Xavier flexes his bossy attitude.

"Like I said little big nuts . . . . I'll handle it; you cool wit dat?"

"Yeah, whatever," answered Enoch as he walks away content.

(Meanwhile) Father Gabriel in route across the USA

Perched on the side of a barren stretch of I-80, 200 miles to their destination, our saintly trio laid stranded credit to a busted wheel axle. By coincidence just so happens road-kill is being devoured by a flock of turkey buzzards at the same location.

"This puts us in a precarious predicament. There isn't a gas station for miles and no cell phone signal . . . What are we going to do now?" Moon inquired.

Grant answers, "I don't know but, I know I ain't feeling those vultures feeding on that animal over there; guess who's next?"

"Paranoia will destroy you," says Gabriel. "Trust the Lord will provide a solution."

As they look around the wasteland they notice, thru the glare of the sun, in the distance a car coming over the horizon toward them. Unfortunately, the sound of an engine choking dampens their spirits as it gets louder. With just enough gas to reach the stranded, the vehicle stalls about 7yards away. Quickly, the men approach the hopeful means of transportation when suddenly a woman and her boyfriend jumps out.

"I thought you said you put gas in the car! You idiot," said the pissed off woman.

Her partner responded, "I did! I put $5.00 in this morning, and I thought that's all it needed."

"I thought you said $25.00. You know the gas needle is broken. Now what are we going to do?"

Over hearing the argument, Gabriel intervenes, "Excuse me, I think I might have a solution. We have plenty of gas . . . maybe we can help each other."

Frightened by the presence of strangers especially in the middle of nowhere, the couple raises their defense by pulling out a rifle from the back seat of the car.

"Who are you people? Get away from us, we don't want any trouble," said the confused man.

"Please, my son put the weapon down. There is no need to fear us. I'm afraid you got us all wrong. We're stranded like you; our vehicle busted an axle. We need to get to Chicago before nightfall, and as I said before; we have plenty of gas. If you are going that far . . . can we hitch a ride," requested Gabriel.

Humbled at Gabriel's request the woman accepts his offer.

"Put the rifle away. Don't you see that these are good men? Sure mister, we'll help each other. Isn't that what Jesus would have done, ain't that right?" She asked.

Moon adds, "Yes, that's exactly what he would've done."

Simultaneously, while fetching the gas can fill with gas, a tow truck pulls up.

"You guys need some help?" asked the driver.

"Why no thank you, we've got it covered," said Gabriel.

"Actually, could you tow the Winnebago to the nearest garage?" Grant asked.

"Sure! It's going to cost you quite a bit though. Actually, it'll be $500.00 to be exact; being that it's a wide load and all," said the driver.

"That's a bit outrageous don't you think? I can't pay that kind of money. What will happen if we left it here locked up?" Grant hypothetically asked.

"I'll tow it anyway, and then you'll have to pay for storage and about an extra $500.00 to get it out of the Impound," said the driver.

"This is highway robbery, no pun intended," Grant aggravatingly states.

"Hey mister, I've got AAA Plus with unlimited mileage; that'll pay for the towing, where would you like it towed to?" volunteered the humbled woman.

"Thank you Jesus, bless your name God and thank you Madame. Send it back to Compton California."

Appropriately perplexed and angered, the driver does his duty with an attitude as the tank to the stalled vehicle is filled and the collaborated company drives off into the sunset toward the Windy city. As they do so, the tow truck driver's eyes flicker with a flame. While driving away, the humbled woman reveals her wings exclusively for Gabriel's eyes to see.

"My friend, you were quick to draw your weapon on us, are you saved? Do you know Jesus, my son?" Moon asked while Gabriel and Grant began to pray to the Creator for thanksgiving.

Instantaneously the confused man confessed without hesitation, "No I'm not saved but, I do believe."

Seizing the opportunity, the three wise men use the time wisely by ministering the teachings and the acceptance of our Lord and Savior. Blessed with words of encouragement, the redeemed man finds his salvation and is truly delivered. As time passes and the destination is now 25 miles within sight, they pull up to a suburban train station.

The Seraphim informs the Men of God, "We must let you out at this train station . . . there is something you must see. It's God's will."

"I understand. How will I know what to look for?" Gabriel inquired.

"You'll know it when you see it. You are gifted and your eyes can see more than the common man," said the Seraphim.

"Thank you once again," said Gabriel.

"May God continue to guide and protect you," said the Seraphim.

As the parties go their separate ways, Gabriel and crew enter the train station. While walking through the dense crowd Gabriel stops at a newspaper stand to buy the Chicago Tribune. *Headline reads: (Priest In NYC Found Dead Hung Upside Down On Cross). (Rabbi, in Brooklyn suffers same fate)*. Startled at the front page news, Gabriel collapses stumbling into the stand but remains conscious.

"Hey Bub, what's your problem? Get away from my stand! You better get your friend before I kick his ass," said the News Stand owner.

Concurrently, Grant and Moon gather Gabriel to his feet while ignoring the arrogant proprietor.

"Gabriel, are you alright?" they asked.

Speechless, Gabriel remains as he shows them the paper. The look on the two men's faces become astonished. Eager to find out the possible correlation, Gabriel reaches in his pocket and pulls out the list to verify the name of the deceased priest. Sadly to say they're names are on it. He then whips out his cell phone to call Bishop Francis. No answer, just an annoying busy signal. As the devil causes confusion; Gabriel fall victim to the pandemonium.

"What do we do now that two of our clergy has died?" asked Grant

"I'm sure God has a contingency plan. What we should be worried about is who or what killed them. It had to take several men to lift their body up so high and hung them like that," Grant implied.

Gabriel divulges, "No, this was the work of one man; the same man I saw in my dream. I need to talk to Bishop Francis."

Moon interjects, "I'm afraid that's not possible."

Slowly Moon reveals yesterday's newspaper which headline says: **Monastery Destroyed By Fire No Survivors. Foul Play Suspected Due To Pummeled Bodies, Bishop Hung upside Down On Cross**.

"I guess this was what the woman was talking about. Father God, forgive me; I've failed you. Grant guides Gabriel to a nearby bench. Adjacent Gabriel's seating sits a Blind man with his Seeing Eye dog. Gabriel stares at the dog and the dog stares back as if it knew him. Suddenly a warm but subtle glow surrounds the dog. Telepathically the dog begins to speak exclusively to him.

"Fear not Gabriel, the Lord thy God has sent me to comfort you in your time of doubt and despair. Satan has sent a facilitator to impede your progress; know that the Lord will make a way. In order to achieve success you only need to gather 3 and at least1000. Substitutes for the fallen will present themselves when you need them most. Have faith in Him and surely He will see you through."

Abruptly, an announcement wail through the station, "Passenger train #7 to Washington DC now boarding at track #2."

Gingerly, the Blind man gets up and walks toward Gabriel's direction, while passing the dog licks his hand. Unaware of what just happened Grant and Moon continue to stand by while Gabriel gathers himself. Rejuvenated with passion, Gabriel stands up with his confidence restored. Together they proceed to the business at hand. As they urgently leave the premises, the News Stand man's eyes flicker a flame.

"We need to move quickly, time is of the essence! We need to acquire Minister Shabazz at once. We need to get to the south side," Gabriel proclaimed.

Together they study the transit map for direction. While doing so a homeless man volunteers his services.

"I've been hanging out at this station for years. I know every person who comes through here and I've never seen you guys before. You look a little lost."

"We look that obvious, huh?" Gabriel asked.

The Homeless man says, "Oh yeah! Where are you guys going?"

"We need to get to S. Prairie Avenue. Do you know what train will get us there?"

"Do I know what train? As a matter of fact, I'm heading that way! I'll be happy to show you guys how to get there, for a goodwill offering . . . I'm kinda in a financial rut. I'll help you, if you help me."

"We don't need him! We can figure it out," blasts Grant.

"Where is your compassion Pastor Grant?" asks Moon.

"Can't you see that he's trying to hustle us?" Grant exposes.

Gabriel says, "I don't think so, that's not how God operates. I'm willing to take my chances besides; we'll be helping a person in need."

"If you say so, I thought time was of the essence . . ." sarcastically added Grant. Gabriel concludes while he stares at the Homeless one.

"If you could see what I can see; you would understand my decision. Trust me."

When looking at the Homeless man, his wings spread out signifying his true position.

"Follow me my good man," said the Homeless.

One level above, they go to catch the proper Iron Horse. When the train arrives, the men get on at the back of the last boxcar as the Homeless becomes firm in his position. He stands guard without conversation, his back turned toward the priests. Not understanding Grant and Moon observe with no questions asked. Gabriel on the other hand fully comprehends, as he sees that there are a few riders who are demons in disguise. Intimidated by his presence the demons remain seated as they refuse conflict with the angelic protection. Gabriel looks at Grant and Moon and they look at him in return.

Grant says to Gabriel, "Do I really want to know what's going on?"

"No you don't, trust me," Gabriel replied.

Fifteen minutes go by and still the Seraphim remains at his post as a Centurion.

Finally he says, "Get off at the next stop; be blessed, oh about that offering."

As the train arrives at their destination, they get off, at the same time Gabriel hands him a $100.00 bill, proudly he accepts but, planned to give it to someone who truly needs it.

"Thank you my friend."

"Thank you, God speed, and be blessed."

(On The Southside of Chi-town)

Its 6 o'clock and all is well. Like most folk at the end of a hard day's work, they sit and enjoy their dinner while viewing the evening news. In the home of Minister Al Malik Shabazz, a hard day's work is teaching his novice to conduct daily disciplines as prescribed by the Islamic faith of Allah through the teachings of The Honorable Elijah Muhammad. Consuming a cup of green tea while reading 'Dante's Inferno', a news flash broadcast on CNN: **Nobel Peace Prized Pope aka: Prime Minister of Peace to be elected as New World Leader. Authorities from Italy and New York have confirmed a link to the Serial killings. Other featured News: Natural Disasters, Hate Crimes, Racial Tension, Rapes and Murder are at an all time high. Gang violence in every major city and suburb in the US is on the rise. To include, a new strand of Influenza has plagued Europe; hospitals overwhelmed.**

DING DONG! DING-DONG! The door bell rang. The butler opens the door.

"Please come in, he's been expecting you."

Routinely they are escorted by The Fruits of Islam to the Minister's Study where he is watching evil through media woes, corrupt mankind.

"Come in gentleman, rest yourselves. Please, have something to eat. Excuse me while I observe how the media continues to destroy the minds of the people by boasting about how the world is in turmoil and how life has become unstable. Socialists believe the Apocalypse is soon at hand, and that the Antichrist is running things. Affecting our youth through song . . . after all the Devil was the Angel of Music," Shabazz elaborates.

Gabriel asked, "And what is your take on the matter?"

"Ahh . . . sin does not have boundaries, color, fear, nor does it discriminate. It is timeless like the difference in ones religion when compared to another. Wars that were fought over opinions and conditions; were far worse than this, but the time has come gentlemen for us to end those differences and fight for whichever God you choose, because in the end the true God will judge you his way . . . . I am ready, let's do this," declared Minister Shabazz.

Unexpectedly shocked and undoubtedly impressed with his disposition, willfully the group continues, now increased by one.

"That was easier than expected," said Grant.

In total agreement yet silent, Moon nods his head to concur. Gabriel speaks with an urgent tone which causes immediate action.

"Great! God is good . . . We'll leave at once."

"Wouldn't you like to dine before our departure? When was the last time you had a home cooked meal?" Shabazz suggested and inquired.

"Yeah, I totally agree, we need to take our newfound brother up on his hospitality besides we need to re-think our next move," suggested Grant.

Moon adds while looking at Gabriel, "You can use the rest even if it is for a few hours."

Willfully he concurs by sitting down on a nearby settee while articulating his gratitude, "Thank you gentlemen for your prudent concerns."

Shabazz says, "I'll make all the arrangements once we figure out our course of action, I am well connected; until then, Mi casa es su casa."

After indulging in fine dining with impeccable service, the 4 men get down to serious business. Together they walk from the dining room back into the study, once entered they continue into a conference room joined by an archway, as they gather around an elaborate table Gabriel experience's another premonition. This time it is sexual yet vividly explicit.

While in this dream like state melodious female voices inundate his mind, chanting the word 'Delphi', images of Greek Goddesses half naked wrapped in white silk groping each other indulging in the sheer decadence of lesbianism; and as quickly as the vision flows, quickly as it goes. Noticing Gabriel in a daze Grant snaps his fingers to bring him out of his exclusivity.

"Now what? I've never seen that look in your eye before; you're about to hit us with something heavy, aren't you?" Grant grumbled.

Bewildered in addition to being exhausted, Gabriel takes his seat and assumes the position as the famous statue; the Thinker. As he sits he tries to make sense of the forewarning as well as veil his unanticipated erection.

Despite the fact of being covered and bent over while sitting Gabriel asks, "Does the word 'Delphi' mean anything to you and if it does could you associate the term with extremely attractive women?"

"BAM! PhilaDELPHIa, excuse my shenanigans. I'm a master at playing scrabble; when you said the word that's the first thing that came to my mind," boasted Grant.

Moon includes, "The Oracle of Delphi, in Greek mythology. Apollo used the Oracle to gaze into the future."

"So what you saying, we're headed to Greece?" wondered Grant.

"Calm down beloved, as farfetched as it may seem I think we're on to something; there is a exhibit premiering in Philly at the Museum of Art this week featuring Greek Mythology," added Shabazz.

Gabriel elaborates, "Gentlemen I think this is where we should concentrate our efforts, according to my list Philadelphia was our next port of call; while we're there we must call on Sister Sophia Papadopoulos, she too must join our quest. You can call it coincidence or call it fate."

"The correlation is a bit uncanny but then again, we're fighting a spiritual battle." Moon concludes.

Grant speculates, "I wonder if she's a cutie."

They all look at him is if he was not supposed to be a part of their group. In unison they shake their heads in disbelief.

Grant response to their actions, "I'm just saying; it would be nice to have some pleasant company besides ya'll to look at."

"Beloved, what ministry you said you belong too?" Shabazz inquired.

Grant answers, "My ministry is to turn around the toxic mindset of gang members in the ghettos of South Central, why do you ask?"

"Just wondering how you've earned your stripes," ended Shabazz.

Next stop, Killadelphia, oops! I mean; the City of Brotherly Love, Cheese Steaks, the home of world renowned record producers: Gamble & Huff (Rest in Peace), recording artist/actors Will Smith, Jill Scott, The Roots, Music Soul-Child and Patti Labelle just to name a few, not to mention the diehard fans of the 76ers, Eagles, Phillies and Flyers; oh Yeah; the home of a proud native and future Mayor, a fellow Howard University alumni, and my long time friend MB (*You know who you are*).

Infomercial #4

'You see, the flesh is capable of enslaving us all; no man/woman is exempt to its will. It is self driven and held high amongst secular delights? So therefore it is sinful and of evil unless you are bound by nuptials under God's decree. As followers of Christ we are empowered by the Holy Spirit to resist such temptation which is a tool of 1 of the 7 Deadly Sins, in this case: Lust. When referencing the Bible **1 John 4:4 says,** *Greater is he that is in you, than he that is in the world.* What Jesus is saying is that, He is greater than he that rules the material world (Satan) and false prophets. If you look beyond your heart and venture deep into your soul you will find Him/ Holy Spirit which will give you the power to rebuke enticement and believe in the Spirit of Truth and Error.

Chapter Fourteen

(Under the Boardwalk)

U nder the boardwalk! Boardwalk . . . there is more that meets the eye as it laid waste to what spills into the underworld. Closely quartered the homeless camp out undercover to a place they call home. Comfort and cozy man-caves carved out of cardboard boxes align these private quarters. Humbly the abode fulfills excitement as it is supported by panhandling, handouts and the fruitful treasures only casino life can bring. First come-first serve, space is always available and so are foolish vacationers who let their guard down. Thousands of spectators struts the wood-grained planks oblivious to what lurks beneath. During daylight hours all is well, but as the sun goes down the malevolent seepage spills into forbidden territory only casino staff knows. As they continue to flock, setting themselves up baited by bright lights and dollar signs, so does the predators because in their minds, 'Crime does pay'. Let the truth be told, this isn't the postcard you see sent by the naïve escapees tricked by brochures, this is the belly of the beast that stain this world.

Wrath in Atlantic City

Rather than using the ominous portal, he defies the odds of any man who could or would walk from NYC to AC in one hour;

leaving much to believe or regard as being possible. Surely the men and women who participate in marathons would die to have such stamina and endurance to overcome their counterparts of which are deemed as mere mortals. Like Hercules, possessing the strength and the will of 100 men makes him a demy-god or something else not yet discovered. As he gallivants about the beach front city, admiring the hardships hidden from tourists that are masked by the bright lights and mammoth billboards used to facilitate as diversions to cloud the minds of motorist as they gingerly cruise through the mean streets that truly plague AC. Religiously patrons gamble their life savings or hard earned cash until the odds are in their favor. In this town you'll lose before you'll win. Place your bets and try to beat those odds . . . . Good Luck! Humorously he appreciates the struggle that spate the chanced city and its shrouded communities. Wrath takes a moment to bask in the sun on the barren beach. When lying down blanket-less, his hands crossed behind his head, and legs in the same fashion, his subconscious nevertheless supernatural mind sinks into an abyss, now somewhere other than this world, he summons his legions to counsel. Posted at various stations throughout the world the Clout of Grim leaves the physical plane forfeiting their bodies to remain for it is not necessary to convene.

"I summon the dark forces to heed my words. Kill the remaining clergy and guide the five to me, east is their direction and east is where they will fall; the priest called Gabriel is mine, do not touch him or I'll have your head; now go and do thy bidding for Satan is king of this world," declared Wrath.

In unison they respond, "By your command!"

Quickly he becomes weary of boredom and decides to explore the treasures the famed boardwalk has to offer. As he begins to walk he can't help but to notice the abundance of homeless people and disabled vets that frequent this attraction. Pleased by the suffering he is entertained by the disparity. Eager to find the location of his next victim Wrath approaches a vagabond for direction. Upon his advance the veteran beats him to the punch with that common question so often spoken . . .

"Could you help an old Vet? Could you spare some change?"

"Only if you promise to use it unwisely . . . . Where is the Hindu Temple?" Wrath queried.

"What that palace looking place? It's on the other side of town, you can't miss it."

Curious about Wrath's clothes the Vet asks, "You're not from around here, are you?"

Wrath replied, "It's quite obvious, huh? Why do you ask?"

"I don't know, maybe it's the way you dress. Your style is very creepy. You look like you're going to a costume party. Hey, I don't know if anybody told you but Halloween is in October, shit you just as crazy as I am! What unit were you with?"

Amused by the jest Wrath replies, "Crazier than you think."

While exchanging conversation with the Vet, three Punk Rockers wearing Gothic apparel stroll by. He looks at them and to himself he says, "Hmm! I can use some new haberdashery to look less conspicuous." Rudely he begins to walk away from the Vet.

"Hey! What about that change?"

Wrath being scrupulous as usual, takes the ring he stole from the broken finger of the Monsignor and tosses it to him and says, "Here take this; I hope it brings you bad luck."

Enthused about receiving a gift and totally unaware of its association with murder, the Vet will soon suffer misfortune when he tries to fence the goods.

"Gee thanks mister! That was nice of him. Strange, but still nice," said the Vet naively spoken.

Swiftly he darts off to catch up with the three. As he approaches, his momentum builds, grabbing them by their collars and scooping them up taking them to a nearby alley.

Instantaneously, the sound of crunching bones begin to crack as, screams of punishment caters to pools of blood. Excited like a kid in a candy store, Wrath strips them of their garments gathering them to his taste; fortunately for him these go-getters were lucky at tables and slots allowing them to hoard in their possession the sum of $5,000.

Now dressed to impress with his pockets filled, at least in his mind; he is ready to hit the casinos and fully embrace the city's motto 'Do A.C.' Pondering his decision on which social establishment to exercise his Gamblers Anonymous rights, the luminous eye in the sky tickles his fancy. Headed to AC's hottest casino, whatever that may be. Taken by the carefree inhibitions that overcome the psyche while engaged in waging bets against all odds, Wrath finds himself the benefactor of good spirits and fun. As he wields the dice with his lustful sway, the crowd goes wild. Back-to-back-to-back, placing 'Place Bets' scoring on wages all or nothing, which enables his winnings to increase causing management to shit a brick. Ignoring the sweat dropping from the Floor Managers' brow he carries on, consumed by the encouraging audience his ego is lifted as the rage in his heart is pacified and distracted. Based on the nature of the business, just like all and every casino that utilizes the oldest profession to sidetrack those who are likely to succeed, these Jezebel's hustle horny men who sneak to blast one off to fill their yearning for the flesh. Normally it is frowned upon, sometimes regulated or favored, in this case an necessity used to lure this high roller away from gaming. Permitted to do her job with no misdemeanor, an admiring eye soon focuses on the big winner.

"I don't know how you're doing it, but can I get a piece of the action?"

Diverted by her curves and voluptuous lady lumps Wrath's arousal enslaves him to his sexual desires.

"Now that depends on what type of action you are referring too," said Wrath as he rolls to hit another four.

The Pit Boss intervenes, "Excuse me sir, I'm afraid you've broken the bank; I must ask you to pass the dice and claim your earnings."

"What are my total winnings?"

"$666,000 to be precise sir," said the Pit Boss.

Wrath bows out while gloating, "Good number! Now that I've taken all of you sucker's money, I'll bid you adieu."

Moving with haste to solicit his business the happy hooker shouts out, "Hey handsome would you like some company or something?"

Wrath's juices begin to flow which waters his mouth; time to quench his palate.

"Hmm, or something . . . Yes, come."

Together they gather his winnings via check and $100,000 cash safely escorted by two security guards.

"I have a room upstairs, we can get right down to business," proposed the high priced whore.

"How convenient," he says as he rudely shuns the officers away without a tip.

On the elevator they begin their nasty escapade as she takes the full ride on her knees.

Enjoying her masterful skill Wrath stutters, "When I get you in the room I'm gonna tear you apart."

Little does she know, he really meant it? Steadily she continues until he releases, at the same time the door opens just short of their floor as she gags. Waiting is a gay married couple with a bird's eye view.

"Oh—my—god! Get a room why don't cha; have some respect," said the Husband.

His wife remained silent but envious, due to the size of Wrath's dangled member. Slowly the door closes as she stands wiping her mouth.

"That was excellent! I want more," requested Wrath.

"Anything you want big daddy, anything you want."

Hours go by well into nightfall, Wrath is sound asleep. Trained to capitalize on all opportunities to roll a trick and being a creature of habit, she tries to vick him for his dough. Slyly she gets out of bed and grabs his pants and her belongings, cautiously she makes her way to the door but before she complete her escape; a clenched fist is wrapped around her neck. While choked, she pleads for mercy.

"Please don't hurt me!"

"I told you I was going to tear you apart. I always keep my promises; especially to sluts like you. Where I'm from, bitches like you come a dime a dozen, you'll fit in nicely; so when you get there tell them that Wrath sent cha," he affirmed as his fist manifests a crunching sound from crushing her throat.

Gently he lays her down on the floor upside down in that sadistic—like signature he wishes to claim, then he looks out the window and surprisingly, in his view is the Hindu Temple; he smiles. Conniving as a committed Psychopath, he refocuses on his merciless mission. Nonchalantly he crawls back into bed to resume his slumber. Sound asleep like a hibernated bear until he is routinely interrupted by housekeeping.

"KNOCK-KNOCK, housekeeping!"

No answer. Customarily, the key enters the keyhole and the door opens as the keeper steps in and repeats her script.

"Housekeep-," snatched before completing of her phrase, she is pulled into the room; meeting her doom.

As the door slams in one fast swoop, he smothers her with a pillow to prevent her from screaming. Drawn to his new habit, he places her breathless body on top of the hooker as if they were one.

"I think I've over stayed my welcome; time to fly the coop."

Like DC comic book character; The Flash, he moves with quickness to the temple as if time had stood still during his motion. Resembling a cat patiently he waits to pounce on his prey. An hour goes by still he waits; finally a car pulls into the parking lot and parks in front. Stepping out of the vehicle is a Mahatma Gandhi lookalike contest winner. Quickly he is approached by our villain. Distressed by the invasion of space, which heightened his suspicion; nervously he flinches with fear.

"Excuse me sir, I didn't mean to startle you. On behalf of my company we would like to make a donation to your temple, we of course would use this as a tax write off; the only stipulation is that I must receive the signature of the head priest . . . . I believe his name is Kraven Patel," concocted Wrath.

Fatefully he replied, "That would be me; who did you say you worked for?"

"I didn't!"

While grabbing him by his collar behind his neck, Wrath forces the defenseless cleric to open the elaborately decorated door. When gaped, he body slams him to the floor. Powerlessly he tries to crawl to safety; able to gain a few feet but to no avail Mr. Mean halts his escape by grabbing his left ankle pulling him back to where he started.

Excepting his fate the priest begins his beseech.

"Not now Gunga Din; I don't want to lose my concentration," jested Wrath while lifting him up in the air over his head then, smashing the poor man across his knee; which resulted in breaking his back.

Unfortunately not built for physical punishment, the priest dies without imploring. Consistently Wrath exercises the expected by nailing the broken body on the door. Hours later, the congregation begins to show up only to find that they have suffered a loss by the hand of a serial psychopath.

Chapter Fifteen

(Testimony of Cause & Affect)

Have you ever stopped and wondered why the world is in its present state? Or why God allows the atrocities committed against man? It is my belief; it is the choices of man that got us where we are today. Daily influences can alter our thoughts; so therefore 'We reap what we sow' enslaved to our karma. Scripture say that we are borne of sin and shaped in iniquity **(Psalm 51:5)**, naturally we are driven by a never ending compulsion to carry out 1 or all of the 7 Deadly Sins: Envy, Lust, Greed, Pride, Sloth, Gluttony and Wrath. It's embedded in our DNA so therefore being of a pessimistic nature it becomes our desire, not our Will; yet there's still hope because God gives us a choice to follow his laws, thus the 10 Commandments were forged.

It seems like there is more bad people doing bad things, than those who rival the opposite. Here's where the problem lies; we base our decisions and our choices on our wants and not our needs. People will always knock heads between good and bad, the only logical space available is up. If you choose down that's where you will stay trying to work your way up; which will be hampered by envious crabs pulling you further down. Instead of taking life for granted and believing that he/she are in control; I recommend trying God's system not the system of Man of which will judge you on your circumstance rather than your accomplishments for example:

An honest, hard working man who has owned his home for 20 years, paid for 5 cars, raised 3 kids who are all college grads, and still happily married to the same woman for 25 years, and on top of that, a veteran of not one but two foreign wars; credit, respect and recognition well deserved. He's truly a pillar of his community, yes? But as soon as he misses a payment due to present financial constraints or stopped by police officers while driving, who rudely issue him a ticket instead of a warning for doing 25 in a 20 zone, the injustice of being judged by man falls into play? In the end God will judge us all, thanks to his mercy our Lord and Savior Jesus acts as our advocate **(1 John 2:1)**. So the choice is yours to live life consequently or die hopelessly. You as an individual will be held accountable. As a solution I suggest that know in your heart that God is true and just and if you obey His rule, He will bless you in more ways that you can possibly imagine. As a Christian I believe in Him and know in my heart that there is light at the end of the tunnel. These days and trails will come and go like seasons, so I try to live my life accordingly in decency and order **(1 Corinthians 14:40)**. Like Jesse Jackson said, 'Keep Hope Alive!'

God is Good; All the time

In my home I have a collection of masks that I've acquired throughout my travels. While looking at them, I began to take a good look at myself and realized that for the last three years I've been hiding behind the mask of ignorance by being in denial and lazy about my medical condition called Type 2 Diabetes. As a result none to say the least, this silent killer was slowly taking me out. Not doing the things prescribed by my doctors, I began to take matters in my own hand. Not eating right, not taking my meds and lack of exercise all contributed to my cloaked demise. Boy was I a fool!

As the saying goes, as I'm sure we've all heard that, 'God works in mysterious ways' and in this testimony I say this to be true. Our bodies naturally deteriorate as we get older; it requires the attention to maintain what was taken for granted . . . . youth. Certain things we learn to appreciate: time, hope, self preservation, family, and love.

Possessing these things can and will fulfill the richness of your heart and prioritize life's purpose.

Earlier in 2013 I was involved in a four car accident of which I was rear-ended resulting in the totaling of my car. Due to God's protection, I sustained common injuries but no broken bones and which I am happy to say that I'm alive and well. When taken to the hospital, I was treated. During my treatment, due to being a diabetic, a blood sugar test was administered to determine how much sugar was in my blood. As a result of this test, RED FLAGS flared as my numbers were critical; 506. They could've sent me into a diabetic coma; a normal reading is 120-140. If I continued to neglect my condition, surely I would've died sooner than later. Thanks be to God for protecting me by placing his yoke around me and revealing the real health issue within me. Now, I diligently do what is required of me if I plan to see my daughters successful in life; happily married and playing with my grandkids. So you see there was a blessing within in accident.

"Thank you Father God in the blessed name of Jesus! Hallelujah to the Lamb . . . . Praise Him!"

This goes to show you that God is good, all the time, if you believe.

Chapter Sixteen

NEWS FLASH

- November 21, 2012 Atlanta, Georgia: An alleged 13yr old girl stabs 2yr old sister because she was going to snitch on a 13 yr old boy hiding in the house.
- December 14, 2012 New Town, Connecticut: Gunman kills himself after massacre shooting 20 Children between ages 6-7; and 6 Adults at Elementary School following murder of mother at home.
- December 24, 2012 Webster, New York: An apparent ambush, home owner, allegedly guns down 4 volunteer fire fighters, killing 2 while crew battle Christmas Eve house blaze then kills himself.
- April 19, 2013 Thousands of law enforcement officers conducted a nearly 24-hour door-to-door manhunt for a Chechnya man, who is suspected of helping his brother plant 2 bombs near the finish line at Monday's Boston Marathon that wounded more than 170 people and left 3 dead. 1 MIT Police Officer was killed and another transit police officer seriously wounded during the violent spree.
- Jul 14, 2013—NOT GUILTY!: Sanford, Florida: Country in civil outrage as George Zimmerman is found not guilty of murder in Trayvon Martin's death. Across the US, multi

cultural protesters demonstrate to seek justice for breach of Civil Rights, preposterous 'Stand your ground Law' and botched murder trial.

- August 2013—Death toll rises as riots continue to 638 dead and 3,994 injured in Egypt; as Muslim Brotherhood Supporters loot and burn Churches around Egypt in apparent retaliation against Christians for ousting Islamic President Mohamed Mursi. Protestors take to the streets to battle police for Mursi's reinstatement.
- August 2013—United States is set for Syria strikes after US Secretary of State, John Kerry confirms evidence of chemical attack was used by Syrian President, Bashar al-Assad and his regime; on his own people killing 1,429 Syrians including 426 children. Allies are half & half for supporting US attack.
- September 16, Oct 3-4 2013—3 Separate Fatal Incidents occurred in Nations Capital faulted by Mental Illness. Each occurrence committed by lone assailant.
- October 10, 2013—NFL Superstar 2-year-old son reported dead after alleged beating by a man dating ex-wife.
- March 3, 2014—In May 2012, Marissa Alexander was sentenced to 20 years in prison after firing a "warning shot" during an argument with her abusive husband has been granted a retrial, but this time she could face 60 years in prison. The case received new attention when George Zimmerman was acquitted of murder and manslaughter after shooting and killing Trayvon Martin. Zimmerman argued his actions were predicated on self-defense, and his case drew unfavorable comparisons to Alexander's.
- March 5, 2014—A pregnant woman drove her SUV into the ocean Tuesday with three young children inside near Daytona Beach in an apparent murder-suicide attempt after claims of talking with demons.

Chapter Seventeen

(*Fear No Evil*)

(Psalms 111:10) *The fear of the LORD is the beginning of wisdom; all who follow his precepts have good understanding. To him belongs eternal praise.*

Driven as a small army of 100 led by its new Commander, the Divine Militia sets out with restored confidence to change things as we know it. Now fully stacked with God's favor and might, little do they know it; this battle is already won. Fighting a spiritual war is like no conflict ever fought before; it takes place in the mind where your personal demons have a better chance of defeating you. Independently, they attack your psyche manipulating your personality and thoughts, persuading you to harm yourself or others. In the Material world several mentally deranged psychopaths who have committed heinous crimes claim that they were told or forced by a demon to do its bidden. In Hell you may be attacked by one or more at the same time working on different aspects of your mind to destroy you. How does one combat this? Do we face our fears or turn from them? Let's see.

"MOVE OUT!" Rashida yelled as the convoy rolled south leaving the deceased city headed toward the outskirts.

Bridge of Fear by Christopher Romo

Utilized as a barrier crossing that hovers over flaming waters, the bridge signifies caution. Riding in the back of a Deuce (Military Cargo truck) is the core group.

"Where are we heading?" Miguel asked.

"We must cross the bridge to get to the wastelands," informed Rashida.

Mathyus adds, "Ahh yes, the Bridge of Fear. It stretches across the Lake of Fire which is made up of all the sewage and waste from the dead, in other words; Hell's toilet, thus it is constantly fueled."

"They say the evil is so concentrated that the fumes play mind games on all who cross it," included Sebastian.

Xavier jives, "Sounds to me like shit is about to get thick."

"Great, that's all we need; mind games," broods Sarah.

Dimitrius pondered, "Is there another way? And are souls in the wasteland?"

Rashida replies, "I don't think so. The bridge is used to keep souls in the city; no one dare cross it because their demons would attack them by bring them to their personal fears."

"Even I want no parts of crossing it," assured Enoch.

"Sarah, does the book say if souls are in the wastelands?" Dimitrius asked.

Sarah opens the book and replies, "It's impossible to read, the pages are hazy as if the ink were wet and splattered."

"It's starting already, evil is upon us as we get closer to the bridge," schooled Lilith.

Mathyus informs, "It is said that in the wastelands your fear is your worst enemy. We must not let the devil see our fears, it gives him strength. In order to find peace within; you must look to your dark side and confront what burdens your heart; if you choose not too; then you'll be condemned to your fear forever, and that's what will torment you; and what will be your personal hell."

"Are we all subject to these mind games?" Sarah wondered.

Mathyus adds, "I'm afraid so . . . The one thing I know about fear, is that it does not discriminate; as a matter of fact, it seeks out the dilemmas' that keeps us trapped or held back. No one is exempt!"

The look on everyone's face divulges dread as they glace at each other for empathy and refuge; like how a dog does when it seeks your attention. Although the look on Dimitrius face suggests that something else is afoot. Noticing the strange appearance, Mathyus switches seats to privately converse with our hero.

"Are you alright? You seem to have that deer staring into the headlights thing going on."

"I'm ok, just a little tired," he replied.

"Come now, tired, or worried? You look troubled," observed Mathyus.

Dimitrius opens up like a desperate client lying on a couch at the psychologist office.

"I guess it's obvious, huh? Haven't you ever considered failure? I mean, I don't know how Moses did it. I don't have the patience to deal with the different personalities. I'm a soldier; we invade, kill, and be out. This is a whole different thing. I'm more stressed out now than if I were headed into battle. Then, after I mediate, I'm calm. Something has got me rattled; and I can't figure it out."

"To answer your question; yes, I have. What you're feeling is normal. It's what gives our souls value. It's the humanistic traits that we possess that make us who we are. The devil feeds on our sins while God feeds on our good intentions; we're rich in spirit and our nature thrives on success, so we fear failure because it's not complementary to our achievement. To overcome this feeling you have to face what is valued to you the most; once you grab that, then you will be able to face your fear and overcome failure. The battles within are won by the struggles in our hearts and minds. I'm so glad God made us this way because if He didn't, we would be like pets waiting for our master to give us what he wants; not what we need . . . . Rest now, you're starting to second guess yourself," preached Mathyus as Dimitrius listen with a keen ear.

"Wow that was deep. After all of that, I think I will grab a few winks. I wasn't expecting such a heavy answer, a simple yes or no would've sufficed."

Exhausted by the lecture Dimitrius tilts his cap over his brow and leans back to catch forty winks or more.

Quiet as a mouse they remain; contemplating their own quandary while approaching the erected structure. The closer they get their anxieties grow. They look to Dimitrius for comfort, but he's in meditation.

"Ain't this great; the one time we need him his mind is somewhere else . . . . Let's go back; this is nonsense," proposed Enoch.

Sebastian blurts out, "Give us a break with the negative talk! Lately you've become more of an arrogant asshole than usual; I wonder what crawled up your ass and died."

Inside Enoch craw Belial laughs and says, "Haaaa! Only if you knew."

Enoch on the other hand snarls at Sebastian as if he were an animal protecting his territory. Now paused at the fearsome crossing, they become more terrified due to the perched demons that await their attempt to cross. Despite the nervous bickering Dimitrius remain in stasis. While deeply engaged in his conscious; he is immersed into a dream which places him in a black chasm. Suddenly a bright light shines upon him as if he were being interrogated by an opposing force. A multitude of heinous actions appear as cries of mercy jingle from women and children, who have suffered a loss since losing a love one by the plunder of rampaged men. Unfortunately, they're classified as victims of the spoil expensed as collateral damage; a costly necessity but senseless still the same. Lifeless bodies, blood and limbs sprawled as a backdrop. In the foreground he sees the devil cheering him on for the dreadful increase of souls contributed to his kingdom. Profusely he begins to sweat as he undoubtedly realizes; although militarily brainwashed he was responsible for annihilating innocent lives. Shunning from this responsibility he turns his face away from the vision, but to no avail restraints grapple his limbs and neck forcing him to accept accountability. During his arraignment; the voices from crowds cheer as a wall of trophies and model airplanes stand as a monument in celebration of his son's accomplishments and hobbies. Standing in front of his shrine with his back facing him is teenager Donnie. Unexpectedly boo's and hisses sound out from imaginary spectators as the great wall came tumbling down; as Donnie is filled with rage while holding a picture frame in his hands of dear ole dad.

As the midst of the drama unfolds, Donnie then turns around and smashes the frame amongst the rubble and says, "YOU WERE NEVER THERE! I HATE YOU!"

Now knowing and accepting the fact that he was a terrible father who missed out on his boy's life; and as a result, he is to be blame for his son's actions. To solve this issue; forgiveness is what he shall seek. Being a student of sound doctrine, he resorts to his biblical teaching acquired while in Purgatory.

"Forgive me Father God, for I accept what I've done; I repent my sins unto you O' Lord in Jesus name," he shouted.

Instantly the disturbed vision disappears as does his shackles.

Then, a comforting voice says, *I forgive you my son.*"

Momentarily his wife appears with encouragement, "My life must have been deemed value, because God choose me as the catalyst to put an end to the Devil's reign; he is afraid of you, he will do everything within his power to stop you, love the Book Keeper as you loved me; all is well with my soul."

Slowly she turns and walk into the darkness as the focused light that shined upon him fades with her steps he blurts out, "Where's Donnie? Where's our son?" Conveniently, he is ignored. As his oneness subsides he awakens with a feeling of gratitude and assurance; but still wonders about his delinquent. Yet in still, his motivation is intact due to his faith once again fueled to do his duty!

"Cross the bridge now!" he demanded.

Instantly the convoy commenced as the demons take flight.

Dimitrius gives warning, "Face your fear with truth and repent. God has got your back; if you believe in Him. I just confronted mine, and I'm victorious."

One by one the demons dive to swarm amongst the trucks and its passengers infiltrating their minds searching for shrouded discovery within. Dimitrius switches seats with the driver and continues the course steady, but as time passes; in their mind's time is at a standstill.

Demon Assault #2: Sebastian

Approached by a half man, half woman split straight down the middle demon; he is bitch slapped into his fear. He is a well cultured Frenchman who is eccentric, flamboyant and witty. Border line gay but have not crossed over; he wrestles with his manhood daily. Fully in tune with his feminine side and prefers her than him; his respect and flair for the finer things in life keeps him on edge. He was an Aristocrat/Socialite from the high society of Paris, in a time when Paris became the fashion cornerstone of the world. Although bred from men of powerful influence, his secret obsession for the love of men lies dormant within. Sauntering softly his fear comes to him as himself masquerading as an elaborate cross-dresser fatuously in awe of being the sweeter man.

"OMG! Are you serious?! This is my fear? Believe me, I've already accepted the fact that I am gay and I don't have a problem being of such," blurted Sebastian.

The demon says, "Your fear is not whether or not you're gay; it is how you became this way."

With a pop of its finger in a 3 snap zigzag fashion, his truth is revealed. In a vision an enlightenment of his past is brought forth. As a young teen of age 15 or so, he was frequently molested by a priest at catholic school which was followed by a string of isolated instances of being sexually assaulted by his uncle, who made him swear not to tell or he would tell his macho father; who believed in exerting physical disciplinary action that his son was in the closet. Terrified of the possible outcome, he completely blocked these incidences out of his mind which caused an adverse affect; leaving him to question his totality as a man.

"It's all coming back to me . . . . I remember now; I suppressed that part of life not because of the pain; it was because of the shame that held me prisoner. I was afraid the world wasn't ready for this Diva Don, so I kept my flamboyancy to myself; but to get pass this I must forgive them as well as myself in Jesus name. As a result from all the drama I must say, that I am happy, carefree and I am gay; I was born this way and proud of it. On the other hand; me being who I am is not my fear, it's how I'll be judged in God's eyes is what I'm afraid of; so if you're done, be gone with your bullshit," declared Sebastian brave and bold.

Defeated by restored confidence while standing on his faith, the demon vanishes and Sebastian stands the victor. Back to reality he goes.

Demon Assault #3: Mathyus

Facing his fear with no fear Mathyus welcomes his demon with valor, "Come to me you obnoxious son of a bitch." Accepting his challenge, a demon disguised as his wife with a severely bruised neck; that resulted from his fury appears in his mind.

"I knew it would be you to give me closure for what I've done," said Mathyus.

"Closure?! You killed me out of jealousy; an uncontrollable rage that negated all that you stood for . . . You're a hypocrite; practicing what you preach has proving difficult when it comes to you . . . You're a liar," verdict the demon.

Mathyus theorized, "My rage was ignited out of love not hate. I thought I was a good man; I tried to do the best that could with what we had . . . . I loved you more than I loved myself, and too see you with another man drove me insane. At first, I didn't understand why, but now I know that it was because I neglected you; I became so obsessed with my work I didn't realize that I had short changed us. As a result of that it drove you to another man's arms."

"It sounds like you've worked it all out, but there's a problem actually, six; that's the amount of men I fucked when you were so caught up within yourself and your God . . . . Now, how does that make you feel?" claimed the demon.

When pondering his next comment he looks toward the sky while swallowing his pride and says, "Because you were an adulteress Hell was inevitable; I just helped speed up the process. . . . Thanks for the closure and may the Good Lord have mercy on your soul come judgment day."

Failing to push Mathyus over the edge with guilt, the demon disappears into thin air as Mathyus gets down on his knees and begin to pray for clarity and closure. Back to reality he goes.

Demon Assault #4: Xavier

Noticing Mathyus and Sebastian as they come out of their crucial conflict, Xavier can't help but wonder when he will face his demon. Anxiously he waits; until finally realizing that he is already in confrontation, due to the double set of hand cuffs secured around his wrist behind his back; as if he were arrested as the scene switches to him now being seated in the back of a squad car. Driving the car is a demon disguised as his old partner when he was a Patrolman: Officer Michael J. Mangam, who he betrayed in order to quench his lustful thirst for a plethora of sexual freebies negotiated with Pimps up, Hoes down. Reflecting about his corrupt nature and betrayal, he understood his dilemma; after all boys play with toys and, hustlers play with money, drugs and bitches. Guess which one he's not? Good cop, Bad cop none the less, a crooked cop; who frequently would flip the script to his personal convenience by taking the law in his own hands. Being a hustler of hustlers governed by a badge gave him respect on the streets as well as crime itself. Protected by the law, he was the law. Daily manipulating the judicial system in his favor without remorse and betraying those who he was partnered, he had it his way although despised by all. He was a man made of brawn which intimidated the average chap; and taken advantage of the penal code was his crime; and therefore those who do should be deemed a criminal thus the case of Detective Dunn. Contained and displaced as if he were a criminal Xavier recognizes his captor; then questions his status, "Oh shit! Mikey is that you? Ah man! What are you doing, Where are you taking me and what have I done?"

Demon Mangam says, "Yeah it's me. I'd hope this day would come. You have a lot to account for; you grimy piece of shit, you're no better than the scum we faced everyday let alone the low-lives who didn't deserve to live. You took advantage of the people and placed yourself above the law. What you did to me was totally fucked up. I was an honest cop, a good cop; I was about to be promoted, which would've got my ass off the streets; until you set me up and got me killed; you dirty son of a bitch! You sold me out for money and a piece of ass and on top of that you got my promotion."

In hopes that this day would never come Xavier knew he had hell to pay.

"I know, I know! Damn it man I'm sorry; I was a fucking freak, I was out of control! There isn't a day that goes by, that I haven't thought about how I fucked it all up. I deserved what I got, I can live with that. At least you died a hero, which is more than I can say for myself. Look enough of this bullshit! Okay, now where're we going, what are you getting ready to do?" he asked.

"Where we're going shouldn't be your concern, but who we're going to see should. There's another reason you are here boy," spoke the demon; that then spat in his face.

Trying to make heads or tails of his situation; the curious ride takes him through his ole stomping ground where most of his dirt was conducted, finally stopping at the notably corrupt 23rd precinct.

"Time to see the man asshole," hollered Mangam the demon cop.

Now brought into the building as they walk down a corridor aligned with betrayed fellow officers, who commence to beating him with their nigger-be-cool sticks; as if he were Rodney King or some poor unfortunate minority scapegoat-ed for something he didn't do, finally they enter a court room filled with victims of his exploits which consisted of Pimps, Hookers, Drug Dealers, Hustlers and Bookies. The demon then kicks him in his groin as he released him to inflict everlasting pain that solidified his redemption.

When forced to take the stand, he is bombarded with fruits, veggies and eggs and a prostitute who spits in his face for service rendered but no payment received.

"Remember me mutha-fucka," she spat.

The audience goes wild as the jury enters the box. Battered and bruised he sits as he is helpless.

"What the hell is this?" Xavier barks.

The room gets quiet when the bailiff cried, "All rise!"

In comes Belial masquerading as a judge. Casually he strolls to the big chair and takes his seat, and then he bangs the gavel, BAM!

"You thought you were big shit earlier; look at you now, all by your lonesome."

"Bring it! I can handle all that you've got; I ain't afraid of you or these fools," ranted Xavier.

"Ahh, which brings us to my point, release him from his shackles."

"You have no fear which means that you are fearless and brave, on top of that you're selfish and greedy; I could use a man of your caliber to reign by my side. You know I'm sitting here looking at you; you remind of that black comic book superhero nigger, 'Spawn'. So, what do you say?" Belial proposed.

Xavier puzzled by the offer says, "That's where you're wrong; the only thing I fear is God. So whatever man, seriously? Me down with you?"

"Going once-going twice; I won't ask you again, what will it be?" Belial retorts.

"Hell no! You must be crazy," Xavier boldly announced.

Belial declare, "Well then I guess I'll kill your entire family; but I'll make them suffer before I do."

"Now that's funny because I don't have any family; their all dead and since I haven't ran across them while I've been here, I guess they're chilling in Heaven," boosted Xavier as he draws confidence as the conversation continues.

"Fuck it then I'll kill your friends then," suggested Belial.

"HAAAAAA! Look around you their already here . . . . HAAAA," laughed Xavier.

Angered by the sarcasm, Belial looks around at the angry mob and gives command, "You want him; you got him, kick his ass!"

Not realizing that he fucked up by removing the cuffs and not having a clue as to how skilled of a fighter Xavier was; surprisingly he witnessed a strength that could only be rivaled by his notorious henchman. At the same time he disappears with the illusion while Xavier establishes his spiritual awakening.

"I admit I was out of control but he was wrong about one thing, I do have fear, the fear of God and in the blessed name of Jesus I ask for forgiveness and I repent all that I've done to dishonor him and myself . . . . After all of that I can use some Alka—Seltza and a drink."

Zapped back to reality he goes. Plop—Plop—fizz—fizz, Oh what a relief it is?

Demon Assault #5: Miguel

Easily targeted during the swarm, due to being an adolescent; Miguel is petrified as he witness the advancement of his demon dressed as a Killer Clown. Sarah, being his big sister of his newfound family, secures him by holding his hand. When attacked his fear consumes his psyche, alone he finds himself engulfed in darkness. Suddenly a light shines spewing a wide spectrum of color, simultaneously circus music commences as a familiar figure approaches.

"Papí, is that you?" He asked.

"Yes mi hijo, who else could get you through what frightens you the most," said Hector, his father.

"What is this place? Where are we? Where did you come from?" inquired Miguel as his anxiety increased.

His Papí says, "Watch and see mi hijo, watch and see."

Briefly they wait until an announcement is made: Ladies and Gentlemen, children of all ages; welcome to the Cinco de Mayo Circus Extravaganza. Hearing the broadcast triggered an eerie shiver up and down his spine. Vividly, he remembers the one and only time his father took him to the circus especially when the Ringmasters introduced the Killer Clowns. In comes a zany squad of murderous clowns with weapons laced with splattered blood. Their faces pruned with infected cuts and contusions while pus secretes from their nose and mouth. Similar to what he did with Sarah when in need of a security blanket as if he were Linus from Charlie Brown; Miguel grabs his father's hand for protection holding on to it for dear life until he feels his father's hand blow up as he loses his grip. Resembling a hand of a clown Miguel looks up at his dad, only to find that his dad has become the things he feared most; he screams and struggles for freedom; but to no avail he is locked within the death grip of his chimera. While trying vigorously to escape the clutch of the colorful boogieman, he blacks out as his fear sends him to his old neighborhood. Finally awake, he finds himself on an errand to acquire some sazón for some 'Arroz con Pollo' his mama preparing for dinner. As he gallivants to the corner store Bodega' he hears gun shots fired, blasting from his destination.

Allowing his curiosity to get the best of him, he peeked into the store window for a look-see.

As the assailant rummage through the cash register he notice that there is a witness to the crime just committed. Once gathered all that was grabber—able he exits and approaches Miguel who is scared shitless as piss trickle down his leg. Without words shared the clowned thief grabs him by his collar and groans out of frustration. Frantic by screeching sirens the masked man shoves Miguel to the ground and darts off down the alley which offered a maze of direction as a sure shot escape route. Although terrified at the tragic event Miguel gets up off the ground and enters the store. Surprisingly having enough time he carries out what he was tasked to do despite the lifeless body that lay on the floor. 'It's been 15 minutes; still the police have not arrived; what was heard by the goon was an ambulance racing to the nearby hospital as frequent as it does. What should've taken five minutes took half an hour. Patiently waiting is his mother who was please to see her hijo safe and sound. Having a keen sense or better known as intuition as all women do; especially when it comes to her child, she notice his stigma as well as his pissed pants.

"Venga aquí, mi hijo. ¿Qué te pasó?" she asked as he stood there quietly in shock.

At the same time his father enters to find his family within a dilemma.

"¿Qué te pasó mi pequeño? He asked.

Still quiet as a mouse he remained. Unfortunately, having witnessed such a heinous act has traumatized the lad to the point of withdrawing himself from interacting with others; thus he became a loner, an introvert. Now segregated from his peers he begins to enjoy the comfort of being home alone as his parents engage in unlawful activities as gang members. He would play self indulged games to pass the time away especially his favorite; hide and go seek. When his cousins would come to visit that was the game of choice until one day while doing so he hid himself in his father's closet where he uncovered a secret compartment. In this partition were weapons, money and the worst possible thing you could've imagined. Hanging on the on a hook on the wall was the same exact mask the robber wore from the murder he witnessed. Using his common sense, he puts two and two together and concluded the obvious; his father and the robber/murderer were one in the same. It was for the love of his father he concealed his feelings; deeper he suppressed this thought, this vision, this conclusion from his mental which caused fear in his heart; until it was the day of which his father took him to the circus for the very 1st time. As the Ringmaster introduced the Clowns it ignited the resurface of his suppression. Upon their entrance the clowns infiltrate the audience conducting zany antics and jest. He is approached by one with a gagged gun when fired sends Miguel back to his clutched fearful attack.

As he resumes his capture, he faces his demon with rationally. He looks to God for the support he needs to face his fear; so he asks the Lord for strength, courage, and wisdom. Immediately he regains his dexterity and halts his struggle.

He stands tall like a man and says, "I know it was you Papí; you were the clown that robbed and killed that man in the store; when you saw me you got angry because I saw you, I knew for a long time but I didn't care because I love you Papa."

His father replied, "I did it for you, I did it for mi familia. It was my initiation; if I didn't do it they would've killed us all."

"I forgive you and hopefully God will too," said the boy all grown up.

"Mathyus and Dimitrius were right, God has got my back. Thank you, Jesus!"

As the specter dissolves away a sense of gratitude and the weight carried is now lifted. Instantly back to reality he goes.

In the mind of a child when affected at an early age may last as a memory that will sit in the back of their minds depending on how enjoyable or detrimental the circumstance, i.e. there are things that I still remember even at my present age of fifty from when I was a young dude growing up in Brownsville, Brooklyn, NY. I'm talking thoughts that came and went that carried no weigh at all. As time moved on during my adulthood I may have never thought about them until a conversation that sparked the thought reveals the calamity or enchantment, then and only then my recollection brought it to view.

Were my thoughts suppressed or stored? I really don't know. In the case of Miguel witnessing a murder caused him to suppress this thought from his psyche which caused fear in his heart, the discovery of his father's secret was the final nail that sealed the coffin until, he look to his faith and sought a higher power (Jesus) for comfort.

Demon Assault #6: Lilith

All hail to the Queen, yet she too is not exempt from the monstrous mind fuck. Although she thought otherwise, being Queen of the Damned granted her immunity from the high flying fiendish ones who beg to differ. Disrespectfully her demon presents himself as a Roman Soldier seeking pleasure from a two bit whore in a time when being Roman was possibly the nastiest Mutha Fuckas on the planet. Now taken back to when sex paved her way and her inhibitions ran free; proudly she was claimed to be the best at pleasuring a man which warranted her jezebel status. A title of which she didn't mind possessing as nymphomania plagued her sinful desires. Fucking her way to the top, kept her furnished with the best quality a drifter or hypocritical nobleman had to offer. She was rich and well provided for from being a student of the oldest profession of the world which provided her with what most men desired: respect, popularity and of course power.

Willfully accepting the vision of assorted Kama Sutra positions before her, she loses her self-respect and her way by succumbing to the tantalizing madness. As he reveals his horse like endowment, she is stimulated by his pursuit of pleasure therefore becoming extremely aroused. Never turning down an opportunity to be dicked down, she removes her dress and welcomes the soldier inside of her. As she enjoys the sexual bonding while absorbing the pressure from his massive man meat; she realizes that she has betrayed her feelings for Xavier. Conflicted thoughts stir inside her heart as her selfishness outweighs her principles, so she continues to enjoy the fuck for what it is worth. After him, a dozen men line up to partake in her juicy offerings; one by one, sometimes two, they exercise their tenderloins never becoming exhausted as if they're cocks were fortified with modern day male enhancements. Allowing her to be drenched inside and out with thick hot creamy man milk as freely as the application flowed. Needless to say no holes, that's right holes, barred anally she is torn a new one. Constantly she quivers and shivers from reaching her climax, due to highly intense multiple orgasms causing a continuous spew throughout her body like never before. As hours go by now finally reaching her lustful fill that is seemingly quenched; exhausted she lay from the vigorous workout.

Yet this is her fear and unfortunately, in addition to the act; sadomasochism demands her attention. In comes a band of masochist raging for sadistical gratification. Faulted by her own inhibitions she finds herself victim to cruel sexual punishment. Pain before pleasure is the claim to fame; a motto governed by few yet isolated by so many. In her mind receiving numerous meat meals is one thing, but being humiliated and getting her ass kicked is another. Abuse is abuse no matter how it is delivered; a lesson soon learned involuntarily. Treated like a guinea pig she is subjected to accommodate their will. She is raped repeatedly by seasoned practitioners violating her sport box as if it were tortured for fun. Administering pain is gratifying yet morbid. Today these practices are labeled as BDSM: Bondage/Discipline, Dominance/ Submission, Sadism/Masochism; undoubtedly some next level shit that I couldn't support or be down with; but hey, to each his own. What was good to her has abruptly grown completely out of control. For hours they commence their exploits running trains and gangbangs, ties that bind and toys, not for tots. Jerking and jabbing, sticking and stuffing and oh yeah did I mention sucking and fucking. Now a victim of total humiliation suggesting as though this extreme was not enough; enters a masked Master and Mistress dressed in black leather accompanied by a Doberman Pincher with an appointment of bestiality slotted for grotesque pleasure, until her sire arrives to save her from despair.

"Enough! What is this? Cease this at once," he bellowed at the top of his voice.

Caught off guard he approaches the situation with frustration and frees her from bondage; pressingly yet insensitive to her worn out state, he inquires about the generous soiree.

"I hope you enjoyed the gift, I must say; I out did myself, quality and quantity; don't you agree, I know how you love some good dick?"

"A gift, this was your doing; how could you? I thought I was worth more to you than that," she cried.

Defensively Belial retorts, "Bitch please, whatever gave you that impression? You're no different than other tramp despite being my favorite . . . Did you forget who I am? I'm the Devil baby, what did you expect; love and affection? I'm not capable of such emotion. What you got was pure unadulterated sex . . . straight up lust. You wanted to fuck and so we did, amongst other nasty little things, I need not remind you. I feed your flesh as you did mine, until our appetite was satisfyingly filled, and then we continued like most animals do."

Realizing her worth her eyes are finally opened to the truth and she says, "You know maybe these people are on to something; I refuse to be your fool any longer, I'll take my chances with Jehovah."

Taken back by her proposition angered he became. Callously he snaps his fingers, sending her back to reality with throbbing soreness, vaginal saturation, and a burning ass.

"Well you know what they say: Hell hath no fury . . . Well, you know the rest," clichéd Belial. "Her being the ultimate harlot, the infamous Whore of Babylon; I thought she would've enjoyed it . . . . women! You can't live with them or without them, besides she was born to condemn as many souls to Hell as possible with her false enchantment. Now why would I fall in love with a trick like that?"

Did she face her fear and overcome it or did she embrace it? Or was it just another fuck or maybe it was just good to her to the very last drip drop.

The Whore of Babylon by SpartaDog

Demon Assault #7: Enoch

10-9-8-7-6-5-4-3-2-1, countdown to his crucial conflict. In the midst of a dark space Enoch is confronted by what lurks deep within. As he struggles with his humanity, confusion contaminates his mind which allows Satan to manipulate his soul. Forced into an unbalanced battle still he fights trying to hold on to discovery. He has found new meaning in life and desires to be blessed by the greatest God in the blessed name of The Christ. His fear is not to be tried in truth; but to be forgiving. He wishes to be a better man who is granted to live his life in abundance as God intended. This is what he wants; this is what he fights for. In his mind, reaching this objective is so farfetched and so hard to believe since his soul is inhabited by Dr. Evil himself; whose plans are purely diabolical in nature. Resistance can be futile but when fighting for your life you have no other choice if you value it. Knowing this fact Satan will cloud your judgment in hopes that you don't have the balls to oppose his fate for you. Recognizing the years of being bamboozled, Enoch daringly defies his captor.

"Greetings Belial, this may come to you as a bit of surprise but an appeal still the same; Release me! I don't want to do this anymore. Suddenly I have a change of heart. I no longer desire to be a part of your royal court! I've come to realize that I can be redeemed to serve a mighty God; so I refuse to be your puppet any longer."

Shocked indeed Belial is outraged to the 2nd power, in response to this he growls like a ferocious lion and grabs his agitator, tossing him across the blackened place. As his punched body aggressively hits the ground, it rolls continuously until it becomes pummeled with scrapes and bruises. Not at his fill and being a glutton for punishment Belial leaps 10ft into the air landing feet first; crushing Enoch's chest. Not allowing him to die Belial continues the ass whipping. A barrage of punches and kicks celebrate upon his torso leaving him to hold on for dear life. Unbelievably, with mustering breath, Enoch finds strength due to his newfound faith; so he forges forth toward intended victory and never minds his consequence.

"Go ahead kill me! I'd rather die than to serve you, finally I realize what you really are; you're nothing."

Ignoring Enoch's gibberish still he continued to bang him up until weighted words devotes true meaning.

"I REBUKE YOU IN THE NAME OF JESUS CHRIST," blurted Enoch with conviction.

In fear of confirmation Belial hightails his way out of the novel saint's meat suit.

However before exiting he gets one off, "Freed from me you are, but you'll never be freed from Hell."

Free at last from the tyranny and strive of the malevolent, Enoch does something he has never done or knew that he could as he gets down on his knees with head bowed, "Lord, I don't claim to be a righteous man but I do desire to be a better man; you of all know that I am a sinner who probably will sin again, please forgive me for the things I don't understand; sometimes I cry when I'm alone because I knew not love until you placed me in the midst of believers who try their best to glorify you, allow my heart to be filled with actions and words that pleases you at all times. May my old life warrant death and my new life promise as your plans for me are presently unrecognizable; nevertheless I have faith in you to see me victorious, so have your way Father God and use me as you see fit for I am ready to do thy bidding in Jesus name, Amen."

While embracing the embellishment of his soul, he is zapped back to reality filled with the glow of love. Excited by the good news, he is blissful about revealing his acceptance to God. Sympathetic and supportive about his transition they applaud him with encouraging words, gestures and glee. For once he feels the love as if he belongs to this family as Thorn licks his hand. Regrettably, as you and I know in most cases; all's well doesn't end well hence this situation due to tattered remains left behind while the evil one vacated the premises. It is because of the devil's invasion and inhumanity Enoch's inhibitions were released and his soul is scared forever. Vengeful and slighted Belial can't let him go without retribution. Knowing that Enoch is new to the religious game; his attack on his walk is swift and well calculated. Helplessly, packaged as damaged goods; his suffering begins to witness a crescendo of demonic visions of revelations soon to come, which automatically drives him insane. They're baffled; the audience witnesses Enoch's strange behavior due to his unorthodox babbling.

"Oh my god!" Rashida exclaimed.

Concurrently, Xavier shouts out, "Yo bro, what's the deal?"

"Qué pasó?" Miguel asked.

Dimitrius guesses, "He's still under attack."

"Somebody, help him," yelled Sarah.

Mathyus concludes, "It's too late there's nothing we can do."

"What about prayer?" Sebastian suggests.

Lilith says, "There's not enough time! Belial has got him now."

Unfortunately, due to time constrains and the lack of wisdom and knowledge not yet acquired left Enoch vulnerable, so Satan takes advantage of the opportunity.

"Rebel without a cause! Then jump since you want to take a leap of faith."

Not strong enough to resist, Enoch submits and screams out, "All is well with my soul, thanks be to God; Hallelujah to the Lamb!"

Recklessly he runs and jumps off the side of the bridge in to the Lake of Doom. On the way down his body begins to burn which gives off the stench of grilled hamburger. Shocked by the extreme measure, words remain silent as Thorn howls for their loss.

"Wow that was deep. Is it me or is anybody else hungry? I could go for a bag of twenty White Castle Cheeseburgers with extra pickles," jested Xavier.

Sebastian replies to Xavier's malicious comment, "Now that was tasteless. No class whatsoever."

On accord, they all look at the cold hearted brutha and shake their heads in disbelief.

"You should be ashamed of yourself. Was that necessary?" Sarah said.

"I agree. Show some dignity, after all he did find God before it was too late; let's hope that God felt the same," proclaimed Dimitrius.

Xavier defends himself, "Sorry guys, I thought it would've broken the tension; you know; bring us out of the shock factor . . . My bad."

Mathyus being the preacher man he is offers a few words via prayer to rest the soul of their loss, "Dear wonderful and gracious

Father; we pray to you now not for ourselves but for our comrade, who for a long time did not know you, but finally realized in his heart that you and only you are the true God and through your precious son Jesus he was shown the light to salvation and was delivered, so therefore hopefully he repented to gain your promise. Father God, use his death as a sacrifice as we learn it as a lesson of obedience unto you; rest his soul my Father and bring him home with you in Jesus name, Amen."

While howling for sorrowed loss, Thorn is faced with his dread.

Demon Assault #8: Thorn

It is believed by many but understood by few, that what distinguishes man from beast is strictly spiritual (*the Soul*). The soul of a man rationalizes his position and governs dominion over all creatures; which is a gift from God that have been corrupted in more ways than some, where as canines are subservient beings driven by hunger and territorial supremacy. When the species interact a consummation is establish which forges a bond as master and pet. Master being man; of course is respectfully granted Alpha status. Humbled and obedient they are to him and only him; such persona should be giving by us to the Creator (*Jehovah*) for his benevolent blessings which are constantly taken for granted, non—deserving yet truly longed for. Discipline, to its owner when shown as a token of appreciation and gratitude; will remain demure and affable, unless commanded otherwise. With distinction they are able to judge human expression whether negative or positive through attitudes of tempered tones or yielding voice. Surely attributes possessed by an intelligent species, who completely comprehend us; as we befall the lesser in understanding them. After all who is fooling who? A dog, as a pet, lays around all day, fed at least twice a day with a nutritious diet, affectionately massaged, cardio exercised and finally walked which leaves you to clean up its mess. When walking one may wonder: who is walking who; a ritualistic task that mocks the responsibility of a mailman: In rain, sleet or snow . . . . Unfortunately, there are pets that fall victim to neglect, abuse and starvation. If a domestic animal suffers these afflictions, they're placed on the defensive and sometimes frighten which is revealed by lowering its head and tucking its tail between its legs while removing itself from the presence of the scolder. More than likely they become homeless; due to their owners' abandonment.

These animals are labeled as Strays. They wander the streets in search of food and shelter or sometimes a kind heart. Forced to fend for themselves; by any means necessary, they involuntarily are strained to live by the desperate codes of survival of the fittest or only the strong survive. Most of the time, they are captured by an authority that brings them to a caged facility (the Pound). There they will stay and be properly cared for until someone claims them or until the allotted time is rendered for death by lethal injection. This is Thorn's fear, this is Thorn's tale. As his demon presents his fear, Thorn is reminded of a time before he became the mighty dog he is today. Regrettably, he was subjected to such a life of cruelty as he was owned by an underground ring of dog fighters and street scum. Thug life persuaded their thug passion by profiting from the lives of gladiator dogs and showmanship. The finest breeds bore the finest prize fighters, as well as top dollar for champion bloodlines home and abroad. Fortunately, Thorn being a Cane Coro stood strong, black and beautiful. He was a pure bred that yielded twenty litters. Classified as a chief producer of cha-ching! He was kept separated from the hellish hounds until one day his owner met with misfortune and was shot and killed over a dispute of pettiness. As a result of being stolen for his manufacturer; Thorn was placed in a foreign kennel with territorial alpha males who were intimidated by his presence, which proved to be a careless move on his new profiteer that resulted in Thorn being assaulted by the savage beasts damaging his loins forever. No longer able to produce and earn his keep, his value has become worthless to the ignorant as abuse introduced itself. Frequently he would find himself on the receiving end of senseless beatings until one day the spirit inside of him spoke giving him a command.

"Stand your ground beautiful one!"

And so he did the very next time his abuser lashed out toward him.

"Grrrrrr!" he growled revealing his teeth expressing his defiance.

Without haste he pounced on him knocking him down then stands on his chest snapping at his face signifying his rebellion. Being the punk that he was, the sucker tries to shoot Thorn. Swift and now fearless with no other option; Thorn attacks and kills the man by ripping out his throat. Left to wander the streets, hungry and now homeless all seemed to be lost until a policeman walking his beat stumbled upon the magnificent stray walking with a limp and whimpering due to a thorn stuck in his paw. Apprehensively they approach one another as if they were meant to be, while removing the splinter with a gentle touch and tender words; reciprocated by the wagging of his tail and the licking of his tongue, confirmation was granted.

"You are safe now. Live, and be happy. I'm taking you home with me; I got someone I want you to meet," said the Cop.

Relieved and humbled Thorn listened to his heart and obeyed his soul. Upon their arrival to his new home a boy of about the age of 12 who was diagnosed with autism routinely approached the car but to his surprise daddy brought home Underdog. Ecstatic about his gift, the boy and dog bond immediately.

"What should we call him poppa?"

"Well, when I found him, he had a thorn in his paw . . . Let's call him Thorn."

Inseparable they become. Listening to his spirit freed him from bondage. Bow-wow-wow-yippy-yo-yippy-yay, feeling good about his new home; he becomes the Atomic dog, caring and adored now that love has finally come his way. Fully content with his blessing; he can concentrate on being man's best friend. Enlightenment of his ideal status there's a saying that goes, 'All dogs go to Heaven' and in Thorn's case he has truly found Heaven on Earth. Satisfied with his soul; he is freed from spiritual bondage and is zapped back into reality.

(Infomercial #5)

What is fear? It is an unpleasant emotion caused by the belief that someone or something is dangerous, probable to cause pain, or peril. The dread of fear is not from God but from Satan. Satan uses fear to keep people from embracing and enjoying life by producing torment and strife, which contradicts Love according to **1 John 4:18**, which says, *'There is no fear in love; but perfect love casteth out fear: because fear hath no torment. He that fearth is not made perfect in love.'* Believing that God is a perfect love; and unbeknownst to you; having this insightful knowledge helps us trust and obey His sanctions. When we think of fear, we associate the word with terror. On the other hand to contradict the popular census in distinguishing a divine difference, one could then ask, **what is the fear of God?** It is to have a deep reverence and respect for the Lord.

Psalms 56:2-3 says, *"²Mine enemies would daily swallow me up: for they be many that fight against me. O thou most High. ³What time I am afraid, I will . . . trust . . . in you."*

Due to pompous arrogance coupled with ignorance, trusting in God is sometimes not so easier said than done, which places us in an awkward position. A situation that allows us to compromise what we know is right from wrong; yet and still we conclude with an irrational decision by taken matters into our own hands and allowing Satan to once again persuade us to be disobedient; which causes fear because we knew better. When convicted and if fear just happens to weigh on your heart; understand that disobedience comes at a high price. A cost of which will result in God removing his hands off of you but never harming you as he promised. The fear of the Lord is a deep rooted reverence that causes believers to want to please Him in the name of Jesus by respecting His word which is found in The Holy Bible. If not in compliance you will be doing yourself an injustice as you won't be able to embrace this beautiful gift called life as our Lord Jesus intended. For most of us there are issues that need to be confronted; issues that may manifest into problems that leave us incomplete if not resolved. Problems that are tucked away and hopefully never uncovered; these things if held on to will own you; and you may find yourself a slave to it. Your attitude will reflect what lies dormant within causing stress and burden. It becomes your fear which are secrets borrowed from Satan to control and block you from God's plan for you. Therefore living a lie leaves you tainted and driven by evil. Befall to being naughty by nature you will become toxic which contaminates and destroys all who come in contact with you. Mercilessly your poisonous venom would rapidly spread like wild fire encouraging evil as the dark forces does 24/7. Your life would be meaningless and have no true value. You'll become bitter, cranky and cruel, like Scrooge. Allowing evil to blend with fear dictating your lifestyle; infectious you become luring people into your web of strife as if Hell was a part of you. It is said that misery loves company. Riding the downward spiral corrupting those who refuse to learn or seek the truth by not taking the responsibility of picking up, reading and understanding God's reference . . . It is my assumption when Judgment day comes; those who refuse to accept this duty will be held accountable and at fault, as well as those who have read it and fully understood it. No one is exempt, so if you must fear anything; be afraid of being made a hypocrite or a fool. And the Good Book says:

(Psalm 27:1-3) *The Lord is my light and my salvation; whom shall I fear? the Lord is the strength of my life; of whom shall I be afraid?* [2] *When the wicked, even mine enemies and my foes, came upon me to eat up my flesh, they stumbled and fell.* [3] *Though an host should encamp against me, my heart shall not fear: though war should rise against me, in this will I be confident.*

(Proverbs 1:33) *But who so hearkeneth unto me shall dwell safely, and shall be quiet from fear of evil.*

(Hebrews 13:6) *So that we may boldly say, The Lord is my helper, and I will not fear what man shall do unto me.*

'Let us thank Him for His wonderful everlasting Word and Truth in Jesus name . . . . Amen'

Chapter Eighteen

(Love *Conquers All*)

HELL

Concerned about what transpired the Commander takes a head count, "Okay! Has everybody gone through their personal bouts with their demons? Have you overcome your fears?"

Without hesitation Sarah and Rashida shout out at the same time, "No!" Astonished, baffled, whatever you'd call it; now without a doubt the gals are uncomfortable.

"I guess you ladies were lucky; they spared you," hunched Xavier.

Rashida replied, "I don't believe in luck."

Rudely Dimitrius interrupts, "Whatever the reason, I've had enough! Let's get off this damn bridge . . . NOW MOVE OUT!"

Commanded the Commander, ordering the convoy to press forward hastily in expectation of removing themselves from their exclusive fear factors.

Once clear of the bridge, they enter a barren wasteland resembling a desert like terrain with mountainous features. In the appointed direction, a road lined with crucifixes made of skeletons with freshly dangled flesh as well as battered bodies posted as if punishment were rendered recent. Serving its purpose of caution, boldly the Militia ignores its heed. In the meantime it's feeding time for the buzzards

Barren Wasteland by Peterson

flying high in the sky; continuously circling until the coast is cleared. As they proceed with said caution, Rashida questions the pass over.

"I wonder why we were spared, it's not like we drenched ourselves in lamb's blood **(Exodus 12:7, 12:13)**, and it can't be a woman thing; didn't you have an episode Lilith?"

"Please don't remind me, it was horrible," said the Babylonian still moist and ready for the next round or two.

Sarah adds her point of view, "Maybe we should be grateful and accept it as a blessing."

"I agree baby girl, haven't you heifers ever heard of the saying, never look a gift horse in the mouth? If I were you, I'd be thankful you didn't have to go through that," encouraged Sebastian.

Even with that being said, still Rashida remained slighted, "I can dig what you're saying but something ain't right; that went down to easy."

"Speak for yourself! Too bad Enoch couldn't be here to agree with you," defended Mathyus. "You better recognize your blessings," he included.

Wounded by his verbal stab Rashida admits to her guilt, "You're right, my bad." Humble but masked; her intuition still leaves her with peach fuzz raised and goose bumps bumping.

While entering the condemned land, staying true to his game, Dimitrius focuses on the ambiance as a tactical soldier should. While concentrating on his mental spot a welcomed visitor, Jessica, spiritually arrives within his mind to give warning.

"You have fallen into a trap my love."

Immediately forced to react with haste, a stern order is given.

"Wait a minute, HALT!"

Automatically the disciplined troops take heed to his command. Thanks to his fair lady, all is revealed to him as he recognizes that they are sitting ducks for an opposing force; due to the high, low terrain features that surrounded them.

"This ain't good. Quick, Rashida have half of the men cover the ridge on both sides and the other half cover our rear . . . . We're in deep shit," informed the eye opened leader. Utilizing the chain of command Rashida barks orders to her subordinates. While the scramble fry hard, in come recklessly a hail of bullets to include the damaging results from a rocket launcher fired, destroying the last vehicle to prevent retreat. Immediately Dimitrius, Xavier, and Rashida jump out of the cargo truck landing in the prone position and begin to return fire in the direction from whence the attack came. Simultaneously the troops do the same. Recognizing the method and reason of attack, Dimitrius orders his men to cease fire.

"This is all too familiar . . . Rashida tell the men to stand down!"

Shocked at the call Rashida poses question, "What was that?"

Xavier adds, "What are you talking about; they have us pinned down."

"Exactly, just do it! Trust me," assured Dimitrius.

Apprehensively Rashida calls to order, "Cease fire! Cease fire! Everybody, stand down!"

"Dude, what the fuck are you doing?" Xavier bellowed.

Dimitrius replied, "They're trying to get us to waste our ammo."

Rashida asks, "How do you know this?"

"Because this is something I would do," declared the Ex-Marine as he removes himself from his cover and stand to reveal what he already knows.

"You can come out now! Show your face, Daxx!"

Silence, then rises above the mystery from the dust, emerges the renegade members of the Lucky 7-3=4.

"As you can see; I've kept my promise. I told you I'd see you again. I must say that I'm impressed. How'd you know it was us?" revered Daxx.

"What? You forgot I wrote the book on this shit," bragged Dimitrius.

Poole adds his $0.02, "Nah Sarge, you didn't write this book."

Duly noted as he gawked at the women; as if they were ripe fruit ready for picking.

"Yeah man, thanks for the ass you brought us! I'm sure they'll be as good as those spic-bitches from the village," anticipated Massey.

Mayweather barks a suggestion, "Fuck all the talk; let's just kill they're asses!"

Xavier being the brawler that he is agrees, "That's what I'm talking about; let's do these fools."

Ignorantly, cattle calls begin to move the crowd as the natives become restless and uneasy.

"Look, they're holding up progress. Let's take 'em down," suggested Miguel.

Daxx implies, "Well that might pose to be a bit of a problem little man."

"He's right, I took you punks out before, I'll do it again; but then that's exactly what he wants because it's not just them . . . now is it?" Dimitrius pondered.

Arrogantly, Daxx then sways his right arm up to gesture the release of a flare shot by Poole to give signal to the Dread of Doom. Marching in unison are Hate Mongers: 500 deep, an unruly but well structured bunch; consisting of the 3rd Reich, Skinheads and the Klu Klux Klan bearing burning inverted crosses and swastikas banners. Surprisingly caught off guard, but now realizing that they were not exempt from confronting their fears, Sarah and Rashida's hearts are seriously wounded. They become angered and restless. Clearly everyone can see their discomfort. Adversely you would expect a nervous breakdown or some sort of introverted behavior; but in their case, familiarity breeds content due to all the drama that has toughened their skin. Their reaction stems from the same place and shyness is nonexistent; so as the saying goes: 'Hell has no fury; like a woman scorn.' Willfully they find themselves releasing their dark sides in pursuit of happiness or revenge. Familiar with disdain, Lilith takes notice to how her girlfriends begin their tempered loom and as a well taught student that has learned her lesson from her eye opener; she gives warning.

"Satan is playing on your emotions! Ignore them or you'll fall slave to them . . . we need to keep moving."

Mathyus wisely comprehends what she is saying and also gives council, "She's right, when it comes to our fears which are attached to our emotions; we tend to lose control and become irrational, our anger and rage fuel our actions which leaves us vulnerable to Satan's will. We become exactly what he wants us to be; suffering souls trapped within ourselves causing confusion and destruction. We become our own enemy, trapped in a living Hell . . . . As for the Devil, mission accomplished."

Daxx grows impatient and decides to antagonize the assault.

"Enough with the psychological bullshit! Let's dance."

Eagerly, he encourages his motley troops who are ready and raring to go. Knowing that this battle would be a loss due to the opposition being 5X the size of his own; Dimitrius decides to hold off until proper contest presents itself.

"Five to one odds, in your favor . . . . I don't think so."

"Well it's not like you have a choice, we're going to kill you bastards, now!"

Announced Daxx as he and his cohorts take one step forward.

Out of nowhere an onslaught of bullets riddles a line between the opponents to prevent the cross over. Astonishingly enough, neither party is aware of who's responsible for the interruption, until the two missing members of the Lucky 7 reveal themselves and report for Good duty.

"Well I'll be damned . . . . Porter, Sanchez; boy it's good to see you guys," hoopla-ed Dimitrius.

"Sanchez and Porter, reporting for duty Sir!"

Respectfully they give honors as they salute their ex-superior. Dimitrius acknowledges the gesture.

"Hold off on the reunion. Let's deal with these scumbags for now," says Dimitrius.

Porter aims his weapon center mass at Daxx's forehead. On the other side stifled and baffled; Daxx is outraged about the additional company.

"Where the fuck did those two come from?"

As the jubilation of two more highly skilled men joining their cause is celebrated, a moment of depression sinks deep within mild mannered Sarah; as her dark side recalls the sad day that she took her own life.

"Ahhhhhhhhh! Wwwwwwwhy!" She cried, at the same time grabbing a semi-automatic weapon from a nearby soldier aiming and firing it at the oppressors.

Sarah Mad by Chris Brimacombe

Fortunately, she was only allowed to get off target-less rounds, aimed without accuracy as Dimitrius was able to snatch the weapon from her.

"Sarah, no!" Mathyus hollered.

Rashida outraged and in full agreement with her comrade speaks her mind, "Right On Sarah!"

"I want them to pay for what they've done! There is no remorse, no shame! I will make it right for all the people whose lives they've destroyed; please God give me strength," cried Sarah.

Lilith again elaborates on the stressful situation and gives warning, "If you kill as a result of revenge, you will seal your fate."

Shocked at how vexed the females have become Mathyus again piggy backs off of Lilith's pertinent information. So, he attempts to refocus them by taming their hearts.

"This is all a mind game, don't you see? The rage in your heart will increase your chances to remain in Hell. Revenge can only be doused out by *Forgiveness and Love*. You must purge this hateful spirit from your soul in order to enter the Kingdom of God or be damned to your fears forever."

Rashida, equally fired up, releases her discrepancies as well.

"Screw that preacher man! Sarah, I'm with you. Those are the bastards that raped me! They're the reason I am here in the first place. They must be held accountable. You don't realize all the bruthas and sistahs they've killed because of their prejudices. Like she said; where is the remorse? It seems like they were rewarded! They asked for hell and they got it. No justice, no peace!"

"I can dig it. I feel your pain Sistah—girl," supported Xavier.

Lilith attempts another plea.

"You people aren't listening to me! Satan is trying to provoke us; we must not give in to his temptation . . . he has set us up for failure."

Standing ready with scythe drawn is Sebastian, who surprisingly has something useful to say, "Take it from me, she's right. The core of one's soul is gauged by the control of one's emotions. If you lose control then you lose your soul. Your fears will rule your life and you will relive your worst nightmares repeatedly. This is nothing but one of his tricks."

With all that was said Dimitrius and Mathyus look at each other with assurance.

"We must be getting close; because the closer we get, the trickier he becomes," said Dimitrius.

"You're right. Now I guess you know what you must do," encouraged Mathyus.

Dimitrius then tenderly draws Sarah close to him and begins to make declaration.

"Well alright then, God has shown us the spirit of our enemy. He's afraid; that's why he sent his army to stop us and try to provoke us into doing something stupid; but we're smarter than that! We now know if you succumb to your rage and possess a vengeful heart; the Devil will claim your soul. You will never be allowed to leave this place. Sarah, Rashida we need you. Sarah, I need your compassion. Rashida, I need your strength. We have a great opportunity to redeem ourselves . . . Let's not blow it by yielding to temptation. I know it's hard, but you must find it in your heart to forgive them. Do this and I *promise* you, the Lord will see us through. As for you Daxx, now is not the time; so step off. We'll dance another day . . . I promise."

Daxx, amused by the resistance, presents a joke but truly wishes a squabble, "What better time than now? Good vs. Evil. Yeah, I know you're out numbered but God is on your side; so that should make it even . . . . Haaaaa!"

Tickled by the jest his army laughs profusely.

Miguel not humored says, "Lo siento señor, the man said not today."

Ignorantly racial slurs sound out from the bigots. Thorn begins to take offense by becoming vicious as he defends the boys honor.

"Check out Baba Louie . . . . Haaaa!" shouted Massey.

The crowd continued the obscenities laced with verbal tongue lashes.

Sarah, now calm, says, "It angers me to know that the cowards are here celebrating instead of burning; it's not fair."

"The reason they're here rejoicing is because they made their deals with the devil for eternal hatred. While in the world they spread hate, in Hell they are hate. They were working for him then as they are working for him now. For committing such heinous acts they solidified their position here. The sad part about it is that they too have a chance to redeem their soul, but are too cold to know what's best for them. They are the Devil's Will," says Dimitrius.

Listening to what Dimitrius was explaining to Sarah, Rashida rationalizes her position.

"Okay, maybe you're right. Sarah look, I've gotten retribution by killing men who had nothing to do with what was done to me. I for one can forgive them if that's what God wants us to do, but I'll never forget. You feel me?"

Sarah nods her head to show that she comprehends.

"I need time, this hurts too deep . . . . Please help me Jesus," she says.

"He already has. I think you are here to keep me grounded; to keep love in my heart. He knew I was going to lose Jesse, that's why he put you in my life," explained Dimitrius.

To support his general, Mathyus elaborates on his comment, "I totally agree; that's why the Lord put love in our hearts. Love, faith, and forgiveness are weapons used to negate evil. They are the only things that can weaken Satan. That's why the world is in the state it's in today; because it doesn't understand the complexity of these concepts. God's greatest weapons graphed for man, and what did we do? We screwed it up. So, use it and let the Devil know that Love conquers all."

On that note, Dimitrius and Sarah look at each other as they embrace. They fully understand that a kiss forged out of pure love will extinguish the situation. As their lips touch, the tender moment elates the atmosphere and begins to purge the mongers fading them into the darkness. Xavier and Lilith take this opportunity to spread the love as well.

While vanishing, Daxx declares a promise, "This ain't over Steele; I'll see you sooooonnnn . . . ."

Miguel finds his departure amusing.

"Now that's funny! He sounds like that Scrubbing Bubbles commercial: 'So you don't have toooooo . . . .'"

"Whew, that was just a little too close for comfort," declared Sebastian.

Relieved of the tension, everyone's stress level takes a dive; especially Sarah and Dimitrius as they are still engaged in their lip-lock.

"Uhh, Yoo-hoo! You can come up for some air now," encouraged Miguel.

Still the loving continued as everyone takes a breather.

Endless Love by SpartaDog

(Infomercial #6) The Good Book says:

(Proverbs 10:12) *Hatred stirs up dissension, but love covers over all wrongs.*

(1 John 3:1) *See what kind of love the Father has given to us, that we should be called children of God; and so we are. The reason why the world does not know us is that I did not know him.*

(Proverbs 15:9) *The way of the wicked is an abomination unto the Lord: but he loveth him that followeth after righteousness.*

(Ephesians 4:31) *Get rid of all bitterness, rage and anger, brawling and slander, along with every form of malice.*

(1 Corinthians 13:4-8) *⁴ Love suffers long and is kind; love does not envy; love does not parade itself, is not puffed up; ⁵ does not behave rudely, does not seek its own, is not provoked, thinks no evil; ⁶ does not rejoice in iniquity, but rejoices in the truth; ⁷ bears all things, believes all things, hopes all things, endures all things.⁸ Love never fails.*

(Luke 6:37) *Forgive, and you will be forgiven.*

(John 15:9-10) *9. "As the Father has loved me, so have I loved you. Now remain in my Love. 10. If you keep my commands, you will remain in my love, just as I have kept my Father's commands and remain in his love."*

Knowing God is to know love, it is a greater love that is His Agape Love. As we learn from the Bible, all things work for the greater good **(Romans 8:28)**. The unrighteous work against what is meant to be good. So therefore the contradiction of love is hate. It is a powerful word that has patronized a demonic fervor which is exploited to destroy all that is good and just. Hate contradicts the teachings of Christ; which constitutes that it stems from evil. Its meaning is defined as: to regard with extreme aversion; detest, being unwilling or disliked. Unfortunately, used by so many, its enthusiasm carries dead weight. Nothing positive can come out of its grotesque personality; which is toxic in nature and infectious to us all. Its contamination causes stress and if not treated properly has the ability to kill. As a result of hate's bliss, we fall victim to negative ramifications which causes chaos that disrupts decency and order in our society. Capitalizing on vile opportunity when anarchy strikes are groups who are discriminative that promotes separatism. These hate groups aka Hate-mongers aka Neo-Nazis, Skinheads, Ku Klux Klan, Islamic Extremist and White Supremacist lie dormant preparing for the day of reckoning. A day of which protest is no longer necessary but physical force is flexed to demonstrate their power and mass. To impose their views upon the people by any means necessary often met by resistance causing damages beyond measure. Are they the Devil's agents; Clout of Grim? Are they demons disguised as men? Either way it goes, they are without question. Hell spawn and surely not Children of God by choice. So let it be known to all men; without love you are already dead. Share its goodness with each other and treat each other with love and kindness. As the song goes; put a little love in your heart. To love one another is to love one's self and to love one's self is to love God with the fullness of your heart. So, If I haven't said it enough; let me say it now . . . . "*I LOVE YOU.*" Love is a splendid thing; it's a godly thing. It's the only thing that there's much too little of. It's what the world needs now. So you may ask yourself; what's love got to do with it? Everything, if we strive to have a better life for our future.

Love is a force of nature. Love is inherently free. Unlike sex; love can't be bought, sold, or traded. Love cares. Love honors the sovereignty of each soul. Love is its own law. Love allows destructive and abusive behaviors to go unchecked. Love speaks out for justice and protests when harm is being done. Love allows you to endure pain.

Chapter Nineteen

(Sticks & Stones)

"A sword never kills anybody; it is a tool in the killer's hand."
—Lucius Annaeus Seneca: 4 BC-AD 65

(Isaiah 54:17), *No weapon formed against me shall prosper."*

"A weapon is as dangerous as the man that wields it."
—Me, Myself and I: 04/2013

Present Truths

In 1941 the United States released an Atomic bomb on the cities of Hiroshima and Nagasaki, Japan in retaliation to an attack on Pearl Harbor, Hawaii. As a result from the destruction, during that time period the cataclysmic event was labeled the greatest weapon deployed on mankind; which gained the US its status as *The Super Power*, until now. With a fading economy and military spread thin due to crucial conflicts spread out all over the world, the US finds itself at a loss of respect and debt, presently trying to reclaim its undisputed title from rival countries who dare step into the ring. Although pressed, the US still remains allies to those who belong to NATO and is first to take a stand to support those countries in need. *God Bless America!*

It is well documented that the excuses used and the fabrication of lies given to draw down on Iraq by the United Nations, was that it possessed Weapons of Mass Destruction.

Led by the Dictator Saddam Hussein, who ferociously flexed his bully mentality upon his own people by extending his might on its neighboring country (Saudi Arabia), who then looked to its allies to defend its honor; and why not since it possesses about 17% of the world's proven petroleum reserves, which ranks as the largest exporter of petroleum, and plays a leading role in OPEC. A cause surely worth defending as American and British forces proudly stepped up to the plate to answer its cry. Although the deeds of support and protection prevailed; the truth shone its light on the real motive which uncovered a plot driven by greed exploited by those doing the protecting.

Today a similar threat has again reared its ugly head 7711.46 Kilometers or 4791.68 miles away from Saudi Arabia, this time in North Korea. Ruled by its Supreme Leader Kim Jong-un, a young successor who succeeded to such powerful position from his predecessor, his father; claims that the said country possesses Nuclear Weapons and is about to test their capabilities on its neighbor South Korea; who boldly stated that it will defend itself if the posing threat is imminent. Supporting the targeted country is the US, who is also hated by the communist and is ready on standby to aid its South Korean ally. All of this, for power and full control of the region.

"Power tends to corrupt and absolute power corrupts absolutely."
—Lord Acton, 1834-1902

(In the Now) traveling to Philly

As they travel par the course via an Amtrak Luxury Train, which was solely provided by the financial endowment of Minister Shabazz, the four men develop a spiritual connection as well as true Disciples of the cloth should. Maxing and relaxing, they share wondrous stories based on their personal experience and ministry; despite their cultural differences, backgrounds, and heritage. Happily, they utilize their open minds to worship God; the most High. Although ethnically called by different names, He proves to be their common bond. But as smooth as the operation seemingly begins, a massive conspiracy is being orchestrated to accommodate their demise. 'Monitor but do not make a move' was the heeded warning duly noted, due to the hunger driven by every demons appetite. Little do they know, watchful eyes have pegged their latest twenty? Those obeying the consequential command of relaying their whereabouts via the dark forces covertly inform the henchman of the hunted's progress. Figuratively speaking, they're being played as puppets, at least in the eyes of the hunter, by strategically manipulating their movement as if they were pieces on a chess board.

*NOTE: *It is my advice to you; my reader: never sleep on the aptitude of a corrupt mind, and you'll always stay one step ahead of the game.*

This is the mentality of the righteous as God protects his Disciples by giving us our right minds and, foresight coupled with hindsight. As for Gabriel, his right mind extends into a vivid flaunting of things to come. Constantly signals flare within his psyche forewarning him to be on the lookout for things unseen. Is it a revelation? Is it just being alert and prepared? Fully aware of the dark plot against them; Gabriel accepts his gift and masters its control. Let us thank God; his eyes are finally open.

UUUUUUURRRRR!!!!! Goes the grinding sound of iron wheels pressing metal on metal; due to the sudden stop that allows the momentum to render bodies tossed around the boxcar as if they were ingredients of a salad?

"What's going on?" Passengers inquired.

Sequentially an announcement begins to fill the speakers: ladies and gentlemen, excuse the sudden delay. There is a stalled vehicle on the tracks a head of us. Once it is removed, we'll be on our way as scheduled. We apologize for the inconvenience and thank you for your patience. During the disruption Gabriel's foresight reveals an enlightened view of Wrath raising a spectacular sword to the sky while blowing a majestic horn. As he comes to his senses, he realizes that this was no mishap.

"Whatever can go wrong, will go wrong," proclaimed Gabriel.

"What was that?" Grant asked.

Moon replied, "Murphy's Law."

"Please tell me you heard of it." Shabazz questioned Grant.

"Of course I have! I didn't hear what he said. What do you think I'm stupid?" Grant asked Shabazz.

"No my beloved; not at all," jived Shabazz.

The line of questioning stems from the same source that causes concern about his qualifications. Pastor Grant develops an aversion toward Minister Shabazz as does Minister Shabazz wonders about Pastor Grant's validity.

"This was not chance, this was done deliberately to impede our progress," presumed Gabriel.

"Are you sure? Moon asked.

Gabriel explains, "As the train stopped, simultaneously I had a vision. Apparently, the demon in my dreams is after the same thing we are. This delay was meant to slow us down."

"Well then, I say if we don't move in the next half hour, we'll use another means of transportation," suggested Shabazz.

Grant says, "Well what do you suggest Minister Moneybags?"

Moon chimes in, "Do I sense dissension or a bit of jealousy even?"

"Nah, I'm not used to being scrutinized, that's all. Especially when it continuously comes from the same source. Maybe, you need to ask him that question," said Grant.

Shabazz takes this opportunity and shines light on his interest in Grant.

"Forgive me, beloved. My concerns about your temperament fascinate me. It's because it's not often I run across men of our persuasion who are bred by the streets, who are willing to dedicate their lives to what God has set forth. Usually, they fall off when the going gets tough but, you on the other hand are able to keep yourself grounded by not forgetting where you came from and being committed to God's work. I find you extraordinary. I applaud you my brother."

"That's right, I was once a thug and deep down maybe I still might be. All I know is that God can make a Disciple out of a convict, drunk, or even a mentally challenged individual. Once the Holy Spirit activates within your heart and soul, anything is possible. You of all people should know that. You know, I'm beginning to wonder about you," retorted Grant.

Seemingly affected by the delusion of evil, once again the Clout of Grim has caused melodrama between the men of assurance. What this proves is that you should never put your faith in man. When given the chance, he will let you down. The greatest weapon forged against man is himself. In order to contradict this concept and achieve fortitude, we must become *Invictus*; the Latin term for unconquered. Please refer to God's word found in **Isaiah 54:17**, which is presented in the introduction of Chapter 1. One must look to the Holy Spirit for confirmation and reassurance.

"Gentlemen, squabbling between us is exactly how the dark forces work. Let's not fall victim to its foolishness, and let our wisdom guide us and grant us victory in the eyes of the Lord. Let's stay focused," declared Gabriel.

As they swallow the bitter with the sweet, the four sit and wait patiently as the half hour passes. Within a few minutes, the train is rudely boarded by gunmen. Diligent yet fearful, they are met with no resistance while committing a search rummaging from boxcar to boxcar until finally entering the compartment where divinity lay.

Aggressively the door slides open as two gunmen dressed in black enter with hand guns drawn.

"You four, come with us. Now!"

Completely caught off guard, the four men have no other choice but to do as they are told. To ease Gabriel's mind, one of the gunmen exclusively flaps his wings signifying comfort and protection. As relief fills his heart, the others do not share his soothing. Grant defies the moment but complies just the same.

"Who are you people, and what do you want with us?"

Silent the gunmen remain. At a steady pace, the four men are shuffled off the train and placed into a black van; still with no resistance. Abruptly the van spins off causing a cloud of dust while leaving most of the train crew astonished as they are clandestine informants of the Clout of Grim and punks playing the devil's game.

"Fear not gentlemen, we are in safe hands," informed Gabriel as the others ponder his mild disposition.

Finally, some questions are answered as the gunmen reveal their purpose, "We are the Protectors of the Righteous; we are Seraphim."

With that being said the gunmen reveal their oddities so all present may witness God's glory.

"Now you too can see what I see," declared Gabriel as the amazing site humbled their hearts which instantly brought them to their knees in prayer.

"Guardian Angels! Well, I'll be dammed," Grant exclaimed.

"Beautiful, simply beautiful," uttered Shabazz.

Moon states from the appreciation of his heart, "Thank you Lord for we are not worthy of your Grace. He truly does love us."

"We are here to get you to Philadelphia. For what is there must be held by your four hands and the hand of the Maiden," said a Seraph.

"What is he talking about?" Grant asked.

Gabriel replies, "I'm not sure, but whatever it is; we must link up with Sister Papadopoulos; she's the key."

Still caught in awe, Moon and Shabazz begin to give thanks in their native tongue, kneeling and perched as if they were in their personal prayer closets. Grant soon joins them as he reflects on the comforting vision from God's warriors. Pleased at the acceptance and reaction to God's perfect timing, Gabriel smiles because he knows that the weight on his comrade's hearts has been lifted as well as their fear; allowing strength, courage, and wisdom to draw from within. As most inquiring minds want to know, Gabriel employs the angelic combatant for much needed council.

"Is there anything else you can tell me? I find that the level of stress and the pressure of it all has got me vexed; so I ask you for clarity and direction."

The Seraph who is committed to seeing God's Will be done enlightens the four with encouraging words, "The Lord our God is pleased with you, and in the honor of his son Christ Jesus, all of your questions will manifest themselves while in the City of Brotherly Love; then you will know what to do."

His curiosity has been met with clever wording yet satisfaction filled his void. However, there are those who don't share the same sentiment.

"Excuse my ignorance; but why are you here? We were not in any danger or even threatened?" Grant asked.

The Seraph answers with zeal, "On the contrary, the train you were on was staffed by Satan's agents of calamity. Demons walk the earth disguised as mortal men; it is our obligation to protect the earth by keeping God's salt from harm's way."

"So I guess it's true of what they say about angels," Grant replied.

"And what is that my beloved?" Shabazz pondered.

Grant bellows, "That they're our guardians."

In agreement they all nod their heads.

"So, will you stay with us until our mission is complete?" Grant asked.

Gabriel enlightens his friend as he looks at the angelic, "I'm afraid not, but we are protected by divinity. I am sure they will come to our aid when necessary."

"Well, that's good to know. I feel better already," said Grant.

The angelic again answers with zeal, "On the contrary, we will be by your side until you leave Philadelphia, war is near and death will follow, plagues will trounce and starvation will compel the people."

The four looked at each other as if thunder had struck.

"Okay! What's with the puzzling statements? Can you give it to us in layman's terms?" Grant requested.

Again the angelic remained silent.

Grant, still unclear, says, "I figured you were not going to answer the question, so I guess as long as you're here we'll be alright . . . . war is near, death will follow . . . . What?"

Shaking his head with disbelief or pure amazement Shabazz smiles at Grant as to suggest that he is amused, "That's right, keep it real my brother."

Focused on the content of the angelic warning Gabriel draws a conclusion, "If we are protected by divinity as we have been as of lately; that can mean only one thing . . . Whatever God has planned is about to come to a head, and our success to see this task through is crucial. Our failure could be detrimental."

"Well it would help if we knew the plan. Right now we're just winging it, gathering folk as we go long. Where are we going with this?" Grant questioned.

Moon interjects with a sound mind, "It sounds to me that the Apocalypse is soon at hand. If you were to breakdown the Angel's message, he stated War, Death, Pestilence/Conquest and Famine . . . . the Four Horsemen."

"So, what does that have to do with us? Are you saying we're the Horseman or something?" Grant cited.

"Don't be ridiculous! I'm not saying that at all," denied Moon.

Shabazz adds, "Well it is a bit ironic . . . the four of us and, him mentioning the Horsemen."

"Whether it's ironic or not, God's plan shall prevail through us. You all knew that this was bigger than anything you could image. Now, I detect fear has reared its ugly head. Get with the program! It's not like you have a choice; you've been chosen," demanded Gabriel.

Moon arrives at a pertinent assumption, "If all that we know is to be true, then we're living in perilous times and the **Word** suggests that these days are noted in the ***Book of Revelation***."

Noticing the change in disposition, the angelic gives further words of encouragement, "When the Church is raptured you will be among the blessed; so go in peace, remain faithful, and fear no more."

"The righteous will be judged not by their deeds, but by their faith," noted Gabriel.

Grant interjects, "Well at last we're covered and all of this won't be in vain; thank you Jesus."

Shabazz smiles; still finding him humorous. As the four curious men glance at each other, the angelic exits without notice. Grant becomes aware of their absence.

"Where did they go? I thought they were going to be with us until we left Philly."

"They're still with us whether seen or unseen; have mercy," reassured Gabriel.

Still burdened with a clouded outlook, the men look to prayer to find answers and to change their perplexed mindset. While engaged in their deep appeal; time continues to travel as they awaken when they arrived at their destination, Killadelphia . . . *Oops! I meant Philadelphia.* Like most cosmopolitan /metropolis or highly populated cities, it can make you feel overwhelmed if you have not frequented all that it has to offer. If you play the street game, you better be a pro, because in this town winners take all. The difference in Philly from the rest; is its die hard citizens whose pride rides high and is not matched by any. So do what you do best or do nothing at all. It takes a Hustler's mentality to gain ground or you'll fall victim to the deception fueled by Satan that keeps this city going. It will take a righteous practitioner to overcome its perilous demise. Slick, trick or honey dip whatever you go by; always be aware that there is someone out to get you. Stay on your P's & Q's G; or you'll be another fool of the game asking Y me or what just happened?

As the van covered in noir travel the blood stream of the Strawberry Mansion section of the city; its passengers can't help but notice the condition mankind has endured. The grimy groveling of the less fortunate dictate the struggle to survive, to compete, and to live. It is as if Hell was on earth for these inhabitants and hope could not be kept alive. Seemingly Famine of every kind has plagued this neighborhood. Respecting the traffic system the vehicle stops at the red light. Like roaches three peddlers swarm the iron chariot in pursuit of an exchange of feeble service for spare change.

"Can we clean your windows?"

Sprits-Sprits! The sounds of squeegee bottles spray away.

"This reminds me of South Central," Grant exposed.

"I'm sure this behavior or means to acquire finances exists in every major city, due to the lack of employment and education," Gabriel speculated.

Moon replies, "You are correct."

"This form of meager labor is a cop out or, if mentally challenged, accepted by its community; it doesn't have to be this way," declared Shabazz.

Grant agrees, "You're right, if the politicians stop politic-in and start caring about the people; maybe just maybe this world would be a better place."

"But in this world Satan rules. It's supposed to be this way until the righteous are raptured and the second coming of Christ enslaves the devil for 1000 years. Peace will reign, then the evil one will be released again in order to test the faith of those left behind. Once that is done, there is the battle at Armageddon. As we know from our studies of the Bible, *only the Church will benefit from the Rapture.*" theologically broken down by Gabriel from *(The Book of Revelation).*

Swiftly the three laborers complete their task and each receives a $10.00 bill out of gratitude. The vehicle then pulls off on its merry way. When viewed through the rear view mirror, one of the laborer's eyes flicker with a flame as he snatches the others money and hauls ass down the nearest alley heading toward the closest liquor store; where every last dime will be spent on poisonous fire water. Homelessness, corruption, greed, addiction . . . all just plain ole sad. No matter which way you look at it; it's fucked up. FYI: Wrath has arrived at the city and immediately finds his way to the museum in question.

"I think this would be a good time to call on our fair maiden," suggested Moon.

Gabriel replied, "I'm way ahead of you. I've already texted her. She's en route via subway to the museum."

Little does she know; she is being followed by the Clout. Tabs kept on her as instructed by El Jefe; Wrath. While waiting for the arrival of all invited, Wrath exercises his might by annihilating the museum guards for entertainment purposes. Simultaneously the van pulls up to the curb in front of the building; Sophia has reached her destination.

"Is that her?" Grant asked as his secular announcement prevails over his priestly disposition.

Shabazz answers with a rhetorical question, "Is that lust I detect; my brother?" Ignoring the meaningless stab; the thought of taking care of business fills Grant's head. Gabriel initiates an introduction by getting out of the vehicle.

"Excuse me Madame; are you the Curator of the museum?"

"Why yes I am, Father Gabriel I presume," she speculated.

As per any respectful greeting they both extend their hands to shake. Once touched, both are hurled into the same vision revealing the unification of the four men each holding one of the four contents of the Arc of the Covenant: The 10 Commandments, 7 Seals, Trumpet of Gabriel and Sword of Michael; transforming their spirits into an extraordinary powerful and majestic creature called ***Gryphon***: a Greek mythological creature with the body, tail, and back legs of a lion; the head and wings of an eagle; and talons as its front feet. It is recognized as the King of all beasts, both land and air . . . . the protector of truth, wisdom, and fortitude, guardian of treasures and worldly possessions. Thus, these possessions of which are priceless, and could be extremely dangerous should they fall into the wrong hands. Hands of which are hell-bent on total world domination.

"Did you see that?" Sofia asked Gabriel as sweat saturates her forehead.

"Yes, yes I did . . . it all makes sense to me now; you're an Oracle," said Gabriel. Excited by the vision; they both separate and venture into the building to discuss their uncanny discovery.

"I knew my gift would someday benefit me! May the Gods smile upon us, for I am truly honored," she says.

Grant, agitated, says, "May the Gods? Great, she ain't even a Christian."

Eager to uncover the mystery, the presence of security goes unnoticed until Moon opens his eyes and expresses his concerns, "Shouldn't there be security officers posted throughout the premises? Where are they?"

"That *is* strange, usually there are three or four guards posted at the main entrance and one guard posted at every entrance of an exhibit; the security force is at least fifty strong," Sofia explained.

Grant concluded, "Something's very wrong here; I can feel it."

Together they venture forth making their way to her office. As she presses the button, the elevator door opens unleashing the stench of death.

"Oh my God, what is that smell?" bellowed Sophia.

Overwhelmingly stunned by the foul odorous blow; once they adjusted to it, yet a monstrous vista slaps them even harder. Inside of the elevator on the walls, are the pummeled bodies of dead security guards, aligned upside down as if they were placed by a skilled contractor commissioned to do wall coverings for Martha Stuart. The floor drenched with stale blood signifying that they've been draining for at least 4hrs.

Simultaneously, Wrath fills the hallways with his ghastly laugh, "MUAAAHHHHHAAAA! The guest has finally arrived!"

"Who the hell is that?" Grant shouted.

Gabriel replies, "It is him; the demon in my dreams."

Grant, terrified, asks, "What does he want?"

"He must want what you came for," guessed Sofia.

Shabazz inquires, "And exactly what might that be?"

"The contents of the Arc," determined Moon.

Gabriel concurred, "That's correct."

Grant anxiously wishes to get to the point, "Well whatever's in the box let him have it . . . it ain't worth dying for."

"But it is my friend; the contents of the Arc are majestic and can be used to put an end to the Four Horsemen . . . . their Heaven sent," Gabriel explained.

Moon concludes, "And I'm guessing; if they fall into the wrong hands, they may try to use them to destroy the world."

"Wow this is deep, I knew . . ." Before Grant was able to finish his statement Wrath shows his ugly face as he opens the ceiling door of the elevator and pokes his head through.

"Boo! Open the box and I'll spare you your lives."

Startled and seemingly frightened all the same; they back up defensively with the quickness; but to no surprise, united they stand and do not flee. You see; they know that there is power in Jesus' name; and fear is not an option.

"I must say that I'm impressed. Thus far, all of the priestly punks that I've met would've fled by now . . . Shocking," complimented Wrath.

Instantly Gabriel announces his defense, "Let the power of Christ compel you away as I rebuke Satan and all Hell spawn just the same."

Feeling the power in the name Jesus, Wrath begins to heed the priest's warning.

"Hisssss!" Retorted Wrath as sweat embraces his brow while sharp pain grasps his attention and brings him discomfort.

Surprisingly, Wrath dashes away with a promise filled with diabolical laughter, "All of you are going to die. MUAAAHHHaaa . . . . !"

"Okay, where are the Angels when you need them?" Grant hollered.

Moon replied, "We didn't need them, the power of saying His name was enough."

"Angels?" wondered Sophia.

Shabazz says, "Yes my sistah. When we get a moment, I'll fill you in."

"Looking forward to it," she replied.

Recognizing his weaponry, Gabriel once again gathers strength from his verbal assault, "Fear not my friends! Let us look to the Lord for our courage."

Once all of the said party gained their composure Gabriel brought forth confirmation.

"As you can see, there truly is power within the name. Surely our words are fearful weapons to those who have chosen to be ignorant . . . glory be to God."

"Did you see the dude's reaction when you said His blessed name?" Grant asked.

To answer his question with a question Gabriel simply says, "Did you?"

Onward they move in pursuit of the Noble prize.

—*(Philippians 4:13) I can do all things through Christ which strengthens me.*

—*(Proverbs 3:25-26)*[25] *Be not afraid of sudden fear, neither of the desolation of the wicked, when it cometh.* [26] *For the Lord shall be thy confidence, and shall keep thy foot from being taken.*

Note: But what about Pastor Grant you might ask? If his faith is intact, why does he seems nervous and on the edge most of the time? He's the prime example of how we are as so-called Believers; *including myself, but I am working on it . . . I guess you can refer to me as a work in progress.* We know and believe in God, we know what God wants us to do, but in most, not less than some cases we are labeled by our disassociated communities, non-believers or outsiders, who seemingly view us as hypocrites that live by a double standard. These local inhabitants have grown up or know us through association or our involvement while we lived our secular lives. Therefore, we are held prisoner to our former way of life and may find it difficult to separate the two. They fear what they don't understand, so consequently leads to a misconception. They think that the degree of sin warrants you a lesser punishment . . . FYI; murder is no different than stealing, and stealing is no different than lying. Sin is sin. Either way we're all held accountable and will be judged.

A word of advice: If you chose to walk this splendid thing called **Righteousness** correctly; you must know it and live it. **2 Timothy 2:15 says, Study to show thyself approved unto God, a workman that need not to be ashamed, rightly dividing the word of truth.** These are powerful words to live by; or powerful words to die by. Although we can appreciate his ability in keeping it real, we shall see later on how this may pan out for him . . . . ***Please do read on!***

Now recovered from the sucker punch and recognizing his disadvantage, Wrath summons dark forces to lend a helping hand.

Out loud he shouts to the sky to bring forth terror, "*Mortuorum ambulantum neco insurgi mei inimicus*" in Latin terms (*Walking Dead rise up to kill my enemy*).

By his command, the lifeless, re-animated security officers arise; unlike your typical slow moving clumsy zombies, but more like the World War Z types; who are determined to run yo ass down and never get tired. Fifty strong indeed, attracted by the stench of living flesh and warm blood motivationally drives them insane.

Cautiously they wander the stairwell until finally reaching the chamber box. Undoubtedly naïve and completely unaware that the hunt was on, Gabriel and crew hastily continue their pursuit of the boxed prize, but stumble upon yet another trial or tribulation. Ominously beastly, baritone growls resonate throughout the property.

"RRRRRRAAAAAAAAAHHHHHHH!!!!!!!!"

Cringing to the ghastly sound that chilled their bones, they ponder an escape.

"I hope that's not what I think it is . . ." Sophia pondered.

Grant explodes, "Whatever it is, we're outta here."

Quickly without any hesitation; equally yoked, they do the mad dash. That's right; run away little boys and girl; here come the monsters. Indeed they came, surrounding them like carnivores with a cannibalistic craving that'll put the hunger of piranhas to shame.

"Oh shit! Oops my bad, we're trapped! Where are those freaking angels when you need them?" hollered Grant.

Closer the living dead men get until suddenly they pause their pursuit as if they were waiting for further instruction. Wrath approaches and the circle opened as if he were royalty.

"In the next room, behind the glass door lays the box. Open it, and like I said before; I'll spare you your lives."

Minister Moon steps in front of Gabriel shielding him.

"And why should we trust you? You're not trustworthy," Gabriel asked.

Wrath answers, "Live or die, those are your choices."

Shabazz interjects, "We'd rather die than to give in to Satan's bitch boy."

Wrath replies, "So be it . . . Kill them!"

By his command the growls become intense, and the lifeless goons draw in for the kill. Suddenly, in comes a light that shines beautiful like a diamond in the sky. Heeding the glare; expeditiously Wrath exits stage right as two Angels appear wielding their justice upon evil; by accelerating their pace to stay ahead of their prey. One by one the angelic duo stomp the dead; as if they were roaches or rats trying to make their getaway when the light turns on. Gallantly their swords and knives swash buck with precision like they were Iron Chefs. Heads begin to roll as the re-animated are re-dying. On the floor, their dead bodies lay awaiting further decay. All while lurking in the shadows Wrath remains quiet as a cowardly mouse waiting for a window of opportunity to retrieve what he has come for. Now, he must resort to plan B; whatever that may be. Finally the divine extermination is completed. Triumphantly the Angels stand tall and looking good as Centurions that just conquered they're mission. As the weight of fear is lifted, the group gives Grant a smidgen of verbal lashing.

"Pastor, you really need to work on your faith," said Gabriel.

Moon sarcastically adds a jab, "Or practice what you preach."

Grant looks at them with puppy dog eyes and says, "You know; he may not come when you want him, but he's always there on time."

"Right on! My brotha, that's what I'm talking about," Shabazz concurred.

Sophia plugs in, "I feel you . . . Oh come on now, surely you all were a bit frightened. I know I was."

"Why yes of course! Due to our human nature, but the Holy Spirit within us gives us our true strength," explained Gabriel.

—(2 Timothy 1:7) *For God hath not given us the spirit of fear; but of power and love, and of sound mind.*

Now within the chamber where the boxed prize is stored, the group allows Sophia to do her daily systems checks by utilizing the proper protocol to unlock the 3 different locks on the sliding glass door. The complication involves Voice recognition, Retinal scan and Fingerprint Identification; all of which must be done in a systematic time frame within each another. Meticulously cracking like a professional safe cracker; she times her sequence just right. Effortlessly, the glass rises. Now they have full access to the prize and all of its wonders inside.

"Good job Sophia," says Gabriel.

Grant excitedly suggests, "Good now let's hurry up and get the stuff, so we can get outta here!"

"Relax my beloved, there's more here than meets the eye," Shabazz warned.

Sophia informs the group of the security features that were placed on the Arc to ward of criminals from stealing its treasures.

"Not so fast! Once the Arc was closed, the priest incorporated a series of traps; it was never to be opened until the proper time. They knew that there would come a day when mankind would need the paraphernalia from Heaven to save the world."

"Well I guess it's about that time," said Grant.

Gabriel informs, "No, not now. This is not the proper place or time; we need to just confiscate the Arc and keep it in our possession. We'll use it at the appropriate time."

"Ah come on! You mean to tell me we have to lug this thing around on top of all the drama?! Are you serious?" Grant protested.

Sophia, wondering what's up with this dude who seems to demonstrate a bad attitude as often as he breathes, asks, "What's his problem?"

"Don't mind him. He just says what's on his mind. As they say in the hood, he's just keeping it real," explained Shabazz.

With the help of the Angelic, the box is lifted with ease and protected beyond measure. Grant gives his stamp of approval.

"Cool, they're carrying it. For a second I thought we had too."

As their movement displays an awkward situation for the King of Terror, Wrath once again makes his presence known.

"Fe—Fi—Foe—Fum, I smell the blood of dead men."

Out classed by his opponents who are fortified with the vengeance of the Archangel Michael, Wrath keeps his distance for he knows that he is no match for the divine duo. Taking advantage of the opportunity, although scared, Grant tries to camouflage his disposition with sarcasm.

"Yeah, yeah, yeah, whatever! As long as we have our guardians, we'll be cool . . . . Right?"

Gabriel and the rest of the crew look at him and shake their heads as they were filled with humor. Being a Master of the Martial Arts and a student of General Sun Tzu; the ancient military strategist and tactician who wrote the hand book on winning ultimate battles called 'The Art of War' Master Moon focuses on which direction the ominous voice hailed. Stealthily he separates himself from the group. As curious as George, he searches the floor until he comes to a hallway without doors. Peculiar it seemed that there would be such a hall in a building like this. Pryingly he ventures down the corridor with caution. The further he goes; his defenses heighten until finally he reaches the end. Strange he thought, but not oblivious to what was behind him. He swiftly does a flying back flip just as Wrath reaches out to grab him. Fluidly he continues his movement as his momentum guides him into a sweep causing the big guy to hit the floor flat on his back before he had a chance to turn around.

"So, this is how you get from one place to another? This is a portal," says Moon as he takes a defensive stance ready for his opponent's next move. Amazed at his newfound discovery, being floored by another man, Wrath slowly gets up in total rage.

"I'm going to squash you like a bug . . . . Aaaaaaahhhh!"

In the blink of an eye he moves toward Moon. Luckily the silent, highly skilled man counters his opponent's moves by utilizing his momentum against himself; causing him to fall victim to a series of sequential flips, kicks and punishing hand hits. Unfortunately for Wrath, the hits keep coming as he realizes that he is no match for the China man. So, instead of sustaining the continuous ass whipping, he escapes into the unknown abyss. Before he returns to his friends, Moon's curiosity gets the best of him. He puts his hand into the perilous void to test its properties. Upon doing so, Wrath grabs his hand and tries to pull him in but, as quick as quick can possibly be, Moon again uses his momentum against him reversing the grip by administering a combination of finger picking, poking, popping, and paralyzing pressure point pinches; which cause temporary paralysis to his victim. However Wrath being the sum of many, and not like the average man; his paralysis only lasted long enough for Moon to pull back. Without hesitation he about faces with folded hands and strolls at a ginger pace to regroup with his fellow clergy.

Wrath, totally taken by surprise says to himself, "Oh shit! What the . . . !"

Meanwhile, as the group continues to exit the building with their minds still focused on the prized package they've acquired; Moon's presence doesn't go unnoticed.

"Wait a minute, where is Moon?" inquired Grant.

Out of the shadows Moon resurfaces, joining as if he never left.

"Where were you?" Grant asked.

Moon replies as he looks toward Gabriel, "I've encountered the fiend that has plagued your dreams. He is merely an *evildoer that is forsaken, so fret not for the worker of iniquity; for he will be cut down like grass and wither as the green herb* (**Psalms 37: 1-2**). I went searching the floor to make sure we were not ambushed upon leaving the museum when I stumbled upon a corridor with no doors. It wound up being a portal used by the demon to get from one place to another. I caught him just before he made his escape."

"An ordinary man you say? That's interesting," said Gabriel.

"Then that means he can be hurt just like us," added Shabazz.

Moon confirmed, "Exactly. He was no match for my skills; although the lap time for my paralyzing blows should've stunned him longer than it did. I barely got away. He tried to bring me into the portal. I'm afraid once you go in there's no coming back."

"Well thank God you're alright," Sophia said.

Grant being shocked, more or less amazed, that little ass Moon's hand game was tight says, "So, he was no match for you huh? What's up? You on some 'Kwai Chang Caine' Kung Fu warrior traveling monk type stuff?"

Once again, the amused clergy laughs as they load the van and passengers all the same. The Angelic vanishes, until needed. Next stop, the nation's capital: Washington DC.

In the interim, Wrath is angered from being bested in a 'mano y mano' bout; which constitutes an extreme measure to regain his advantage. Unable to accept failure and replaying the ever changing event, which causes him not to be the best that he can be; he decides to offset the odds by stacking his deck with iniquitous trump cards despite his instructions from Belial. His pride is damaged so his defiance warrants his own redemption, at this point anything goes.

Vigorously he shouts out at the top of his lungs to his agents to cause despair, "I summon the dark forces to hear my cry, bring forth vengeance to edify my plight and see my enemies crumble to the wages of death; for we are strong and never few! Quench my thirst with blood and bring on the bittersweet pleasures of pain: *Omnes Neci!*"

In Latin terms, *(kill them all)*, leave nothing alive. By his order, the diabolical cohorts target the righteous for total annihilation. God is Watching!

Arc Light by Christopher Romo

Chapter Twenty

(The Devil's Playground)

F inally the couple releases themselves from the clenched lip
lock. Dimitrius takes this opportunity to express his gratitude
by commending his troops on maintaining their discipline and
composure.

"I applaud you all for your bravery and obedience. Your discipline
to order is a compliment to your character and strength; clearly Satan
doesn't know who he is fucking with . . . . HOORAH!!!"

The crowd goes wild as they're happy to oblige their Commander
in-Chief.

"FORWARD!" Rashida belts out a command, ordering movement
toward the next domain of horror.

Overwhelmed by the ghastly stench of death that seems to become
more intense as they exit the wasteland, Miguel speaks his mind as he
covers his nose.

"Lo que apesta aquí."

"You got that right, little man! I don't know what he said but
whatever it was, I agree. It smells like hot ass and trash up in this
piece," Xavier said as he too covered his nose.

Mathyus schools them on a lesson.

"Death, my friends, is the last stop for the living; based on how
you lived will dictate whether or not you would have a good death.

Living in Hell surely can't be good; so yeah it stinks because this is their home."

"He's right, so suck it up and keep it moving before I throw up on all of you," demanded Dimitrius.

As they enter the dreary dark domain, the humidity becomes as thick as peanut butter and their sweat as sticky as jelly jam.

"What is this place?" Dimitrius asked.

Mathyus once again educates them.

"We are in a place where the sins of man are stored like condiments on a shelf. Deep down in the belly of the beast we are; also known as the Devil's Playground."

"They say that this is his bath house; his fountain of youth," says Sebastian.

Lilith includes, "No one dare enter this place; it is forbidden."

"No one but us," Xavier boldly states.

Sebastian interjects, "No wonder I never came to this place. Besides being off limits, why would anybody want to?"

"Are there souls here?" Miguel wondered.

Sarah answered, "I don't think so. I don't have any information on this place."

"I can answer that question," says Lilith. "The wise one is right, this is Belial's playground. Even he needs to have some fun once in awhile. This is where he waddles in man's sins and is thoroughly entertained by their misery. You won't find souls here, unless they are punished, the only thing you'll find here is disease and things that go bump in the night."

"Things that go bump in the night, like what?" Her lover asked.

"I'm afraid it gets worse . . . It's also a feeding ground for his pets," she continued.

Sebastian replied, "Something tells me we're in deep shit."

"I'm not worried about the things that go bump, what I'm worried about is the disease," vexed Dimitrius. "How do we inoculate ourselves against that?"

"I have an idea! Why don't you bless some water or something and give it to us as medicine if we need it? It worked with the bullets," suggested Miguel.

Mathyus piggy backs off of Miguel's suggestion, "Better yet, we can use it as a vitamin to build our immune system as well as a preventive measure."

"Good thinking kid! How old did you say you were again?" Xavier asked.

Miguel responded, "Old enough to be a man."

"A man indeed, mi amigo buen trabajo," Dimitrius intertwines languages.

Sarah proposes, "I think before we go any further, we should do it now."

Dimitrius hops out of the vehicle first, then Xavier, then Rashida.

"I agree with Sarah. This would be . . . ."

Before he could finish his sentence, a giant Anaconda quickly snatches Dimitrius around his waist and lifts him up in the air. Luckily for him, although power wrapped, his hands remained free. As the reptile applies the tight squeeze, our soldier boy remains calm. Not able to say that about the rest of the gang, with exception of Thorn who commences on biting chunks out of the snakes tail. Anxiety attacks plague them all.

"Oh shit!!! Oh damn!!! Oh my god!!! AAAAAHHHH!!!!"

Cries shout out as their fearless leader becomes a hearty meal for the Devil's pet. At the same time to be heard, the click-clacks of weapons locked and load begin to chatter as the Militia prepare to fire.

"Don't shoot! They might hit Dimitrius," bellowed Mathyus.

Rashida yells, "Hold your fire!"

Analyzing the dilemma she notices his freed hands.

"Dimitrius catch!"

Immediately she places the weapon on automatic then hurls it to him. As he understood the nature of the beast, he knew not to squirm or his body would become mush, instead of reaching out to grab the tossed hand cannon, he waited until it reaches him. By doing so, he allowed the snake to remain focused on its kill and not the sudden movement. Finally when the hand cannon is in his possession, Dimitrius plays dead. Due to the dreadful drama Sarah faints and stumbles to the ground. Immediately Lilith and Miguel come to her aid providing comforting arms. In the midst of action, Xavier pulls an

Snake by Chris Brimacombe

axe from a truck and begins to hack away at the enormous monster. Enthusiastic to get its grub on; the snake opens its mouth wide for consumption. Simultaneously, our hero springs to life and begins to blast into the maneater's mouth. RRRAAATTA-TAAAT-TAAAT! The sound of barraged bullets blasting fills the air, striking the beast until its grip is released. Now free from reptilian bondage, he reaches down to his right leg boot holster to draw his bowie knife. Not sure whether or not the creature was dead; he two hand tomahawk-ed the blade deep into its body and begins to slide down its trunk splitting it open as he traveled in a downward spiral. Shocked and amazed at the heroic scene, all eyes and mouths remain opened wide. As he hit the ground, the massive body of the snake falls lifelessly into a pile of fresh dead meat in which an enormous crocodile plunges to confiscate its remains then darts off to feast on the gifted kill. Startled at the horrendous sight all parties jumped back in unison. Confused as to cheer or stunned from the action before them, they all remained nervously silent. Strangely they look at each other as to say, "?"

Sebastian is the first to break his silence with two snaps and a twist.

"If this is what we have to look forward to, I'll just turn my lily white ass around. I'd rather deal with demons and zombies than be a snack for Jurassic Park . . . . Okay!"

Ignoring the flamboyant gesture, Dimitrius gets back to the business at hand.

"As you were! Where was I? Oh yeah, the medication."

Feeling hyper about what just went down, Mr. Dunn expresses his admiration.

"Man I tell you what; God knew what he was doing when he chose you! You's a bad Mam-ma-Jam-ma," he says as he pats Dimitrius on the back while he retrieves Sarah from their concerned friends.

Lilith bearing witness to the phenomenon, proclaims to herself assurance, "Every time I view these extraordinary encounters it gives me confirmation that I've made the right decision . . . thank . . . Thank you God, in Jesus' name."

Although she struggled with humbling words toward her new found faith, recognizing and accepting Jesus as her savior proves that she is now on the winning team; and it feels good.

Whilst her open eyes awaken, Sarah remains in her comfort zone realizing that she was in her hero's arms. Noticing her rising from her catnap with compassion he questions her status.

"Are you alright Sarah?"

Comforted yet ironically, she replied, "You have got to be kidding, right? I thought for sure you were dead."

"Yeah, I know, believe me; I wasn't expecting that either. I was caught sleeping . . . that usually doesn't happen to me."

Listening to their conversation, Lilith educates them, "Your senses are off due to the stench of sin."

Sebastian also adds his $0.02, "No wonder you don't have any information on souls up in here. They were either eaten, or died from the plague. I wonder what miracle is going to get us out of this nightmare."

"The miracle of our faith and God's mercy will see us through," encouraged Mathyus.

Dimitrius being reminded about the inoculation says, "Quickly, gather whatever water we have and bring it to me."

Hastily within a few minutes, the troops do what they are commanded by placing their canteens in front of their fearless leader per his request.

With a stern tone in his voice he says, "Mathyus do your thing."

Standing over the assembled canteens, Mathyus raises his arms to the sky and asks God for another blessing.

"Father God, once again we come before you with humbled hearts; to ask you for yet another blessing. Bestow your healing power to this water, so that we may use it to uplift your Kingdom in Jesus' precious name, Amen."

Suddenly, thunder clap slaps the sky and the common water begins to shimmer with that familiar glow only Dimitrius and Father Gabriel know exclusively. Slowly as the shimmer fades, what was once useless is now medicinal to some and dangerous to others.

"El agua es bastante," says Miguel.

Dimitrius jokingly responds as he sips the ice cold quencher.

"Yeah, and it tastes as good as it looks. Thank you Father! Drink everyone; that's an order!"

Now that the medicine is administered, they are fortified and enriched with God's healing grace; which will keep all evil at bay, thus they are now immune from the ghastly things that can claim their flesh.

"Porter, Sanchez . . . . front and center! We need to talk," ordered Dimitrius.

They hurry up and huddle, the ex-marines gathered to discuss their new position.

"Do you know and understand what we are doing here?" Dimitrius asked.

With certainty, the two newbies glance at each other.

"You know, as I was growing up my Mama would keep me and my brothers and sisters in church, so that we could build our own relationship with God, but like most kids; I did everything but that. Deep down I always knew I would wind up here. That's okay though because I accepted my fate and before, I fought for what I thought was right and now I fight for God," Sanchez explained.

Porter piggybacks off of Sanchez testimony.

"In my heart I know the Lord, and I always tried to do what was right. Although we were mercenaries, we didn't live up to the stigma that was attached to being so. We fought against tyranny as soldiers should, so now we have an opportunity to fight for God's justice; and to answer your question, yes we know exactly why we are here."

Pleased at the testimonies given Dimitrius nods and group hugs them to show his approval.

"Now that that's out of the way, we need to come up with a plan to protect ourselves while we're in Monster Fest."

In unison they confirm, "Road March! Weapons stacked."

"I'll inform Rashida, she's next in command," Dimitrius acknowledged.

Courageously the mighty military men convey the strategy to Rashida. Willfully she accepts her duty and humbly carries out the plan with no friction. Strategically like a well oiled machine they organize themselves in decency and order. Each man ready to march behind one another with weapons drawn and muzzles pointed opposite the next.

"Fine group of troops you have here Ma'am," Porter complimented.

Rashida replies with a sarcastic tone, "Who are you calling Ma'am? I work for a living, don't you forget it."

Having heard the statement before, Porter smiles and says, "Apologies."

"Don't let it happen again. You got it?"

The expression of nodding his head indicated that he got it.

To himself he says, "Feisty, I like that."

She, on the other hand, rolls her eyes and smiles as she turns her back to walk in the opposite direction.

Rashida receives word that they are ready so she signals Dimitrius who with an authoritative command bellows, "FORWARD, MARCH!"

Highly motivated and feeling real groovy, they begin to sing army cadence in harmony.

"Helicopters hovering-hovering over head—picking up the wounded and leaving the dead, Air borne-or-or-or-orne, Rangerrr-er-Kill-stab mutilate!"

As they proceed to get what they need to camouflage their fear, through the muck and the mire they go **(Psalms 40:1-3)**. Unknowingly they are being watched by a pair of prying eyes. Although they're oblivious yet alert as to what to expect from their surroundings, only Thorn, as keen as his senses are, notices the spy game that lurks within the trees. Irately he begins to growl toward the trees as if another canine had entered his marked territory. His roar served as a warning, as well as an alarm, to those of less ardent.

"What's the matter with Thorn?" Sarah asked.

Miguel answers back, "He is nervous. He keeps staring at the trees."

"Then that means there is something over there," Xavier spoke out loud.

"Oh my God, not another supersized monster," anticipated Sebastian.

Dimitrius belts an order to his trusted, highly skilled, fearless colleagues from another space in time.

"Porter, Sanchez, check it out."

Without hesitation the two soldiers tactically make their way to the tree line. Pressing upon their advance they notice the crumbling of trees far off, as if something huge had set a b-line headed straight for them. Both acknowledged the spectacle as they signal each other at the same time. Right arms half way up halted them where they stood with open eyes and keen ears locked on all, if any, hazard. While standing still like statues, the soft pitter-patter of two sets of feet slowly give way to the pin dropped silence. Instantly they gaze at each other and point their weapons toward the direction of the approaching soft shoes. Emerging from the follicle shaped line of the bushes; a man and a woman desperately reveal themselves.

"Run, salvese quien pueda!" they say as they expeditiously dart pass the ready-made soldier boys.

Harmless and frightened, the two appeared but left the soldiers curious of their hasty departure. Concurrently the forest trees topple then separate as the cause of such destruction now reveals itself. As its shadow darkens the sky, 5 stories high the Gargantuan stood; brazenly strong and barbaric, carnivorous and malevolent . . . nonetheless magnificent.

"OMG! It's Paul Bunion, the barbarian," shouted Sebastian.

All while viewing from a far, the Militia bears witness to something they've never knew existed. Expeditiously they begin to prepare for an attack.

"All weapons aimed and hold, on my mark!" Dimitrius hollered.

As they focus on their defense, Miguel's attention is drawn on the two unknowns that fled from the tree line.

Sharply focused like a lost pup he recognizes his bloodline.

"Mama, Papa!" he shouted as he dashes his way to reunite with them.

Recognizing the voice of their youngin they reciprocate fittingly by crying out, "Mi hijo!"

Together they run as their concerns are now refocused on La Familia. Once embraced, tears of joy soothe their emotions as lost love has finally found their wounded hearts. Meanwhile astounded by the giant, the little green army men pondered their next move while Thorn goes berserk. Stopped and stared at the assortment of fresh fleshed victuals, its hunger entertained a buffet style feast. At first the thought of two snacks brought about satisfaction, but now the thought of 100 brought him one of the 7 Deadly Sins: Gluttony. Aggressively forward, the giant moved in for the feast. As he gets closer, his saliva drooled from its mouth anticipating the flavor of such a hearty meal.

"Aim center mass at its head and let's blow it clean off!" Dimitrius shouted. "Fi . . . !"

Just before the command is completed, out of nowhere the giant is blindsided by another giant a bit shorter, but not by much, who had also laid eyes on the extensive meal and wishes the spoils for himself.

"Hold your fire!" Dimitrius yelled.

Simultaneously, Sebastian dramatically faints and his body droops to the ground as Sarah screams. Frazzled, the men head back to join the observing crowd, Sanchez and Porter scoop up Miguel and his parents while the clash of the titans continues.

Viciously the massive men fight, delivering blows with intent to maim as the winner takes all. Their bodies roll about the land causing destruction to anything in their path. Kicks and flips, punches and blows continuously volley until finally a choke hold tightly yoked around the first spotted giant's neck cuts off all circulation and then the crunching sound of bones breaking of the elder's neck and collar. To the victor go the spoils. It's time to claim his prize when the readied command is unpaused.

"Ready, aim, fi . . . !"

"WAIT! STOP! Don't shoot! Hold your fire!" Miguel's mom shouted. "He was protecting us! He's a good boy. Please, don't kill him," she pleaded.

Gentle as a lamb the giant seemed, unlike the others who are filled with evil to their rotten core and angered with malice to the fullness of their hearts. Intimidating at first glance, then afterwards you can see that, he was just a boy.

"His name is Johan (*Yo-hon*), our protector," she says.

"I am Hector Vasquez and this is my wife Lucy; and this my son, Miguel."

Astounded at a loss for words, Miguel gets down on his knees and begins to thank God for finding his lost treasures; as he symbolizes the sign of the cross.

"Gracias a Díos por los padres."

Mathyus gladly welcomes the boy's family with kindness.

"Thank God you two are alright, the boy always knew in his heart that one day he would find you. In which his faith has made it so, welcome."

Xavier asks, "What are you doing here?"

"Better yet, how did you survive?" Dimitrius inquired.

Hector explains while holding Miguel in his arms, "We came here to get away from the demons. Although it is forbidden, we'd rather deal with the creatures; they are big and clumsy. You can hear them coming a mile away. We figured our chances were better if we stayed here, and on top of that we helped Johan by removing a splinter the size of a toothpick from his foot and ever since he has protected us."

"I must admit, your survival skills must be all that," said Porter.

Hector replied, "I am from the slums of Tijuana and the Barrios of LA, my wife is from the streets of NYC, it don't get any tougher than that, Homes."

"So I guess you can handle yourself with a weapon?" Dimitrius asked.

Quickly Lucy whips out a switch blade and begins to butterfly it with precision.

Hector then throws a handful of bullets in the air and blasts each one before they hit the ground.

"Well that's good enough for me, join the party," Xavier boosted.

Quiet kept Rashida with negative thoughts flowing through her brain.

"Bullshit! Something's not right with these two. There ain't no way anyone could survive out here with just a handgun and a switch blade."

Sanchez welcomes Hector and Lucy with a sarcastic remark, "Bienvenido a la revolución."

The look on the couples face warranted a nod of uncertainty.

"So is it safe to say that you know how to get us out of here without running into anymore uninvited guests?" Sebastian asked after the coast became clear and the giant seemed at ease.

Complacent the big boy appeared as his friends were safe and sound.

"Yeah we can show you the way, and Johan will see that we'll make it through." Hector implied.

Happy to hear his name, Johan reaches down to the ground and opens his palm for La Vasquez family to climb aboard.

As they step, Miguel demonstrates his level of maturity by asking the simplest but pertinent question, "Papí, will Johan protect my friends like he has protected you and Mama?"

Surprisingly Johan answers and says, "YES, I WILL PROTECT THE GOOD."

The facial expression by all proved to be shocking as Sebastian lays claim to his astonishment.

"Oh my god, he can talk!"

"Of course he can talk. Although he is mystical, he *is* part human," Lilith enlightened. **(Genesis 6:1-7)**

Mathyus expounded on her accusation, "She is right, when the mutinous angels were cast out from Heaven with Lucifer; they fell to earth and inhabited it. While disguised as mortal men, they found themselves attracted to the women and fornicated with them. God became outraged by their actions and as punishment; He struck their offspring to be as giants who roamed the earth, as menacing creatures."

"If that is true, how is it that big boy over here is the opposite? How did we get so lucky?" Xavier asked.

"Call him a freak of nature or better yet, a part of God's big plan." Dimitrius concluded.

Sarah includes, "Thank you Jesus!"

"What about the others? Once they get wind that baby boy is down with the get fresh crew, I'm sure they'll be hell to pay," added Porter.

Sanchez also inserts, "That's not the only thing we have to worry about. What about Cerberus the three headed dog that guards the devil's realm?"

"Is that what we have to look forward to?" Sebastian asks as he again suffers an anxiety attack. "That's it, we're dead!"

"Stop this foolishness! God has granted us a gift, a protector and this is how you act? Where's your faith now?" Mathyus scolded.

Dimitrius bravely says, "I agree. We'll deal with it when the time comes just like we have with everything else. Rashida, give the command."

"FALL IN! Road March Formation . . . . Weapons Stacked . . . . MOVE OUT!" she ordered.

Mathyus begins to sing an old Baptist hymnal, *"There's an army rising up; to break every chain, to break every chain, break every chain."*

Together they march in accord, now fortified with formidable strength from a sacred time, a time before Jesus, the time before the great flood of Noah; when the world was corrupt and God deemed it necessary to go back to the drawing board. Although he was spawned from the seed of the wicked his virtue is weighted as a diamond in the rough who currently leads the way to a righteous path. God is good; God is great; even in the darkness his light always shines through.

> **(Romans 13:12)** *". . . let us therefore cast off the works of darkness, and let us put on the armor of light."*

> **(2Timothy 2:3-4)** *"Thou therefore endure hardness, as a good soldier of Jesus Christ. No man that warrant entangle himself with the affairs of this life; that he may please him who has chosen him to be a soldier.*

In the Interim

As the Militia's optimistic momentum grows; the dark forces in Hell become destabilized; and a change of attitude slowly arise into view, as doubtful souls become hopeful. Like an infectious virus the cause of good incapacitate the infamous light bringer to discomfort as he begins to suffer from something he's never felt before; an allergic reaction to the brand new feeling that fills the air. Actions like itching, scratching, hocking, runny eyes and nose are common to a mortal man, but grossly abnormal to the majestic.

"What the fuck is happening to me? Am I catching a cold or something? Nah, it can't be. Down here I am God, this type of shit happens every day to the hairless apes, not me."

Hot and cold flashes, body aches and pain plague his being as he coughs up green mucus to verify infection. Dizzy he becomes as he passes out on the floor. Falsely misunderstood due to never bearing witness to the demise of their ruler, his humbled servants become the town criers.

"The King is dead!" rumored the damned.

An honest conclusion as his body releases its bowels and urine spills to a gathered puddle. Catching ear of such tale, mutinous demons buck for their new position.

"Finally the time has come for Hell to be ruled by a new king. Let us battle for its spoils and let the victor reign supreme."

Like wildfire, the buzz spreads throughout the demonic network as it reaches Wrath who defies them all. Deemed precedent over all ; he is detoured from his duty in the material world. Courageously he redirects himself while in the dark void to teleport him homeward bound. Upon his arrival, the battle royal ceremony commences. Demons flying high above, whirling and swirling about, whooping and howling as the first battle is underway. Clash, Bash, and Slash undergo as one stands to remain victor awaiting its next opponent. Casually Wrath strolls on to the field and presents himself as champion when he shakes the victor's hand and tears the entire arm off. Then, he uses it to behead the so called frontrunner.

"When the bell tolls, let's see who will remain standing . . . . Next!"

Due to his fierce reputation and brawn, no contest persists as he boldly walks off the battle field.

"Where is my king? Show me the body," he insists.

Quickly the audience and participants swallow their pride and bitch up, as expected, with heads hung low and tails tucked.

"He's in his chamber."

Onward to Belial's chamber he went. Upon his arrival he approaches the darkened room to find his king wrapped in a cocoon. Bewildered and unspoken, he remained by his side pondering his next course of action and realizing that he is now in charge.

"He deserves a proper burial . . . he *was* my king. I'll take him to where he frequented the most. I'll take him to his playground where he'll enjoy his eternal slumber safely and, be without interruption."

*Note: The one good thing I guess you could say about the immorally demented is that their loyalty lies true to their code as well as the respect for each other's craft. Bullshit!

Carefully Wrath picks up the cocoon and enters the dark abyss. Within seconds, he arrives at the playground where unexpected company dwells. In search of a tomb to place his king, he continued to walk until he found such. Underneath his masters' recreation area lie a grotto tucked away in seclusion; this would be an excellent crypt, he thought. Without haste his plotted direction guides him to the desolate tunnel below. Upon his arrival he summons the master's pooch by tooting his silent whistle. Responding to the deaf toned shrill, a grisly roar sounds out as Thorn heard the pitch as well; which merits him to respond with a bothersome howl.

"What's got him spooked?" Rashida asks Mathyus.

"I don't know. Let's hope it's not as big as his first caution," Mathyus quipped.

Dimitrius includes, "Dog's hearing is keener than ours. Something else is out there and he knows it. Keep a sharp eye out for anything unusual and prepare for the worst.

"What can be worse than what we've already seen?" Xavier asked.

Sarah adds, "I would hate to imagine that there is something worse out here."

Those that knew remained silent and cautious all the same. At the same time, deep into the hole in the ground Wrath went; as deep as he could've possibly gone. Finally he laid Belial to rest.

"Rest now my king. Soon the days of reckoning shall reign and you shall have your throne upon the trinity, the secular, and the so called righteous. This I promise. This I will obey. In the interim, I will rule with an iron fist and bring forth pandemonium as the mortals will suffer total chaos and gloom."

After his vow he begins to punch at the stone, knocking down slabs, creating a wall to seal off his master's tomb. As he exits the cavern, he is greeted by the family pet. Triple licks vested the familiar as the welcome is reciprocated with heartfelt instruction.

"Guard him with your life."

Obedient, the three headed beast sustained as it sat at the entrance of its master's dead quarters. Surrendering to his new responsibility, into the abyss he went still unaware that his enemies' location was so near. Heavily laden with a new agenda; completing his master's plan is expedited as his loyalty proves him worthy to be king. Back to the material world he went to see his mission to conclusion.

Meanwhile

While continuing through the jungle swamp the Militia are encroached with the infestation of insects bugging and toads croaking.

> **(Psalm 78:45)** *He sent among them swarms of flies, which devoured them, and frogs, which destroyed them.*

Pests they are, as to the meaning of their existence is questioned.

"Hey Mathyus, answer me this. What's the purpose of bugs and why did God make so many?" Xavier inquired as he swats his way with every step as he moves forward.

"That's easy my friend, to answer your question, insects represent the various problems that frequent mankind every day. As they are many; a chosen few actually serve with a purpose. For example we could not have honey without Bees, the soil we plant seeds in must meet a certain grade in order to produce a harvest; it is the dung from bugs that provides its nutrition. Flowers pollinated from the assistance of crawlers and Bees. The Trees and greenery are cultivated to produce the air we breathe; it's the bugs that feed on its chlorophyll which to provides nutrition used to sustain us. Then again there are insects that serve as Pestilence, their soul purpose is to cause harm and spread decease. They also serve as a constant reminder that we are being punished for our inadequacy toward God's laws. They feed off the dead and live amongst the trash.

Cerberus by Christopher Romo

Needless to say according to the Book of Revelation; two of the four Horsemen which *a*re named Death and Pestilence will defile the earth causing death and destruction," Mathyus taught.

"Well thank goodness we've got one of them on our side, so that won't be happening," said Sarah.

> **(Revelation 6:8)** *And I looked, and behold a pale horse: and his name that sat on him was Death, and Hell followed with him. And power was given unto them over the fourth part of the earth, to kill with sword, and with hunger, and with death, and with the beasts of the earth.*

"Damn, all of that? Dude, you give the longest explanations, but you got to love it. I appreciate you old man," accepted Xavier as he continued to swipe, swing, and swat.

Dimitrius provides comfort with warm counsel, "Don't worry if anyone gets stung the medicine will prevent sickness."

"Thank God!" Sarah blurted.

Seemingly to test the theory from above, a swarm of jumbo mosquitoes muster formation to take an attack position. As the minuscule buzz from flies is drowned out by a loud hum, the alert minute men leave no stone unturned and immediately takes a defensive stance.

"Where is that noise coming from?" Rashida asked.

Dimitrius informs, "It's surrounding us but mainly from above . . . . Look to the sky, it's a bird, it's a plane, no it's big ass mosquitoes . . . . Target practice anyone?!"

"Look at the stingers on them jokers, the venom won't kill you before the stinger would," stated Xavier as the swarm dive bomb toward their prey.

Realizing that an attack was underway below Hector orders Johan to help the others, so without hesitation he begins to swat the menacing bugs as bullets pick off those that slipped the giant's mitt. While exterminating the bugs; feasted the toads below as they took full advantage of the gifted spoils.

Noticing the commotion from a far, Cerberus becomes inflamed with rage; and lets out an earth rattling roar, "RRRAAAAHHHH!"

Demanding the attention drawn from the bug slaughter, all eyes shift to the direction of the ominous roar.

"It's Cerberus," shouted Sanchez.

Sebastian looks at Dimitrius and sarcastically says, "Well, I guess the time has come to deal with the bigger problem, now hasn't it?"

Ignoring Sebastian's quip until confirmation of the pest control was completed, Dimitrius ask Johan to pick him up to get a better look at the latest threat.

"Johan, lift me up big fella," he said.

As his right hand is crowded with Miguel and family, he reaches down with his left allowing Dimitrius and Rashida to climb aboard.

While rising, Hector announces a warning, "He's charging straight at us."

When in full height and in view, Rashida can't believe her eyes.

"What *is* that?"

"My men said it's the devil's pet Cerberus, he guards the entrance to the last realm; we must be near," he said.

"Right now he's in attack mode, what are we going to do?" She asked.

Calmly he looks into Johan's eyes and says, "Can you handle him; big fella?"

Quickly Johan places all parties down to the ground and counter charge toward Cerberus path. When they meet Johan jumps around the dog's backside and straddles, as he wraps his left arm around 1of the heads and throws a series of punches to another with his right, while the third head bites him on his right leg. Scrapping like titans they fought while the others make their way to the exit. Now scurrying across a rocky terrain just outside the jungle swamp they flee to the bound that ends this dreadful place. As they approach they stop and stare at the raged battle that their friend is deeply engaged. Bloody the fight as it made a blood stream flow; freely down cracks and crevices it dripped until finally ladled upon Belial's cocoon; drenching its shell with warm fresh blood as it absorbs it like a sponge. Within seconds the cocoon starts to quiver and catches a flame igniting what lies within. Vengeful as Hell is; it is fueled by the purest of evil which manifest itself from the carcass of Mr. Evil himself; which give birth to something more than expected.

Continued the scrap scuffed, while on his back Cerberus heads begin to snap at the giant; during so Johan places his two feet on Cerberus' chest kicking the beast off him. Quickly he snatches a tree and bashes the body of the three headed K9 as if it were a club. Silent the wounded dog lay as Johan jumps in the air and pounces hard with both feet, landing center mass; crushing its back. Finally the battle came to its end as Johan is victor. Celebrated cheers sound out as Johan raises his hands as champion. Louder the cheers become as they all proclaim their appreciation of him being on their side, when all of a sudden the ground begins to tremble as if there were an earthquake. BOOM! The mountain top blows and lava spits out instantly becoming a volcano. As it spews out, liquid magma gathers at the foot of the mound, the melt begins to take shape forging into a fearsome creature feared by those from medieval times. Stupendous it stood with its wings spread out wide, as if it were stretching from relief of a long awaited slumber, and then its furnace fires burned and its mouth aimed its searing breath toward them.

"A Fire-Breathing Dragon," shouted Sebastian as he grabbed the closest person next to him which happened to be Lilith; who seemed to be just as terrified as she grabbed hold of Xavier's arm.

Gallantly Johan stood between his friends and the great beast as if he were a shield; ready to pounce if the situation demanded it. Ready, aimed to shoot Sanchez draws his weapon.

Immediately Porter knocks down Sanchez's extension and says, "All that's going to do is piss him off."

"He's right, everybody hold your fire," suggested Dimitrius.

(Job 41:19-20) *"Out of his mouth go burning lamps, and sparks of fire leap out. Out of his nostrils goeth smoke, as out of a seething pot or caldron. His breath kindleth coals, and a flame goeth out of his mouth."*

"Hector, show us the way outta here," commanded Dimitrius.

"Si mi amigo, follow me," he replied.

"Run everybody and keep running, don't stop," Dimitrius suggested.

Eager to remove themselves from the awkward setting they ran, lead by Hector into a gully which was like no gully ever seen before by man. Mystified they stood as they are stunned by its magnificent wondering all awhile; where are we? Is this Hell or Outer Space?

Chapter Twenty One

(Trick or Treat)

HELL

L uckily being able to dodge the living flame-thrower, they escape the hazardous killing field. As the coast seemed clear they enter into the Celestial Realm: Land of the Demons. A place where blue black is the sky and shooting stars fly constant, the full moon remains crimson with blood, and rancid air that gives way to what is ruthless and sinister. Blissful challenges persist as Satan's minions vie for absolute power; as he who possess the prize, possesses the throne. Once again an opportunity has knocked and opened the door. Hovering up above and buried deep blow; a squadron of repugnant fiends awaits. Unaware of their presence, they stop to make heads or tails as to they're whereabouts.

"What is this place? Is it the realm where we'll find Satan?" Dimitrius curiously inquired.

Eager to figure out and answer his question, Mathyus and Sarah rummage through the Book of Souls to determine the place of cosmic uncertainty.

"There's nothing in the book about this place, we're officially off the grid," she said.

"Something isn't right with this picture; I need to check this out. There aren't too many places I haven't been and this is definitely one of them," Sebastian claimed as he morphed back to his gruesome self and, then he vanished right before their very eyes.

"Wait a minute I thought this was supposed to be the place where the devil lived? It seems to me that someone bullshitted us," declared Xavier as he looked around cosmic atmosphere.

Dimitrius intervenes with sound mind, "Whatever this place is we're here, and together we'll get through. Let our faith be our strength and guide, or would you rather go back through the land of the lost? You decide. Besides if that was the Devil's playground; then what is home?"

Mathyus adds, "They say that an idle mind is the Devil's playground."

"I can dig it. People's minds are screwed up. They're are dying every day, there's a murder every hour and a rape every minute, not to mention the sick, and the all out assault on mankind; black on black crime and let's not forget the thievery, the jails are filled with kats who fell victim to socialism just trying to survive, the system is flawed," declared Rashida.

Xavier adds to the convo, "I'm hip, they have that: I gotta get yours before you get mine attitude. As far as the system goes, it only works if you respect it."

"Right! If you ask me home is where he's having most of his fun," said Sarah.

Dimitrius concludes, "That was on point, I couldn't have said it better."

"Whenever you guys are done shooting the chew, we need to figure out where and what this place is," stated Mathyus.

Sanchez walks over to Hector and says, "Well homes, you led us here; where are we?"

With a dumbfounded look on his face Hector says, "I don't know."

"WHAT!" they all shouted in their heads including his son, as they look astounded at what was said.

"This place wasn't here! Ask Lucy; it use to be a gully."

Little did they know that the Will of Hell had altered itself to gain the advantage?

To support Hector's claim Johan says, "He is telling the truth, Hell has its own mind; it changed again."

"I had heard that Hell has a Will of its own, and it will suit itself in its own defense. I bet if we did go back; we would not be where we were. Hell is alive my friends; and has become our #1 enemy," said Mathyus.

Xavier out of frustration blurts out, "Damn it! Well isn't that just great?! We just went from the kitchen into the frying pan . . . . anything goes people."

Sitting back watching the degrading of their faith; Hell dispatches a mischievous sprite to further their demise. From the darkened sky a shooting star falls to the ground 100 yards away from their location, dust splatter clouds their view. As the powder cloud clears; from it a man exhumed with the stature of Tattoo from Fantasy Island or Austin Power's Mini Me dressed as a Referee. Slowly he approaches floating through the air while sucking his teeth.

"Tisk, tisk! What a stupor? Are we confused once again?"

Xavier trips on the comical site; on what he thought was a hallucination.

"Get a load of the great Gazoo?"

Instantly the little funny looking guy transformed into his real demonic body, which was twice the size of Xavier and beyond grotesque to look at.

"Now, as you were saying. Would you prefer me like this or the lesser of the two?"

Startled at the flash scare they reminded silent. As quickly as he changed, just as quickly he changed back.

"What was that? No answer; that's what I thought. Allow me to introduce myself; my name is Gemini; and yes like the zodiac sign I have a duo personality wrapped up in lil-ole-me as you just bared witness. As for each and every one or shall I say two of you here's where the trouble lie within. The problem is that you don't know who you really are; you struggle daily with your alter ego to gain face with your emotions or better yet your desires. You resist temptation when in reality, you love it. You've already confronted your own demons. Consider this is your opportunity to confront yourself; lets get down to the real nitty gritty to find out what truly makes you tick. If in the end you conclude that you like the person who stands before me today then you may leave. If not, then you will remain here forever in the Celestial Realm: Land of the Demons and become as happy and content as we are . . . . Let the games begin!"

Simultaneously the sound of a whistle blows and the setting changes into the Acropolis under the moonlight, the serious moonlight.

Defiant in times of necessity Dimitrius rejects the invite with firm vigor.

"Screw this! We don't have time to play games. Snatch the midget and blast anything that moves."

"Right On! My sentiments exactly," Xavier agreed.

Mathyus concurred as well, "Good move; I bet that threw him off guard."

Subsequent to the snatching of Gemini, he quickly turned back into the true Hell raiser he is while growling and uttering these words, "Fools! You dare defy me? Surely this day you all shall die."

Without hesitation Sanchez and Martin blast the creature into smithereens.

"I thought he said grab the dude?" Hector said.

Lucy defends their course of action, "Did you see him change? That was not the dude."

Due to their unexpected clash, aggravated demons begin to pop up from everywhere grabbing hold of a gang of soldiers from above and below. Bullets defensively fly as their targets are able to dodge the majority which resulted into diminishing half of them (Militia) gone.

"They're killing my men," hollered Rashida while running and exhausting her ammo.

Realizing that in an instant their numbers have dramatically dwindled, Dimitrius comes up with an elaborate escape plan. While Johan smashes and bashes his way creating a path of least resistance, the others followed allowing his brawn to be their might.

"Porter! Hand me your bandoleer; everybody who has them drop them on my command," said the fearless leader.

Xavier expresses his enthusiasm, "Damn it man! I wish I had a few of them shits; I'd blow their asses to Kingdom Come."

With a wink from his eye Dimitrius retorts, "Right On! My sentiments exactly."

In cahoots they both reciprocate with a smile.

"We're gonna make sure these bastards feel the pain and glory," declared the mercenary leader.

Ahead of the horrid herd they find themselves at a safe space due to the feeding of their sacrificial buddies. Once the feast was over the pursuit continued as the angry demons drew near. When they reached the anticipated mark and, dared to cross the line, sway is given to the disciplined to drop the bomb.

"Bombs away!" bellowed Dimitrius.

Pulling pins are pulled and tiny bombs are slumped to the ground; at the same time they continued forward as deadly demons synchronize with the timely explosions, BBOOMM! BBLLAAMM! PPOOWW! Screeches and howls from demons cry out as their body parts are disfigured and some dismantled or dismembered '*take your pick*'.

As the coast seemed cleared of present danger, a head count is taken to see who is left to be accounted for. Lo and behold, the core group remains standing with the exception of Sebastian who has never returned from his excursion.

"Has Sebastian returned yet?" Dimitrius asked.

Mathyus replied, "I don't think so; he would've made a grand entrance knowing him."

"Something's wrong then, that's not like him," feared Sarah.

Miguel comforts her with inspiring words as he walks over to her and hugs her to reinforce his feeling, "Don't worry Sarah, God will keep him safe."

"You're right Miguel. God will protect him only if he believes. I hope he has figured it out, all he has to do is claim it and believe in Him and God will shine through like a beacon in the night. I pray he has Jesus in his heart, well he did survive his demon assault, he'll be fine." she said as Mathyus and Thorn include themselves in the hug to show their compassion for their friend and for those who just lost their lives.

(John 8:12) *Then spoke Jesus again unto them saying, "I am the light of the world: he that follow me shall not walk into darkness, but shall have the light of life.*

Delusions of Grandeur

"Don't worry guys Sebastian is capable of handling himself; he'll run before he'll let anything happen to him," said Xavier.

Unaware that Hell was up to no good; Sebastian finds himself caught in a maze as he continually pops in and out of the same realm as if he were going around in circles.

"What the heck is going on? It's like I'm on a merry-go-round or something."

As plains shift and dimensions collide Hell finally manipulates Death to the grotto where the dark one's cocoon lies.

"What is this place? Where am I?"

Slowly he begins to explore the cave as light is provided from a glow that seems so close but yet, so far. As he gets closer he experiences an illusion of which places him in a time when he first fell victim to his pride and reveled on the top of the world.

Lights, Camera, Action: Pop—Pop! Go the flashes from photographers and paparazzi as the glamorous fashion show moves underway.

"That's it ladies! Strut your stuff like Gazelles crossing the Serengeti, be proud, be bold, be magnificent. . . . Shucks be me!"

The cheers from the audience validate his status and once again he personifies vogue. It's his greatest triumph as he is named Fashionista Extraordinaire, but as abruptly as he was consumed by the glorified hallucination; the dismal darkness consumed his reality.

"What was that? Who is messing with me? Why? Why?! I was the best, I was a Diva, the fashion cosmopolitan was my baby; I had it all and I want it back!"

BINGO! The voice of reasoning in his head fills the cave, "Do you really want it? If you want it; you can have it," said the Chimera.

"Who are you?" Sebastian asked.

"Who I am doesn't matter. All that matter is that I can give you what you've been missing . . ."

"Get away from me Satan; you're not God," commanded Sebastian.

"Oh but, I am God. God of this world and the world from whence you came, all that matters is that I can give it all to you like it was," said the Chimera.

"What do you want from me?" he asked.

"Nothing really, I just what you to be happy; that's all. Enter the cocoon and remain inside until it hatches. That is all that is required; and then you will have all your hearts desire."

"Sounds good and all but something doesn't seem right with this," said Sebastian.

Tempting, the Chimera continued, "We all have needs and wish for desires; it's a rarity to be able to have them all within reach, just do what is required and it's all yours.

"What do you get out of this?" Sebastian asked.

Suddenly the glimmer dims down to a spark as Hell become sensitive to the piercing query; at the same time Belial's face emerges from the cocoon, "To be a part of you."

Instantly Sebastian tries to escape by pop-locking his way in and out; but to avail he is brought back to the cavern of gloom. Accepting his capture, Sebastian tries to put things into prospective.

"I know what you are up too, I've heard of this; Hell has become you while you become something else, but you need Death in order to complete the puzzle."

Applause claps out as if he was on a game show; but there is no audience.

Again the Chimera states its intention, "Right you are, with you we'll become all that I can be, without you I am what I am, still your superior weakened by the poison that infects Hell as your friends' faith grows stronger."

Sebastian continues to fight for his freedom.

"I hate to spoil your party but, that poison that you are referring to resonates throughout my soul. It's because of the renewing of my mind, my spirit; I no longer serve you; I now serve JESUS CHRIST."

Instantly, without hesitation Sebastian is hocked out of the cocooned cavern as if he were phlegm from a cleared throat; back into the Playground where skin and bone remain after the dragon had finished its fill of bodies dispensed from the magical realm. Quickly realizing where he is; he musters up as many weapons he can find and loads them into a jeep that was left behind.

"Thank God Mathyus had me study Proverbs and Ephesians. It's because of the spirit of my mind that I am free and I'm glad I know that there is power in the name of JESUS!"

Onward back into the Celestial Realm he went to meet up with his friends . . . . POOF!

Leaving a misty cloud of smoke behind he sings, "Oh happy day! Oh happy day! When Jesus washed, oh when He washed, my sins away . . . . Lord have mercy; By Jove I think I've got it!"

God is Watching!

(Ephesians 22-24) [22] *that, in reference to your former manner of life, you lay aside the old self, which is being corrupted in accordance with the lusts of deceit,* [23] *and that you be renewed in the spirit of your mind,* [24] *and put on the new self, you be renewed which in the likeness of God has been created in righteousness and holiness of the truth . . . .*

(Proverbs 22:1) *A good name is to be chosen rather than great riches.*

Meanwhile back at the Demon domicile, tension weighs heavy as Belial's essence subliminally encourages Hell to bang down its gavel.

As the survivors expeditiously move forward but proceed with caution, in the darkened sky up above; demons prepare for a shifty attack only the scrupulous can adore. Like vultures they circle upon their prey; waiting patiently to dive down to feast; for in these parts food is famine. Hover no more, when violently the lighting crack as if it was a cow bell signaling that dinner is served. A hopeful advantage granted from an attack above, given to the minority due to both oppositions dwindle down to few. As a result from the last debacle the mystified monsters learned a meaningful lesson as they adjust by hollowing-out their being to a more vaporous form. When ineffective blessed bullets spray like insecticide; immunity is established as to whom now have the upper hand.

Screeches and shrieks howl; as the hideous vultures descend meeting a barrage of upward hale, but to the administration now given the spoil.

"The bullets are not working," said Porter as they continue to fire without a kill.

Again, grenades are tossed; this time to no avail.

"What are you prepared to do now?" Mathyus asked Dimitrius.

"What would you do?" Dimitrius asked Mathyus.

Lilith intervenes, "I'd play the game, but under set conditions."

"She's right, give them what they want. We don't have much of a choice." Sarah includes.

Mathyus disagrees, "That's where you're wrong; there's always a choice my dear."

While they contemplate their next move, the demons halt their pursuit as if their attack was fueled by the fear radiating from the blessed. Being practitioners of tactical strategy and war; Dimitrius, Sanchez and Porter notice the demon freeze. At the same time they glance at each other for confirmation.

Porter says, "Is it me or does it seems like the demons are kinda soft."

They silently concur with a nod.

"Listen up! Put your weapons down, then get down on your knees and begin to pray. On my mark," said Dimitrius with assurance.

Sanchez says, "I hope you know what you're doing?"

"Have I'd ever let you down? Don't doubt me now. Where's your faith? Now pray for traveling mercy, like never before," Dimitrius instructed to all with open ears and to those who knew fear before they knew their own hearts.

"Do what he says everyone because prayer changes things," shouted Mathyus.

So together they were obedient and did just that. Individually they petitioned to God asking for safe travel while embarked in this evil place. Knowing that their supplication was pure in heart but not as complex, Mathyus prayed for the removal of the reprobated spirits that befall them. **(Mark 9:17-29)**

As a result from such powerful meaningful words that were expressed from the goodness of their hearts, suddenly the demonic marauders disassembled and squandered away. Although new to the discipleship there is always one who can't leave well enough alone.

"Why didn't you think of this in the first place? We could've been outta here without loss of soldiers and good men. You risked the lives of your company, if we were under military law, you would've been court marshaled for your incompetence," bitched Sanchez.

Porter defends his superior with an aggressive shove and these stern words, "Back off Sanchez."

Simultaneously Rashida drop kicks Sanchez; landing on top of him in a straddle and says, "If anybody has the right to bitch; it's me. Those were my men and they knew the score. Take it down soldier, that's an order."

"Besides, this ain't the military's law; it's God's Law. A righteous man must fall before he rises again **(Proverbs 24:16)** unfortunately, that was number five," revealed Mathyus in an authoritative way.

Accepting the schooling from the wise old man, Sanchez still looked at Dimitrius with angered eyes.

Dimitrius wisely puts Sanchez back into proper perspective, "Its okay, I understand where you're coming from but understand this; we're soldiers in a fight that has no boundaries, no rules; if I had it my way we wouldn't be here at all, but we are. Mistakes are made by men who are imperfect, the only perfect man that walked the earth was Jesus Christ, and he too had his moments. So don't judge me because Judgment day is coming and you too will be judged."

Slapped back into reality as he swallowed his pride Sanchez nods his head to show lesson learned.

"We've got a lot to learn," said Porter as he pats Sanchez on his back with a That-a-Boy.

Onward they walked finally as the coast seemed clear.

"Hell No!" Says Hell as it's not done yet.

As a plethora of lifeless demons blanket the ground; Hell begins to consume each and every one of them by absorbing its entirety of the deceased into the dirt to give birth to something beyond compare; conjured from the linkage within, the dead bodies mesh into an abomination. Suddenly the ground begins to tremble as cracks split open, while smoke fills the air and everyone begins choking. Busting from underneath, a pair of giant red arms exhume as a gigantic demon arise; equal to the gargantuan in stature.

"What the hell is that? Johan, handle your business," Xavier blurted.

As he listened, he obeyed. Knowing that they are out matched Johan has an overwhelming feeling of engaging his integrity while embracing his true purpose. While Johan stepped to the vast imp; the rest of the crew dipped, cut out or skedaddle . . . *take your pick.* Ran they did until finally without a doubt; vacating the Home of the Demons as if they were bad tenants.

Quickly Johan bum-rushes the super demon, in an attempt to save the others.

"You dare defy me? I am Hell! Satan to the tenth power!"

Serious blows bang down by Johan but seemingly have no effect as Hell absorbs them like the Hulk; who has the ability to gain strength as blows are landed. Wisely Hell uses a 'Rope-a-dope' style to gain the advantage. Johan continue to bash but regrettably due to fatigue, he proves to be no match, as it snatches Johan's still beating heart from his chest; which leaves him lifeless as his body collapsing to the ground. At great expense due to his sacrifice his heroic distraction granted his temporary friends enough time to escape. As cruel and rude as it could be; Hell with its sharpened claws shreds Johan's body and feeds his carcass to some pterodactyl like scavengers that patiently hover above.

Caught up in its own hype and totally full of itself, Hell boasts about its body as well as its formidable power. Needless to say that its vanity boosted its ego, its pride engulfed sin, and its conceit willfully morphs him back from whence it came.

During his departure it proudly proclaimed, "Nothing can stop me . . . . I am truly a God; Satan ain't got shit on me!"

Diablo by SpartaDog

Diablo vs Johan by SpartaDog

Hell bent—Hell boast—Hell bound and beyond . . . . Foolish pride surrenders to its will; encouraging it to be a force on its own.

During their escape Miguel would occasionally look back to witness the bionic brawl. Unfortunately, while doing so he glimpsed his newfound friend's ending. Tears begin to roll down his face as he kept the bad news exclusive.

"Before we go any further, let's wait for Johan," requested Hector.

Boldly yet saddened Miguel informs the others, "He's not coming . . . the giant devil killed him; I saw it with my own eyes."

Flabbergasted the group stood as Dimitrius attempts to soothes the lad with comforting words, "Its okay mi amigo, Johan served his purpose as God intended; without him we could not have made it out of there alive. His total existence was to protect and serve us in our fight for God. So you see we all serve a purpose, only mighty Johan could've gotten us safely through; he's a fallen soldier that will never be forgotten."

With humbled spirits, once again they prayed for their loss. While doing so they are unexpectedly rudely interrupted by a grand entrance no other could've conjured. A raging whistle blows as bells ring loudly; in come assisted sounds of self manufactured theme music from Grace Jones: Pull up to the Bumper. Cheer and laughter spry while Sebastian arrives in a vehicle fully stocked with blessed hardware. A welcomed entrevue indeed; for they thought him be dead.

"Pull up to my bumper, baby. In your long black limousine," he sang as everyone is elated to see their friend,

"Oh my god!—Welcome back!—Good to see you!—Glad you can make it!" they all said.

"Ahh, so much love! I missed ya'll too," he replied as tears of joy began to roll down his face.

"What took you so long? What happened?" Dimitrius and Xavier asked.

"Give him a minute; don't you see he's all choked up," Sarah compassionately defends.

Thoughtlessly they ease up per her request. Willfully Sebastian accommodates them as a brand new patriot would, "Belial is in some kind of cocoon morphing into something else. His consciousness tried to consume me as if I were an ingredient to a recipe. I barely escaped because I was caught in a loop until I spoke the wonderful name of Jesus. It was like Hell released me and spit me out of that drama like mucus."

"That's exactly what is going on, **Satan and Hell are becoming one**; and he needs Death to complete the ritual; and if that happens . . . ." Mathyus tries to explain as Lilith completes his sentence providing the crucial factor.

"Then Hell on Earth and the Underworld would be one in the same."

"Then the demons will be at full throttle; and mankind would end as we know it." Mathyus concluded.

Realizing that their mission has just become more complex; the fire inside of their hearts begins to smolder due to added weigh as their significance become clearer.

"We mustn't fail," said Rashida.

Dimitrius replied with valor, "Failure is not an option!"

"That's my boy," said Mathyus.

Then Sarah says, "No, That's my man."

"Get it together people, now move out!" Rashida belted as 33.3% of what's left of the heroic army march to keep its date with the Devil.

Chapter Twenty Two

(7)

In the Now: The Material World

As Hell becomes Satan; and Satan begets' the same; the Great Tribulation manifests itself while the Abomination of Desolation teeter totters the scale of balance, forging a way to bring forth the Antichrist into the Material World. Prophetic predictions come to fruition when 7 Cataclysmic events par the course to a New World Order as Church and Government become one in the same.

"7? What about 7, and why?" you may ask.

Well let me show you substance within this great number, and how it has impacted our lives.

The Human body is made up of 7 sections: 1 Head, 2 Arms, 2 Legs, 1 Torso and a Spirit that guides you; equaling 7. Here's more as it pertains to our being: The Holy Bible speaks of The 7 Signs, 7 Seals, 7 Trumpets, and the 7 Deadly Sins: Lust, Greed, Gluttony, Sloth, Wrath, Envy, and Pride. Let's not forget created by man the 7 Heavenly Virtues: Chastity, temperance, charity, diligence, patience, kindness, and humility. God created Heaven and Earth in 6 days; and on the 7th He rested (The Sabbath), there are 7 Continents on which we live, there are 7 Seas, and 7 Original Wonders of the World, 7 Days in a week, 7 notes on a musical scale, there are 7 colors of the rainbow,

7 is "neutral" on the pH scale; pure water has a pH of 7, we human mammals have 7 layers of skin and, let us not forget Snow White and the 7 Dwarfs, James Bond: Agent 007 and The Magnificent 7 starring Yul Brenner and his ultimate supporting cast, the cute Dragon Lady in the 'Game of Thrones' when its all said and done will reclaim 7 Kingdoms. In the beginning of this story Dimitrius and crew started out as 7. When I was growing up in Brooklyn, NY as a young teen, my peers and I played a game called '7 Minutes in Heaven' with the opposite sex; needless to say a game of which I hope and pray my daughters have not and will not play. Psychologically, after 7 years of marriage there's an itch that must be scratched which is warranted by the unfaithful.

On a serious note, the number 7 actually signifies God's Divine Perfection or Conclusion gifted to us as our humanity seemed to glorify things of less importance i.e. power, control, and greed. In order to negate the efforts to exalt evil; we were fearfully and wonderfully made to serve God's purpose; which is to worship him, praise him and to fellowship with each other to celebrate; as for what we have in common by sharing thanksgiving with one another. Last but not least the 7 last words spoken by Jesus which are actually phrases.

1. **(Luke 23:34)** *Father, forgive them, for they do not know what they do.*
2. **(Luke 23:43) Truly,** *I say to you today, you will be with me in paradise.*
3. **(John 19:26-27)** *Woman, behold your son. Behold your mother.*
4. **(Matthew 27:46), (Mark 15:34)** *My God, My God, why have you forsaken me?*
5. **(John 19:28)** *I thirst.*
6. **(John 19:29-30)** *It is finished.*
7. **(Luke 23:46)** *Father, into your hands I commit my spirit.*

(Psalms 139:14) *I will praise thee; for I am fearfully and wonderfully made: marvelous are thy works; and that my soul knows very well.*

(Revelation 7: 11-12) *And all the angels stood round about the throne, and about the elders and the 4 beasts, and fell before the throne on their faces, and worshipped God. 12. Saying, Amen: Blessing, and glory, and wisdom, and thanksgiving, and honor, and power, and might. Be unto God forever and ever. Amen.*

Infomercial #7

Without discipline and loyalty to give the Lord his honor and praise, the spirit man within will be deprived. Depravity of the spirit is due to our compromise when presented with temptation. In order to stand firm against our own foolish negotiation, we must set God's Word as the standard for how we live our lives when managing our conduct. If you start your day with the His Word and prayer, He will guide your way and protect you. This action is referred to as 'Putting on your armor,' Then when the Holy Spirit gives a warning, obey it, because giving consideration to temptation opens a door for Satan and his clout. Remember **Proverbs 24:16**, *a righteous man will fall 7 times, he will rise again, but the wicked stumble into calamity.* What this means is that no matter how many times you make mistakes or sin, God will forgive you as long as you keep trying and stay faithful to Him. This statement does not give you a pass to be a bad ass upon your death bed, and then and only then you ask for forgiveness, because you think it's the right thing to do. Surely it can be if you are sincere; in which He knows your true heart. God is watching!

Chapter Twenty Three

(The Chase)

Gabriel In Route to Washington DC

Unaware that a merciless posse is on their trail; Gabriel and crew move forward without fear; for they know that God is on their side. As they travel I-95 South, for the usage of this magnificent highway and byway; benefactors are corralled and boundary-ed by conventional traffic lanes. As socialism mandate, taxes are levied as frequent patrons must stop to pay commerce listed as tolls, of which seem to be highly exaggerated by eastern states utilized to financially milk consumers as they go. To expedite Gabriel's travel, the van is conveniently registered with the EZ Pass system; but for some strange reason, amber lights flash stating that the failsafe composition is down; which compel thousands of travelers to pay cash forced by hand. While approaching the Maryland congested toll booth they notice that the cash lanes are also out of order causing a major pile up. Negative attitudes begin to arise as frustration weighs heavy on selfish impatient commuters; in addition to road rage revving its tempered engine. Aggressive horns toot to voice insurgence, while safety is no longer taken into consideration.

"Once again it looks as though evil has manifested to stifle routine conditions; by hampering safe travel; thanks to the Clout of Grim.

Diligently, they exercise their mayhem on faithless souls who have not yet found comfort and humility in the Son of God—aka—the Son of Man. Our humanity is tested against one another daily by God and Satan, both vying for our greatest treasure; our Souls. But the choice is yours as to who will gain favor. Do we give in to the moment as it may dictate a questionable outcome, a temporary fix or tangible gratification; or do we exercise our faith by demonstrating our obedience to God? And by putting our trust in Him to guide us to make better decisions?" Gabriel poses several questions to his cohorts.

Moon replied, "Our ignorance is merely a result of our laziness, rather than be inquisitive about religion people prefer to ignore it; as it surely impacts their lives due to the loss of its absence."

"This is true, not to take a stab at you my brother," says Shabazz as he directs his statement toward Grant. "People are disenchanted as they peg us as hypocrites. Pastor Grant's lack of faith gives them the ammunition to deny what we as discipline men practice daily; it's due to this kind attitude which shines bright to them because it is what they are use to seeing; and when it comes from us as a result; they lose hope and may not consider having faith at all."

"You know you're right, I have been short on the faith thing because of dealing with the supernatural, not due to lack of believing in God. My humanity reveals my weakness as my spirituality gives me my strength that allows me to hold on. The people of my community needed someone to plant seeds that guided them to Christ and me being a hustler from them streets, to see me make a 360 to become a better man, and set a positive example by providing hope, obliged me to be a self ordained preacher. So now you know the truth. I never went to theology school; I learned everything from prison ministry," confessed Grant.

The judgmental look on the group's faces appeared astonished for a quick second then tenderness filled their hearts and together they all said in unison, "To God be the glory, Amen."

"I knew it, just couldn't put my finger on it, but that's alright. God choose you for this mission; not man," said Shabazz.

Gabriel smiled which gave gesture to acceptance and a nod for welcomed approval.

"I applaud you for your initiative," said Moon while Sophia pats him on his back with a 'That-A-Boy.'

"Somebody had to do something! My people were killing themselves because they lacked spirituality and did not know God. I had to handle my business the best way I saw fit." Grant confessed.

Gabriel concurred, "You did what was necessary; and God delivered you. Well done my friend."

While kudos is given, behind them along line of cars continue to rant outrage. Suddenly, a Tractor Trailer begin to barrel its way forward at a high rate of speed muscling puny vehicle aside as if it were wiping water off a windshield.

Crashed sounds of bent metal and broking glass burst as automobiles make contact with the brazen iron horse destroying everything in its path.

"What the . . . . ?" said them all as the monster truck aggressively disrespects all in its path.

Noticing par the course of the big bad truck of which seemed to be heading straight for them, Gabriel and company contemplated their hasty move.

"We must get out of the vehicle now," suggested Sophia.

"But what about the Arc?" Gabriel said.

Moon added, "The Arc is no good to us if we're dead!"

"He's right we'll be killed if we stay in here," Shabazz agreed.

"Now, where is your faith? Summon the Angels to take the Arc and let's scram," said Grant.

As his words were spoken in came blinding light beholding the Angelic; securing them by flexing their wings which barricaded them upon impact. Being magical and majestic, possessing the ability to halt time; and then fast forward it to gain the advantage; clueless to the naked eye; those who bared witness as commuters saw a collision that actually gave the impression of an illusion. Only by the Grace of God the Angelic manipulated the collision seven seconds which allowed enough time for the van to maneuver to the opposite side of the toll booth out of harms way. Granted the oblivious driver eyes flickered with burning flames proclaimed success; as he thought he'd completed his mission until he saw the damn van safely drive away.

"What just happened?" Sophia asked.

Gabriel replied, "The Angels intervened."

Grant uttered "I would've been more impressed if they just zapped us to DC . . . I guess that's asking too much, but I am grateful."

"Amen to that my brutha," said Shabazz.

Now filled with vehicular vengeance, the mad driver punched down the gas pedal in hot pursuit causing a car to bust through the toll booth; killing the poor helpless soul inside while creating an explosion. Through the wreckage it raged as its horn sounded out with a terrifying roar. After being saved by Heaven as quickly as they showed up, quickly they vanished. Realizing that the menacing pursuit was still afoot, quickly Grant puts the pedal to the metal to haul ass.

"Oh shucks, we're outta here!"

Spin-outs burn rubber as screeched tires grasps the ground for traction.

"Don't worry folks I got this, back in the day I was known as the Driver, because I was the best getaway man in Mob City," boasted Grant.

Shabazz says, "Well that's a blessing in disguise; do your thing beloved."

Keeping it street, Grant hits him off with modern day colloquialism, "Fo' sho, ya-hurd."

"What was that?" Gabriel inquired.

Sophia suggests, "Don't worry; it was nothing."

In the meantime the demon truck is gaining ground due to the van only reaching a maximum speed limit of 85 miles per hour.

"He's gaining on us," yelled Sophia as Satan's rep's eyes burn with fury and vehicles between them bashed and sprawled all over the highway behind them.

Skillfully Grant begins to bob & weave the vehicle between traffic while receiving vulgarities from road raged addicts; who now find themselves victim to something worse; a menacing 18 wheeler reckless speed demon. Due to the slippery side stepping Grant has complicated, the Clout of Grim unify their efforts by indulging other members casted along the roadways to prevent their enemy from exiting at an off ramp. Hearing their cry, the motorcycle gang called Hell Riders ride to intercept the Holy one's progress.

"Get off at the next exit!" Sophia suggested.

As their vehicle pulls into the slow lane, hale fires of bullets riddle the passenger side preventing them from entering the ramp.

"There are more of them on our tail, we can't get off. We're going to have to ride this out. It's a good thing we have enough gas," Moon said as more bullets riddle the rear door shattering the glass.

On each side of the van; motorcycle marauders aim their illegal weapons toward the front of the vehicle. Noticing the sabotage; and utilizing his common sense in lieu of experience while escaping cops and robbers; Grant smashes the van into the cyclist on both sides causing them to lose control and to meet their maker upon the guard rails. Not dumb enough to make the same mistake, two more riders sped up pulling in front of them and began shooting at the windshield. Needless to say that everyone ducked the incoming as it explodes the glass. Afterward, one of the cyclists courageously stands on the seat of his bike and jumps on the hood of the van; attempting to climb in the absent window as his bike crashes and explodes into a steel grate. Quickly Moon jumps out of his seat with a flying kick knocking the stooge off the hood landing him under the modern day mechanical chariot. As for the other rider, he begins to shoot at the tires but misses; due to their close proximity which becomes nearer as Grant decides to run him over. CRUNCH! Frantic as they appeared surprisingly Grant maintains his composure. Staying in full control as his street roots took over his savoir-faire.

Gabriel says, "I don't know how much more of this we can take."

"There's a rest area two miles ahead; Damn it! There's construction there as well," Grant informed.

Unexpectedly, a bunch of pitter-patter rains down, *'Rat-ta-tat-tat!'* then two bludgeon sounds thumps the roof while passing the overpass. Ardently a dynamic duo from the MC gang contributes to the hot pursuit by jumping off the miniature stone bridge that extended across the freeway; amazingly as well as accurately timing their descent flawless. One of the bikers stands tall wielding a machete held by both hands cocked over his head as if he were going to drive it thru a vampire's chest and the other, unloading bullets from his assault rifle that riddled the top of the vehicle on the way down which softens the metal shell. 'What the hell is that?' is the question as lead rain drops fall; in addition to a razor sharp piece of steel piercing the metal hull, slicing Grant's shoulder, resulting in a gash that may require a stitch or four but, nothing more?

"AHH shit!" he cried as he slammed the brakes.

Anchored by his blade gouged into the roof, still one adversary remains intact, but this sudden move, or should I say lack of movement, causes the rifle man to be tossed through the air landing directly in front of them. As Grant and goon lay eyes on each other; a nonverbal message was understood by both, 'Kill or be killed.' Simultaneously the bad man eyes flicker, unfortunately signaling Grant to punch the gas which causes him to be tagged as a hit and run offender when he mowed the punk down and continued to proceed without remorse.

"Can somebody do something about that fool on the roof," yelled Grant.

Quickly Moon snatches the covering off of the Arc and rips it in half. Then he wraps the ends around each of his hands forming mitts. Still dedicated to execute his mission, the bladed man vigorously begins to hack away at the roof, sporadically submerging his blade harpooning for the catch of the day; Gabriel. Concentrating on various variables pertaining to the cut man's thrust depth and speed; Master Moon times his counter action just right. As the sucker on the roof jabs his blade into the top, Moon grabs and snaps it in one motion during his staled retraction. Now realizing he's without his primary weapon, the stooge then results to whip out his hand gun, but before he could act on that impulse, he was bombarded with a combination of kicks, hits and ass whips which leave his body pummeled and his mind humbled with the thoughts of retirement. Expeditiously the master got back into the vehicle, all awhile Gabriel and company are impressed with Moon's fighting skills, especially Grant.

"You's a bad man, you're on that Monkey Hustle tip; you look and act like you can't fight, but in reality you'll bang a joker up."

"Very impressive Master Moon," complimented Gabriel.

Onward they go, moving cautiously down the highway until they come to a traffic flow from three lanes reduced to one.

Still the speed demon continued his pursuit, disregarding the hampered lane as it barreled its way thru; causing a pile up of which stifled his progress to a complete failure. Realizing that he's a few miles behind his enemy, he jumps out of the truck and continues on foot with a double barreled shot gun cocked and loaded. Committed to his aid and dedicated to their cause members of the MC crew also continue the hunt as they bob & weave, in & out of the snail moving traffic flow.

"We are at a stand still and those goons are still after us; we need to get out of this truck and hightail it out of here before it's too late," said Sophia.

Gabriel's response, "I think you're right; we need to move."

Together they all disperse, abandoning their only means of transportation, carrying the Arc; and now fully exposed for the whole world to see. Due to the Arc being of a product of divinity and used as God's hotline to speak to Moses, the infectious radiance illuminated, humbly infecting all who laid eyes on it. To gaze upon the Arc released what was fine in all men, whether bad or good. The trials and tribulations were no longer a concern as temptation took a back seat to its toxic oppression. For those who did not know God; now wanted to be close to God; God saw this and was pleased. So He sent down an anointing to save all who wished to be **Born Again** in the blessed name of Jesus. **(Mark 16:16)** *He that believeth and is baptized shall be saved; but he that believeth not shall be damned.* As Gabriel and company walked to the rest stop, irritated commuters had become pleasant; and began to abandon their vehicles to join them on their march to safety. Once they reached the rest stop, over 200 people gather around them at a duck pond that was untouched by man; due to a conservation act that demanded respect. Overwhelmed with the wondrous feeling from the Holy Spirit, Gabriel and clergy began to exercise their theological prowess on the people as God has given them the right too. Splish—Splash, water cleansed as submerging commenced until all in attendance were new in their hearts. Now surrounded by a newfound congregation, the wicked that dared followed aborted their mission. A loud chant proclaiming **'PROTECT THE RIGHTEOUS'** cried out as evil witnessed their deliverance when; saved souls found their salvation. So they continued to drive by with their tails tucked and brows drenched with sweat due to having to explain their failure to El Jefe: Wrath, who does not take failure lightly.

Humbled, the people became as a collection plate is passed around without asking.

"Blessed is he that asks for no favor, but appreciate the goodness that's shared in their hearts," said Gabriel to his fellow clergy.

Master Moon says, "Through us God has done a great thing today."

"God is good," said Grant.

All at once they replied, "All the time."

"Our mission here is done, we must be on our way," suggested Gabriel.

Noticing that their truck was in no condition for travel, the new saints had prayed to God for traveling mercies and in an instant, lo and behold a State Trooper pulled up with *the Glow of Love* surrounding him; which was oh so familiar to Gabriel and his men, not yet the woman.

"Come!" said the Angelic Trooper.

Together they exited and waved goodbye while lights flashed as far as any eye can see.

"How's your shoulder?" Sophia asked Grant who fell asleep once he knew that they were safe.

Feeling fatigue from all of the excitement she decides to join Grant in his slumber; so she says goodnight to all, only to realize that they have beating her to the punch.

Chapter Twenty Four

(The Siege)

(Simultaneously in Hell)

Now realizing the diabolical master plan Hell has conjured; Dimitrius decides to keep Sebastian closely guarded due to his significance, "Sebastian, get in the middle of the platoon, we can't take any chances. Platoon! Guard him with your life; that's an order."

Although reduced in numbers due to an error from their Commander; obeying his command they remain disciplined to the cause. So they marched until they came to a gorge that spelled trouble. Dimitrius notices the dubious terrain and privy not to fall victim to an ambush, silently with a combination of waves of his hand, gestures are given that signaled Sanchez and Porter to scout the narrow entrance from above to get a better assessment, but only go halfway. Midway up they scaled the walls on both sides, not reaching the top as the coast seemed cleared; which raised suspicion.

"I smell a rat," Sanchez said aloud.

Porter replied, "I know, something ain't right."

Back down they went, but on the way down shots are fired from above; barely missing them as they jump down escaping the onslaught.

"Cover them!" commanded Rashida, initiating an insurgence to counter the slaughter.

Returned fire allotted Dimitrius and Rashida enough time to run and grab Bazookas' from the jeep. At the same time Hector and Lucy fired RPG's at the base of each wall, causing them to collapse. Once the mountainous walls crumbled, they too fired their Bazookas for GP.

"I had a hunch we were going to be ambushed, it was too quiet," said Dimitrius.

Not expecting them to possess the firepower they had, the awaited ambushers become aggravated.

"Why that sneaky Son of a Bitch, how did he know we were waiting?" Daxx pondered out loud.

Sgt. Poole says, "He wrote the book on this shit, remember?"

The look on Daxx's face grimaced as he is forced to use Plan B.

Dimitrius on the other hand boastfully barks orders as he is confident, "Okay, listen up, follow my orders and ask questions later . . . . Trust me! I was chosen because this is what I do. We are out numbered, so the logical thing to do is to do the unexpected. They expect us to retreat, but we're going to shove it down their throats. Bazookas' and RPG's blast off as we go. Hold off on using your bullets unless you have too. Keep the jeep in between us, so we can access it at all times, Mathyus stay in the jeep. If there's a gorge then there's a valley; we'll take the higher ground and wind up on top of them. Also, when you see the ridgeline, head toward it. If it comes down to hand to hand, Rashida, your men are proficient in Martial Arts. Xavier, protect Sebastian, I'll need my enforcer to handle his business; and ladies stay by my side. Stay together! Last but not least, pray to God for deliverance. NOW MOVE OUT!"

Abruptly Mathyus yells out, "What about the demons and their fireballs? I'm sure there's more."

Dimitrius responds, "We'll fight fire with fire, when they charge up we'll use Heat Seekers. That's why we're gonna use artillery instead of bullets, they'll do more damage . . . . Now If it's alright with you; can we move?"

With a smile on his face and at the top of his lungs Mathyus yells, "IN THE NAME OF JESUS, MOVE OUT!"

Expeditiously they went with a sense of urgency forging their way boldly as the opposition can't believe their eyes.

"What the fuck? They're charging," Poole bitched.

Daxx concludes, "Good, they'll be heading for the ridgeline to gain higher ground, but that's what he thinks. There's no place to go; we'll trap his ass. I've got your punk ass now!"

"Are you sure?" Poole inquired.

Daxx glances at him with a menacing look sprawled all over his face and says, "One more time Poole, one more time! Come on; we'll head him off at the pass."

Off they go to who the hell knows. Courageously the group moved with vigor with Sebastian still as nervous as he wants to be, he grabs hold of Xavier's shirt tail.

"Dude, let me go, don't worry I got you. Why do you think he assigned me to you? Beat downs is what I do, so relax and keep your hands off the merchandise."

"Whatever you say my good man, whatever you say." Sebastian complied.

As they begin their battle trek, Dimitrius assesses the dynamics of the valley and the road to higher ground. It appears to begin behind some kind of structure ahead. Chased by Hate Mongers and haters on foot, primitively throwing spears and shooting arrows, mixing gunfire and whatever to include the kitchen sink, still together they plowed through the rubble, throwing the opposition off guard, blasting ballistics and bombs until they arrived at the dilapidated ruins.

"What is this place?" Dimitrius asked before entering the unknown.

Sarah revealed, "These are the Aztec ruins, a lot of people died here; they were considered some of the cruelest people the world has ever seen; fitting that this would be here."

Forcing them to enter the horrid structure; demon kamikaze dive bombers release fireballs to urge them on. Countering the sinister attack they are met by an upward mine-field strategically structured to blow them to kingdom come. Due to their heartless sacrifice, successfully their mission was not impossible as Dimitrius and crew take refuge in the wrecked complex. So, up the steep staircase they went, then into the dark temple.

"Rashida, set up the seekers on the perimeter. Sanchez, you handle the sharpshooters. Porter, come with me. The rest of you start making your way to the other side and stay together! Hector, Lucy and Xavier take a squad of Rashida's men with you and guard the less able. I'll feel better knowing that my people are protected in case some of those bastards slip by; and if they do I'm sure you'll have something for them."

"Yes sir," said the willful team as they respectfully tended to their business as directed.

"Go with God," said Sarah as she grabs Dimitrius' hand and kisses it expressing her concern.

Pleasantly he reciprocates with a warm caress to her face and a soft kiss and says, "Star of the show, remember?"

She then smiles letting him know that she has faith in him. Once that was confirmed, together Dimitrius and Porter jumped in the jeep and proceeded thru what appeared to be a court yard lined with Totem poles. On the walls there are thousands of illustrations depicting sacrificial ceremonies.

While driving, Porter's interest is drawn to the decorative wall covering in which he wisely concludes, "The writing's on the wall Sarge, this ain't just an ancient ruin; it's a temple, and we're in the sacrificial chamber. Like the lady said a lot of people died here."

"Well let's get thru this without dying, shall we?" suggested Dimitrius.

So they continued to drive until they came to an exit. Dimitrius then vacates the vehicle to verify that the escape route led to the ridgeline. Once that was established swiftly they begin to rig up some explosives to booby-trap their escape route.

In the meantime the lesser continued on foot as instructed until they came to the tombstone totem poles. Thorn begins to growl as the hairs on his neck rises.

"Halt!" Hector yelled.

Urging Xavier to ask, "Why are we stopping?"

Mathyus adds, "There's something out there that's got Thorn on edge."

Filled with fear and having knowledge of their whereabouts, Hector begins to show signs of anxiety. Lucy also expresses her discomfort as temple lanterns ignite on their own.

"What's going on?" Xavier inquires with Sebastian clinging close to him.

Suddenly the temperature drops as the ground begin to quake. Instantly it stops as sheiks howl and the totem poles begin to unravel. The look on Hector and Lucy's faces dictate surrender in their eyes, but one look at Miguel undoubtedly brought courage back to their souls.

"They're alive; the poles are moving!" Sarah screamed.

Limb by limb detach as Pygmy bodies start to take shape with hatchets and cleavers clutched in their hands indicating that these little fellows were Head Hunters; with a cannibalistic appetite to boot.

"Run! Stay together," said Hector.

At the same time Rashida's men open fire, chopping them down, but to no avail they kept up their pursuit as their bodies reform using interchangeable parts. With precision, cutlery is thrown, slicing and dicing the soldiers' heads off while boomeranged back to its rightful masters hands. Headless bodies roll on the floor confirming their death.

"Oh my god, they're all dead and they're still coming; the bullets don't work," Sarah cried.

Miguel, grown in his mind, suggests, "They're made out of wood and wood burns."

Fast and furiously, the Hunters over run and by pass them; then tauntingly surrounds them. Xavier big bad and ballsy as ever, steps out of the crowd and with verve begins his beat-down with Thorn at his side barking and chewing at the wooden people. Terrified by the ominous chant conducted by the undying advantage, all seemed doomed.

"Where's soldier boy when you need him?" Sebastian muttered when suddenly the raved up jeep skids its way on to the scene with flamethrowers flaming.

"GET DOWN!" He shouted.

As Dimitrius and Porter administer the killer flame, although burning the enemy to a crisp; it just so happened Xavier is singed as well.

"Damn it man, you burned my Fro, Bro!"

Aztec Totem Poles by Christopher Romo

"Sorry dude, got a bit reckless wit it," said Dimitrius.

Porter says, "Sarge we gotta get the people outta here."

"You're right, take them to the exit and wait, don't enter until I get there . . . . Xavier and Sebastian stay with me," Dimitrius barked.

Lilith says, "We shouldn't separate, we should stay together."

Porter says, "Don't you worry your pretty little head, I've got you covered . . . Trust me."

Gallantly they moved in opposite directions. Porter and group on foot as Dimitrius' trio drive the jeep toward the entrance.

"What are we doing?" Xavier asked.

Dimitrius replied, "We have to gather Rashida and her men and at the same time set a trap in motion to finally get rid of them bastards."

"Cool I'm down," said Xavier.

Sebastian, not liking what he has heard, says, "Ahh, am I being used as bait?"

Together Dimitrius and Xavier looks at him with raised eyebrows.

"That's what I was afraid of," he confesses.

Quickly with his hand he begins to illustrate the Holy Trinity: in the name of the Father, the Son and the Holy Spirit across his body. As they approach the temple doors Rashida and one of her men are heavily defending it like he knew they would. Urgently, the jeep pulls up to the commotion allowing Dimitrius and his boys to admire the fiasco.

"That's right! Hold it down Sistah girl; that's what I'm talking 'bout," flattered Xavier.

Gallantly she replied, "It's about time ya'll showed up, we're running out of bullets."

"Keep shooting! I've got a plan, when we get back cease fire and hurry up and get out of the way; listen for our signal," said Dimitrius as he circled about the perimeter informing what's left of the Militia and Sanchez to vacate their positions and head to the back exit.

Upon doing so, Satan's minions slithered within the unattended cracks and swirled about the tattered property as if they were ghost looking for something to haunt or scare.

"Here we are you Sons of bitches. You're looking for Death? Here he is! Now come and get him," shouted Dimitrius.

Now that they've got their attention, immediately they race back to Rashida's position. Hooping and Hollering, horn beeping and yelling, followed by screeches and howls from the angry phantoms in pursuit of what was important to Hell itself. Continued firing at the Mongers knocking on the door; Rashida and friend hear the noise and wisely determine that that was the signal.

"That must be it, move!"

Without pause they did as they were instructed. Noticing the cease fire, the Mongers bust the doors wide open and carelessly enter. Simultaneously the revved up jeep traveling about 75 in a 25 mile an hour zone is fearlessly followed by the high flying ghouls, gaining ground and about to pounce.

At the same time Dimitrius and Xavier jump out of the vehicle leaving Sebastian unattended and still seated and says, "You know what to do?"

"I think so," he says apprehensively.

At the point of collision and audience gathering, the jeep explodes while Sebastian does a perfectly timed disappearing act reuniting him with his peers at the rear. KA-BOOM! All that were in pursuit are destroyed while 4 + 1 is safe and sound.

"That shit was all that; if I must say so myself," said Rashida.

Xavier boasted, "It was better than that; that shit was groovy baby."

"I hope Daxx and his misfits were amongst the dead," Dimitrius ponders.

And the Soldier says, "That's too bad the guy in the jeep didn't make it. Together the others laughed as they begin to quick time back to reunite with their friends.

Patiently waiting at the rear exit is Porter and company pondering their next move.

"What was that?" Miguel said as the explosion of the jeep is echoed throughout the dreadful temple.

Porter explained, "Sounds like an explosion."

"What are we going to do if they don't make it?" Hector asked all who were listening.

Mathyus says, "Have faith son; they'll be here in due time."

"They'll make it; they always do; you don't know the sergeant like I do," encouraged Porter.

Lucy adds, "But what if they don't? We can't just stay here."

During their contemplation they hear pitter—patter of feet heading their way.

"STOP! Who goes there?" demanded Porter.

While trotting Sanchez responds, "It's us Papí!"

Partially reunited, anxiety begins to rear its ugly head.

"You heard that explosion?" Porter asked.

Sanchez replied, "Heard it? We felt it . . . Not too many people could've survived that blast."

Hector suggests, "Okay, I say we get the hell out of here while we can."

"We're going to wait," yelled Sebastian as he reunites with them at a blink of an eye.

Sarah rushes him with welcomed arms.

"Are you alright? Where are the rest of them?"

He looks her in her eyes and says, "I don't know."

Hector arrogantly says, "We'll give them 10 minutes, if they're not back, my family and I are leaving."

"That's your choice, the rest of us are going to wait . . . all agree?" Mathyus questioned.

Miguel begs to differ with La Familia.

"Papí, I'm going to wait. You and Mama' should too."

"You're coming with us mi hijo," Hector said with raged filled eyes and veins popping out of his brow. Violently, he walks up to Miguel and slaps him across his face.

"You do what you are told; you're coming with us."

Mathyus, who has been holding down Miguel as a fatherly figure, jumps at Hector only to be shoved to the ground. Sarah and Lilith help him up to get on his feet.

Sarah belittles by him saying, "You should be ashamed of yourself; beating children and old men."

Aggressively he heads toward her as if he were going to attack her, when abruptly Lilith jumps on his back.

"Bitch, get off me," he said as he shrugs her off to the ground as well.

One of the soldiers then grabs him in a yolk around his neck from behind and begins to squeeze the life out of him until he turns blue. Fearful for her husband's life Lucy shoots the soldier in his back. Sanchez then reciprocates by belting her over the back of her head with the butt of his weapon.

"Oh my God!" Sarah shouted.

Sebastian cried, "What the hell just happened?!"

They were appalled.

Now pissed off that one of their comrades is dead due to a domestic squabble; the band of mad Militia demands retribution.

"Eye for an eye, a tooth for a tooth, give them to us . . . Pay back's a bitch."

Being morally and spiritually sound Mathyus tries to reason with the vengeful men.

"I'm afraid you're using the scripture to justify lynching. Read the rest of it; then you'll know what it truly means. **(Matthew 5: 38-48)** We can't let you do that son, we need to forgive them and let them go their merry way . . . That's how God would've wanted it."

> **(Luke 6: 36-37)** [36] *Be ye therefore merciful, as your Father also is merciful.* [37]*Judge not, and ye shall not be judged: condemn not, and ye shall not be condemned: forgive, and ye shall be forgiven.*

"We hear you pops, but that ain't happening . . . You forgive them! We'll never forget," said the uncommon valor.

Rebelliously the pseudo army draws their weapons on the lesser as they force demands. Now finding themselves in a precarious situation; they are forced to do what Hector wanted from the get go. Porter and Sanchez each pull the pins from a grenade in response to the fickle movement while the others move into the gully.

Porter yells, "Watch out for the booby traps . . . You got this dude? I need to guide them thru; they'll never make it."

Sanchez nods his head as Porter carefully hand him his grenade. Swiftly he moved to lead them thru the hazardous maze of doom. Slowly Sanchez followed by backing up stepping in the footprints Porter left along his departure. Eager to let 1 go, the pissed off soldiers begin to shoot forcing Sanchez to toss the grenades during his retreat. *Rat-ta-tat-tat-buck-buck-buck!* Bullets riddled him; as the grenades are dropped; then blast off causing the booby traps to explode. BOOM-BOOM-BOOM! The entrance rocks fall, crumbling below, ricocheting stones given the consistency of big bullets smashing all and everything within a quarter mile radius to include the newly found nemeses.

A tremendous smoke cloud develops due to the debris as could be seen by Dimitrius and crew from a distance.

"What was that?" Rashida said.

"Oh no!" Dimitrius hollered; as he picks up his pace. Upon their arrival bodies are sprawled all over.

"What happened here? All of my men are dead," said Rashida rummaging through her lifeless soldiers.

Xavier says, "Where are our people?"

Knowing that the booby traps were set, Dimitrius' only thought is that they had set them off.

"Lord, please noooooo!"

God is Watching!

Chapter Twenty Five

(Against All Odds)

HELL

Searching through the rubble no bodies, limbs or signs of their friends are found. Only their weapons lay waste to ground. Dimitrius begins to dig and toss boulders, Xavier and the lone soldier joined in all teary eyed and emotional. Together they dug until they were able to make a hole only to find Daxx and his ex-team pointing their weapons directly in their faces. POW! A shot is fired striking the lone soldier right between the eyes at close range. Alone he is not, for he is now dead with his friends forever lounging on the battlefield.

"Surprise ass hole! I told you I would see you soon," said Daxx feeling cocky as ever.

Dimitrius yelled, "What did you do to my people?"

"Where are they?" Xavier included.

"They're dead, and you'll be joining them in just a few minutes, but first I want to see you down on your knees begging me for your lives," answered Daxx.

Chuckles sound stemming from the rest of Daxx's men. Based on their awkward position Dimitrius realizes that he and his team are at a disadvantage, so he presents an offer that Daxx and his goons could not refuse.

"You know I always pegged you guys to be punks. Put down your weapons and let's do the mano y mano thang. It'll be the three of us against four of you. Besides, one of us is a woman, and if you beat us, have your way with her."

Comprehending what he is trying to establish and knowing that these type of guys think with their little head as oppose to their bigger Rashida says, "I wish they would! I could use some good loving from some real men right about now . . . After all I'm a lover and a fighter. If you want some, come and get it."

In order to make the offer encouraging, she pulls down her pants and turns around to reveal her sweet ass; which tantalized them even more. Catching a glimpse at her fatty, all men from both parties at once say, "DAMN!" Unable to turn down an opportunity for a lay, like fools, they fall for Dimitrius' ploy.

"Stand back," Poole demanded as he and his cohorts blast the rest of the stones minimizing them to have better access to the booty.

"Weapons down! Get ready boys! After we kill these fuckers, we're gonna have some fun with the sweet ass nigger bitch," said Daxx as they all step into the imaginary arena, weaponless.

Shocked, but not amazed, Dimitrius' plan worked thanks to Rashida.

"Alright people let's do this," he said.

Xavier announced, "Finally, some fun!"

Like gladiators they pair up while Rashida stands aside. Poole and Daxx circle Dimitrius as Mayweather and Massey do the same for Xavier.

"What the hell are ya'll doing? I thought we were going to fight, not dance," said Xavier as he flinched toward them causing them to jump. Then he laughs and says, "Ha—Ha—Ha! That's what I thought, without their weapons . . . straight up bitches."

Rashida laughs at the jest causing them to make their move. While circling, Mayweather bends down and grabs a handful of dirt and throws it at Xavier eyes.

Accustomed to such sucker tactics, he closes his eyes and listens for the scuffles from their feet; and the change of wind as a person moves. As contact is made from his back and front by both enemies,

Xavier snatches one then head butts his opponent's head splitting his skull straight down the middle. Mayweather's lifeless body hits the ground like over weight luggage. One down three to go. Pissed off that his partner has met his demise, Massey whips out his bowie knife and slices across Xavier's left shoulder, then his right forearm, and then his left hand. Fortunately for Xavier; pain ain't no thang. He ignores it as if it were nothing but a scratch.

"Because you cheated, I am going to rip your fucking head off," he said as he runs toward Massey who in turn flips the big guy on his back.

"Okay, funs over," Xavier said while he gets up off the ground, brushing the dirt and dust from his clothes.

"Let's try that again nigger," boasted Massey.

In the meantime Daxx and Poole rush Dimitrius to the ground only to find themselves intertwined in a series of wrestling moves that once gained him the title of State Champion back in high school. Rashida, no longer thrilled at the senseless brawl, resorts to drastic measures. While boys will be boys continuing the scuffle, she quietly retrieves her weapon to take matters into her own hands. Ignored and stealthy she walked up to both parties to blast her adversaries with two to the back of their heads; gangster style. However for some reason her weapon is jammed. Out of the blue, a sniper's rifle is fired completing her task accordingly. One by one they go down until Xavier and the vivacious woman are left standing. As a result Daxx's bad boys are slain in an instant.

"Who did that? We had everything under control," said Xavier.

She replied, "I don't know, but I'm glad they did. We don't have time for this bullshit, we need to keep moving and hopefully, if they're still alive, find our friends."

"You're right, although dude said they were dead, there's nothing here to support that." Xavier said.

Rashida says, "Still, that doesn't explain, who shot them."

"Whoever did it must be on our side," he said.

Still Dimitrius brawls his nemesis rendering a series of bone dislocation and choke holds. While caught up in a death grip around his neck; Daxx sees his men laid wasted, while not discouraged as they were granted an honorable death in battle.

"Time to say goodbye Daxx," said Dimitrius as he lifts him above his head and pile drives him into the dirt, then yokes his neck applying pressure to compose a crunching sound followed by piercing snap.

Finally, Daxx is done. Suddenly the rocks begin to move which forces Rashida to point her weapon in the direction. Out from the rubble and rocky debris Miguel reveals himself with a smoking rifle in hand.

"Mi amigo, is that you?" Dimitrius asked.

"Sí mi amigo, It's me," he replied.

Dimitrius asked, "Do you know what happen to them?"

"My father went crazy and wanted to leave. Everyone else wanted to wait until you got back. Then things got out of hand and he hit me. A fight broke out between him and the soldiers. Mathyus wouldn't let them have him so, we went into the gully. Shots were fired, so then I hid. Then, there was an explosion and everybody disappeared."

"What do you think could've happened to them; where could they have gone?" Rashida asked.

Miguel answered, "I think they're dead."

In turn Xavier answered, "Since there is no trace of them. I think Hell pulled another rift and is holding them captive."

"I think you're right detective. Death became the prize; and now Hell has him along with our friends. That was his plan all along. By using Daxx and those creeps, we allowed him to separate and distract us from the mission, now he has us by the balls by taking our people." Dimitrius derived.

Rashida retorts, "Why that conniving Son of a Bitch!"

Together they walked into the unknown with inexplicable circumstances mounting. Once there were 113, now there are 4; or could it be possibly more . . . or none?

God is watching!

Chapter Twenty Six

(Chocolate Blue)

Meanwhile in the Material World: Washington DC

Hardships and hammy-downs plagued these streets as polished white buildings gleam and Men of Power continue to bicker over a fair way of life for us all. As the Political Party continues to private party with the Tea party; the locals continue to drop the bomb in a struggle that is constant to those of less fortune, and for those Block Boys who find themselves as joy riders on the Love boat aka Lovely which is Embalming fluid mixed with PCP, surely a high that warrants death as you literally become the walking dead. Crazy as this may seem, Lovely was the choice by popular demand until the mayor of this fare city was busted for drug addiction to Crack Cocaine. Bad things happen to bad people and sometimes good things happen to good people, thus Sin plunders its way with selfish intent; beguiling its way between both worlds feeding off each other as the Clout of Grim conduct our symphonic demise.

On a common day just like those in any other town, evil demands attention and we as weaklings give in to it for example, two under age black male youths walk into a liquor store to purchase two 40oz. of Old Gold (That's Old English in case you didn't know). The clerk asked them for ID. Viewing the transaction is the store owner who steps in and allows the boys to purchase without further question. Upon their exit, his eyes flicker a flame.

Nearby is the neighborhood park where children are playing Dodge ball. On the sideline are alternates warming up while awaiting their turn. While practicing the ball is thrown missing its target and rolls into the bushes. Eager to retrieve it is little Susie who is outgoing and truly a team player. While doing so she is confronted by a stalker who snatches her up from behind and begins to molest her on the spot while his eyes flicker a flame.

It's Friday night and they just got paid. White collar workers forge their way during rush hour anticipating a dynamite weekend of bar hopping in Georgetown. In order to 'turn it up' a notch they'll need a pool full of liquor, then they'll dive in, but that's not enough; so they call the local drug lizard to acquire some blaze. As one hand washes the other, so do bad batches and overdoses slowly creep into view. The drug dealer doesn't care, he just got paid so his eyes began to flicker a flame as he moves on toward his next victim.

Is this everyday living for the masses that seem to routinely contribute to their own demise? Or is it due to lack of opportunity or education? How about ignorance? Nevertheless, victims indeed. They're simply trying to handle the struggle on their own; never seeking God as their beliefs are in question. Never guided by Faith, but by selfishness and personal gain acquired from someone other than themselves. Whatever it may be, the lack of motivation drives them to a senseless power that merits a stingy attitude, Drug Addiction, Poverty or Prison. As Washington expands its infrastructure; urban inhabitants who once plagued these streets are forced to relocate to urban domains due to rent increase and ghetto modification; made for people who can afford to ride the gentrification. This system may backfire as urbanites are now mix and mingling with toxic people who were deprived in many ways; whose mission is to plague the fortune with a 'you better get yours because I gotta get mine' consciousness steered by immorality. To counter the onslaught of this maniacal madness is God's fortitude and love. His Grace is spreading throughout the world as people's eyes are finally opening and their Faith and understanding is growing rapidly. Worship groups and Christian cells are saving lives as backsliders and newfound saints are spiritually reborn in Jesus name. So let us wait patiently; and build on knowing that God will make a better life starting with you and me because without the *Blood of Jesus* we're dying of thirst and, don't even know it.

Gabriel & Crew in DC

Hassled no more by the merciless Clout, entering the Nation's capital seemed an easy task despite the watchful eye of Big Brother whose sight is on every corner; who had just tagged them while driving south on New York Avenue toward the Mecca.

"I've arranged a safe haven to rest, less conspicuous I may add," said Shabazz.

While cruising, Gabriel notices the monumental stately hood that is surrounded by an urban jungle that is merely mentioned or frequent by travelers. Just like Atlantic City and Killadelphia . . . . Oops, I've done it again! I meant Philadelphia. Ignored is the mundane lifestyle of its minority resident's lamenting the songs of the Have and the Have-Not's, are forced to illegally hustle to survive; as the Politicians rule by way of a bipartisanship that helm's the entire country.

"Why do they call DC Chocolate City?" Gabriel asked.

Shabazz begins to answer; when Grant interjects his reasoning, "I got this my Balailian brutha," he states as he applies pressure to his wound. He then says, "There are more Blacks per capital, per square mile that live in this great city; thus the name Chocolate was derived."

Gabriel shakes his head up and down and replies, "I see, I understand but I thought there would be more Indians due to the football team being called the Redskins."

Together they all laughed including Gabriel who didn't realize that he had jokes. The squad car then stops at the light. Gabriel watches pedestrians acquire free newspapers from an unmanned newsstand with a story headlined on the back page highlighting 'The International Gospel Fest' on the Mall this weekend. Quickly he gets out of the vehicle to obtain a copy, when he has a premonition of Wrath smiling and then laughing as if he were pleased. Immediately he jumps back into the car and shares his thoughts.

"I just experienced another vision of our demon friend; he seemed to be pleased; at all cost this must not come to fruition. As you all know, a few members that intended to join us have befallen to Satan's malicious agents. One thing is for certain; he and his followers will try to impede our mission because this is I'm afraid is the final stand, this is where we will substitute our losses and gain many; one prayer, one voice to our God in the name of Jesus. The *Unification of Christianity* is the key to all of our answers. At all cost we must not fail. Everything rides on what we accomplish here in Chocolate City. So beware of the malevolent and keep your faith."

"How soon before we arrive at our destination?" Sophia inquired.

Shabazz answers with a quip, "Walla! We're already here my lady."

Slowly the cop car pulls into the main campus of the HBCU and parks in front of the Chapel. **PAUSE!**

NOTE: At this time of the day at high noon the campus is congested due to students flowing to and from their classes in order to complete assignment deadlines, while others enjoy the Greek Life for what it is worth. Brilliantly the university sustains a ratio of 10 to 1, that's woman to men; and proudly produces the cream of the crop i.e. Doctors, Lawyers, CEO's; and top notch Professionals while maintaining its social prowess with binding cultural experiences, everlasting camaraderie laced with promiscuity to boot. Heaven on earth is this great HBCU; that's Historically Black Colleges and Universities; in case you wanted to know.

Ask me how I know? Well I should know due to my tenure 81'-86'and a semester in 92'. (I took a break to serve in the Army from 87'-91 and served in War campaigns:

Desert Storm and Desert Shield) Afterwards I went back to complete what I started. And I must admit; those were truly the greatest days of my life besides my loving wife giving birth to my children. Strong friendships and bonds that were established from day #1 are still intact 33 years later. Thankfully I belong to an elite group of positive, strong men that I can honestly say are my friends; and my brothers from another mother. (From the Class of '81. They know who they are) Yes we beat the odds as we all graduated. I'm talking bout

Kats from far and wide. I can honestly say that I've bared witness to some of the most affluent minded people the world has ever produced, to include some of the finest women that has ever walked the earth. Thank you God for the gift!

*NOW YOU MAY CONTINUE

As the ordained men and lady exit the squad car they are greeted by a clergyman of the premises.

"Welcome Gentlemen, Madame, which one of you would be Minister Shabazz?"

"That would be me, my good man; thank you for being here on such short notice," he said.

"Ahh, it's nothing; anything for an alumni; especially a righteous one . . . I hope the accommodations meet your approval?" the clergyman said as they walk into the Chapel carrying the Arc as if it were a coffin, two by two.

"We need a safe place to put this," said Grant.

Gabriel advises, "I think we should keep it in our line of sight."

"Everything looks great! Is there a resting area? It's been a long trip," Shabazz inquired.

"Why yes, it's downstairs next to the kitchen; which is fully stocked . . . Please feel free to use it as well. Minister Shabazz has taken care of everything and by the way, Brother Minister your donation is highly appreciated," said the honored Clergyman.

Gabriel again extends his gratitude, "Thank you, you don't know how helpful you really are. God sees this and I'm sure you will receive his blessing." The Clergyman wisely proclaim, "I already have, good night Gentlemen; Madame see you in the morning."

After they got situated the group takes some time out to prepare for the unexpected and enrich their spirits with food, prayer and strategy. All awhile they are being guarded by the Seraphim who stood outside the door protecting them as God ordered.

Following their trail Wrath exhumes from the dark abyss which places him in Union Station; while eager passengers hastily run to catch their scheduled train departing. He looks around and sees nothing of importance. While doing so a little boy notice and stares at him as if he resembled a character from PlayStation. Wrath observes the boy staring; the boy then sticks out his tongue at him. Wrath reciprocates the same. During this tit-for-tat, the boy's eyes widen as he begins to piss in his pants due the serpent-folk like tongue Wrath revealed. His mother becomes aware of him pee-peeing on himself; and begins to whip his ass in public. As the violent juvenile assault takes place, concerned commuters who bear witness; threaten to call DYFS for Child Abuse. Amused about the embarrassment Wrath begins to laugh out loud so that the entire city can hear his jolly. Like a trumpet his eerie voice echoed as it travel throughout the hallways finally escaping the building into the atmosphere. Sounding his alarm, he is able to kill two birds with one stone, by signaling his agents that he has arrived and warning those that feared him that their end is near.

Hearing Wrath's sinister song send chills up and down their spines, "Is that who I think it is?" Sophia asks as she moved closer to Master Moon.

"Be calm my child; that was just a mere warning; letting us know that the demon is in the city," he explained while holding her hand for comfort.

Grant blurts out, "Well if we heard him, so did the Goon squad."

"Perhaps your right, we need not worry; we have God's Blessing," said Sophia as she reminds herself of the guardians.

Gabriel suggests, "Let us now eat everyone, and afterwards rest; because tomorrow is going to be a beautiful day, a day that the Lord has made, we should be joyful and glad in it." **(Psalms 118: 24)**

A few hours pass as good food, wine, and spirits are shared amongst them. Like children they are complacent with their accommodations, as familiarity breeds a subtle welcome; so does the wellness of their hearts. Gabriel takes heed to his own words and retires after a hearty dinner prepared by Sophia. Being new to the comradeship, she is thoroughly entertained by the bond to which these men have established in such a short period of time. With a watchful eye she recognizes the fellowship that brings them strength, courage and wisdom.

Satisfied with their valor she removes herself to accompany the Angel on guard. As she opened the door gingerly he stood tall and devoted; for his presence demanded respect and caution.

"Surprisingly quiet evening," she said upon her approach.

Rudely, he ignored her while maintaining his stature.

"What's the matter, you only talk to men?" she quipped.

Still sturdy he stood as well as quiet. Suddenly a multitude of distress calls shrieked from various locations within the neighborhood. Distracted from his duty due to his oath to uphold and protect mankind, the Angel expeditiously moseys to their aid; thinking due to; and not bound by Kronos time, he can go and come back in a jiffy. Little did he know the opportunity opened the door to new discovery that was shrewdly planned? Rain drops begin to fall as lightening blaze the sky. Simultaneously, the dark void opens as Wrath and at least twenty others step out like an invading barbarian horde. Startled at his arrival, she stood in conflict, but welcomed him the same.

Proudly he stroked her face with a comforting hand and said, "You've done well and as promised, you are now an agent of my dread. Accepting her reward; she kneeled to receive her sell out."

"Foolish actions gain foolish reward" he said.

Swiftly with a swing of his axe, her head is severed from her pretty little body. Now a rolling rock on the ground, suddenly Wrath gets the urge to kick her head through some uprights located on the opposite side of the campus. Unaware of the developments just outside the front door, the men begin to seek rest as it is surely needed.

"Where's Sophia?" Grant asked.

Shabazz answers him, "She's probably sound asleep, which is what we should be doing. I'm beat."

Moon sets up a cot on the floor next to the Arc, never leaving it out of his site. In his mind this symbolic chest and company is the closes he's ever been to God; and cherishes every moment as it is a gift from Heaven. So, protecting it is the least he can do; this is not a bad idea as Wrath smashes through the front door tossing Sophia's body across the pews, landing in the Pulpit.

"Guess who's coming to dinner? Ha . . . . . !"

Immediately the Angelic arrived only to be shackled with bloody cuffs by twenty or more Clout. Occupied and now limited, the Angel is useless as he was caught off guard.

"How is this possible? How are you restraining me?" he asked.

Conveniently Wrath answers him, "Angels are bound by blood. Lucifer was once an Angel who cried tears of blood when cast out of Heaven. Wisely he kept them for a rainy day; and as you can see it's raining cats and dogs . . . . Ha . . . !"

Instantaneously the men gather themselves and converge to the Alter where the Arc lie and Moon stands in front of them in his defensive stance. Despite the danger humbly they all take a second to notice her headless body.

Grant bellowed, "Ahh, Baby Girl!"

Casually Wrath walks down the center aisle followed by more of his Clout and candidly says, "It doesn't matter who dies first; because you all must die. So I did what any gentleman would've done. Ladies first . . . Who said chivalry was dead?"

"May you rot in hell," Shabazz hollered.

Wrath retorts, "Been there, done that."

"Get Gabriel and the Arc out of here, I'll be alright. Go!" Moon commands.

"We need four people to carry it. It's too heavy," said Shabazz.

"I think now is the time we should open it," Gabriel suggested.

Expeditiously the men grabbed the Arc and proceeded to open its cover when wisely Grant reminded them of the booby traps installed.

"What about the traps?"

At same time ascending from the rafters is a member of Grim. He lands on top of the Arc, crushing the hull. Immediately the traps are triggered causing a chain reaction of poisonous gas and darts to be released into the air. Quickly Gabriel and crew exit the side entrance leaving Moon and the Arc inside.

"What about Moon and the contents?" questioned Shabazz.

In the meantime Moon, noticing the drama, leaps into the rafters escaping the deadly entrapment. Seemingly not affected is Wrath and his death squad; due to their souls having being dead already; so with a nod of his head, Wrath demands are understood by the excess Clout that stood by waiting for their next command. In hot pursuit they go. As Gabriel departs he drops the flier on the floor.

During their escape Gabriel notice the grappled Angel; who in turn notice their getaway, so the defenseless angel begun to call out to Heaven for assistance, but due to the tainted blood stains that hinder his need; all communication is temporally out of order. Five minutes later, Moon return to the floor for unfinished business. Courageously the adversaries circle each other as Wrath set forth his vengeance upon Moon due to his previous ass whipping. Moon in turn delights at the opportunity to defend God's honor, Shaolin style.

Round and round they go until frustration grabs hold of Wrath's inpatient ego. Rushing the china man proves to be a mistake as Moon counters his approach with a series of flips and dips which allows him to be untouched, also ending his volley with kicks starting from his lips down to his hips. As a result Wrath is knocked on his ass again, lying down on his back in the center isle. Annoyed beyond measure once he gathered himself, Wrath begins to snatch pews up one by one; and violently hurls them at Moon as if he were target practice. Dodging them like dodge balls Moon's stamina increases as Wrath's decreases.

"I hate that Bruce Lee shit!"

Noticing that Wrath grows weary of the standoff, quickly Moon shifts his concentration on gathering the contents of the box. Hastily he spins off smacking and slapping, kicking and whipping the goons who had recently confiscated the items. While delivering his formidable beat down he acquired all that he had hoped for; by retrieving Gods' tools, then swiftly exiting the demolished building to reunite with the righteous fugitives. Upon his departure fire is set by the unholy in an attempt to deface Holy ground. Raged and insane Wrath exit the building as well; and pick up the flier that Gabriel dropped; mercilessly he approaches the defenseless Angel.

"What do you call an Angel who has lost his wings?"

No response is given due to the fact that he is mad . . . no pun intended. Swiftly with a swing of his merciless axe; he detaches the wings from the Angels body that's bound by restraints. Then he proceeds to viciously quarter him like a chef does a chicken; shameless he stood.

"Sushi!" he boasts.

As the Angel's light diminishes piece by piece, finally a flash of blinding light bursts as it disintegrates his supported Clout. Baffled by what just happened as he now stands alone, Wrath bowed down on his knees for he knows that there was a divine intervention that took place. 'You see; even the Devil and all his demons must bow down to God.' God is watching!

Meanwhile, frantically Gabriel and crew jumped into the squad car only to realize that the tackled Angel had the key.

"Where is the key?" Grant hollered.

"Oh no! I think the Angel has it!" Shabazz said.

Gabriel remains stressed as the rest of them manage to stay focused on their escape.

"Look in the visor for the spare, or in the tool box for a screwdriver," Grant suggests.

"Why didn't I think of that?"

Lo and behold, there was a screwdriver in the toolbox. Quickly Grant snatches it from Shabazz and pries it into the key slot breaking it off. With a little push, tug and pull the engine turns over. Hastily they begin to pull off, when they observe Master Moon making his way toward them quick, fast and in a hurry. Knowing that Moon is always good for a grand entrance, Gabriel rolls the window down then, slides over to make room for his arrival. Fully aware that they recognize his status, he does a flying kick which guides him directly through the right rear passenger side window without a scratch.

"I have the contents of the Arc," said Moon.

Gabriel advises, "Careful we must not touch them until the time is right."

"A minute ago you said the time was right," Grant retracted.

"Obviously it wasn't because God did not allow it so," said Moon as he reveals to Gabriel the items enclosed with cloth wrapped around them.

"Thank goodness that you're alive!" Gabriel expressed his appreciation.

Moon replied, "Thank God for his Mercy and Martial Arts."

Grant says, "AMEN TO THAT BROTHER!"

"Bless you He did, yes indeedy." Shabazz agreed.

Examining the situation that they barely escaped, Gabriel begins to ask his own questions.

"What kind of demon dare defies The House of God, kills Angels, and still manages to stalk us as if nothing can stop him? There's more to this one, he's more than just a demon, he is *pure evil* in the flesh. Everywhere he goes bereavement follows. I am afraid gentlemen, unless we rid ourselves of this creature, surely we will die; as God intended, but all awhile fulfill our mission in His honor. So you may ask yourself; Are you willing to die for the cause?"

Willingly upon their declaration they answered, "YES!"

"To be honest I didn't think we were going to survive this far. That's why I chose to get my life together and allow it to mean something worth living for. I guess that's why I took on prison ministry and hit the mean streets reppin' the Lord. The people saw my heart and allowed me to share Jesus with them. I'm grateful that I was chosen for such a task. He saw something in me; and I am willing to die for it. After all, what is life if there's nothing to die for?"

From his heart Grant expressed his convictions with compassion and in truth.

"I hear you my brutha, but now is not the time for speeches. Put the pedal to the metal and get us the hell outta here," blurted Shabazz.

Expeditiously tires begin to screech as burning rubber dig deep into the black tar, leaving applaudable skid marks to be idolized by local ghetto boys inspired to be would-be Getaway drivers, or something that has never crossed the racial barrier; i.e. an Indy 500 Champion. Unfortunately, these are examples of minds that are terribly wasted, whose dreams are inspired by contradiction implanted in a corrupt system that was established over 200 years. Most of us don't even know it exists; i.e. The Willie Lynch Syndrome.

Actually corruption has been around as long as Satan. It started with him. No wonder it is still here flourishing in a world that knows better, but does not believe that there is a better way; because the majority isn't washed in the Blood of Jesus, that cleanses us into a new life of abundance as God intended. Instead we suffer and chase the malevolent carrot that Satan dangles in our faces, as it represents an easier profitable way due to our own stupidity and selfishness.

> **(Romans 8:28)** *And we know that all things work together for good to them that love God, to them who are the called according to his purpose.*

> **(1 John 1:7)** *But if we walk in the light, as he is in the light, we have fellowship one with another, and the blood of Jesus Christ his Son cleanses us from all sin.*

> **(John 10:10)** *The thief comes only to steal and kill and destroy; I came that they may have life, and have it abundantly.*

"The Goodness and Mercy of the Lord has done it again," Gabriel reminded them as they make their way to nowhere, somewhere, anywhere away from there.

Grant asks, "Where are we going?"

"Just drive until we are clear from the malevolent," Gabriel suggested.

Moon inquires as he elementarily attempts to understand the enemy in hot pursuit of them.

"He wishes to gain possession of the contents of the box, but why?"

"The four items if possessed by the righteous will manifest a great beast fortified with God's vengeance. If Satan got his hands on such power; he would then unleash it on Heaven for the big payback, and on top of that the four Horsemen will ride on earth forever," Gabriel explained.

Shabazz includes, "If you think it's bad now; it'll be Hell on earth."

Moon derived, "That was the vision you saw when you touched Sophia's hand."

"How did you know?" Gabriel asked.

"You usually tell us about your visions; that one you didn't," he replied.

Appreciating Moon's awareness Gabriel then opened the wrappings to reveal God's power tools.

"The vision we shared illustrated a battle beyond any battle unlike ever before."

While Gabriel tells his unsung story, Shabazz fiddles around the radio stations to gather the latest news talk. WLIB 98.3 (And here now the news: its official Prime Minister of Peace elected *New World Leader*. Out with the old, in with the New Currency that trumps all.)

Heavily weighed by the top story; Shabazz cites an undesirable warning, "The world as we know it has just gotten worse. Now correct me if I am wrong, but doesn't the Book of Revelation say something about this?"

"Indeed it does but not in Layman's terms. **Revelation 17-21** reveals the ordeal in its entirety. Many scholars and clergy are baffled at the implications of these chapters; due to its cloudy interpretation and discovery of its true meaning. Misconceptions render clarification as Kings bow down to a new world order. Religion and Government become one; while the Antichrist rears his ugly head, bearing false religion and peaceful doctrine to confuse Christians and nonbelievers that he is God. Fear not for our Lord Jesus will break the Seals and release the four Horsemen to incarcerate the Devil; and render punishment to the new order, to regain his kingdom for a thousand years with peace and pure harmony. Until he releases Satan to sift out his worshipers; to learn who are true. As of today this inaugural event proves that the Antichrist is here on earth and has been for along time whether he knew it or not," Gabriel proclaimed.

Granted his explanation confirms their understanding, still clarification was required.

"So the great beast is birth to combat the Horsemen?" Moon asked.

Gabriel accepted, "Yes, even the great flood of Noah had to be seized. A Gryphon or a Phoenix is Heaven's honorable beasts formidable to halt the Horsemen."

"You know all this time I thought the four Horsemen were spawned from Hell. I guess that's what you get when you don't attend a School of Theology," said Grant.

"You think? How did you getaway with Bible Study? I'm sure somebody asked about The Book of Revelation?" Shabazz wondered.

Grant retorted, "I told them to stay away from it. You know how it is in the hood, anywhere else for that matter. People are afraid of things they don't know or comprehend."

Knowingly and willing to except his answer, Shabazz grins and shakes his head in agreement. Still they ride until tomorrow to bring forth a new day the world has never seen. God is watching!

In the Interim

At the site where the Angel died, Wrath gets down on his knees and begins to scoop the ashes; and smear them on his face; as if he were marking himself for war. Sirens scream while lights flash as fire trucks, an ambulance, one cop and a boat load of campus police attempt to tame the destruction. Upon their arrival duly personnel approaches him as if he was a victim. As they seize him and lay him on the stretcher, they check for his vital signs.

"We're not getting any readings, the equipment is malfunctioning."

"That's impossible I calibrated them this morning."

Eagerly the EMT used the apparatus on himself . . . And it worked.

"It's working fine; here try it again."

Still no readings. Tired of all the drama Wrath snatches both of them into one big group hug and commences to crush them like Bears do. Bones begin to snap-crackle-pop as they break; leaving him to enjoy the fatal sound as if it were music to his ears.

As he drops the bodies a cop witness the kill and, draw his weapon and says, "Hold it right there. Put your hands up where I can see them. Move away from the vehicle, now!"

"Why yes officer, anything you say."

Gryphon vs. The 4 Horsemen by SpartaDog

315

Swiftly Wrath accelerates his movement catching the officer off guard; who finds himself a victim at this monster's mercy. Unfortunately over powered, the gun is shoved into his mouth; and unloaded as many times as many bullets it held. Splattered with warm blood, Wrath enters a euphoric state seemingly comparable to busting a nut. Witnessing the calamity Fire Fighters stood as their eyes catch a burning flame.

"Turn them!" he demanded as he finished his quiver.

Willingly they obeyed by assaulting the campus patrol, turning them into Clout or giving them a choice that they could not refuse. Calmly Wrath climbs into the squad car and pulls off sounding the siren with boldly blinking lights; as if he were in pursuit of an urgent matter.

"Haaaaaaa!"

Into the night he went fumbling and bumbling making short stops and starts, due to his lack of driving skills. While recklessly cruising he reached into his pocket to review the flier; first he read it, then he sniffed it; to gain Gabriel's scent like every hunter would. Based on the information, he now knows where his mission will end.

Simultaneously he is sucked into the dark abyss to rendezvous with the hunted. Callously he waited until the vehicle reached sixty miles an hour in a twenty-five mile an hour zone; allowing it to zoom into oncoming traffic. Head on—smash—bash, the collision brought; as passengers on an approaching bus are tossed about upon impact like 'Shake'n Bake.' To their advantage, posted traffic cameras catches it all, while violations add up daily revenue for the district; that is faulted by tourist who don't know better.

Cloaked within the abyss he stood, admiring the damage caused by his vile mind. Apparently he's a clever fella, utilizing his idle mind for treachery and causing chaos. Nearby is a construction site with earth movers and dump trucks shaking and moving about. He stares at them intrigued with their mass and power. Maliciously he begins to explore the possibilities; and conjures a wayward scheme that'll gain him the advantage once more. Like a manic premeditated he is satisfied with the thought of his demented surprise; so he smiles signifying his pleasure.

Chapter Twenty Seven

(*Truth or Consequences*)

HELL

Like Moses and the 12 Tribes of Israel, Dimitrius and what's left of his crew; walked with a sense of purpose in hopes of reuniting with their friends, unknowingly Hell being the stubborn bitch that it is; begs to differ. With every step they moved forward, they took 2 steps back. Naive to this hindrance they walked; and walked; and walked until Dimitrius eyes were finally opened to draw a conclusion.

"STOP! This is nonsense; for long as we've been walking we're not getting anywhere."

Laughter fills their ears when finally Belial's face appears in the sky in HD.

"Look, up there," Miguel shouted while pointing upward toward the motion picture.

Belial then spoke his bogus propaganda, "Now don't you feel like rats in a maze? Excuse my absence, out on a sabbatical. Even God rested on the 7th day, believe it or not I too grew weary of the same ole, same ole. Shit was getting boring, until now! Hell and I have established a new alliance; one that will go down in the history books as the worst thing that could've possibly happen."

"Forget all of that. Where are our peeps?" Xavier inquired.

Belial retorts, "Hold your horses fearless one, all in due time. What are you going to do now? All of your army is depleted; and I have your friends including the Reaper. Things are surely looking bright from where I stand. I'll tell you what; meet me at the top of the hill, it's time to put this baby to rest; besides I have a surprise for you."

Baffled they stood while Belial vanished.

"This is starting to look like a bust. I say when we get up there, kill the bastard. Surely we'll get the same results," said Rashida out of frustration.

Countering her suggestion Dimitrius replied, "That's not what I was tasked to do besides, how do you kill the Devil?"

Xavier quipped as he clenched his fist and then punches the palm of a hand, "I can think of a few ways to waste his ass; let's do this."

Together they ventured forth at a timely trot until they came to what appeared to be a scorched forest at the base of the would-be hill. Haunted it appeared while inundated with dead carcass, riddled with maggots and flies; drenched in the stench of death. As they proceed; they gazed at the corpses with suspicion; surprisingly Rashida recognizes who and what they were as a tear falls from her eye.

"Oh my God, my men; these are my men," she cried as she is stunned hard enough to knock her to her knees.

Unrecognizable their bodies rest, resembling life size stick figures wrapped in their signature action gear with name tags explicit to the naked eye. Angered and about to explode, she speaks her mind and uses the Lord's name in vain as it is purely set on revenge.

"Jesus H. Christ, if you don't take this mutha-fucka out, I'll do it! I swear to God!"

Quickly Dimitrius does what Mathyus would've done by quoting scripture.

(Exodus 20:7) ***Thou shalt not take the name of the Lord thy God in vain; for the Lord will not hold him guiltless that taketh his name in vain.*** *(See 10 Commandments)*

-Also-

(Romans 12:19) *Dearly beloved, avenge not yourselves, but rather give place unto wrath: for it is written, Vengeance is Mine; I will repay, sayeth the Lord.*

Immediately she is humbly reminded to stay in her lane. Honoring her soldiers' death, they gathered as many name tags as they could; and respectfully prayed for their souls to be delivered unto the Kingdom of Heaven.

Feeling her pain Xavier gives her his shoulder to cry on and holds her like a good friend would.

"I know this is a hard thing to swallow and at the rate we're going; it doesn't seem possible, but have faith honey . . . We're gonna win this gig."

As tears roll down her face she is comforted.

Miguel adds assurance, "Now don't you feel empowered to do what we have to? We have to be stronger now than ever before! This is a sign; everyone is not going to make it to Heaven."

"You're right mi amigo, even Moses didn't make it to the Promised Land and we must find strength in our weaknesses. The odds have been against us from the beginning, so do we ride or die, or do we say fuck it?" Dimitrius questioned.

Xavier looks at Rashida. Rashida looks at Miguel.

Miguel looks at Dimitrius and says, "Jesus died for us; it's time to repay the favor. Vamanos!"

Impressed with Miguel's gallantry Dimitrius pats him on his back and compliments his maturity.

"Spoken like a true man."

To their surprise finding strength from within themselves, and from each other, they determine that it's all or nothing and that the greater cause is worth dying for.

Before they leave, Dimitrius encourages them to find their inner peace and take a squat in a Yoga position on the ground.

"In order to be complete, we must sync our minds with our bodies to form a union that finds strength, vitality, and tranquility. I usually do this before and after battle. Join me."

Without hesitation they do as instructed to close their eyes and explore their minds until finally reaching their spirit within. A ½ hour passes when Dimitrius awakens to find that he is all alone. Patiently he rises, thinking due to their lack of discipline his comrades ceased their oneness earlier than he; so he called out to them and received no response. Little did he know that just like Mathyus and them, they were consumed? Turning himself around and around looking in all directions to no avail. Realizing that he was alone, wasting no more time wondering; he concludes that he must challenge the mission on his own.

Hut 2-3-4; hut 2-3-4 . . . He marched until reaching the end of the burnt tree line. Just inside of the limits he stood before the base of the hill to assess his view. On top of the hill he could see that it was occupied by demon spawn, but there was an innocence that shined like fire flies; more like stars amongst the darken sky. Trying to make sense of what he was looking at which appeared to be the setting of The Crucifixion with lit torches and a restless crowd in an arena chanting 'Death' as if they were from Spartacus the TV series. Accepting his fate, he proceeded to face the showdown with nerves of steel; and honor. While approaching, a motley crew of demons pushed and shoved him which encouraged the crowd to cry out for his blood. As he walked down a makeshift street of lined peasants; incoming fruit, eggs, and stones are tossed at him bouncing off his physique like he was a corny act at the Apollo. Ignoring their ignorance he did, until a stone knocked him upside his head; sending him to his knees. The crowd goes wild as they delivered a staggering blow. While on the ground they began to taunt him, spit on him, curse him and yes whip him until blood exposed his injuries by popular demand. Trapped in a sense of insanity he bears the brunt of his punishment. Could it be that his sacrifice weighed as much as life itself? Or is it what measures a man's heart in time of despair? To flex his strength he dug deep within himself to a place where he can lament; unnoticed by the populous standing ovation.

Steady his heart beats like the fire that burns furiously inside the vengeance of an angered man; instigated by the confusion that manipulates his emotion, he is rendered senseless while waiting for his mind to give direction. Would it be wrong to give in to Satan's madness by losing his composure? Or should he rely on the training that was taught by the suited mentor that nurtured him to be the righteous man he is today? Being all that he can be by recognizing the change within that developed a different man, a better man. Admirably looking to his Spirit deep within and allowing it to guide him to a conscience decision.

Jesus said as referenced in the Bible, **(Matthew 6:33)** *"But seek ye first the kingdom of God, and his righteousness; and all these things shall be added unto you."*

Yet retribution can easily be obtained. Transcend retaliation too is not wise, let's not entertain the enemy. Patience is the solution; don't give in to your adversary. Let them see that love is the better way and you shall prevail. Although you may be weak in might, in time love will find a way to shine. It takes the better man to forgive, especially while enduring pain. Impress yourself as well as others by watching the superior man take shape within you.

> **(Matthew 5:44)** *"But I say unto you, Love your enemies, bless them that curse you, do good to them that hate you, and pray for them which despitefully use you, and persecute you."*

Have no fear from your display of humility, your rival will yield; and realize that the impossible has occurred as the faith of a mustard seed has taken hold to the soil within him.

> **(Matthew 17:20)** *"And Jesus said unto them, Because of your unbelief: for verily I say unto you, If ye have faith as a grain of mustard seed, ye shall say unto this mountain, Remove hence to yonder place; and it shall remove; and nothing shall be impossible unto you."*

On the ground he groveled, finding him a spectacle beholds unto brazen followers; that were heartless to say the least. Mocking a malice scorn, crudely a crown of thorns is mashed on the base of his forehead; while in tandem scalding water is thrown on him, forcing him to rocket to his feet where a dilapidated cross await his carry.

"What the heck is this?" he thought, recognizing the scenario and the part of which he is cast.

As blood begins to trickle down his brow it runs into his eyes which appear as tears of blood. Mindlessly the crowd is entertained as though they were prompted to do so . . . or else. Dancing in a ritualistic bounce are naked vixens' vicariously viced for their lustful pleasure; despite the heinous brutality. Thorn becomes restless because he is confused by witnessing his alpha mauled while collared by a Roman demon.

Weighed by the splintered structure to drag along cobbled stone streets burdened his bear. A difficult task for anyone even one who was physically Adonis-ed in stature.

One can only imagine the pain and strife Jesus had to suffer. With this thought in mind Dimitrius channeled his thoughts on his Savior; and then sheds a tear for his greatly appreciated sacrificial task. You never know about another man's life, until you wear his shoes. Seeing this Belial was pleased, but falsely tamed by the illusion. You see, he thought Dimitrius' whine was due to the cruelty that he inflicted; unknowing that Dimitrius was in tuned to his heart and soul. One mind, one body in tune to his will. Practicing what he'd preached now came in handy. During the drama he is approached by a familiar face that seemed displaced within. It's Miguel with a bucket of water. Kindly he rationed out a tin cup to quench the scourge thirst.

"Thank you mi amigo," Dimitrius said.

Unknowingly enslaved to the game, Miguel has served his purpose; then casually walks away. Recognizing his dilemma, Dimitrius rationalizes his friends' position. Willfully he continued his trek not knowing what to expect. Seemingly the unexpected presented itself as Belial is thrown off guard by Miguel's actions. What just happened? He thought, while brushing it off as a glitch.

As the weight of the cross stock piled his muscles, he tripped on a jagged stone rendering him flat on his face. Laughter chimed to what they thought to be his embarrassment. Suddenly extending from the mob a helping hand sympathizes with his demise.

"Let me help you, give me the cross," he said.

Welcoming the handout, Dimitrius finds gratitude for it is Xavier his friend. Helping him to stand Xavier commandeers the dead wood. Signaled by his empty gaze, as if he were a deer staring into headlights, he could see that Xavier was a day dreamer. Staggered steps continued his march with trusted friend by his side. Again Belial is baffled as good deeds infect his preposterous charade.

From a clap of his hands, a bolt of lightning shocks the stage. Freezing rain begins to fall while boisterous thunder bangs the boom. Winged demons take flight, filling the sky resembling vultures circling the awaited dead. Pestilence remains pest, swarming about as if someone had left the light on. On the low ground snakes slither along chasing rats that infest the neighborhood. Overwhelmed by it all Thorn begins to pace and whine with raised hair claiming his back; still leashed.

Despite him being in control, Belial begins to second guess his certainty, "That's twice these imbeciles rebelled willfully unknown. Something's not right. I am not going to allow them to fuck this up. Bring in the Reaper, it's time I take what I need."

Grappled by hunched demons, Sebastian is brought to thy master's bidding. Held in front of Belial he stood helpless and afraid; until an unexpected rage crazed his heart. Allowing his fear to fuel his instigation once they let him loose, swiftly his scythe is raised and wield with deadly purpose. Slicing and dicing his way like the Tasmanian Devil from Bugs Bunny cartoons; whirlwind through them sending limbs and heads flying until finally once again he is face to face with Belial.

"You want me? You got me," said Sebastian, huffing and puffing.

"Wow, now that was entertaining! Downright exciting even! Can we get a round of applause; for that spectacular display on how to handle a giant Ginsu." prompted Belial. Claps and cheers are rendered as obeyed. Quickly Belial takes hold of Sebastian's face and kisses him on the mouth. Victimized by the lip-lock Sebastian is caught, he then begins to drain the final ingredient of what was left of the Reaper's sought after power. Sebastian is now stripped of his sovereignty and as timid as a lamb. Simultaneously Belial grabs hold of his scythe and then shoves him to the ground to join his friends. Now fortified with the Reapers strain, his inoculation is completed allowing him to become Hell's Diablo on impulse which was his initial plan. Styling and profiling, stretching and flexing and bone cracking, he exercised his right by demonstrating his ability to morph with the greatest of ease. Feeling a new oneness with the underworld, Belial proclaimed his majesty, and holds the scythe over his head to symbolize his victory. In comes a dragon in which he mounts and fly about as Diablo for his kingdom to see. One lap then two, then he returned while receiving a round of applause. When landed he took a bow acknowledging their cheers.

"Finally, true power beyond measure. I was bad before, but I'm worst now."

Lustful celebration carried on that would've put Sodom and Gomorrah to shame. While Belial releases his inhibitions, fornication and sodomy exploits the mass orgy for the mob; as a gift from Belial: The Almighty Devil. From where he stood, he was seating on top of the world, but something still aggravated his craw.

Still Dimitrius and Xavier trekked the rocky road while Sebastian laid waste to his inferiority by curling up in a corner crying all alone. Gathered like cattle, the leftovers viewed their redeemer a prisoner to ruffians. Helpless they stood back wondering what to expect. Gallantly they began to pray; as they trust and believe in the Lord's reliance.

Although his plan seemed foolproof, still there was a rebellious undertone that bothered him like an itch that needed to be scratched.

"Bring in the rest of the prisoners," he barked.

In comes the rest of Militia escorted by wingless demons. Shackled together is Sarah and Mathyus, Rashida and Porter; and Lilith all by her lonesome, but where are Hector and Lucy? Immediately eye contact is made between Lilith and Belial; which urges her to plea for Dimitrius clemency.

"Belial, stop this. These people don't deserve this."

Incoming! by SpartaDog

"Why don't they? They've been granted perdition. This is where they belong. Furthermore, they were sent here to destroy me," said Belial as he caresses the asses of two concubines; one on each of his sides.

After his statement he then rolled his eyes at her in disappointment.

"Piss off, bitch! You're going to pay for your insolence. I've already taken care of the accountant and in a minute I'll take care of you. Sit tight, don't go anywhere."

Standing on his throne for all of Hell to hear, he reveals his logic to the Militia.

"It's time you'll know the truth and nothing but the truth, so help me god. Tonight you will learn why you've been chosen to rebel against yours truly."

In an attempt to show faith, Dimitrius, although occupied with a heavy burden, still shoots for a dig to throw Belial off his game.

"Speak, and let the truth set you free."

Belial snaps, "Spoken like a true hero, but in this story the hero must die!"

Admiring from a distance from each other; the Militia and Dimitrius express their sorrow by shedding tears of love and sadness for each other. Their emotions shine through as all could see. Noticing the twinkle in their eyes Belial commits to sabotage their tears of joy. Comfortably he took a squat in his chair and spotlighted the pulpit.

"I guess you're wondering, why the reenactment of the catastrophic event that changed it all. Till this day, your Royal Highness is still sulking over the death of his precious son. How could he do that? He treats his kids like orphans. Even when I was His favorite . . . until He dogged me. The real reason I had to leave was because I became a threat, my popularity surpassed His and He couldn't stand it because He's a jealous God, and due to His insecurity I was condemned to Hell. The Boy Wonder was forsaken as well as mankind and, I devoured it like a wolf does sheep. After all it's better to rule in Hell, than to serve in Heaven."

Dimitrius defends his belief with words of truth.

"The Bible says that you are a liar."

(John 8:44) *Ye are of your father the devil, and the lusts of your father ye will do. He was a murderer from the beginning, and abode not in the truth, because there is no truth in him. When he speaketh a lie, he speaketh of his own: for he is a liar, and the father of it.*

"Jesus was sacrificed to liberate us from our sins as part of God's divine plan that delivered our salvation," said Mathyus who was fed up with Satan's gas.

Using her defiant swag Rashida too adds a quip, "Go ahead! Preach my brother!"

"SILENCE . . . ENOUGH!" Belial screamed.

Quiet it got, as the ruthless mob shut up at the drop of a dime. Forward, he went ahead and began to deliver his bogus speech.

"When a man looks deep into his soul, there he will find his true self. Let me paint you a picture."

Disrespecting his command, the rebel forces continued to pray to their God.

Reacting to their prayers, Belial disrupts their flow by morphing into his alter ego. Mercilessly he throws a fire ball at Lilith which sets her a flame and burns her to a crisp. Immediately Sarah screams which draws Xavier's attention. She then becomes woozy and buckles. Quickly, Porter stops her fall and begins to fan her.

"LILITH!" Xavier yells, immediately snapping him out of his trance however, sending him to a place of sadness that had sulk his heart.

Stunned by Belial's heartless deed, still the defiant stood anxiously waiting for the so-called announcement.

"Whatever comes out of his mouth, don't believe the hype! He's not capable of telling the truth. The Bible says, **(Proverbs 3:5)** *Trust in the Lord with all thine heart; and lean not unto thine own understanding.* Trust in Him at all times; especially now," said Mathyus.

Meanwhile, Dimitrius and Xavier reach the top of the hill. Upon their arrival a barrage of stones are hurled at them sending the crowd into frenzy.

"Stone them!" they suggested because they did not expect them to complete the death march.

Xavier, filled with sadness, conveniently turns to his madness and being the beast that he is, he digs deep within his brawn then tosses the crusty cross at them. Simultaneously he is rushed; which forces him to fight for which he stands. A banging—battle-bruiser he became; as his brut strength generously busts their asses. Mindlessly his rage rumbled as ravenous ruckus; purely motivated by his revenge for his true love, until too many rushed him at once pinning him to the ground.

Dimitrius on the other hand, once powerful now found meek, with battered body ladled with bumps and bruises is snatched by excess demons; who then bind him to the majestic symbol that has so meaningfully lasted forever. As he lay on the cross his Manifest Destiny flashes before his eyes. Dreadfully death becomes him. Understanding his fatality; and not afraid to die; he welcomes it with open arms . . . . Literally. Hastily the cross is raised on the peak of Calvary over looking the valley; set between two others for all of Hell to see. Empty the cross at his left, but not so at his right. Not able to identify the tormented soul, yet there was something familiar about him. Not so open to what was inevitable, his friends drop to their knees; and increased their petitions to God, for they know that . . . **He was watching!** Surely one thing is for certain; and a matter of fact; and that all true Christians know: *'When Praises go up, Blessings come down.'*

Pleased at how his charade has turned out; Belial begins to speak in tongues; chanting demonic cuts as if he pulled them from his library on iTunes. After the dark mantra; he then delivers, according to him, what they've been waiting for . . . . *The Truth*; fueled by calamity and trickery. Motivationally he spoke the untruth which was what he was totally capable of. Obviously, another lie that complements his mission to gain the advantage over Heaven's Glory. Hearing his voice tamed the mob who closely listened with keen ears. Joyfully he gazed amongst them admiring the attendance; as if it were a sold out concert. Having all eyes on him pumped his adrenaline, which foolishly applauded his vanity. Singled out from his audience, the speech is designated especially for the Militia. Rain drops began to spill, soaking the playing field with no delay of game. Belial's speech:

"On this wondrous day the Son of Man died. As we all know, this catastrophic event changed everything. Actually it set me back not one but, two millenniums. Finally, we have an opportunity to make this right. Ok, here it comes. I'm about to drop the bomb on you bastards. Little did you know, ***all of you contributed to his fall!***. Let me break it down:

Mathyus: The prisoner who was spared by the people by popular demand, instead of facing death you were passed over in which Heaven's pride and joy took your place. *Barabbas* the name, scorn forever in the book of life as swapped meat.

Sarah: My dear Sarah, when you're around him you stay moist, raring to go; now don't you? That's because you're the soul of *Mary Magdalene* . . . . You know what? I'm beginning to think there is some truth about the 'Di Vinci Code'.

Rashida: The tough girl. Look at your hands; they're rough, scarred and strong. *It was you who wove his crown.* Good choice of medium you used; very creative, very original.

Unexpectedly, ***Miguel*** and ***Xavier*** have already done their parts of being the *Water boy* and a big black field hand nigger. Tote that barge, lift that bail. It amazes me how you were able to fulfill your duties before I put this scene in motion, but that's not important. I guess it's embedded in their DNA.

Porter: You were the *Captain of the Guard; who task mastered the march and nailing.* You leashed the ferocious hound that I based all of my hellhounds, so ***Thorn*** truly was my best friend.

And ***Sebastian, the Grim Reaper***: You were *the soldier; who delivered the final* blow by taking your sword; and stabbing Him through the rib-cage which pierced His heart. Why do you think I chose you for that job? Taking life was you're forte, you were good at it. You sealed the deal, you earned it my boy.

And now to put the nail in the coffin, last but not least, the star of the show, ***Dimitrius: the Redeemer***. You were the standard as to how I measured the integrity of men . . . . You betrayed your faith; which proved one thing is for certain; when placed in a precarious situation and given an ultimatum, every man has a price and can be bought. You took a gamble; and lost . . . And boy did you? So ask yourself, who could've committed such a vile act? This is the part I like . . . . Going once, going twice; *Judas Iscariot, The Betrayer, The ultimate Traitor.*" The Good book says:

> **(Matthew 26: 14-16)** *Then one of the twelve, whose name was Judas Iscariot, went to the chief priests and said, "What will you give me if I deliver him over to you?" And they paid him thirty pieces of silver. And from that moment he sought an opportunity to betray him.*

"That's right, the Apostle who served Him up to be slaughtered. This is why you were chosen to redeem yourself and was granted the name, Redeemer. And that's the Gods' honest truth."

Stunned by the shocking news, all in attendance took a deep breath, including the Militia whose astonishment punished their hearts for the man they grew to love, but betrayed their God. Dimitrius on the other hand, being a practitioner of defying the odds, wisely turns a negative into a positive by applying his lessons to be used as weapons to soften Satan's heart; after all, the more knowledge and faith you have in God's word, the stronger the Holy Spirit dwells within you. Properly he applies the application.

"If this is true, then there is hope for you yet! Don't you see, it's all about *'Forgiveness'*? Let us look at what the Word says, **(Matthew 6:14)** *For if ye forgive men their trespasses, your heavenly Father will also forgive you.* If God forgave me, surely he'll forgive you."

Hearing this scripture ignited their spirits within as *'the Seed of Righteousness'* had begun to grow. Spreading like wildfire the word has sung. Sinners who clandestinely desired to leave are heading to Calvary with hopeful intention. Out of nowhere and everywhere souls flocked, spewing from the darkness like rats and roaches do when the lights go out. They now believe that they can be saved; as did those who jumped on the bandwagon by accepting Jesus at the time of death; after living their trifling lives. The time is now or never to be redeemed. The Redeemer has planted the seed; and restored their faith in God with his sacrifice, thus the rebellion is born. Instead of being a symbol of defeat; he realizes what the gleaming mouse meant from day one; that he was the *Beacon of Hope* that ignited the souls of the damned. From miles around they gathered to see the Redeemer fulfill the prophecy; and deliver them to Jehovah's Kingdom. Together they express their insubordination at the foot of the hill without fear. He is their Deliverer.

"In the name of Christ Jesus, we rebuke you Satan," they proclaimed.

Pissed off to the max Belial breaks his cool, "INSOLENCE! Silence you fools! You dare rebuke me? KILL THEM, KILL THEM ALL!"

Suddenly, from the sky high flying demons begin to swoop down and snatch random bodies from the new arrivals. Usually they would've dispersed, but there is a change in their hearts that allows them to stand their ground to fight for their deliverance. The rebellion is in full affect. Dimitrius although exhausted from hanging on the cross finds humor due to the lack of tyranny. While the rebels revolt, he glances at his friends; and winks his left eye. His laughter irritates his foe causing him again to express his dissatisfaction.

"What the hell are you laughing at?" he bitched while looking around to see joy brewing from the hearts he tried to despair.

He begins to question his disposition. For a moment Belial's heart was caught off guard; which rendered him tender mercy as he watched his plot flip the script. Seemingly, what bothered him deep down in his craw was to witness the reenactment. Lurking within his heart and soul was the Angel he once was, but unfortunately, being one with Hell; no longer permitted him to feel those emotions. Rattled by the verbal sucker punch, he gathered himself; and resulted to an extreme measure.

"I don't want His forgiveness, I have all that my heart desires and soon I'll have all of the Material World as well; which brings me to my next surprise. There is someone I want you to meet . . . Hell you already know him. Come on out and say hello to daddy . . . Here's Donnie!"

Strutting onto the scene with the swag of a rebellious twit, a thug, a pants hanging off his ass type of fool is Donnie. Representing what claimed property does when their salads have been tossed in penal systems mocked present in the 21st Century. He was defiant then; and more so now; for he is the devil's protégé.

"What's up Pops? How's it hanging?"

Tickled by Donnie's jest, Belial start dying laughing.

"Oh my God, no, no . . . ." Dimitrius rants.

Belial boasts, "He sold his soul to me a long time ago just so he could pay you back for being a shitty father. You got to love his ingenuity."

"Donnie, what are you doing? Why are you with him?" Dimitrius asked his long lost son.

"Why do you care? You didn't seem to care when I was alive, why now?" Donnie inquired.

"Because you are my son and although I wasn't around, I never once stopped loving you and your mother." he said.

"You were never there, I hate you and I hate everything about you. I hated you so much that I blamed mom for choosing you to be my father, so she had to pay," Donnie retorts.

(Exodus 20: 12) *Honour thy father and thy mother: that thy days may be long upon the land which the Lord thy God giveth thee.* See the 10 Commandments

Dimitrius rebutted, "What happened son? Am I to be blame for all your bad decisions, especially conspiring with the devil? Did you hate life so much that you rebuked God? Forgive me if I am at fault, but believe me, hurting you was not my intention."

Donnie shouted, "Bullshit! Well you did and now I'll make it right for all the children who missed out on daddy's wayward love. What I'm about to do, I am obliged to do. I thought you should know while you were alive, because soon you will be dead."

"What are you talking about? What are you going to do?" Dimitrius asked as he looked into his eyes and saw the pain in his heart.

Slowly Donnie turned his back and walked away.

"Tell him boss, he'll get a kick out of this . . ."

Little did Dimitrius know the devil had plans for Donnie long before Donnie was born?

"Wow, what a reunion! That went better than I expected. I knew I'd made the right choice; my boy. Anyway, here's the grandiose: The world has chosen a new leader, one who speaks of peace, love and harmony, boisterous is he that the whole world adores him. He has a following that mirrors Christ. Recently he amalgamated the world's currency into one and soon he will unify the church and government. When that takes place there shall be a New World Order, led by your son . . . . The Antichrist! He will take possession of this saint and trick them, all awhile preparing the world for my arrival. During this period, the four Horsemen will ride and the world will suffer. It'll be Hell on earth and I shall be king. Are you ready to be all that you can be sonny boy?" said Belial.

"Yes, let's get this party started," he said.

Now fortified with the reaper's power, with a snap of his fingers, Donnie is sent to the world to do his duty. Devastated by such harsh news Dimitrius swallowed his throat, his pride and whatever else you could've imagined. Hit with such a low blow, he hung his head with a loss of words. Noticing the affect that weighed on his friend, Mathyus encourages the revolt by claiming Jesus' name.

"Hail to almighty God, maker of Heaven and earth, glory be to the Father-Son and the Holy Ghost. Hallelujah to the Lamb!"

Despite their discovery, they were not discouraged because deep within they know that the Lord has truly blessed them with a second chance, as well as goodness and flourished them with gladness. To encourage their friend, they began to sing an old Negro spiritual to help draw his strength.

"We shall overcome . . ."

"Although it saddens me to see my son being used as a puppet, I must let him go and focus on what I was tasked to do. They say that God works in mysterious ways, to look at you all proves this to be true. He knew that I would not be able to lead his people out of here. The sole purpose of the prophecy was to restore Faith in Him to his people.

Look at them, out of the wood work they come. I do believe in my heart that your time has come," proclaimed a man who has falling 7 times.

Fed up with it all, Belial looks at Sebastian and waves his right hand; which sends him to the foot of the cross with his ole trusted scythe. Unable to resist he stood helpless. Up close and personal Belial became as he mounted the cross on Dimitrius' left.

He says, "No, I think your time has come . . . . Rest in peace, Mutha Fucka!"

Again from a wave of his right hand, Belial engages the scythe from Sebastian's grasp and plunges it into Dimitrius' rib cage; at the same time piercing his heart. With his last sight he glances at the cross on his right and recognizes the man who hung by his side.

"The Priest," he said.

Instantly death had come to him; as he expected. Screams cry out as Sarah then falls to the ground. Miguel begins to rant loosely his native tongue causing him to hyperventilate. Mathyus in turn grabs his heart as it grabs hold of his lifeline. Rashida holds her head down in disbelief. Porter falls to his knees while Sebastian, ashamed of his participation, wanders off to a dark place where no one dare reach him. Outraged like a crazed Hulk, Xavier's anger causes him to break his captors hold.

"AHH, you Son of a Bitch," he yelled.

Keenly focused on Belial, he tosses them around like stuffed animals, heading straight for him for revenge. Universally they shared the same feeling of not able to conceive what just happened or believe their eyes. Silently they hoped that this was not true. Their open hearts could not embrace him down. No longer among them; fearless and proud. He was finally dead . . . . Nuff said!

Witnessing his death outraged the masses. He brought them closer to their dreams; which took them to a jubilation that had just swept away with his last breath. When you feel the fire burning deep within, igniting what your heart desires, a higher foundation establishes the ground for which you stand. Torment provoked by the fear that was brought on by evildoers came to a grinding halt because a new light shines; which over shadows their meaningless past. With his death came a new beginning, one that was certain and comfortable to bare. Tomorrow they'll wake up to a new day filled with fresh air. Surely, God has answered their prayers. Happy faces filled with dreams that are laced with the peace from the inner man. A divine conscience rages to worship their true king by bring offerings that please our God. Always wanting to be free from Hell's bondage, they embrace Heaven's love with open arms. Not if Belial could help it, but for now he's concentrating on the rage of an angry black man; looking for payback. Step by step his anger increased, approached by henchmen to block his path. One by one, they continued until finally there were no more. Nothing but space and opportunity sat between them and out of the blue, Hector and Lucy stepped in to fill the void.

"Hold your horses big fella, you don't want to do nothing stupid," Hector said with his weapon drawn; and his wife's as well.

Curiously, the big black Silverback tilted his head to the right and then the left to figure out what they were doing, and then it hit him like a slap in his face.

"You've been working for him the whole time! You sold us out," he concluded.

Watching with tearful eyes was Miguel who surprisingly took a stand and spoke like a man, "Some things never change. You were a piece of shit then and you're a piece of shit now, both of you. All you really care about is yourselves! You're not my mother and father; you're the devil's bitches."

Distracted by Miguel's renouncement they were; which gave Xavier what he needed. Big, black-brown, and beautiful as ever, like a Kodiak, he moved swiftly, knocking them down and snatching their weapons. Then he gathered them to apply a bear hug. Squeeze he did until he heard the crackling of their bones and the breath that left their mouths. After he crushed the little, big man's parents, he looked at him for validation. Nodding his head, Miguel approved. Meanwhile, Belial realizes that the threat was real. So he morphs into the Diablo to stand 15ft. above ground.

"You still want me? Come and get me," he said.

Being a brutha from Brownsville, Brooklyn; Who never ran and never will (The original home of Mike Tyson and myself), Xavier put up his dukes and welcomed the challenge. According to Belial's memory, handling Xavier should be a breeze since he was able to put down the giant. Like gladiators they collided, delivering blows that would've crumbled the average man. Deadly bangs that battled the bulge rendered Belial pummeled on the ground; due to Xavier being a natural brawler.

"I'm gonna tear you apart," he proclaimed.

Unexpectedly, Belial morphed back to himself in defeat, the fearful look on his face instantly turned into a smile.

Xavier thought, "What is he smiling about?"

> **(Eph. 6:11)** *"Put on the whole armor of God that you may be able to stand against the wiles of the devil."*

Chapter Twenty Eight

(So shall it be Done?)

In the Material World: The Vatican, Rome

The early morning sunrise gleams through the window that yonder breaks of the newly appointed Pope, aka 'The Prime Minister of Peace'. While lying in his bed, exhausted from all of the hoopla; deeply submerged within his dreams, he is filled with joy, harmony and glee, but without notice he is about to play a major role in the devil's master plan. Unbeknowst to him an intruder had infiltrated his boudoir still he slept while the ghastly spirit hovered over him. Adjacently the wicked specter aligned itself, sizing him up for the take over. Tossed and turned the Pope suffered discomfort; which placed him on his back. What a fine opportunity to confiscate his body, Donnie thought, and so he did just that by laying directly on him, allowing his body to absorb him like Bounty the quicker picker upper.

While doing so the Pope abruptly opened his eyes realizing too late that something had imprisoned his soul and taken possession of his body. Possessed and knowing it can be torture on its own, yet he tried to fight to no avail. Donnie on the other hand is where he wanted to be fitting like fingers in a glove.

"Time to go to work," he laughed.

And so it is written, the seals will be broken and then enter the Horsemen; watch them ride . . . There will be war, there will be death, there will be starvation, and there will be disease that will spread throughout the land. Life as we know it will cease to exist and deviltry will claim its people. Filtered millions will be sifted as followers of Satan and the New World Order or true Disciples of God: the Father of Emmanuel who is the Son of Man (Jesus).

(Proverbs 19:21) *Many are the plans in a man's heart, but it is the Lord's purpose that prevails.*

Washington DC

As time marches on, nothing stays the same. All seemed normal on this the day of reckoning, although oblivious to the spiritual warfare that was cloaked amongst them. Ritualistically the people continued their daily routine per usual, slaved to an order soon to be orchestrated by Orwell's belief (Big Brother). Oblivious that this day had finally arrived, the weight of the scales have been balanced, and judgment will soon be rendered accordingly. Fortunately, on God's behalf, there are those who are fully aware of the blackened nightmare and are willing to take a stand to defend his honor.

Nonstop they drove, where they'll stop? Nobody knows. With no direction in mind, they're just riding on borrowed time until the time is right. Like cowards they escaped the stressful quandary; barely dodging another bullet to stay alive. *'Applause granted as I commend their move. Shucks if I were in the same predicament I'd have ran too!'* Nevertheless, being safe and sound soothed them for now.

"Did you see what they did to the Angel? They chopped him in to pieces," ranted Grant.

Shabazz then asked, "Since when are demons powerful enough to destroy angels?"

"Obviously this demon is of a higher class, its nature feeds on the torment of others. Punishes his victims; then disembowels them purely for pleasure," derived Moon.

Gabriel concludes, "Nonetheless we are marked men."

Abruptly Shabazz reaches into his pocket and pulls out a healthy wad of cash to distribute amongst his friends and says, "Okay if we just so happen to get separated, here's some cash, find yourself a hotel and lay low. Remember we'll regroup tomorrow at the event around 1400 hrs."

$1000.00 each he generously shared.

While trying to rationalize their dilemma, mysteriously the gruesome abyss opened in front of them; which headed them off at the pass. In comes Wrath driving a dump truck barreling straight for them. SMASH-BAM-CLINGLING-LING!!! The sound sprang as the unexpected murder weapon stepped out of its vehicular boundary by crashing into the holy fugitives' vehicle. Now lifeless victims they lay, since the head on collision tragically claimed their lives. Smoke filled air clouded the site, while dead bodies lay waste sprawled about. Satisfied with his results casually he strolled up to the wreckage and began to calculate.

"1+1=2+1=3, where is the 4th?" he asked while looking inside and saw that both driver's air bag had been deployed. Curiously he looked around, and then he site specks of trickled blood which aligned the escape route of the sole survivor. Just like a hunter he bends down and swipes his finger across the puny pedals and then sniffs and tastes the blood to acquire useful information about his prey. Haphazardly he begins to rummage through the bodies in search of the prizes from the box. Nothing, he found. Raged he became as he must continue his pursuit. Per usual he tagged his fashionable signature amongst his victims, he then ignited the gas that dripped on the ground; which mixed with the dead-pool of blood.

On foot the sole survivor stumbled his way about, now blocks away, until finally collapsing on the ground underneath Cherry Blossom trees that were in full bloom. Surrounded by tourists, who ignored him; and homeless people that thought he was one of them, due to his freshly tattered clothing spackled with blood. Dazed he was, but still focused on the task that he now must fulfill on his own.

Consciously yet fidgety he grappled the bag to assure that the treasures were still in his possession. Thank God they were, he thought, or his friends would've died for nothing.

"What I am to do now that I'm alone?" he sighed and then grew a pair after he thought 'what would Gabriel do?'.

All alone he became stronger in his mind as his duty survived him to call on his faith to see him through.

"I must and I will labor, O' Lord to see this to the end so help me God." He proclaimed.

(Matthew 9:37) *Then said He unto his disciples, the harvest is plenty, but the laborers are few.*

For the seed within has grown to be a plentiful harvest, not to be condescending to his charitable heart of which he drew strength and dignity, but welcoming the responsibility that God has provided him. At a high cost, he became a new man as a result of what was given unto him. Once upon a time this would've been mission impossible, but he is fearless now and with God's blessing, he will bring it to fruition; along with renewing his mind.

(Romans 12:2) *And be not conformed to this world: but be ye transformed by the renewing of your mind; that ye may prove what is that good, and acceptable, and perfect, Will of God.*

(Ephesians 6:10-13) *[10]Finally, my brethren, be strong in the Lord, and in the power of his might. [11] Put on the whole armor of God; that ye may be able to stand against the wiles of the devil. [12] For we wrestle not against flesh and blood, but against principalities, against powers, against the rulers of the darkness of this world, against spiritual wickedness in high places. [13] Wherefore take unto you the whole armor of God; that ye may be able to withstand in the evil day, and having done all, to stand.*

Tired and weary of being chased exhaustion yoked his strength, so he then crawled to the nearest bench and fell asleep. Time steadily passes, until the sunrise slowly came into view. As hungry birds chirp and gather, they find his body to be a good place to perch upon. Bothered by the noise he awakened. While sitting, he is approached by a stray white cat. The cat begins to purr which allows him to feel the compassion radiating from it as it began to glow. Now being able to see what his friend saw, he now knows that God is with him. Camped amongst the homeless; he blends in accordingly, but not unnoticed to those who were dying of thirst. The broken men and women gather around him to sacrifice their well being by protecting him from harms way, but why? Was it that he was in possession of the majestic treasures or that God's Grace and Mercy had finally fell upon them when they saw goodness in his eyes? Kindly a woman who once was a nurse that now suffers from mental illness pampered his shoulder wounds. Recognizing that this man was of a divine nature, their thirst for the Blood of Jesus had quenched their hearts. Filled with Saving Grace, their cup had runneth over; so they will be judged not by works, but by their faith.

> **(Romans 2:4-6)** [4] *Or do you show contempt for the riches of his kindness, forbearance and patience, not realizing that God's kindness is intended to lead you to repentance?* [5] *But because of your stubbornness and your unrepentant heart, you are storing up wrath against yourself for the day of God's wrath, when his righteous judgment will be revealed.* [6] *God "will repay each person according to what they have done."*

Accepting their kindness, he rose to face this glorious day knowing that God has not abandoned him. He then hailed a cab; which immediately stopped to acquire him. Strange he thought since it was always hard for a black man to catch a cab in most metropolitan cities. As he took his seat, the door locks engaged as they pulled off.

"Where to Pastor Grant?" the driver said as he looked into the rear view mirror.

"How do you know my name?" pondered Grant who said it out loud.

Conveniently the cabby revealed his flaming eyes while giggling. Recognizing that he was being chauffeured by a member of the Clout, without hesitation Grant puts the driver in a headlock; which caused the cab to recklessly swerve in traffic. Bobbing and weaving the vehicle veered, until finally jumping a curb smashing into a tree that resulted in killing the driver. Cautiously Grant climbs out of the cab and stumbles his way into the dawns early light.

A ½ hour goes by as Police and Ambulance sirens holler with urgency while venturing toward the crime scene. Little did they know keen eyes were also drawn to attention? Once arriving in the dump truck, Wrath slowly pulls up to get a better look at the dead body. Inconvenienced by the yellow tape, he inconspicuously walks over to the cab to identify the dearly departed. Swamped with essential personnel only, noticing Wrath's invasion of the crime scene, two officers casually get out of their squad car and approaches him to prevent contamination.

"Hey you, move away from the vehicle . . . Now! This is a restricted area," said Officer #1.

Wrath complies and then replied, "No problem officer, anything you say."

Officer #2 asks, "What are you stupid or something? Can't you see that this is a crime scene? Now get out of here, before I haul your ass in for obstruction."

Tired of the conversation including the disrespect, Wrath does what he normally does by making examples of those who piss him off. So he provokes them into arresting him.

"Fuck you!" he said.

"Okay smart ass, that's it! You're under arrest," they both said while aggressively approaching him.

"Bullshit!" defied Wrath.

Deemed to be too fast for them, he rushes them then smashes their heads together knocking them out cold, and then he tosses their bodies into the wreckage and sets it aflame. Witnessing the onslaught were essential personnel who skedaddled to save their own lives. Afterwards he then confiscated the squad car and began to laugh while flashing lights flicker and sirens scream. While cruising, he then reaches into his pocket again to view the whereabouts of his next destination. He grins to show his gratification and heads toward the Lincoln Memorial singing Lil Wayne's, 'No Worries'.

In the Interim

Back on campus, the crime scene is being investigated by Law Officials from a collaboration of various agencies which consisted of: the FBI, CIA, Local Authorities and Campus Police. Customarily, CSI Forensic teams join forces to try and make heads or tails of what had happened. Not routine to usual tactics and assumptions, a Private Investigator combs the scene and derives what they all missed. Apparently this horrid scene was linked to the killing spree that has plagued the North East Corridor.

"Who's in charge here?" he asked aloud.

Everyone embroiled in their work ignored him accept for an officer who was tasked to conduct crowd control.

"I don't know; I'm kinda new. I think it's that guy over there," he said while pointing in the direction of a detective who was talking to Campus Security.

"Ahh, Det. Chavez, I know him; thanks," said the Dick.

After they finished talking, the Private Eye approached him speculating, "The press is going to have a field day with this one . . . . Especially when they find out that it is linked to the serial killings in Italy, New York, New Jersey and Philly,"

"What makes you think this had anything to do with those murders?" Det. Chavez questioned.

The Dick answered, "They all share a common denominator: the religious factor. Besides, all of this blood and no body? Surely this is on another level."

"A cult perhaps, either way it goes, savages to say the least," said the Detective.

"I concur," said the Dick.

"Come take a walk with me, there's something I would like to show you," suggested Det. Chavez. Together they strolled from the gruesome site conversing about the possibilities; they find themselves in an alley off campus.

"This is it," said Chavez.

Slowly the Detective turned around and revealed his flaming eyes. Simultaneously the Dick revealed his wings.

"I've known this about you for a while, besides I can smell you."

Detective Chavez says, "Is that so? Did you smell the others behind you? Turn around."

And so quickly he did, fast and in a hurry.

"I guess you think you've got the drop on me. I am exactly where I want to be . . . For the murder of my brother, my friend and fellow Angel, I condemn you to your doom. Today is the day he shall be avenged and as for you, your time has come; it is for you whom the bell tolls."

The look on the corrupt Detective's face only proved that he was afraid. ATTACK! Bum rushed him they did. As people walk by, all that they could hear is cutlery being utilized by a master; with each kill flashing lights sparked which indicated his victory until there were no more. Afterwards he then took to the sky in search of the fantastic four. While in flight, he remembered there was something that needed to be done, so over the campus he flew in a circular pattern until reaching maximum speed, suddenly he stopped mid air and boldly clapped his wings; which released a blinding light, which resulted in an erasing of all in attendance minds of the horror show just performed. If you didn't know any better, it appeared as a typical day on the yard. With the exception of a six man crew of Mexican construction workers rocking steady to the beat, raising sheet rock and brick to restore beauty to the Chapel's overhaul. God is watching!

Fumbling and bumbling his way about 14th street, Grant arrives at a grand hotel. Tattered down, his clothes falsely represent who he really is. Casually he approaches the front desk. From the second he walked into the hotel via valet, the Bell Captain halted the vagabond in his tracks.

"Excuse me; we don't have any money or food to give you so, keep it moving."

Grant looks at him with a sense of sorrow and retorts, "Didn't your mother ever tell you that you should never judge a book by its cover?"

At the same time, he slams his doe on the desk. Quickly attitudes change; as they accommodated him appropriately.

"What time is checkout?" he asked.

"Noon sir," replied the front desk rep.

Finally somewhere descent, as the military would say; to shit, shower, and shave. Tuckered out, soaking his muscles as he lay in the tub allowing Calgon to take him away. Traumatized he began to shed tears until he was asleep as dreams about his friends slowly come in to view.

"Isn't it funny how life demands more than what most individuals are prepared to do? Doubts and fear cloud the mind which forms a bias opinion or illogical judgment. When you look deep within your heart, it is there you would find the Spirit Man that will guide you to a place where you're true power dwells," said Gabriel in his ghostly form.

"Find you're chi, and let it furnishes you with Faith, Hope and Joy. You must know that God's plan was for the better man you've become," added Moon who also presents himself as an apparition.

"You have the power within you in storage, release it, reflect on the measurement of the man that you've become and you'll find your heart to be true. Draw its power and fortify your faith with truth and love," declared Shabazz.

Simultaneously, the three spirits laid hands on him; and give him the Benediction:

> **(Jude 1:24, 25)** *Now unto Him that is able to keep you from falling, and to present you faultless before the presence of his glory with exceeding joy, to the only wise God our Savior, be glory and majesty, dominion and power, both now and forevermore. Amen.*

And just like that, they were gone. In tune to his responsibility which humbled his heart, he begins to pray for the honor that God has bestowed upon him. After praying within his temporary prayer closet, he then calls the front desk for directions to local shops to purchase new gear.

HELL

It is said that being absent from the body is to be present with the Lord, but in the case of the three blind mice, God had other plans. Straight to Hell they went to serve their purpose accordingly. Transported to Calvary to take their places for which they stand. As for Gabriel, vivid the scene proved as his place neighbored Dimitrius who just died on the cross. Immediately he recognized the condemned man, due to them crossing paths once before; which meant that he was now in the spiritual war on another level.

It's the same war and now the same battle. As to what purpose is his question? One he dared not ask. God's plan is supreme and to be able to continuously fight for Him was enough. While hanging, he can see the uprising as well as the fear that has grasps Satan's heart brought on by a big angry black man. Finally a break, that gave true meaning to visions of old and clarity to his present condition. The twinkle in his eye brought him gratification, that seemed to be uncommonly good to be able to watch sinners who covertly desired to be dismissed, but was afraid because they thought that their condition had no hope and that they were punished forever. In the foreground he could see his fellow clergy as they too march for the liberation of freed men. Gloriously the rebellion is in full bloom. He also notices the sadness beaming from the core Militia, who has suffered a great loss of which is represented by the body neighboring him on the cross. What dreams may come as he thought, why the reenactment of Jesus death? From the look in everyone's eyes all seemed to be mystified; due to his body being lifeless before but strangely enough they thought as he is now alive and kicking. Mathyus notices Gabriel's movement and realizes that this ain't over.

"Sarah, look the thief next to him is alive."

Not only was he observant, but keen ears pinpointed a new existence. Suddenly Thorn breaks his master's grip and barrels toward Gabriel's cross. Finally he reaches the wooden structure and healed. Gabriel stares into his eyes and both could see the goodness that only God could've brought. Once upon a time He came to him as a soft white glow and now He comes as a feeling of comfort and love.

Together they comprehended the message that God was still there. The core Militia gathered at the base of Dimitrius' cross; including Sebastian who listened to his heart and not his mind. Forming an unbreakable chain, they held hands to express their solidarity, although they were missing Xavier who had redemption weighing heavy on his mind. Master Moon as well as Minister Shabazz entered the circle of faith by extending their hands to join the others.

"I take it that you know him?" Mathyus asked Moon.

"Yes, and soon you will too," reciprocated Moon.

The look on Gabriel's face approved their unification, so together they wept out of sadness and glee.

In the Meantime in the Material World: Wash DC

Once Grant purchased his clothing, valiantly he makes his way to settle the Lord's business. Along the way he is stopped by a beggar for spare change.

"Excuse me my friend, can you spare some change?"

Casually Grant reached into his pocket and said, "Of course my good man, buy yourself some breakfast while you're at it."

Exclusively, the beggar revealed his wings to assure him that God has sent a protector cloaked in many disguises. First he was a Private Investigator, and now he's a vagabond, deep down he is God's fury manifested into a man to protect and serve as all of His soldiers can.

"You're an Angel! Lord have mercy! Thank God for His wondrous Glory. I thought I would've had to do this alone. I hope you're stronger than the last Angel that filled the position before you," Grant said.

"Don't worry. I am Michael; I've tussled with worst than them," the Arch Angel declared.

Together they strutted to the Mall where the Million Man March commenced on the day of Atonement, which was a great idea, but as soon as it was over; let's just say, things went back to the way they were.

Spacious yet crowded, many facets of Christianity congregated as one body to share God's Love. It's a celebration, a time of Liturgical Praise, Fellowship, Song, and Jubilation. It's *The International*

Gospel fest 2014. Let them rejoice in his name and see His Love flow everlasting! Goodwill and Peace to all men that believe that Christ Jesus is their Savior.

> **(Psalm 149:3)** *Let them praise his name in the dance; let them sing praises unto him with the timbrel and harp.*

Brewing behind the Lincoln stone is an evil more condensed than stale blood and more dangerous than an infectious disease that claims its victim by breath of foul air. Enslaved to a contrite world of which the masses are trifling, ignorant, lazy and selfish, hopefully he'll find them all to be off guard and then he'll have his way with them the good old fashion way; execution style.

The chimes of good spirits spread like wildfire cleansing their hearts of all that was negative that had bothered them before such a day arrived. Worship and praise filled their vocals; which reached out for the whole world to hear, but to another species of men the sound became an irritant; and their cries were not heard forever more . . . .

Out from the murky shadows he came, snarling at all that was good, leaving a trail of dead grass with every step he made. Clearly he did not belong, but a righteous attitude would prompt that it's never too late to convert, so they welcomed his nasty disposition in hope that God will fill his spirit with the Holy one. Condescendingly, he ignored their foolish quips as well as their dumb ass suggestions of wanting to be saved; as if he had a chance to be any different than he already was. He marched on until he reached the center, and then stopped to reassess his position.

Due to the discomfort that engaged his craw, "I can feel the presences of the Guardians; surely the odds are stacked against me. I think it's time to level the playing field." Rudely aloud, he called on his minions, "Beware mortals as I summon the Dark Forces to heed my call; bring on the black rain for the Clout of Grim arises! Rise to edify my plight and rid our fare of angelic puritans; come now! And do thy bidden."

Upon his request the sky diligently obeyed by assembling a darkened sky that turned this sunny beautiful day in to an unforeseen gloomy forecast with a high probability of rain. Surrounding the Mall were his minions awaiting their next command.

"Ah, now that's better."

So he continued his march without a care. Despite having his pure evil dim their sunny delight, the Believers continued their celebration as if they were not there at all.

Fully aware at the other end of the Mall Pastor Grant and his Angelic friend notice the blunted change of climate.

"There is something unnatural about the change in weather, the demon is here with his minions, we must hurry," said the Angel.

Heaven faulted by providing insufficient personnel, surplus-ing the need for more it generously filled the void by replenishing its count of Seraphim to even the odds. Lightening strikes twice while beams of light fall to the ground unseen by the naked eye. Archangel Michael observes familiar faces within the crowd; as they belong to his garrison.

"Fear not Pastor, we are fully stocked and fiercely strong. Today is a good day," he said while they synchronize their defenses.

Although unseen by man, Wrath could feel that the enemies were plentiful in attendance.

"Move in for the kill," he commanded, and so they did, sifting through the crowd for Grant and the Crown Jewels until met by the foot soldiers of the Lord.

Angels vs. Demons; to live is to die for is all that truly mattered to the God they serve, so let the battle begin and release the dogs of war.

Surprisingly the crowd remains oblivious to the battle royal that has fully commenced amongst them. Demons bouncing in and out of humans making it difficult to combat, but astute are the Angels who are there to distract them from hampering Grant's mission.

"Let them play, for they're doing exactly what we want them to do," said the Angelic horde.

Dying without death is just as bad as being defeated without competing. Somewhere along the lines the rules were changed. What was important had just become irrelevant, for the demons that is, because God's joy filled the void in all men and the stench of evil had no place there. Estranged during his pursuit, Wrath felt as his mission should've been a breeze. Finding the mortal should've been a simple task, especially since his minions were plentiful in attendance. More eyes, more views; at least that's what he thought. Cloaked amongst the people until the time was right, the Angels kept him hidden throughout the fold of the benevolent as each Born Again Saint is profound in learning from the teachings of Christ; and are inspired to be as such. The devil is a liar and they proved just that while the evil that saturated the festival attempts to undermine their common goal to rejoice in Christ and fellowship with thanksgiving.

Slowly time passes by, so many people Wrath impatiently thought.

"Where is he? It's like trying to find a needle in a haystack."

Until finally as he came closer to the stage, so did Grant and his guardian. Grant, paranoid as he is, was able to feel the presence of evil which prompts him to grasp hold of his Rosary Beads. Treated like a diplomat he is surrounded by unearthly guardians that have his best interest at heart. Escorted to the center of the stage, Grant unveiled the holy trinkets to the Archangel who took them for safe keeping.

"You've done well Pastor," said Michael, "The Antichrist is here and these will come in handy to befall the Horsemen at another space in time."

"Noooooo!" Wrath bellowed as Michael confiscated the trinkets and passed them on to another Angel whose plans were to ascend to Heaven, but hastily Wrath intercepted the exchange by utilizing his acceleration. Thus he grabbed the tote, and now possesses the prized goods. Although his mission is halfway completed, yet the death of the four is still at hand.

"Forgive me Michael for my carelessness," said the faulted Angel.

Without saying a word Michael looked at him with forgiveness, and then took matters into his own hand.

Boldly and aggressively Wrath made his way up the stage tossing people to and fro like rag dolls until he came to a band of angels that halt his next move.

"Don't worry about him, handle your business Pastor and see the Coming of our King is true," said Michael.

Utilizing the Abyss, he plotted its whereabouts all over the stage trying different avenues to get at Grant to halt his prayer until finally he was able to snatch him from the Angels grip and enclose him in the dark void. Streamlined, the abyss started to close, but committed the Angels were by halting the dark hole from sealing. Suspended midstream, the abyss froze.

"Your time has come priest. Yield to me and I shall be merciful," said Wrath.

Grant feeling the fire that burned deep inside his heart says, "God is the only one who determines when it's my time and if it is, then it is what it is."

"As you wish," obliged Wrath.

From out of the blue The Archangel cried, "Nonsense! Pastor, continue. I'll handle the monster, say the prayer."

Wrath temporarily distracted, takes his eye off his mark and suits up for battle. In the meantime Grant steps out of the abyss and falls flat on his face; back on the stage. Now that the darkness has been brought into the light, the battle that was cloaked is now revealed to the common eye. The rain finally came like a monsoon.

Pandemonium struck fast, causing mass confusion as angels and demons commence the battle royal. Human assaults became harder once the people knew that they truly exist. The people became baffled, frightened, and helpless at this point to see the spiritual warfare up close and personal.

A measure of hypocrisy in the sense of not relying on the teachings of their God until the man who stood alone said, "Let us look to the Lord for he is our salvation. Together, let us pray on one accord."

As a unified front committed by all Believers who truly believe this to be true, they began to recite the Lord's Prayer knowing that this will change things, so the masses did just that as Jesus did:

(Matthew 6: 9-13) *"This, then, is how you should pray:*

'Our Father in heaven, hallowed be your name, [10] *your kingdom come, your will be done, on earth as it is in heaven.* [11] *Give us today our daily bread.* [12] *And forgive us our debts, as we also have forgiven our debtors.* [13] *And lead us not into temptation but deliver us from the evil one.'*

Battle Royal by SpartaDog

Suddenly, the rain had abruptly stopped as the sun gave way to a new horizon. Tranquility had succumbed and clarity had given way to their hearts. Birds began to sing as Peace besieged the planet. All became humbled in their spirits. Demon spawn descended back to Hell; including Wrath who failed his mission.

"Wait, what is this? This can't be! I've failed my master," he shamed.

Despite his failure, yet he still possessed the tools from Heaven that may be used maliciously. So away he went with his tail tucked back to Hell to face his punishment with no fear. Afterwards all seemed well and the prayer brought on a new attitude amongst the people. Unknowingly, taken matters into his own hand the Archangel followed him back to the Dark Realm in pursuit of the heavenly possessions.

In the meantime, the Angels flew high in celebration of their victory. Grant fell to his knees crying, due to his success, and at the same time honoring his friends. He then closed his eyes and paid homage to his friends.

"We did it, Gabriel! It is done! I'm going to miss you my friends."

The jubilation carried on as the day proved to be a glorious one. Yet deep in their hearts they knew that something was coming, but no one had a clue. Suddenly, it came as a flash. A blinding light magnificently, vibrant set as a spectacle for the whole world to see. Simultaneously Grant opens his eyes and, realizes that he is back in Compton.

"Well I'll be damn! I am home, thanks be to God in the blessed name of Jesus."

Counting his blessings Pastor Grant devoted his life to the Word and his studies by enrolling in a School of Theology. He dedicated a sworn Oath to give God all that was required to become a Saint amongst sinners, and a true Disciple. For his devotion God granted him a Mega-Church that dwarfed them all. Praise God for his Goodness and Mercy!

In the Interim—HELL

Gathered at the top of the hill at the foot of the crosses are the Militia plus three. Mortified about their loss and mystified about the new, they continue to grieve.

Apparently who are still alive due to a temporary setback orchestrated by Xavier, who was fueled with rage and gall?

"I'm gonna tear you apart and there is nothing you can do to stop me," said Xavier as he approaches Belial who groveled along the ground until his frightful frown turned into a smile; which left Xavier wondering?

"What are you smiling about?" he asked while he was about to lay down the hammer that would've ended it all.

In mid swing his arm was stopped by an arm of equal brawn and perhaps more might.

"Well, say hello to my little friend . . . just in time bud! Now kill the bastard," commanded Belial.

Shocked that Wrath was able to stop his swing, Xavier shrugs his arm free from Wrath's grip and then steps back to assess the situation.

Wrath in turn smiles at Xavier and says, "As you wish sire, by your command."

The two men circle each other while Xavier ripped off his shirt. Admiring his opponent for his physique and stature Wrath applauded him for what it was worth . . . . Nothing! Ding-Ding-Ding! The bell rang signaling the brawlers to have at it. Slamming their bodies as if they were Sumo wrestlers and throwing deadly blows with unimaginable power that was expected of men of such caliber. Combinations mixed with blocks and dodges that powered the wind only made them angrier. Fancy footwork beguiled them both; which caught them off guard due to their size and stature. Wrath possessing the strength of 100 men granted him the advantage, but skilled at the sport of fisticuffs proved Xavier to be a formidable opponent. Punches continue to mangle their faces as well as kicks and flips punished their bones. Like gladiators it must end in death or lay waste to blood.

"It's a shame we're enemies. I have yet fought a man with such power and zeal until now. We could've made a fearsome team . . . someone I would've fought beside many of battles and surely we would've been victor," said Wrath paying him a compliment.

Xavier replied, "Shut up and fight."

Evenly matched, seemingly, they appeared until stamina became the deciding factor. Grappled on the ground they squabbled until

Wrath captured Xavier's neck in a yoke that choked; cutting off the air to his brain until he was comatose. Belial became elated.

"Is he dead? I told you to kill him," he inquired.

Out of respect for the contest and the measure of his opponent Wrath did the unexpected and lied to his master while he gathered his breathe and measured his win.

"Yes Sire, he is dead."

Things just got worse the helpless Militia thought, as another strong icon fell to the rave of the devil. The fall of all that made them physically and mentally strong, but not spiritually at least that's what Mathyus believed in his heart.

"Fret not people, the Lord our God will still get us through this . . . . Believe!"

For the first time they were truly on their own and at the mercy of Satan. Witnessing the downfall was all who bravely denied slavery as they reclaimed their hearts and refused to bow down. Freedom reigned; as did their faith, hopes, and dreams. Their show of strength in numbers cautioned him which radiated fear in his soul. Foil not the solidarity, suggesting his impeachment they demanded. Tormented for an eternity granted them the way of the damned, a lifestyle forced upon them as punishment yet was his entertainment. Living and knowing that Devil gets his strength from their fear and if there was no fear, then there could be no evil. If there was no evil, then there could be no Satan. If there was no Satan then there would be no Hell. Damned are the dead who once feared his power. An alternative could be a blessing knowing that there was another power that encourage them, one that he feared with great respect and undisclosed admiration. Being the Devil always kept him one step ahead of the rest; which allowed him to discretely notice their unification, but not allowing them to see how it weighed heavy on his pride. Unlike the rest of the heartless minions, a soul he still possessed due to once being an Angel from Heaven. Once again the trickster, he attempted to be.

Thunder and Lightening violently consume the sky while he weasels his influence before they notice that slowly but surely his mojo was dwindling. So he morphs back into the Diablo to breach their bravery.

"Who's gonna stop me now? Finally, I won! Finally I've beat Jehovah, I can't wait to destroy His puny world," he ranted.

Then he began to rejoice, dancing and prancing his way about until suddenly a blinding light, magnificently vibrant, set as a spectacular flashed before their eyes.

Chapter Twenty Nine

(Resurrection)

HELL

(John 6:40) And this is the will of Him that sent me, that every one which seeth the Son, and believeth on Him, may have everlasting life: and I will raise Him up at the last day.

(1 Thessalonians 4:14) For if we believe that Jesus died and rose again, even so them also which sleep in Jesus will God bring with him.

(1 Thessalonians 4:16) For the Lord himself shall descend from heaven with a shout, with the voice of the archangel, and with the trump of God: and the dead in Christ shall rise first.

The light tamed the hostility and controlled the ruckus which soothed their hearts and pampered their souls. For the first time, Hell was calm. Even Belial's heart was modest due to the familiarity from the warmth of the light that once shone upon him. Wrath, on the other hand, found it to be a discomfort that drove him to crawl into the residue of the abyss; which cloaked his existence. Scattered the garrison of demons dispersed to far corners away from the epiphany. The crowd remained in awe for they knew not what to expect, but deep down they knew it was going to be something good.

With comfort allied pity and sorrow, still they had compassion for their brethren who sacrificed it all. Tenderly Sarah, Miguel, and Mathyus walk over to the cross of which Dimitrius draped. Two of them calmly wept while uttering their petitions, as Miguel stood strong like a pillar of stone. Sarah caresses Dimitrius' foot and gazes at the face of the man she once loved for a short but meaningful time. Privately she reflected on their joy as the beautiful light touched the hearts of every man, woman and child; taking them to a place of comfort and bliss in their personal lives. After the brief reflection, a soothing complacency came over them as the illumination merged with Dimitrius' body. What was once exclusive is now all inclusive. In the material world the same light brought forth the same message at the same time it does in Hell. EVERYONE; I mean EVERYONE, focuses on the spectacle.

"Look at his body! It's glowing," said Miguel.

As Dimitrius remains lifeless on the cross, the voices of Heavenly Saints: Moses, Elijah and John 'The Baptist' exude from his body. Instantly all in attendance muster to their knees as humility bestow respect, gratitude and fear. Belial too befalls to his knees with his head bowed not because he is humbled, but because he is afraid. Quiet he stood with keen ears on God's Messengers.

"Children of our Father we greet you in the name of our Lord and Savior: Jesus Christ. With repentance of your sins and, restoration of your souls, you must declare your petitions by voice to the Lord and plant the Seeds of Righteousness amongst thy brethren as they shall grow as they do in your hearts. Love one another as God has loved you. If you know love then, you'll know God because God is love. To gain God's Favor you must have Forgiveness in your hearts and remorse for you selfishness," instructed Moses.

"Trust in the Lord with all thine heart and, lean not to your own understanding, for a renewing of your mind is mandatory. Finally, rebuke the devil and, declare Jesus, Lord and Savior. If you cannot then you are doomed. Until all things are restored then and only then will Jesus return to bring you to the Kingdom of God," cautioned Elijah.

"Those of you who reside in Hell know this; Hell is no more and, the Kingdom of Heaven resides in your hearts, build a relationship with our God and, he'll prosper you as promised. Fear not the devil and his minions for they are as powerful as you allow them to be. You now have power in the name of Jesus. Grace and Peace unto you beloved," enlightened John 'The Baptist'.

Slowly the light that filled Dimitrius' body subsided as he then opened his eyes to live once again. His wounds were healed and his strength builds as he smiles at Gabriel, who reciprocated the same.

"Padre, good to see you again despite the circumstances," said Dimitirus.

Gabriel says, "To you the same my friend; your faith has triumph as God intended.

"God is good! If you're here that means you are dead?" determined Dimitrius.

"What it implies is that we're playing our roles in God's purpose."

"I can see now you and Mathyus is going to be a trip."

Gabriel says, "Mathyus? Who's Mathyus?

In the material world the instruction gave them true meaning, a sense of direction that gained them Glory if they so choose; it's *'Free Will'* that'll guide them to make the right decisions, until then Jesus will remain in Heaven as our advocate.

> **(Acts 3:20-21)** [20] *and that He may send Jesus Christ, who was preached to you before,* [21] *whom heaven must receive until the times of restoration of all things, which God has spoken by the mouth of all His holy prophets since the world began.*

As for Belial, where does he stand? Intimidated by the revolt and now the divine element that has claimed his majesty. Trying to regain his kingdom in Hell would be senseless and maybe detrimental he thought.

"This is a bust . . . I'm outta here; to hell with this place He can have it," he declared.

Realizing that he has lost, resulting to an extreme measure accelerated his plan. Like a coward he chooses a gutless alternative and fled to die another day. Suddenly without a trace, he vanishes into thin air. Not caring or concern about the safety of his master; Wrath had already beat him to the punch by transporting himself somewhere else as he entered the abyss fleeing when, the light first burn bright.

Grateful they all stood, giving praise and celebration of their emancipation. Finally the Prophecy had come true but, they all thought, 'When are they leaving?' Suddenly the sky turned blue and the sun smiled upon them, the birds began to sing, while the flowers spring. What was once ugly scorched with fire and brimstone is now blissfully sweet; as herbal essence of frankincense and myrrh filled the air, resembling the Promised Land. What a beautiful place indeed! God brought Heaven to Hell, which stifled its existence.

But as we know Hell has a mind of its own so it attempts to fight back.

From underneath the ground volcanoes emerged than violently erupted. Panic struck as the ground trembled. Fear had once again reared its unsightly head, '*but the God I serve is a magnificent God, who is **capable of ALL** things'*. With that being said in an instant what was molten and hot blossomed in to magnificent palms, pines and redwoods . . . . trees that is. Once again God stifled Hells' fury and tamed its rage by protecting the people as promised. Celebrate they did with supplication and glee chanting Jesus! Jesus! Jesus!

As the people rejoice the Militia is overjoyed beyond compare. In unison they helped Dimitrius and Gabriel off the Christian symbols of the ultimate sacrifice. Together they inundated them with happiness and love. Immediately Sarah tears of joy drips down her face saturating her lips, so she hugs and kisses him like never before.

"You're the hero right?" she said as she whimpers like a child.

As they gathered around our heroes, approach a wobbly man gathering his common sense. Holding his head and dragging his feet.

"What did I miss?" he asked as everyone turned to listen to the familiar voice with bright eyes without bushy tales.

"Xavier!" They shouted as he is received with joy and laughter especially from Miguel and Sebastian who became closer to him during the struggle.

Rashida too showed her appreciation for him by shaking her head up and down and then raised her fist to show their solidarity.

"Dimitrius! I thought you were wasted . . . . Happy to see you my friend," proclaimed Xavier.

Patiently Mathyus and some of the others waited until Sarah had her fill with Dimitrius so that they could express their gratitude. All in the circle listened closely as they bonded.

"I must say we did it, thanks to your dedication and commitment to see this to the end. I am proud to be a part of such a dynamic task, especially with a man of your caliber as God seen fit to lead us thru the belly of the beast. Like I said before and, I'll say it again my friend; it was because we trusted in Him with our hearts and maintain our Faith is how we beat the devil. Thank you for giving all of us inspiration and the drive to carry on. To God be the glory for his foresight as well as his hindsight." said Mathyus.

Dimitrius humbly replied, "Hallelujah to the Lamb; I too appreciate all that you've done for me. Without your knowledge and providing me with the armor and shield that gave me strength and protection; not to mention your consult . . . I couldn't have done it without you. Thanks to all of you for the love and trust we share. I don't know about you but, if I had to do it all over again I would, because God knew something that each and every one of us didn't know and, that is that His Love for us is infinite."

"Is this really over? What about the demons?" Porter asked.

"That's a good question, there are many realms here, chock full of spawn, their probably trying to escape hell. That guardian fella may have his work cut out for him." Mathyus wondered.

Sarah enlightened, "If that is true then they'll enter Purgatory; I can't imagine the outcome."

"Now that's an unpleasant thought. Like I said a few minutes ago; if I have to stay here and do it again, I will. Can any of you say the same?" Dimitrius proclaimed.

Proposed the question he did as the others contemplate. Immediately Xavier steps up by his side, then Porter, Master Moon casually strolls to the roll call; while Rashida beats him to the punch. Establishing his manhood was Miguel who stood on his brave heart and volunteered; Mathyus to move in the direction of the brotherhood only to hand over Thorn to Miguel. Standing seven strong, the Militia vows to continue the fight because the Spiritual Warfare is continuous and relentless. Suddenly the ground began to tremble as trees begin to fall, step by step seemingly they've experienced this before, when introduced to the giant one. Again he appears as if he never left smiling and feeling good.

"Oh my God; it's Johan," shouted Sarah.

Cheers rang out loud as his presence brought them exceeding joy and strength, especially for Miguel who could not believe his eyes. Neither could Gabriel and crew as their eyes opened wide so did their throats swallow with uncertainty.

"PROTECT THE RIGHTEOUS," proclaimed Johan the Champion.

"Yesssssssssssss! Miguel shouted while he and Thorn run toward their buddy.

Mathyus enlightened them, "He was brought back to us to assist us with God's fight. He proved his loyalty by sacrificing his life to save ours."

"Thanks be to God for his Mercy to provide us with such power, we'll need all that we can get," Dimitrius welcomed.

Now they stand as Soldiers of the Lord through and through, as they knew in their hearts that their mission was not impossible nor was it done.

"If you do this you will need a base to call home. Myself, Mathyus and the lady will set up base here in the Promised Land. After all of that I don't have much fight left in me and, because they didn't step up I would guess their feelings are mutual," Gabriel concluded while glancing at Brother Minister.

"I too think I'll sit this one out besides, the new saints will need to be schooled, the three of us are clergy, we'll have our work cut out for us," declared Shabazz.

Sebastian adds his whimsical expression, "If you don't mind, I'd like to sit this one out as well. This is where I belong, amongst the birds and the bees and, trees not thieves and whatever else you might run into, besides I'll keep the misses company."

"I'd like that, we have a lot to talk about," said Sarah.

The Ascension by SpartaDog

Gathered at the edge of the hill they overlooked the horizon, and the start of a new day. Holding hands as they sing songs of joy to God. While doing so the sky opened up and a different light pulled the souls of the deceased from the ground. While viewing the ascension they can see Enoch, Lilith, the Crusaders, Sanchez, the Vasquez's and finally Jessica on their way to Heaven as if the Rapture had taken place.

"See I told you; everybody wasn't going," confirmed Miguel.

"I don't think that this is the Rapture, Jesus hasn't returned yet; I think it was to comfort us by showing us that our comrades didn't die in vain," explained Mathyus.

"It's stuff like this that gives us strength. Thanks be to God," said the Redeemer; Opps! I meant Dimitrius.

As the magnificent light dimmed behold an Angel appeared, demanding authority as he stood beautiful draped in armor and ready for battle. Astonished but not fearful the Militia knew in their hearts God had blessed them with something greater . . . but why?

"Fear not beloved; I am The Archangel Michael; I come to aid you in what's yet to come. The henchman has in his possession a greater power that can tip the scale of righteousness and sin. I will stay by your side until we conquer the malevolent. This I am sworn and this I will obey in the glorious honor of God thy Father."

Content with their new development satisfaction filled the void of uncertainty. Together they smiled although they were smaller in numbers but stronger in every possible way.

"The Angel that kicked Lucifer out of Heaven," said Sarah as she sighed with relief.

Mathyus responded, "God's might at hand a blessing indeed."

"Thanks be to God for his power and his Glory." Dimitrius proclaimed.

"If the Archangel is here with us, than the world from whence we came must be in good standings. Pastor Grant has completed the mission as God knew he could," determined Gabriel.

Mathyus says, "Sounds like a story I would like to hear some day."

Gabriel then replied, "And some day you shall, we're going to be here for a very long time."

Fortified with glory and honor they stood strong, driven by what was in their hearts that finally gave them peace, and a place called home that is now filled with love. Who was once persecuted for their sins are now graciously rewarded with yet a more meaningful purpose in life. For God is mighty and forever strong are his children.

In the Interim

Deep down in the belly of the beast hiding in an underground grotto, Wrath sits quietly in the dark where Belial's cocoon once laid. Contemplating his next move he realizes that he is now King of what was left of Hell, and that he possessed the prize the devil had hoped for.

"MUUUUAAAHHHHHHAAAAAA!" His laughter hauntingly echoed about.

Infomercial # 8

There is a movement that is conspired amongst God's people that has taken the world by storm. Soon His true believers will be tested as the world will succumb to a New World Order. The Antichrist continues to campaign falsities that will brainwash the foolish, while eager righteous men grow in numbers. The Horsemen will ride giving waste to what they are tasked. Thus, the people will be punished for their disobedience. The Wrath of God is vengeful and swift and His judgment is just. It's never too late to repent your sins in Jesus name, especially when it comes genuinely from the heart. Remember as stated in Chapter #1: The Awakening:

> **(2 Chronicles 7:14)** *If my people, which are called by my name, shall humble themselves, and pray, and seek my face, and turn from their wicked ways; then will I hear from heaven, and will forgive their sin, and will heal their land.*

Although this scripture took place in the Old Testament it is universally applied during these modern times, because God's Word is true and never changes. This may be something to seriously consider; Why? because unfortunately, Satan has surfaced and in this world he is king, but that will all soon come to an end as he too

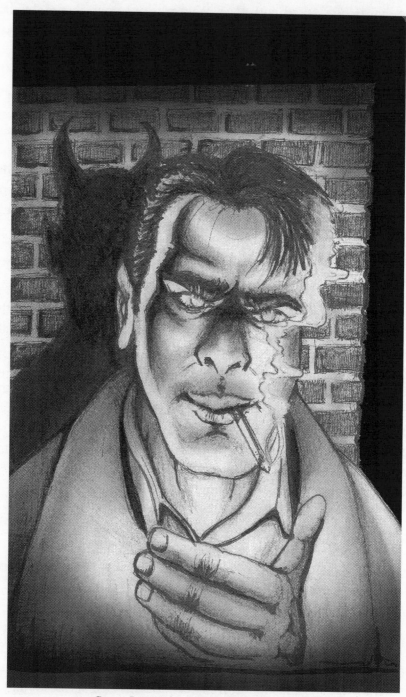

Satan Incognito by Christopher Romo

will be judged and enslaved for a thousand years and then he will be freed to test God's Christians that are true. Hopefully that'll be me and you, through the existence of our lineage because it is my belief that we will not be here to see God's plan, as we'll be dead awaiting the church to arise (Rapture). Continue to praise and worship Him and speak your salvation into existence. Stay obedient to his Precepts and Commandments while you establish and build your relationship with Him. Always know that the devil is diligently on his grind and will continuously put temptations before you. Trials and tribulations build soldiers in God's Army. Thus, the weight of expectation is what keeps you grounded in the Word of which is God's promise. Continue to study to show thyself to be true unto Him and, He'll bless you with more than you can imagine. But it's your choice, your commitment. Thank God that He is a Forgiving God, as His Mercy is based on His Love for us all. Treat each other with Love and Respect and allow our Fellowship to be blissful as we reap a harvest that'll be ever so plentiful. Speak kindly as words can be used as weapons. Once you say them, you can't retract them; the damage has already been done. As Christian ideology promotes Forgiveness; it's okay to forgive but never forget, don't be foolish. Retaliation is fueled by vengeance; which is the Lord's to bear not ours.

It is our responsibility to stand for what is right, and fight for the greater good. Edmund Burke, a philosopher from the 18th Century once said *"All that is necessary for the triumph of evil is that good men do nothing."* What does this mean? Perpetuating wrong by not doing what is right, for example: Everyone in your neighborhood know who are the local drug dealers, yet the community continues the affliction brought on by these profiteers that capitalizes off of your docile imprudence; which is driven by fear. As a result of your loyalty to this madness which leads to the disintegration of the integrity of the community as a whole, you sat back and support the demise by doing nothing. So the crisis continue as actions to combat this dilemma taken are none. Don't let fear dictate your life, as it did to those who wouldn't stand for what was right; even when what was being done was wrong i.e. *'The Enslavement and Oppression of any man'* Although it was more physical yet abolished; today modern day slavery is mental as well as economical; which mean that it affects us all. Let us strive for a better tomorrow instead of embracing the selfishness/lawlessness of carefree men. We should listen closer to the merit which speaks to our humanity that says 'we are all brothers and sisters' and that there is no room for *Prejudice*. *Pray to God in supplication for clarity, patience, strength, courage, wisdom, protection, Hope, forgiveness and most of all Love*. These virtues will cover you if you believe them to be true. Remember our choices are determined by our gift giving Free Will. Here are a few scriptures that will encourage you as you study His never changing Word. After all, *the Lighter Side of Darkness can be found in you.*

(Deuteronomy 28: 1-14) *"Now it shall come to pass, if you diligently obey the voice of the Lord your God, to observe carefully all His commandments which I command you today, that the Lord your God will set you high above all nations of the earth.* [2] *And all these blessings shall come upon you and overtake you, because you obey the voice of the Lord your God:* [3] *"Blessed shall you be in the city, and blessed shall you be in the country.* [4] *"Blessed shall be the fruit of your body, the produce of your ground and the increase of your herds, the increase of your cattle and the offspring of your flocks.* [5] *"Blessed shall be your basket and your kneading bowl.* [6] *"Blessed shall you be when you come in, and blessed shall you be when you go out.* [7] *"The Lord will cause your enemies who rise against you to be defeated before your face; they shall come out against you one way and flee before you seven ways.* [8] *"The Lord will command the blessing on you in your storehouses and in all to which you set your hand, and He will bless you in the land which the Lord your God is giving you.* [9] *"The Lord will establish you as a holy people to Himself, just as He has sworn to you, if you keep the commandments of the Lord your God and walk in His ways.* [10] *Then all peoples of the earth shall see that you are called by the name of the Lord, and they shall be afraid of you.* [11] *And the Lord* *will grant you plenty of goods, in the fruit of your body, in the increase of your livestock, and in the produce of your ground, in the land of which the Lord swore to your fathers to give you.* [12] *The Lord will open to you His good treasure, the heavens, to give the rain to your land in its season, and to bless all the work of your hand. You shall lend to many nations, but you shall not borrow.* [13] *And the Lord will make you the head and not the tail; you shall be above only, and not be beneath, if you heed the commandments of the Lord your God, which I command you today, and are careful to observe them.* [14] *So you shall not turn aside from any of the words which I command you this day, to the right or the left, to go after other gods to serve them.*

(Psalms 1-6) *Blessed is the man that walks not in the counsel of the ungodly, nor stand in the way of sinners, nor sit in the seat of the scornful. 2 But his delight is in the law of the LORD; and in his law does he meditate day and night. 3 And he shall be like a tree planted by the rivers of water, that bring forth his fruit in his season; his leaf also shall not wither; and whatsoever he does shall prosper. 4 The ungodly are not so: but are like the chaff which the wind drive away. 5 Therefore the ungodly shall not stand in the judgment, nor sinners in the congregation of the righteous. 6 For the LORD know the way of the righteous: but the way of the ungodly shall perish.*

(Matthew 6:33) *But seek ye first the kingdom of God, and his righteousness; and all these things shall be added unto you.*

(Psalms 91) *He who dwells in the secret place of the Most High shall abide under the shadow of the Almighty.* [2] *I will say of the Lord, "He is my refuge and my fortress; My God, in Him I will trust."* [3] *Surely He shall deliver you from the snare of the fowler and from the perilous pestilence.* [4] *He* *shall cover you with His feathers, and under His wings you shall take refuge; His truth shall be your shield and buckler. [5] You shall not be afraid of the terror by night, nor of the arrow that flies by day, [6] nor of the pestilence that walks in darkness, nor of the destruction that lays waste at noonday. [7] A thousand may fall at your side, And ten thousand at your right hand; But it shall not come near you. [8] Only with your eyes shall you look, and see the reward of the wicked. [9] Because you have made the Lord, who is my refuge, Even the Most High, your dwelling place, [10] No evil shall befall you, nor shall any plague come near your dwelling; [11] For He shall give His angels charge over you, to keep you in all your ways. [12] In their hands they shall bear you up, lest you dash your foot against a stone. [13] You shall tread upon the lion and the cobra, the young lion and the serpent you shall trample underfoot. [14] "Because he has set his love upon Me, therefore I will deliver him; I will set him on high, because he has known My name. [15] He shall call upon Me, and I will answer him; I will be with him in trouble; I will deliver him and honor him. [16] With long life I will satisfy him, And show him My salvation." AMEN!*

'GOD IS WATCHING! Heaven awaits'

Heaven's Gates by Hillary Wilson